Praise for *Combat*

"American troops go to hell and back to save the free world. Push comes to shove, then Fire-away! And Carrumph!"
—*Kirkus Reviews*

"Editor Coonts has gathered an impressive group of technothriller authors for this testosterone laden anthology. These John and Jane Wayne meet *Star Wars* tales offers a chilling glimpse into warfare in the 21st century. The most successful focus is not on weird military technology, but on the men and women who must actually fight . . . best of all is Ing's tightly wrapped tale, "Inside Job.""
—*Publishers Weekly*

"War is as inevitable in this new century as it was in the past. A thought-provoking, plausible, and exciting look at the "interesting times" the proverbial ancient Chinese curse says that we are condemned to live through."
—*Library Journal*

"Dean Ing masterfully delivers the goods in "Inside Job" . . . This anthology reads quickly. It has the kind of pages that keep you turning them long into the night, your sleepless eyes glued like a terrified double-agent on the run from the bad guys . . . can be considered a mission success."
—*Readers and Writers Magazine*

"As the Bush administration undertakes a review of the who, what, when and where of military spending, *Combat*—through the eyes of ten well-respected experts—offers a realistic look at what American men and women may face on the battlefields of the not-so-distant future."
—*The Ocala Star-Banner*

EDITED WITH AN INTRODUCTION BY
STEPHEN COONTS

COMBAT

Volume 2

STEPHEN COONTS

DEAN ING

BARRETT TILLMAN

FORGE®

A TOM DOHERTY ASSOCIATES BOOK
NEW YORK

To the memory of the seventeen sailors who
lost their lives on the USS *Cole*

This is a work of fiction. All the characters and events portrayed in this
book are either products of the author's imagination or are used ficti-
tiously.

COMBAT Volume 2

A Forge Book
Published by Tom Doherty Associates, LLC
175 Fifth Avenue
New York, NY 10010

www.tor.com

Forge® is a registered trademark of Tom Doherty Associates, LLC.

ISBN: 0-812-57616-0
Library of Congress Card Catalog Number: 00-048451

First edition: January 2001
First mass market edition: February 2002

Printed in the United States of America

0 9 8 7 6 5 4 3 2 1

Contents

INTRODUCTION

The milieu of armed conflict has been a fertile setting for storytellers since the dawn of the written word, and probably before. The *Iliad* by Homer was a thousand years old before someone finally wrote down that oral epic of the Trojan War, freezing its form forever.

Since then war stories have been one of the main themes of fiction in Western cultures: *War and Peace* by Leo Tolstoi was set during the Napoleonic Wars, Stephen Crane's *The Red Badge of Courage* was set during the American Civil War, *All Quiet on the Western Front* by Erich Maria Remarque was perhaps the great classic of World War I. Arguably the premier war novel of the twentieth century, Ernest Hemingway's *For Whom the Bell Tolls*, was set in the Spanish Civil War.

World War II caused an explosion of great war novels. Some of my favorites are *The Naked and the Dead, The Thin Red Line, War and Remembrance, From Here to Eternity, The War Lover,* and *Das Boot.*

The Korean conflict also produced a bunch, including my favorite, *The Bridges at Toko-Ri* by James Michener, but Vietnam changed the literary landscape. According to conventional wisdom in the publishing industry, after that war the reading public lost interest in war stories. Without a doubt the publishers did.

In 1984 the world changed. The U.S. Naval Institute Press, the Naval Academy's academic publisher, broke with its ninety-plus years of tradition and published a novel, *The Hunt for Red October,* by Tom Clancy.

This book by an independent insurance agent who had never served in the armed forces sold slowly at first, then became a huge best-seller when the reading public found it and began selling it to each other by word of mouth. It didn't hurt that President Ronald Reagan was photographed with a copy.

As it happened, in 1985 I was looking for a publisher for a Vietnam flying story I had written. After the novel was rejected by every publisher in New York, I saw *Hunt* in a bookstore, so I sent my novel to the Naval Institute Press. To my delight the house accepted it and published it in 1986 as *Flight of the Intruder.* Like *Hunt,* it too became a big best-seller.

Success ruined the Naval Institute. Wracked by internal politics, the staff refused to publish Clancy's and my subsequent novels. (We had no trouble selling these books in New York, thank you!) The house did not publish another novel for years, and when they did, best-seller sales eluded them.

Literary critics had an explanation for the interest of the post-Vietnam public in war stories. These novels, they said, were something new. I don't know who coined the term "techno-thriller" (back then newspapers always used quotes and hyphenated it) but the term stuck.

Trying to define the new term, the critics concluded that these war stories used modern technology in ways that no one ever had. How wrong they were.

Clancy's inspiration for *The Hunt for Red October* was an attempted defection of a crew of a Soviet surface warship in the Baltic. The crew mutinied and attempted to sail their ship to Finland. The attempt went awry and the ringleaders were summarily executed by the communists, who always took offense when anyone tried to leave the workers' paradises.

What if, Clancy asked himself, the crew of a nuclear-powered submarine tried to defect? The game would be more interesting then. Clancy's model for the type of story he wanted to write was Edward L. Beach's *Run Silent, Run Deep*, a World War II submarine story salted with authentic technical detail that was critical to the development of the characters and plot of the story.

With that scenario in mind, Clancy set out to write a submarine adventure that would be accurate in every detail. Never mind that he had never set foot on a nuclear submarine or spent a day in uniform— his inquiring mind and thirst for knowledge made him an extraordinary researcher. His fascination with war games and active, fertile imagination made him a first-class storyteller.

Unlike Clancy, I did no research whatsoever when writing *Flight of the Intruder*. I had flown A-6 Intruder bombers in Vietnam from the deck of the USS *Enterprise* and wrote from memory. I had been trying to write a flying novel since 1973 and had worn out two typewriters in the process. By 1984 I had figured out a plot for my flying tale, so after a divorce I got serious about writing and completed a first draft of the novel in five months.

My inspiration for the type of story I wanted to write was two books by Ernest K. Gann. *Fate Is the Hunter* was a true collection of flying stories from the late 1930s and 1940s, and was, I thought, extraordinary in its inclusion of a wealth of detail about the craft of flying an airplane. Gann also used this device for his novels, the best of which is probably *The High and the Mighty*, a story about a piston-engined airliner that has an emergency while flying between Hawaii and San Francisco.

Gann used technical details to create the setting and as plot devices that moved the stories along. By educating the reader about what it is a pilot does, he gave his stories an emotional impact that conventional storytellers could not achieve. In essence, he put you in the cockpit and took you flying. That, I thought, was an extraordinary achievement and one I wanted to emulate.

Fortunately, the technology that Clancy and I were writing about was state-of-the-art—nuclear-powered submarines and precision all-weather attack jets—and this played to the reading public's long-standing love affair with scientific discoveries and new technology. In the nineteenth century Jules Verne, Edgar Allan Poe, Wilkie Collins, and H. G. Wells gave birth to science fiction. The technology at the heart of their stories played on the public's fascination with the man-made wonders of that age—the submarine, the flying machines that were the object of intense research and experimentation, though they had yet to get off the ground, and the myriad of uses that inventors were finding for electricity, to name just a few.

Today's public is still enchanted by the promise of scientific research and technology. Computers, rockets, missiles, precision munitions, lasers, fiber optics, wireless networks, reconnaissance satellites, winged airplanes that take off and land vertically, network-centric warfare—advances in every technical field are constantly re-creating the world in which we live.

The marriage of high tech and war stories is a natural.

The line between the modern military action-adventure and science fiction is blurry, indistinct, and becoming more so with every passing day. Storytellers often set technothrillers in the near future and dress up the technology accordingly, toss in little inventions of their own here and there, and in general, try subtly to wow their readers by use of a little of that science fiction "what might be" magic. When it's properly done, only a technically expert reader will be able to tell when the writer has crossed the line from the real to the unreal; and that's the fun of it. On the other hand, stories set in space or on other planets or thousands of years in the future are clearly science fiction, even though armed conflict is involved.

In this collection you will find ten never-before-published techno-thriller novellas by accomplished writers, a category in which I immodestly include myself. I hope you like them.

In this, the second of three volumes of original novellas from the *Combat* collection, you will find original novellas by Dean Ing, Barrett Tillman, and me.

No one knows more about U.S. Naval Aviation than Barrett Tillman. When he was growing up in Oregon, his father owned and flew a Douglas Dauntless dive bomber. Barrett fell in love with the plane and military aviation. A professional writer all his adult life, he met and interviewed many of the surviving fighter aces of World War II, American,

German, and British. When he wasn't editing *The Hook* magazine or working for the Champlin Fighter Museum in Mesa, Arizona, he has written over a dozen scholarly books on the planes of World War II and the men who flew them, and four well-received novels. His history of naval aviation during the Vietnam War, *On Yankee Station*, written with John B. Nichols, is a classic.

Written two years ago, long before the terror strike of September 11, 2001, Dean Ing's *Inside Job* seems almost prophetic. Dr. Ing didn't look into a crystal ball when he wrote this tale of Arab terrorists willing to commit genocide on their way to paradise; he merely assumed that the 1993 bombers of the World Trade Center and the criminals who committed other atrocities throughout the world were not yet finished. He was right. This is, in my opinion, the most chilling tale in the *Combat* collection.

STEPHEN COONTS

AL-JIHAD

BY STEPHEN COONTS

One

Julie Giraud was crazy as hell. I knew that for an absolute fact, so I was contemplating what a real damned fool I was to get mixed up in her crazy scheme when I drove the Humvee and trailer into the belly of the V-22 Osprey and tied them down.

I quickly checked the stuff in the Humvee's trailer, made sure it was secure, then walked out of the Osprey and across the dark concrete ramp. Lights shining down from the peak of the hangar reflected in puddles of rainwater. The rain had stopped just at dusk, an hour or so ago.

I was the only human in sight amid the tiltrotor Ospreys parked on that vast mat. They looked like medium-sized transports except that they had an engine on each wingtip, and the engines were pointed straight up. Atop each engine was a thirty-eight-foot, three-bladed rotor. The engines were mounted on swivels that allowed them to be tilted from the vertical to the horizontal, giving the Ospreys the ability to take off and land like helicopters and then fly along in winged flight like the turboprop transports they really were.

I stopped by the door into the hangar and looked around again, just to make sure, then I opened the door and went inside.

The corridor was lit, but empty. My footsteps made a dull noise on the tile floor. I took the second right, into a ready room.

The duty officer was standing by the desk strapping a belt and holster to her waist. She was wearing a flight suit and black flying boots. Her dark hair was pulled back into a bun. She glanced at me. "Ready?"

"Where are all the security guards?"

"Watching a training film. They thought it was unusual to send everyone, but I insisted."

"I sure as hell hope they don't get suspicious."

She picked up her flight bag, took a last look around, and glanced at her watch. Then she grinned at me. "Let's go get 'em."

That was Julie Giraud, and as I have said, she was crazy as hell.

Me, I was just greedy. Three million dollars was a lot of kale, enough to keep me in beer and pretzels for the next hundred and ninety years. I followed this ding-a-ling bloodthirsty female along the hallway and through the puddles on the ramp to the waiting Osprey. Julie didn't run—she strode purposefully. If she was nervous or having second thoughts about committing the four dozen felonies we had planned for the next ten minutes, she sure didn't show it.

The worst thing I had ever done up to that point in my years on this planet was cheat a little on my income tax—no more than average, though—and here I was about to become a co-conspirator in enough crimes to keep a grand jury busy for a year. I felt like a condemned man on his way to the gallows, but the thought of all those smackers kept me marching along behind ol' crazy Julie.

We boarded the plane through the cargo door, and I closed it behind us.

Julie took three or four minutes to check our cargo, leaving nothing to chance. I watched her with grudging respect—crazy or not, she looked like a pro to me, and at my age I damn well didn't want to go tilting at windmills with an amateur.

When she finished her inspection, she led the way forward to the cockpit. She got into the left seat, her hands flew over the buttons and levers, arranging everything to her satisfaction. As I strapped myself into the right seat, she cranked the left engine. The RPMs came up nicely. The right engine was next.

As the radios warmed up, she quickly ran through the checklist, scanned gauges, and set up computer displays. I wasn't a pilot; everything I knew about the V-22 tiltrotor Osprey came from Julie, who wasn't given to long-winded explanations. If was almost as if every word she said cost her money.

While she did her pilot thing, I sat there looking out the windows, nervous as a cat on crack, trying to spot the platoon of FBI agents who were probably closing in to arrest us right that very minute. I didn't see anyone, of course: The parking mat of the air force base was as deserted as a nudist colony in January.

About that time Julie snapped on the aircraft's exterior lights, which made weird reflections on the other aircraft parked nearby, and the landing lights, powerful spotlights that shone on the concrete in front of us.

She called Ground Control on the radio. They

gave her a clearance to a base in southern Germany, which she copied and read back flawlessly.

We weren't going to southern Germany, I knew, even if the air traffic controllers didn't. Julie released the brakes, and almost as if by magic, the Osprey began moving, taxiing along the concrete. She turned to pick up a taxiway, moving slowly, sedately, while she set up the computer displays on the instrument panel in front of her. There were two multifunction displays in front of me too, and she leaned across to punch up the displays she wanted. I just watched. All this time we were rolling slowly along the endless taxiways lined with blue lights, across at least one runway, taxiing, taxiing . . . A rabbit ran across in front of us, through the beam of the taxi light.

Finally Julie stopped and spoke to the tower, which cleared us for takeoff.

"Are you ready?" she asked me curtly.

"For prison, hell or what?"

She ignored that comment, which just slipped out. I was sitting there wondering how well I was going to adjust to institutional life.

She taxied onto the runway, lined up the plane, then advanced the power lever with her left hand. I could hear the engines winding up, feel the power of the giant rotors tearing at the air, trying to lift this twenty-eight-ton beast from the earth's grasp.

The Osprey rolled forward on the runway, slowly at first, and when it was going a little faster than a man could run, lifted majestically into the air.

The crime was consummated.

We had just stolen a forty-million-dollar V-22 Osprey, snatched it right out of Uncle Sugar's rather loose grasp, not to mention a half-million dollars' worth of other miscellaneous military equipment that was carefully stowed in the back of the plane.

Now for the getaway.

In seconds Julie began tilting the engines down to transition to forward flight. The concrete runway slid under us, faster and faster as the Osprey accelerated. She snapped up the wheels, used the stick to raise the nose of the plane. The airspeed indicator read over 140 knots as the end of the runway disappeared into the darkness below and the night swallowed us.

Two weeks before that evening, Julie Giraud drove into my filling station in Van Nuys. I didn't know her then, of course. I was sitting in the office reading the morning paper. I glanced out, saw her pull up to the pump in a new white sedan. She got out of the car and used a credit card at the pump, so I went back to the paper.

I had only owned that gasoline station for about a week, but I had already figured out why the previous owner sold it so cheap: The mechanic was a doper and the guy running the register was a thief. I was contemplating various ways of solving those two problems when the woman with the white sedan finished pumping her gas and came walking toward the office.

She was a bit over medium height, maybe thirty years old, a hardbody wearing a nice outfit that must have set her back a few bills. She looked vaguely familiar, but this close to Hollywood, you often see people you think you ought to know.

She came straight over to where I had the little chair tilted back against the wall and asked, "Charlie Dean?"

"Yeah."

"I'm Julie Giraud. Do you remember me?"

It took me a few seconds. I put the paper down and got up from the chair.

"It's been a lot of years," I said.

"Fifteen, I think. I was just a teenager."

"Colonel Giraud's eldest daughter. I remember. Do you have a sister a year or two younger?"

"Rachael. She's a dental tech, married with two kids."

"I sorta lost track of your father, I guess. How is he?"

"Dead."

"Well, I'm sorry."

I couldn't think of anything else to say. Her dad had been my commanding officer at the antiterrorism school, but that was years ago. I went on to other assignments, and finally retired five years ago with thirty years in. I hadn't seen or thought of the Girauds in years.

"I remember Dad remarking several times that you were the best Marine in the corps."

That comment got the attention of the guy behind the register. His name was Candy. He had a few tattoos on his arms and a half dozen rings dangling from various portions of his facial anatomy. He looked at me now with renewed interest.

I tried to concentrate on Julie Giraud. She was actually a good-looking woman, with her father's square chin and good cheekbones. She wasn't wearing makeup: She didn't need any.

"I remember him telling us that you were a sniper in Vietnam, and the best Marine in the corps."

Candy's eyebrows went up toward his hairline when he heard that.

"I'm flattered that you remember me, Ms. Giraud, but I'm a small-business owner now. I left the Marines five years ago." I gestured widely. "This grand establishment belongs to me and the hundreds of thousands of stockholders in BankAmerica. All of us thank you for stopping by today and giving us your business."

She nodded, turned toward the door, then hesitated. "I wonder if we might have lunch together, Mr. Dean."

Why not? "Okay. Across the street at the Burger King, in about an hour?" That was agreeable with her. She got in her car and drove away.

Amazing how people from the past pop back into your life when you least expect it.

I tilted the chair back, lifted my paper and sat there wondering what in hell Julie Giraud could possibly want to talk about with me. Candy went back to his copy of *Rolling Stone.* In a few minutes two people came in and paid cash for their gas. With the paper hiding my face, I could look into a mirror I had mounted on the ceiling and watch Candy handle the money. I put the mirror up there three days ago but if he noticed, he had forgotten it by now.

As the second customer left, Candy pocketed something. I didn't know if he shortchanged the customer or just helped himself to a bill from the till. The tally and the tape hadn't been jibing and Candy had a what-are-you-gonna-do-about-it-old-man attitude.

He closed the till and glanced at me with a look that could only be amusement.

I folded the paper, put it down, got out of the chair and went over to the counter.

"So you was in the Marines, huh?"

"Yeah."

He grinned confidently. "Wouldn't have figured that."

I reached, grabbed a ring dangling from his eyebrow and ripped it out.

Candy screamed. Blood flowed from the eyebrow. He recoiled against the register with a look of horror on his face.

"The money, kid. Put it on the counter."

He glanced at the blood on his hand, then pressed his hand against his eyebrow trying to staunch the flow. "You bastard! I don't know what you—"

Reaching across the counter, I got a handful of hair with my left hand and the ring in his nose with my right. "You want to lose all these, one by one?"

He dug in his pocket, pulled out a wadded bill and threw it on the counter.

"You're fired, kid. Get off the property and never come back."

He came around the counter, trying to stay away from me, one hand on his bleeding eyebrow. He stopped in the door. "I'll get you for this, you son of a bitch."

"You think that through, kid. Better men than you have died trying. If you just gotta do it, though, you know where to find me."

He scurried over to his twenty-five-year-old junker Pontiac. He ground and ground with the starter. Just when I thought he would have to give up, the motor belched a cloud of blue smoke.

I got on the phone to a friend of mine, also a retired Marine. His name was Bill Wiley, and he worked full time as a police dispatcher. He agreed to come over that evening to help me out for a few hours at the station.

It seemed to me that I might as well solve all my problems in one day, so I went into the garage to see the mechanic, a long-haired Mexican named Juan.

"I think you've got an expensive habit, Juan. To pay for it you've been charging customers for work you didn't do, new parts you didn't install, then splitting the money with Candy. He hit the road. You can work honest from now on or leave, your choice."

"You can't prove shit."

He was that kind of guy, stupid as dirt. "I don't have to prove anything," I told him. "You're fired."

He didn't argue; he just went. I finished fixing the flat he had been working on, waited on customers until noon, then locked the place up and walked across the street to the Burger King.

Of course I was curious. It seemed doubtful that Julie Giraud wanted to spend an hour of her life reminiscing about the good old days at Quantico with a retired enlisted man who once served under her father, certainly not one twenty-five years older than she was.

So what did she want?

"You are not an easy man to find, Mr. Dean."

I shrugged. I'm not trying to lose myself in the madding crowd, but I'm not advertising either.

"My parents died twelve years ago," she said, her eyes on my face.

"Both of them?" I hadn't heard. "Sorry to hear that," I said.

"They were on an Air France flight to Paris that blew up over Niger. A bomb."

"Twelve years ago."

"Dad had been retired for just a year. He and Mom were traveling, seeing the world, falling in love with each other all over again. They were on their way to Paris from South America when the plane blew up, killing everyone aboard."

I lost my appetite for hamburger. I put it down and sipped some coffee.

She continued, telling me her life story. She spent a few more years in high school, went to the Air Force Academy, was stationed in Europe flying V-22 Ospreys, was back in the States just now on leave.

When she wound down, I asked, as gently as I could, why she looked me up.

She opened her purse, took out a newspaper clipping, offered it to me. "Last year a French court tried the men who killed my parents. They are Libyans. Moammar Gadhafi refused to extradite them from Libya, so the French tried them in absentia, convicted them, sentenced them to life in prison."

I remembered reading about the trial. The clipping merely refreshed my memory. One hundred forty people died when that Air France flight exploded; the debris was scattered over fifty square miles of desert.

"Six men, and they are still in Libya." Julie gestured at the newspaper clipping, which was lying beside my food tray. "One of the men is Gadhafi's brother-in-law, another is a key figure in Libyan intelligence, two are in the Libyan diplomatic service." She gripped the little table between us and leaned forward. "They blew up that airliner on Gadhafi's order to express the dictator's displeasure with French foreign policy at the time. It was raw political terrorism, Mr. Dean, by a nation without the guts or wit to wage war. They just murder civilians."

I folded the clipping, then handed it back.

"Ms. Giraud, I'm sorry that your parents are dead. I'm sorry about all those people who died on that airliner. I'm sorry the men who murdered them are beyond the reach of the law. I'm sorry the French government hasn't got the guts or wit to clean out the vermin in Tripoli. But what has this got to do with me?"

"I want you to help me kill those men," she whispered, her voice as hard as a bayonet blade.

TWO

I grew up in a little town in southwestern Missouri. Dad was a welder and Mom waited tables in a diner, and both of them had trouble with the bottle. The afternoon of the day I graduated from high school I joined the Marines to get the hell out.

Sure, I killed my share of gomers in Vietnam. By then I thought life was a fairly good idea and wanted more of it. If I had to zap gomers to keep getting older, that was all right by me. It helped that I had a natural talent with a rifle. I was a medium-smart, whang-leather kid who never complained and did what I was told, so I eventually ended up in Recon. It took me a while to fit in; once I did, I was in no hurry to leave. Recon was the place where the Marine Corps kept its really tough men. The way I figured it, those guys were my life insurance.

That's the way it worked out. The guys in Recon

kept each other alive. And we killed gomers.

All that was long ago and far away from Julie Giraud. She was the daughter of a Marine colonel, sure, a grad of the Air Force Academy, and she looked like she ran five miles or so every day, but none of that made her tough. Sitting across the table looking at her, I couldn't figure out if she was a fighter or a get-even, courthouse-stairs back-shooter. A lot of people like the abstract idea of revenge, of getting even, but they aren't willing to suffer much for the privilege. Sitting in Burger King watching Julie Giraud, listening to her tell me how she wanted to kill the men who had killed her parents, I tried to decide just how much steel was in her backbone.

Her dad had been a career officer with his share of Vietnam chest cabbage. When they were young a lot of the gung ho officers thought they were bulletproof and let it all hang out. When they eventually realized they were as mortal as everyone else and started sending sergeants to lead the patrols, they already had enough medals to decorate a Panamanian dictator. Whether Julie Giraud's dad was like that, I never knew.

A really tough man knows he is mortal, knows the dangers involved to the tenth decimal place, and goes ahead anyway. He is careful, committed, and absolutely ruthless.

After she dropped the bomb at lunch, I thought about these things for a while. Up to that point I had no idea why she had gone to the trouble of looking me up; the thought that she might want my help getting even with somebody never once zipped across the synapses. I took my time thinking things over before I said, "What's the rest of it?"

"It's a little complicated."

"Maybe you'd better lay it out."

"Outside, in my car."

"No. Outside on the sidewalk."

We threw the remnants of our lunch in the trash and went outside.

Julie Giraud looked me in the eye and explained, "These men are instruments of the Libyan government—"

"I got that point earlier."

"—seventeen days from now, on the twenty-third of this month, they are going to meet with members of three Middle East terrorist organizations and a representative of Saddam Hussein's government. They hope to develop a joint plan that Saddam will finance to attack targets throughout western Europe and the Middle East."

"Did you get a press release on this or what?"

"I have a friend, a fellow Air Force Academy graduate, who is now with the CIA."

"He just casually tells you this stuff?"

"She. She told me about the conference. And there is nothing casual about it. She knows what these people have cost me."

"Say you win the lottery and off a few of these guys, what's she gonna tell the internal investigators when they come around?"

Julie Giraud shook her head. "We're covered, believe me."

"I don't, but you're the one trying to make a sale, not me."

She nodded, then continued: "Seventeen days from now the delegates to this little conference will fly to an airstrip near an old fortress in the Sahara. The fortress is near an oasis on an old caravan route in the middle of nowhere. Originally built by the ancient Egyptians, the fortress was used by Carthaginians and Romans to guard that caravan route. The Foreign Legion did extensive restoration and kept a small garrison there for years. During World War ll the Germans and British even had a little firefight there."

I grunted. She was intense, committed. Fanatics scare me, and she was giving me those vibes now.

"The fortress is on top of a rock ridge," she explained. "The Arabs call it the Camel."

"Never heard of it," I retorted. Of course there was no reason that I should have heard of the place—I was grasping at straws. I didn't like anything about this tale.

She was holding her purse loosely by the strap, so I grabbed it out of her hand. Her eyes narrowed; she thought about slapping me—actually shifted her weight to do it—then decided against it.

There was a small, round, poured-concrete picnic table there beside the Burger King for mothers to sit at while watching their kids play on the gym equipment, so I sat down and dug her wallet out of the purse. It contained a couple hundred in bills, a Colorado driver's license—she was twenty-eight years old—a military ID, three bank credit cards, an expired AAA membership, car insurance from USAA, a Sears credit card, and an ATM card in a paper envelope with her secret PIN number written on the envelope in ink.

Also in the wallet was a small, bound address book containing handwritten names, addresses, telephone numbers, and e-mail addresses. I flipped through the book, studying the names, then returned it to the wallet.

Her purse contained the usual feminine hygiene and cosmetic items. At the bottom were four old dry cleaning receipts from the laundry on the German base where she was stationed and a small collection of loose keys. One safety pin, two buttons, a tiny rusty screwdriver, a pair of sunglasses with a cracked lens, five German coins and two U.S. quarters. One of the receipts was eight months old.

I put all this stuff back in her purse and passed it across the table.

"Okay," I said. "For the sake of argument, let's assume you're telling the truth—that there really is a terrorists' conference scheduled at an old pile of Foreign Legion masonry in the middle of the god-damn Sahara seventeen days from now. What do you propose to do about it?"

"I propose to steal a V-22 Osprey," Julie Giraud said evenly, "fly there, plant enough C-4 to blow that old fort to kingdom come, then wait for the terror-ists to arrive. When they are all sitting in there plot-ting who they are going to murder next, I'm going to push the button and send the whole lot of them straight to hell. Just like they did to my parents and everyone else on that French DC-10."

"You and who else?"

The breeze was playing with her hair. "You and me," she said. "The two of us."

I tried to keep a straight face. Across the street at my filling station people were standing beside their cars, waiting impatiently for me to get back and open up. That was paying business and I was sitting here listening to this shit. The thought that the CIA or FBI might be recording this conversation also crossed my mind.

"You're a nice kid, Julie. Thanks for dropping by. I'm sorry about your folks, but there is nothing on earth anyone can do for them. It's time to lay them to rest. Fly high, meet a nice guy, fall in love, have some kids, give them the best that you have in you: Your parents would have wanted that for you. The fact is they're gone and you can't bring them back."

She brushed the hair back from her eyes. "If you'll help me, Mr. Dean, I'll pay you three million dollars."

I didn't know what to say. Three million dollars

rated serious consideration, but I couldn't tell if she had what it takes to make it work.

"I'll think about it," I said, and got up. "Tomorrow, we'll have lunch again right here."

She showed some class then. "Okay," she said, and nodded once. She didn't argue or try to make the sale right then, and I appreciated that.

My buddy, Gunnery Sergeant Bill Wiley, left the filling station at ten that night; I had to stay until closing time at 2 A.M. About midnight an older four-door Chrysler cruised slowly past on the street, for the second or third time, and I realized the people inside were casing the joint.

Ten minutes later, when the pumps were vacant and I was the only person in the store, the Chrysler drove in fast and stopped in front of the door. My ex–cash register man, Candy, boiled out of the passenger seat with a gun in his hand, a 9-mm automatic. He and the guy from the backseat came charging through the door waving their guns at me.

"Hands up, Charlie Dean, you silly son of a bitch. We want all the money, and if you ain't real goddamn careful I'm gonna blow your fucking brains out."

The guy from the backseat posted himself by the door and kept glancing up and down the street to see who was driving by. The driver of the car stayed outside.

Candy strutted over to me and stuck his gun in my face. He had a butterfly bandage on his eyebrow. He was about to say something really nasty, I think, when I grabbed his gun with my left hand and hit him with all I had square in the mouth with my right. He went down like he had been sledgehammered. I leaped toward the other one and hit him in the head with the gun butt, and he went down too. Squatting, I grabbed his gun while I checked the driver outside.

The driver was standing frozen beside the car, staring through the plate-glass window at me like I was Godzilla. I already had the safety off on Candy's automatic, so I swung it into the middle of this dude's chest and pulled the trigger.

Click.

Oh boy!

As I got the other pistol up, the third man dived behind the wheel and slammed the Chrysler into gear. That pistol also clicked uselessly. The Chrysler left in a squall of rubber and exhaust smoke.

I checked the pistols one at a time. Both empty.

Candy's eyes were trying to focus, so I bent down and asked him, "How come you desperate characters came in here with empty pistols?"

He spit blood and a couple teeth as he thought about it. His lips were swelling. He was going to look like holy hell for a few days. Finally one eye focused. "Didn't want to shoot you," he mumbled, barely understandable. "Just scare you."

"Umm."

"The guns belong to my dad. He didn't have any bullets around."

"Did the driver of the car know the guns were empty?"

Candy nodded, spit some more blood.

I'll admit, I felt kind of sorry for Candy. He screwed up the courage to go after a pint or two of revenge, but the best he could do for backup help was a coward who ran from empty pistols.

I put the guns in the trash can under the register and got each of them a bottled water from the cooler. They were slowly coming around when a police cruiser with lights flashing pulled up between the pumps and the office and the officer jumped out. He came striding in with his hand on the butt of his pistol.

"Someone called in on their cell phone, reported a robbery in progress here."

I kept my hands in plain sight where he could see them. "No robbery, officer. My name's Dean; I own this filling station."

"What happened to these two?" Spittle and blood were smeared on one front of Candy's shirt, and his friend had a dilly of a shiner.

"They had a little argument," I explained, "slugged each other. This fellow here, Candy, works for me."

Candy and his friend looked at me kind of funny, but they went along with it. After writing down everyone's names and addresses from their driver's licenses while I expanded on my fairy tale, the officer left.

Candy and his friend were on their feet by then. "I'm sorry, Mr. Dean," Candy said.

"Tell you what, kid. You want to play it straight, no stealing and no shortchanging people, you come back to work in the morning."

"You mean that?"

"Yeah." I dug his father's guns from the trash and handed them to him. "You better take these home and put them back where they belong."

His face was red and he was having trouble talking. "I'll be here," he managed.

He pocketed the pistols, nodded, then he and his friend went across the street to Burger King to call someone to come get them.

I was shaking so bad I had to sit down. Talk about luck! If the pistols had been loaded I would have killed that fool kid driving the car, and I didn't even know if he had a gun. That could have cost me life in the pen. Over what?

I sat there in the office thinking about life and death and Julie Giraud.

At lunch the next day Julie Giraud was intense, yet cool as she talked of killing people, slaughtering them like steers. I'd seen my share of people with that look. She was just flat crazy.

The fact that she was a nut seemed to explain a lot, somehow. If she had been sane I would have turned her down flat. It's been my experience through the years that sane people who go traipsing off to kill other people usually get killed themselves. The people who do best at combat don't have a death grip on life, if you know what I mean. They are crazy enough to take the biggest risk of all and not freak out when the shooting starts. Julie Giraud looked like she had her share of that kind of insanity.

"Do I have my information correct? Were you a sniper in Vietnam, Mr. Dean?"

"That was a war," I said, trying to find the words to explain, taking my time. "I was in Recon. We did ambushes and assassinations. I had a talent with a rifle. Other men had other talents. What you're suggesting isn't war, Ms. Giraud."

"Do you still have what it takes?"

She was goading me and we both knew it. I shrugged.

She wouldn't let it alone. "Could you still kill a man at five hundred yards with a rifle? Shoot him down in cold blood?"

"You want me to shoot somebody today so you can see if I'm qualified for the job?"

"I'm willing to pay three million dollars, Mr. Dean, to the man with the balls to help me kill the men who murdered my parents. I'm offering you the job. I'll pay half up front into a Swiss bank account, half after we kill the men who killed my parents."

"What if you don't make it? What if they kill you?"

"I'll leave a wire transfer order with my banker."

I snorted. At times I got the impression she thought this was some kind of extreme sports expedition, like jumping from a helicopter to ski down a mountain. And yet . . . she had that fire in her eyes.

"Where in hell did a captain in the air farce get three million dollars?"

"I inherited half my parents' estate and invested it in software and internet stocks; and the stocks went up like a rocket shot to Mars, as everyone north of Antarctica well knows. Now I'm going to spend the money on something I want very badly. That's the American way, isn't it?"

"Like ribbed condoms and apple pie," I agreed, then leaned forward to look into her eyes. "If we kill these men," I explained, "the world will never be the same for you. When you look in the mirror the face that stares back won't be the same one you've been looking at all these years—it'll be uglier. Your parents will still be dead and you'll be older in ways that years can't measure. That's the god's truth, kid. Your parents are going to be dead regardless. Keep your money, find a good guy, and have a nice life."

She sneered. "You're a philosopher?"

"I've been there, lady. I'm trying to figure out if I want to go back."

"Three million dollars, Mr. Dean. How long will it take for your gasoline station to make three million dollars profit?"

I owned three gas stations, all mortgaged to the hilt, but I wasn't going to tell her that. I sat in the corner of Burger King working on a Diet Coke while I thought about the kid I had damn near killed the night before.

"What about afterward?" I asked. "Tell me how you and I are going to continue to reside on this planet with the CIA and FBI and Middle Eastern terrorists all looking to carve on our ass."

She knew a man, she said, who could provide passports.

"Fake passports? Bullshit! Get real."

"Genuine passports. He's a U.S. consular official in Munich."

"What are you paying him?"

"He wants to help."

"Dying to go to prison, is he?"

"I've slept with him for the past eighteen months."

"You got a nice ass, but . . . Unless this guy is a real toad, he can get laid any night of the week. Women today think if they don't use it, they'll wear it out pissing through it."

"You have difficulty expressing yourself in polite company, don't you, Charlie Dean? Okay, cards on the table: I'm fucking him and paying him a million dollars."

I sat there thinking it over.

"If you have the money you can buy anything," she said.

"I hope you aren't foolish enough to believe that."

"Someone always wants money. All you have to do is find that someone. You're a case in point."

"How much would it cost to kill an ex-Marine who became a liability and nuisance?"

"A lot less than I'm paying you," she shot back. She didn't smile.

After a bit she started talking again, telling me how we were going to kill the bad guys. I didn't think much of her plan—blow up a stone fortress?— but I sat there listening while I mulled things over. Three million was not small change.

Finally I decided that Julie's conscience was her

problem and the three million would look pretty good in my bank account. The Libyans—well, I really didn't give a damn about them one way or the other. They would squash me like a bug if they thought I was any threat at all, so what the hell. They had blown up airliners, they could take their chances with the devil.

Three

We were inside a rain cloud. Water ran off the windscreen in continuous streams: The dim glow of the red cockpit lights made the streams look like pale red rivers. Beyond the wet windscreen, however, the night was coal black.

I had never seen such absolute darkness.

Julie Giraud had the Osprey on autopilot; she was bent over fiddling with the terrain-avoidance radar while auto flew the plane.

I sure as hell wasn't going to be much help. I sat there watching her, wondering if I had made a sucker's deal. Three million was a lot of money if you lived to spend it. If you died earning it, it was nowhere near enough.

After a bit she turned off the radios and some other electronic gear, then used the autopilot to drop the nose into a descent. The multifunction displays in front of us—there were four plus a radar screen—displayed engine data, our flight plan, a moving map, and one that appeared to be a tactical display of the locations of the radars that were looking at us. I certainly didn't understand much of it, and Julie Giraud was as loquacious as a store dummy.

"We'll drop off their radar screens now," she muttered finally in way of explanation. As if to emphasize our departure into the outlaw world, she snapped off the plane's exterior lights.

As the altimeter unwound I must have looked a little nervous, and I guess I was. I rode two helicopters into the ground in Vietnam and one in Afghanistan, all shot down, so in the years since I had tried to avoid anything with rotors. Jets didn't bother me much, but rotor whop made my skin crawl.

Down we went until we were flying through the valleys of the Bavarian Alps below the hilltops. Julie sat there twiddling the autopilot as we flew along, keeping us between the hills with the radar.

She looked cool as a tall beer in July. "How come you aren't a little nervous?" I asked.

"This is the easy part," she replied.

That shut me up.

We were doing about 270 knots, so it took a little while to thread our way across Switzerland and northern Italy to the ocean. Somewhere over Italy we flew out of the rain. I breathed a sigh of relief when we left the valleys behind and dropped to a hundred feet over the ocean. Julie turned the plane for Africa.

"How do you know fighters aren't looking for us in this goop?" I asked.

She pointed toward one of the multifunction displays. "That's a threat indicator. We'll see anyone who uses a radar."

After a while I got bored, even at a hundred feet,

so I got unstrapped and went aft to check the Humvee, trailer and cargo.

All secure.

I opened my duffel bag, got out a pistol belt. The gun, an old 1911 Colt .45 automatic, was loaded, but I checked it anyway, reholstered it, got the belt arranged around my middle so it rode comfortable with the pistol on my right side and my Ka-Bar knife on the left. I also had another knife in one boot and a hideout pistol in the other, just in case.

I put a magazine in the M-16 but didn't chamber a round. I had disassembled the weapon the night before, cleaned it thoroughly, and oiled it lightly.

The last weapon in the bag was a Model 70 in .308. It was my personal rifle, one I had built up myself years ago. With a synthetic stock, a Canjar adjustable trigger, and a heavy barrel custom-made for me by a Colorado gunsmith, it would put five shots into a half-inch circle at a hundred yards with factory match-grade ammunition. I had the 3×9 adjustable scope zeroed for two hundred. Trigger pull was exactly eighteen ounces.

I repacked the rifles, then sat in the driver's seat of the Humvee and poured myself a cup of coffee from the thermos.

We flew to Europe on different airlines and arrived in Zurich just hours apart. The following day I opened a bank account at a gleaming pile of marble in the heart of the financial district. As I watched, Julie called her banker in Virginia and had $1.5 million in cold hard cash transferred into the account. Three hours after she made the transfer I went to my bank and checked: The money was really there and it was all mine.

Amazing.

We met for dinner at a little hole-in-the-wall restaurant a few blocks off the main drag that I remembered from years before, when I was sight-seeing while on leave during a tour in Germany.

"The money's there," I told her when we were seated. "I confess, I didn't think it would be."

She got a little huffy. "I'd lie to you?"

"It's been known to happen. Though for the life of me, I couldn't see why you would."

She opened her purse, handed me an unsealed envelope. Inside was a passport. I got up and went to the men's room, where I inspected it. It certainly looked like a genuine U.S. passport, on the right paper and printed with dots and displaying my shaved, honest phiz. The name on the thing was Robert Arnold. I put it in my jacket pocket and rejoined her at the table.

She handed me a letter and an addressed envelope. The letter was to her banker, typed, instructing him to transfer another $1.5 million to my account a week after we were scheduled to hit the Camel. The envelope was addressed to him and even had a Swiss stamp on it. I checked the numbers on my account at the Swiss bank. Everything jibed.

She had a pen in her hand by that time. After she had signed the letter, I sealed it in the envelope, then folded the envelope and tucked it in my pocket beside the passport.

"Okay, lady. I'm bought and paid for."

We made our plans over dinner. She drank one glass of wine, and I had a beer, then we both switched to mineral water. I told her I wanted my own pistol and rifles, a request she didn't blink at. She agreed to fly into Dover Air Force Base on one of the regularly scheduled cargo runs, then take my duffel bag containing the weapons back to Germany with her.

"What if someone wants to run the bag through a metal detector, or German customs wants to inspect it?"

"My risk."

"I guess there are a few advantages to being a well-scrubbed, clean-cut American girl."

"You can get away with a lot if you shave your legs."

"I'll keep that in mind."

That was ten days ago. Now we were on our way. Tomorrow we were going to case the old fort and come up with a plan for doing in the assembled bad guys.

Sitting in the driver's seat of the Humvee sipping coffee and listening to the drone of the turboprops carrying us across the Mediterranean, I got the old combat feeling again.

Yeah, this was really it.

Only this time I was going to get paid for it.

I finished the coffee, went back to the cockpit, and offered Julie a cup. She was intent on the computer screens.

"Problems?" I asked.

"I'm picking up early warning radar, but I think I'm too low for the Libyans to see me. There's a fighter aloft too. I doubt if he can pick us out of ground return."

All that was outside my field of expertise. On this portion of the trip, I was merely a passenger.

I saw the land appear on the radar presentation, watched it march down the scope toward us, as if we were stationary and the world was turning under us. It was a nice illusion. As we crossed the beach, I checked my watch. We were only a minute off our planned arrival time, which seemed to me to be a tribute to Julie's piloting skills.

The ride got bumpy over the desert. Even at night the thermals kept the air boiling. Julie Giraud took the plane off autopilot, hand-flew it. Trusting the autopilot in rough air so close to the ground was foolhardy.

I got out the chart, used a little red spotlight mounted on the ceiling of the cockpit to study the lines and notes as we bounced along in turbulence.

We had an hour and twenty minutes to go. Fuel to get out of the desert would have been a problem, so we had brought five hundred gallons in a portable tank in the cargo compartment. Tomorrow night we would use a hand pump to transfer that fuel into the plane's tanks, enough to get us out of Africa when the time came.

I sat back and watched her fly, trying not to think about the tasks and dangers ahead. At some point it doesn't pay to worry about hazards you can't do anything about. When you've taken all the precautions you can, then it's time to think about something else.

The landing site we had picked was seven miles from the Camel, at the base of what appeared on the chart to be a cliff. The elevation lines seemed to indicate a cliff of sixty or seventy feet in height.

"How do you know that is a cliff?" I had asked Julie when she first showed the chart to me. In reply she pulled out two satellite photos. They had obviously been taken at different times of day, perhaps in different seasons or years, but they were obviously of the same piece of terrain. I compared them to the chart.

There was a cliff all right, and apparently room to tuck the Osprey in against it, pretty much out of sight.

"You want me to try to guess where you got these satellite photos?"

"My friend in the CIA."

"And nobody is going to ask her any questions?"

"Nope. She's cool and she's clean."

"I don't buy it."

"She doesn't have access to this stuff. She's stealing it. They'll only talk to people with access."

"Must be a bunch of stupes in the IG's office there, huh."

She wouldn't say any more.

We destroyed the photos, of course, before we left the apartment she had rented for me. Still, the thought of Julie's classmate in the CIA who could sell us down the river to save her own hide gave me a sick feeling in the pit of my stomach as we motored through the darkness over the desert.

Julie had our destination dialed into the navigation computer, so the magic box was depicting our track and time to go. I sat there watching the miles and minutes tick down.

With five miles to go, Julie began slowing the Osprey. And she flipped on the landing lights. Beams of light seared the darkness and revealed the yellow rock and sand and dirt of the deep desert.

She began tilting the engines toward the vertical, which slowed us further and allowed the giant rotors to begin carrying a portion of our weight.

When the last mile ticked off the computer and we crossed the cliff line, the Osprey was down to fifty knots. Julie brought the V-22 into a hover and used the landing lights to explore our hiding place. Some small boulders, not too many, and the terrain under the cliff was relatively flat.

After a careful circuit and inspection, Julie set the Osprey down, shut down the engines.

The silence was startling as we took off our helmets.

Now she shut down the aircraft battery and all the cockpit lights went off.

"We're here," she said with a sigh of relief.

"You really intend to go through with this, don't you?"

"Don't tell me you still have doubts, Charlie Dean."

"Okay. I won't."

She snapped on a flashlight and led the way back through the cargo bay. She opened the rear door and we stepped out onto the godforsaken soil of the Sahara. We used a flashlight to inspect our position.

"I could get it a little closer to the cliff, but I doubt if it's worth the effort."

"Let's get to work," I said. I was tired of sitting.

First she went back to the cockpit and tilted the engines down to the cruise position. The plane would be easier to camouflage with the engines down. We would rotate the engines back to the vertical position when the time came to leave.

Next we unloaded the Humvee and trailer, then the cargo we had tied down in piles on the floor of the plane. I carried the water jugs out myself, taking care to place them where they wouldn't fall over.

The last thing we removed from the plane was the camouflage netting. We unrolled it, then began draping it over the airplane. We both had to get up on top of the plane to get the net over the tail and engine nacelles. Obviously we couldn't cover the blade of each rotor that stuck straight up, so we cut holes in the net for them.

It took us almost two hours of intense effort to get the net completely rigged. We treated ourselves to a drink of water.

"We sure can't get out of here in a hurry," I remarked.

"I swore on the altar of God I would kill the men who killed my parents. We aren't going anywhere until we do it."

"Yeah."

I finished my drink, then unhooked the trailer from the Humvee and dug out my night-vision goggles. I uncased my Model 70 and chambered a round, put on the safety, then got into the driver's seat and laid it across my lap.

"We can't plant explosives until tomorrow night," she said.

"I know that. But I want a look at that place now. You coming?"

She got her night-vision goggles and climbed into the passenger seat. I took the time to fire up the GPS and key in our destination, then started the Humvee and plugged in my night-vision goggles. It was like someone turned on the light. I could see the cliff and the plane and the stones as if the sun were shining on an overcast day.

I put the Humvee in gear and rolled.

Four

The Camel sat on a granite ridge that humped up out of the desert floor. On the eastern side of the ridge, in the low place scooped out by the wind, there was an oasis, a small pond of muddy water, a few palm trees, and a cluster of mud huts. According to Julie's CIA sister, a few dozen nomads lived here seasonally. Standing on the hood of the Humvee, which was parked on a gentle rise a mile east of the oasis, I could just see the tops of the palms and a few of the huts. No heat source flared up when I switched to infrared.

The old fort was a shattered hulk upon the skyline, brooding and massive. The structure itself wasn't large, but perched there on that granite promontory it was a presence.

I slowly did a 360-degree turn, sweeping the desert.

Nothing moved. I saw only rock and hard-packed earth, here and there a scraggly desert plant. The wind had long ago swept away the sand.

Finally I got down off the hood of the Humvee. Julie was standing there with her arms crossed looking cold, although the temperature was at least sixty.

"I want you to drive this thing back into that draw, and just sit and wait. I'm going to walk over there and eyeball it up."

"When are you coming back?"

"Couple hours after dawn, probably. I want to make sure there are no people there, and I want to see it in the daylight."

"Can't we just wait until tonight to check it out?"

"I'm not going to spend a day not knowing what in hell is over the hill. I didn't get to be this old by taking foolish risks. Drive down there and wait for me."

She got in the Humvee and did as I asked.

I adjusted my night-vision goggles, tucked the Model 70 under my arm and started hiking.

I had decided on South Africa. After this was over, I was going to try South Africa. I figured it would be middling difficult for the Arabs to root me out there. I had never been to South Africa, but from everything I had seen and heard the country sounded like it might have a future now that they had made a start at solving the racial problem. South Africa. My image of the place had a bit of a Wild West flavor that appealed to my sporting instincts.

Not that I really have any sporting instincts. Those all got squeezed out of me in Vietnam. I'd rather shoot the bastards in the back than in the front: It's safer.

The CIA and FBI? They could find me anywhere, if they wanted to. The theft of a V-22 wasn't likely to escape their notice, but I didn't think the violent death of some terrorists would inspire those folks to put in a lot of overtime. I figured a fellow who stayed out of sight would soon be out of mind too.

With three million dollars in my jeans, staying out of sight would be a pleasure.

That's the way I had it figured, anyhow. As I walked across the desert hardpan toward the huts by the mudhole, I confess, I was thinking again about South Africa, which made me angry.

Concentrate, I told myself. Stay focused. Stay alive.

I was glad the desert here was free of sand. I was leaving no tracks in the hard-packed earth and stone of the desert floor that I could see or feel with my fingers, which relieved me somewhat.

I took my time approaching the huts from downwind. No dogs that I could see, no vehicles, no sign of people. The place looked deserted.

And was. Not a soul around. I checked all five of the huts, looked in the sheds. Not even a goat or puppy.

There were marks of livestock by the water hole. Only six inches of water, I estimated, at the deepest part. At the widest place the pond was perhaps thirty feet across, about the size of an Iowa farm pond but with less water.

The cliff loomed above the back of the water hole. Sure enough, I found a trail. I started climbing.

The top of the ridge was about three hundred feet above the surrounding terrain. I huffed and puffed a bit getting up there. On top there was a bit of a breeze blowing, a warm, dry desert breeze that felt delicious at that hour of the night.

I found a vantage point and examined the fort through the night-vision goggles, looked all around in every direction. To the west I could see the paved strip of the airport reflecting the starlight, so it appeared faintly luminescent. It too was empty. No people, no planes, no vehicles, no movement, just stone and great empty places.

I took off the goggles and turned them off to save the battery, then waited for my eyes to adjust to the darkness. The stars were so close in that clear dry air it seemed as if I could reach up and touch them. To the east the sky was lightening up.

As the dawn slowly chased away the night, I worked my way toward the fort, which was about a third of a mile from where the trail topped the ridge. Fortunately there were head-high clumps of desert brush tucked into the nooks and crannies of the granite, so I tried to stay under cover as much as possible. By the time the sun poked its head over the earth's rim I was standing under the wall of the fort.

I listened.

All I could hear was the whisper of the wind.

I found a road and a gate, which wasn't locked. After all, how many people are running around out here in this wasteland?

Taking my time, I sneaked in. I had the rifle off my shoulder and leveled, with my thumb on the safety and my finger on the trigger.

A Land Rover was parked in the courtyard. It had a couple five-gallon cans strapped to the back of it and was caked with dirt and dust. The tires were relatively new, sporting plenty of tread.

When I was satisfied no one was in the courtyard, I stepped over to the Land Rover. The keys were in the ignition.

I slipped into a doorway and stood there listening.

Back when I was young, I was small and wiry and stupid enough to crawl through Viet Cong tunnels looking for bad guys. I had nightmares about that experience for years.

Somewhere in this pile of rock was at least one person, perhaps more. But where?

The old fort was quiet as a tomb. Just when I thought there was nothing to hear, I heard something . . . a scratching . . .

I examined the courtyard again. There, on a second-story window ledge, a bird.

It flew.

I hung the rifle over my shoulder on its sling and got out my knife. With the knife in my right hand, cutting edge up, I began exploring.

The old fort had some modern sleeping quarters, cooking facilities, and meeting rooms. There were electric lights plugged into wall sockets. In one of the lower rooms I found a gasoline-powered generator. Forty gallons of gasoline in plastic five-gallon cans sat in the next room.

In a tower on the top floor, in a room with a magnificent view through glass windows, sat a first-class, state-of-the-art shortwave radio. I had seen the antenna as I walked toward the fort: It was on the roof above this room. I was examining the radio, wondering if I should try to disable it, when I heard a nearby door slam.

Scurrying to the door of the room, I stood frozen, listening with my ear close to the wall.

The other person in the fort was making no attempt to be quiet, which made me feel better. He obviously thought he was very much alone. And it was just one person, close, right down the hallway.

Try as I might, I could only hear the one person, a man, opening and closing drawers, scooting something—a chair probably—across a stone floor, now slamming another door shut.

Even as I watched he came out of one of the doors and walked away from me to the stairs I had used coming up. Good thing I didn't open the door to look into his room!

I got a glimpse of him crossing the courtyard, going toward the gasoline generator.

Unwilling to move, I stood there until I heard the generator start. The hum of the gasoline engine settled into a steady drone. A lightbulb above the table upon which the radio sat illuminated.

I trotted down the hallway to the room the man had come out of. I eased the door open and glanced in. Empty.

The next room was also a bedroom, also empty, so I went in and closed the door.

I was standing back from the window, watching, fifteen minutes later when the man walked out of a doorway to the courtyard almost directly opposite the room I was in, got into the Land Rover, and started it.

He drove out through the open gate trailing a wispy plume of dust. I went to another window, an outside one, and waited. In a moment I got a glimpse of the Land Rover on the road to the airport.

In the courtyard against one wall stood a water tank on legs, with plastic lines leading away to the kitchen area. I opened the fill cap and looked in. I estimated the tank contained fifty gallons of water. Apparently people using this facility brought water with them, poured it into this tank, then used it sparingly.

I stood in the courtyard looking at the water tank, cursing under my breath. The best way to kill these people would be to poison their water with some kind of delayed-action poison that would take twenty-four hours to work, so everyone would have an opportunity to ingest some. Julie Giraud could have fucked a chemist and got us some poison. I should have thought of the water tank.

Too late now.

Damn!

Before I had a chance to cuss very much, I heard a jet. The engine noise was rapidly getting louder. I dived for cover.

Seconds later a jet airplane went right over the fort, less than a hundred feet above the radio antenna.

Staying low, I scurried up the staircase to the top of the ramparts and took a look. A small passenger jet was circling to land at the airport.

I double-timed down the staircase and hotfooted it out the gate and along the trail leading to the path down to the oasis, keeping my eye on the sky in case another jet should appear.

It took me about half an hour to get back to the oasis, and another fifteen minutes to reach the place where Julie was waiting in the Humvee. Of course I didn't just charge right up to the Humvee. Still well out of sight of the vehicle, I stopped, lay down, and caught my breath.

When I quit blowing, I circled the area where the Humvee should have been, came at it from the east. At first I didn't see her. I could see the vehicle, but she wasn't in sight.

I settled down to wait.

Another jet went over, apparently slowing to land on the other side of the ridge.

A half hour passed, then another. The temperature was rising quickly, the sun climbing the sky.

Finally, Julie moved.

She was lying at the base of a bush a hundred feet from the vehicle and she had an M-16 in her hands.

Okay.

Julie Giraud was a competent pilot and acted like she had all her shit in one sock when we were planning this mission, but I wanted to see how she handled herself on the ground. If we made a mistake in Europe, we might wind up in prison. A mistake here would cost us our lives.

I crawled forward on my stomach, taking my time, just sifting along.

It took me fifteen minutes to crawl up behind her. Finally I reached out with the barrel of the Model 70, touched her foot. She spun around as if she had been stung.

I grinned at her.

"You bastard," Julie Giraud said.

"Don't you forget it, lady."

Five

Blowing up the fort was an impractical idea and always had been. When Julie Giraud first mentioned destroying the fort with the bad guys inside, back in Van Nuys, I had let her talk. I didn't think she had any idea how much explosives would be necessary to demolish a large stone structure, and she didn't. When I finally asked her how much C-4 she thought it would take, she looked at me blankly.

We had brought a hundred pounds of the stuff, all we could transport efficiently.

I used the binoculars to follow the third plane through the sky until it disappeared behind the ridge. It was some kind of small, twin-engined bizjet.

"How come these folks are early?" I asked her.

"I don't know."

"Your CIA friend didn't tip you off about the time switch?"

"No."

The fact these people were arriving a day early bothered me and I considered it from every angle.

Life is full of glitches and unexpected twists—who ever has a day that goes as planned? To succeed at anything you must be adaptable and flexible, and smart enough to know when backing off is the right thing to do.

I wondered just how smart I was. Should we back off?

I drove the Humvee toward the cliff where we had the Osprey parked. The land rolled, with here and there gulleys cut by the runoff from rare desert storms. These gulleys had steep sides, loose sand bottoms, and were choked with desert plants. Low places had brush and cacti, but mainly the terrain was dirt with occasional rock outcroppings. One got the impression that at some time in the geologic past the dirt had blown in, covering a stark, highly eroded landscape. I tried to keep off the exposed places as much as possible and drove very slowly to keep from raising dust.

Every so often I stopped the vehicle, got out and listened for airplanes. Two more jets went over that I heard. That meant there were at least five jets at that desert strip, maybe more.

Julie sat silently, saying nothing as we drove along. When I killed the engine and got out to listen, she stayed in her seat.

I stopped the Humvee in a brushy draw about a mile from the Osprey, reached for the Model 70, then snagged a canteen and hung it over my shoulder.

"May I come with you?" she asked.

"Sure."

We stopped when we got to a low rise where we could see the V-22 and the area around it. I looked everything over with binoculars, then settled down at the base of a green bush that resembled grease-wood, trying to get what shade there was. The temperature must have been ninety by that time.

"Aren't we going down to the plane?"

"It's safer here."

Julie picked another bush and crawled under.

I was silently complimenting her on her ability to accept direction without question or explanation when she said, "You don't take many chances, do you?"

"I try not to."

"So you're just going to kill these people, then get on with the rest of your life?"

I took a good look at her face. "If you're going to chicken out," I said, "do it now, so I don't have to lie here sweating the program for the whole damned day."

"I'm not going to chicken out. I just wondered if you were."

"You said these people were terrorists, had blown up airliners. That still true?"

"Absolutely."

"Then I won't lose any sleep over them." I shifted around, got comfortable, kept the rifle just under my hands.

She met my eyes, and apparently decided this point needed a little more exploring. "I'm killing them because they killed my parents. You're killing them for money."

I sighed, tossed her the binoculars.

"Every few minutes, glass the area around the plane, then up on the ridge," I told her. "Take your time, look at everything in your field of view, look for movement. Any kind of movement. And don't let the sun glint off the binoculars."

"How are we going to do it?" she asked as she stared through the glasses.

"Blowing the fort was a pipe dream, as you well know."

She didn't reply, just scanned with the binoculars.

"The best way to do it is to blow up the planes with the people on them."

A grin crossed her face, then disappeared.

I rolled over, arranged the rifle just so, and settled down for a nap. I was so tired.

The sun had moved a good bit by the time I awakened. The air was stifling, with no detectable breeze. Julie was stretched out asleep, the binoculars in front of her. I used the barrel of the rifle to hook the strap and lift them, bring them over to me without making noise.

The land was empty, dead. Not a single creature stirred, not even a bird. The magnified images I could see through the binoculars shimmered in the heat.

Finally I put the thing down, sipped at the water in my canteen.

South Africa. Soon. Maybe I'd become a diamond prospector. There was a whole lot of interesting real estate in South Africa, or so I'd heard, and I intended to see it. Get a jeep and some camping gear and head out.

Julie's crack about killing for money rankled, of course. The fact was that these people were terrorists, predators who preyed on the weak and defenseless. They had blown up an airliner. Take money for killing them? Yep. And glad to get it, too.

Julie had awakened and moved off into the brush out of sight to relieve herself when I spotted a man on top of the cliff, a few hundred yards to the right of the Osprey. I picked him up as I swept the top of the cliff with the binoculars.

I turned the focus wheel, tried to sharpen the dancing image. Too much heat.

It was a man, all right. Standing there with a rifle on a sling over his shoulder, surveying the desert with binoculars. Instinctively I backed up a trifle, ensured the binoculars were in shade so there would be no sun reflections off the glass or frame. And I glanced at the airplane.

It should be out of sight of the man due to the way the cliff outcropped between his position and the plane. I hoped. In any event he wasn't looking at it.

I gritted my teeth, studied his image, tried by sheer strength of will to make it steadier in the glass. The distance between us was about six hundred yards, I estimated.

I put down the binoculars and slowly brought up the Model 70. I had a variable power scope on it which I habitually kept cranked to maximum magnification. The figure of the man leaped at me through the glass.

I put the crosshairs on his chest, studied him. Even through the shimmering air I could see the cloth he wore on his head and the headband that held it in place. He was wearing light-colored trousers and a shirt. And he was holding binoculars pointed precisely at me.

I heard a rustle behind me.

"Freeze, Julie," I said, loud enough that she would plainly hear me.

She stopped.

I kept the scope on him, flicked off the safety. I had automatically assumed a shooting position when I raised the rifle. Now I wiggled my left elbow into the hard earth, settled the rifle in tighter against my shoulder.

He just stood there, looking right at us.

I only saw him because he was silhouetted on the

skyline. In the shade under this brush we should be invisible to him. Should be.

Now he was scanning the horizon again. Since I had been watching he had not once looked down at the foot of the cliff upon which he was standing.

He was probably a city soldier, I decided. Hadn't been trained to look close first, before he scanned terrain farther away.

After another long moment he turned away, began walking slowly along the top of the cliff to my right, away from the Osprey. I kept the crosshairs of the scope on him until he was completely out of sight. Only then did I put the safety back on and lower the rifle.

"You can come in now," I said.

She crawled back under her bush.

"Did you see him?" I asked.

"Yes. Did he see the airplane?"

"I'm certain he didn't."

"How did he miss it?"

"It was just a little out of sight, I think. Even if he could have seen it, he never really looked in the right direction."

"We were lucky," she said.

I grunted. It was too hot to discuss philosophy. I lay there under my bush wondering just how crazy ol' Julie Giraud really was.

"If he had seen the plane, Charlie Dean, would you have shot him?"

What a question!

"You're damned right," I muttered, more than a little disgusted. "If he had seen the plane, I would have shot him and piled you into the cockpit and made you get us the hell out of here before all the Indians in the world showed up to help with the pleasant chore of lifting our hair. These guys are playing for keeps, lady. You and me had better be on the same sheet of music or we will be well and truly fucked."

Every muscle in her face tensed. "We're not leaving," she snarled, "until those sons of bitches are dead. All of them. Every last one."

She was over the edge.

A wave of cold fear swept over me. It was bad enough being on the edge of a shooting situation; now my backup was around the bend. If she went down or freaked out, how in the hell was I going to get off this rock pile?

"I've been trying to decide," she continued, "if you really have the balls for this, Charlie Dean, or if you're going to turn tail on me when crunch time comes and run like a rabbit. You're old: You look old, you sound old. Maybe you had the balls years ago, maybe you don't anymore."

From the leg pocket of her flight suit she pulled a small automatic, a .380 from the looks of it. She held it where I could see it, pointed it more or less in my direction. "Grow yourself another set of balls, Charlie Dean. Nobody is running out."

I tossed her the binoculars. "Call me if they come back," I said. I put the rifle beside me and lay down.

Sure, I thought about what a dumb ass I was. Three million bucks!—I was going to have to earn every damned dollar.

Hoo boy.

Okay, I'll admit it: I knew she was crazy that first day in Van Nuys.

I made a conscious effort to relax. The earth was warm, the air was hot, and I was exhausted. I was asleep in nothing flat.

The sun was about to set when I awoke. My binoculars were on the sand beside me and Julie Giraud was nowhere in sight. I used the scope on the rifle to examine the Osprey and the cliff behind it.

I spotted her in seconds, moving around under the plane. No one else visible.

While we had a little light, I went back for the Humvee. I crawled up on it, taking my time, ensuring that no one was there waiting for me.

When we left it that morning we had piled some dead brush on the hood and top of the vehicle, so I pulled that off before I climbed in.

Taking it slow so I wouldn't raise dust, I drove the mile or so to the Osprey. I got there just as the last rays of the sun vanished.

I backed up to the trailer and we attached it to the Humvee.

"Want to tell me your plan, Charlie Dean?" she asked. "Or do you have one?"

As I repacked the contents of the trailer I told her how I wanted to do it. Amazingly, she agreed readily.

She was certainly hard to figure. One minute I thought she was a real person, complete with a conscience and the intellectual realization that even the enemy were human beings, then the next second she was a female Rambo, ready to gut them all, one by one.

She helped me make up C-4 bombs, rig the detonators and radio controls. I did the first one, she watched intently, then she did one on her own. I checked it, and she got everything right.

"Don't take any unnecessary chances tonight," I said. "I want you alive and well when this is over so you can fly me out of here."

She merely nodded. It was impossible to guess what she might have been thinking.

I wasn't about to tell her that I had flown helicopters in Vietnam. I was never a rated pilot, but I was young and curious, so the pilots often let me practice under their supervision. I had watched her with the Osprey and thought that I could probably fly it if absolutely necessary. The key would be to use the checklist and take plenty of time. If I could get it started, I thought I could fly it out. There were parachutes in the thing, so I would not need to land it.

I didn't say any of this to her, of course.

We had a packet of radio receivers and detonators—I counted them—enough for six bombs. If I set them all on the same frequency I could blow up six planes with one push of the button. If I could get the bombs aboard six planes without being discovered.

What if there were more than six planes? Well, I had some pyrotechnic fuses, which seemed impractical to use on an airplane, and some chemical fuses. In the cargo bay of the Osprey I examined the chemical fuses by flashlight. Eight hours seemed to be the maximum setting. The problem was that I didn't know when the bad guys planned to leave.

As I was meditating on fuses and bombs, I went outside and walked around the Osprey. There was a turreted three-barreled fifty-caliber machine gun in the nose of the thing. Air Force Ospreys didn't carry stingers like this, but this one belonged to the Marine Corps, or did until twenty-four hours ago.

I opened the service bay. Gleaming brass in the feed trays reflected the dim evening light.

Julie was standing right behind me. "I stole this one because it had the gun," she remarked. "Less range than the Air Force birds, but the gun sold me."

"Maximum firepower is always a good choice."

"What are you thinking?" she asked.

We discussed contingencies as we wired up the transfer pump in the bladder fuel tank we had chained down in the cargo bay. We used the aircraft's battery to power the pump, so all we had to do was watch as three thousand pounds of jet fuel was transferred into the aircraft's tanks.

My plan had bombs, bullets, and a small river of blood—we hoped—just the kind of tale that appealed to Julie Giraud. She even allowed herself a tight smile.

Me? I had a cold knot in the pit of my stomach and I was sweating.

Six

———

We finished loading the Humvee and the trailer attached to it before sunset and ate MREs in the twilight. As soon as it was dark, we donned our night-vision goggles and drove toward the oasis. I stopped often to get up on the vehicle's hood, the best vantage point around, and take a squint in all directions.

I parked the vehicle at the foot of the trail. "If I'm not back in an hour and a half, they've caught me," I told Julie Giraud. I smeared my face with grease to cut the white shine, checked my reflection in the rearview mirror, then did my neck and the back of my hands.

"If they catch you," she said, "I won't pay you the rest of the money."

"Women are too maudlin to be good soldiers," I told her. "You've got to stop this cloying sentimentality. Save the tears for the twenty-five-year reunion."

When I was as invisible as I was going to get, I hoisted a rucksack that I had packed that evening, put the M-16 over my shoulder, and started up the trail.

Every now and then I switched the goggles from ambient light to infrared and looked for telltale heat sources. I spotted some small mammal, too small to be human. I continued up the ridge, wondering how any critters managed to make a living in this godforsaken desert.

The temperature had dropped significantly from the high during the afternoon. I estimated the air was still at eighty degrees, but it would soon go below seventy. Even the earth was cooling, although not as quickly as the air.

I topped the ridge slowly, on the alert for security patrols. Before we committed ourselves to a course of action, we had to know how many security people were prowling around.

No one in sight now.

I got off to one side of the trail, just in case, and walked toward the old fortress, the Camel. Tonight light shone from several of the structure's windows, light visible for many miles in that clean desert air.

I was still at least five hundred yards from the walls when I first heard the hum of the generator, barely audible at that distance. The noise gradually increased as I approached the structure. When I was about fifty yards from the wall, I circled the fort to a vantage point where I could see the main gate, the gate where I entered on my last visit. It was standing open. A guard with an assault rifle sat on a stool near the gate; he was quite clear in the goggles. He was sitting under an overhang of the wall at a place where he could watch the road that led off the ridge, the road to the oasis and the airfield. He was not wearing any night-vision aid, just sitting in the darkness under the wall.

The drone of the gasoline generator meant that he could hear nothing. Of course, it handicapped me as well.

I continued around the structure, crossing the road at a spot out of sight of the man at the gate. Taking my time, slipping through the sparse brush as carefully as possible, I inspected every foot of the wall. The main gate was the only entrance I noticed on my first visit, yet I wanted to be sure.

A man strolled on top of the wall on the side opposite the main gate; the instant I saw him I dropped motionless to the ground. Seconds passed as he continued to walk, then finally he reversed his course. When he disappeared from view I scurried over to a rock outcrop and crouched under it, with my body out of sight from the wall.

If he had an infrared scope or any kind of ambient light collector, he could have seen me lying on the open ground.

I crouched there waiting for something to happen. If they came streaming out of the main gate, they could trap me on the point of this ridge, hunt me down at their leisure.

As I waited I discovered that the M-16 was already in my hands. I had removed it from my shoulder automatically, without thinking.

Several minutes passed as I waited, listening to the hypnotic drone of the generator, waiting for something to happen. Anything.

Finally a head became visible on top of the wall. The sentry again, still strolling aimlessly. He leaned against the wall for a while, then disappeared.

Now I hurried along, completed my circumnavigation of the fort.

I saw only the two men, one on the gate and the man who had been walking the walls. Although I had seen the man on the wall twice, I was convinced it was the same person. And I was certain there was only one entrance to the fort, the main gate.

I had to go through that gate so I was going to have to take out the guard. I was going to have to do it soon, then hope I could get in and out before his absence from his post was noticed or someone came to relieve him. Taking chances like that wasn't the best way to live to spend that three million dollars, that's for sure, but we didn't have the time or resources to minimize the risk. I was going to have to have some luck here or we had no chance to pull off this thing.

This whole goddamn expedition was half-baked, I reflected, and certainly no credit to me. Man, why didn't I think of poisoning their water supply when we were brainstorming in Germany?

In my favor was the fact that these people didn't seem very worried about their safety or anything else. A generator snoring away, only two guards? An open gate?

I worked my way to the wall, then turned and crept toward the guard. The generator hid the sounds I made as I crept along. He was facing the road.

I got about ten feet from him and froze. He was facing away from me at a slight angle, but if I tried to get closer, he was going to pick me up in his peripheral vision. I sensed it, so I froze.

He changed his position on the stool, played with the rifle on his knees, looked at the myriad of stars that hung just over our heads. Finally he stood and stretched. For an instant he turned away from me. I covered the distance in two bounds, wrapped my arm around his mouth, and jammed my knife into his back up to the hilt.

The knife went between his ribs right into his heart. Two convulsive tremors, then he was dead.

I carried him and his rifle off into the darkness. He weighed maybe one-eighty, as near as I could tell.

One of the outcroppings that formed the edge of the top of the ridge would keep him hidden from anyone but a determined searcher. After I stashed the body, I hurried back to the gate. I took off my night-vision goggles, waited for my eyes to adjust. I took off my rifle, leaned it against the wall out of sight.

As I waited I saw the man on the ramparts walking his rounds. He was in no hurry, obviously bored. I got a radio-controlled bomb from the rucksack, checked the frequency, and turned on the receiver.

The Land Rover was in the courtyard. When the man on the wall was out of sight, I slipped over to it and lay down. I pulled out the snap wire and snapped it around one of the suspension arms. The antenna of the bomb I let dangle.

This little job took less than thirty seconds. Then I scurried across the courtyard into the shelter of the staircase.

The conferees were probably in the living area; I sure as hell hoped they were. My edge was that the people here were not on alert. And why should they be? This fort was buried in the most desolate spot on the planet, hundreds of miles from anyplace.

Still, my life was on the line, so I moved as cautiously as I could, trying very hard to make no noise at all, pausing to listen carefully before I rounded any corner. My progress was glacial. It took me almost five minutes to climb the stairs and inch down the corridor to the radio room.

The hum of the generator was muted the farther away from it I moved, but it was the faint background noise that covered any minor noise I was making. And any minor noise anyone else was making. That reality had me sweating.

The door to the radio room was ajar, the room dark.

Knocking out the generator figured to be the easiest way to disable the radio, unless they had a battery to use as backup. I was betting they did.

After listening for almost a minute outside the door, I eased it open gently, my fighting knife in my hand.

The only light came through the interior window from the floods in the courtyard. The room was empty of people!

I went in fast, laid my knife on the table, got a bomb out of the rucksack. This one was rigged with a chemical fuse, so I broke the chemicals, shook the thing to start the reaction, then put the package—explosive, detonator, fuse and all—directly behind the radio. As I turned I was struck in the face by a runaway Freightliner.

Only partially conscious, I found myself falling. A rough hand gripped me fiercely, then another truck slammed into my face. If I hadn't turned my head to protect myself, that blow would have put me completely out.

As it was, I couldn't stay upright. My legs turned to jelly and I went to the floor, which was cold and hard.

"What a pleasant surprise," my assailant said in highly accented English, then kicked me in the side. His boot almost broke my left arm, which was fortunate, because if he had managed to get a clean shot at my ribs he would have caved in a lung.

I wasn't feeling very lucky just then. My arm felt like it was in four pieces and my side was on fire. I fought for air.

I couldn't take much more of this. If I didn't do something pretty damned quick he was going to kick me to death.

Curling into a fetal position, I used my right hand

to draw my hideout knife from my left boot. I had barely got it out when he kicked me in the kidney.

At first I thought the guy had rammed a knife into my back—the pain was that intense. I was fast running out of time.

I rolled over toward him, just in time to meet his foot coming in again. I slashed with the knife, which had a razor-sharp two-sided blade about three inches long. I felt it bite into something.

He stepped back then, bent down to feel his calf. I got my feet under me and rose into a crouch.

"A knife, is it? You think you can save yourself with that?"

While he was talking he lashed out again with a leg. It was a kick designed to distract me, tempt me to go for his leg again with the knife.

I didn't, so when he spun around and sent another of those iron-fisted artillery shots toward my head, I was ready. I went under the incoming punch and slashed his stomach with the knife.

I cut him bad.

Now he grunted in pain, sagged toward the radio table.

I gathered myself, got out of his way, got into a crouch so I could defend myself.

He was holding his stomach with both hands. In the dim light I could see blood. I had really gotten him.

"Shouldn't have played with you," he said, and reached for the pistol in the holster on his belt.

Too late. I was too close. With one mighty swing of my arm I slashed his throat. Blood spewed out, a look of surprise registered on his face, then he collapsed.

Blood continued to pump from his neck.

I had to wipe the sweat from my eyes.

Jesus! My hands were shaking, trembling.

Never again, God! I promise. Never again!

I stowed the little knife back in my boot, retrieved the rucksack and my fighting knife from the table.

Outside in the corridor I carefully pulled the door to the radio room shut, made sure it latched.

Down the stairs, across the courtyard, through the gate. Safe in the darkness outside, I retrieved my M-16 and puked up my MREs.

Yeah, I'm a real tough guy. Shit!

Then I trotted for the trail to the oasis. It wasn't much of a trot. My side, back, and arm were on fire, and my face was still numb. The best I could manage was a hell-bent staggering gait.

As I ran the numbness in my side and back wore off. I wheezed like an old horse and savored the pain, which was proof positive I was still alive.

Julie Giraud was standing beside the Humvee chewing her fingernails. I took my time looking over the area, made sure she was really alone, then walked the last hundred feet.

"Hey," I said.

My voice made her jump. She glanced at my face, then stared. "What happened?"

I eased myself into the driver's seat.

"A guy was waiting for me."

"What?"

"He spoke to me in English."

"Well . . ."

"Didn't even try a phrase in Arabic. Just spoke to me in English."

"You're bleeding under your right eye, I think. With all that grease it's hard to tell."

"Pay attention to what I'm telling you. He spoke to me in English. He knew I understood it. Doesn't that worry you?"

"What about the radio?"

"He knew I was coming. Someone told him. He was waiting for me."

"You're just guessing."

"He almost killed me."

"He didn't."

"If they knew we were coming, we're dead."

Before I could draw another breath, she had a pistol pointed at me. She placed the muzzle against the side of my head.

"I'll tell you one more time, Charlie Dean, one more time. These people are baby-killers, murderers of women and kids and old people. They have been tried in a court of law and found guilty. We are going to kill them so they can never kill again."

Crazy! She was crazy as hell!

Her voice was low, every word distinctly pronounced: "I don't care what they know or who told them what. *We are going to kill these men. You will help me do it or I will kill you.* Have I made it plain enough? Do you understand?"

"Did the court sentence these people to die?" I asked.

"*I* sentenced them! *Me!* Julie Giraud. And I am going to carry it out. *Death.* For every one of them."

Seven

The satellite photos showed a wash just off the east end of the runway. We worked our way along it, then crawled to a spot that allowed us to look the length of it.

The runway was narrow, no more than fifty feet wide. The planes were parked on a mat about half-way down. The wind was out of the west, as it usually was at night. To take off, the planes would have to taxi individually to the east end of the runway, this end, turn around, then take off to the west.

"If they don't discover that the guards are missing, search the place, find the bombs and disable them, we've got a chance," I said. "Just a chance."

"You're a pessimist."

"You got that right."

"How many guards do you think are around the planes?"

"I don't know. All of the pilots could be there; there could easily be a dozen people down there."

"So we just sneak over, see what's what?"

"That's about the size of it."

"For three million dollars I thought I was getting someone who knew how to pull this off."

"And I thought the person hiring me was sane. We both made a bad deal. You want to fly the Osprey back to Germany and tell them you're sorry you borrowed it?"

"They didn't kill your parents."

"I guarantee you, before this is over you're going to be elbow-deep in blood, lady. And your parents will still be dead."

"You said that before."

"It's still true."

I was tempted to give the bitch a rifle and send her down the runway to do her damnedest, but I didn't.

I took the goddamn M-16, adjusted the night-vision goggles, and went myself. My left side hurt like hell, from my shoulder to my hip. I flexed my arm repeatedly, trying to work the pain out.

The planes were readily visible with the goggles. I kept to the waist-high brush on the side of the runway toward the planes, which were parked in a row. It wasn't until I got about halfway there that I could count them. Six planes.

The idea was to get the terrorists into the planes, then destroy the planes in the air. The last thing we wanted was the terrorists and the guards out here in this desert running around looking for us. With dozens of them and only two of us, there was only one way for that tale to end.

No, we needed to get them into the planes. I didn't have enough radio-controlled detonators to put on all the planes, so I thought if I could disable some of the planes and put bombs on the rest, we would have a chance. But first we had to eliminate the guards.

If the flight crews were bivouacked near the planes, this was going to get really dicey.

I took my time, went slowly from bush to bush, looking at everything. When I used infrared, I could see a heat source to the south of the planes that had to be an open fire. No people, though.

I was crouched near the main wheel of the plane on the end of the mat when I saw my first guard. He was relieving himself against the nearest airplane's nosewheel.

When he finished he zipped up and resumed his stroll along the mat.

I went behind the plane and made my way toward the fire.

They had built the thing in a fifty-five-gallon drum. Two people stood with their backs to the fire, warming up. I could have used a stretch by that fire myself: The temperature was below sixty degrees by that time and going lower.

No tents. No one in sleeping bags that I could see.

Three of them.

I settled down to wait. Before we made a move, I had to be certain of the number of people that were here and where they were. If I missed one I wouldn't live to spend a dollar of Julie Giraud's blood money.

Lying there in the darkness, I tried to figure it all out. Didn't get anywhere. Why that guy addressed me in English I had no idea. He was certainly no Englishman; nor was he a native of any English-speaking country.

Julie Giraud wanted these sons of the desert dead and in hell—of that I was absolutely convinced. She wasn't a good enough actress to fake it. The money she had paid me was real enough, the V-22 Osprey was real, the guns were real, the bombs were real, we were so deep in the desert we could never drive or hike out. Never.

She was my ticket out. If she went down, I was going to have to try to fly the Osprey myself. If the plane was damaged, we were going to die here.

Simple as that.

Right then I wished to hell I was back in Van Nuys in the filling station watching Candy make change. I was too damned old for this shit and I knew it.

I had been lying in the dirt for about an hour when the guy walking the line came to the fire and one of the loafers there went into the darkness to replace him. The two at the fire then crawled into sleeping bags.

I waited another half hour, using the goggles to keep track of the sentry.

The sentry was first. I was crouched in the bushes when he came over less than six feet from me, dropped his trousers and squatted.

I left him there with his pants around his ankles and went over to the sleeping bags. Both the sleeping men died without making a sound.

Killing them wasn't heroic or glorious or anything like that. I felt dirty, coated with the kind of slime that would never wash off. The fact that they would have killed me just as quickly if they had had the chance didn't make it any easier. They killed for political reasons, I killed for money: We were the same kind of animal.

I walked back down the runway to where Julie Giraud waited.

I got into the Humvee without saying anything and started the motor.

"How many were there?" she asked.

"Three," I said.

We placed radio-controlled bombs in three of the airplanes. We taped a bomb securely in the nosewheel well of each of them, then dangled the antennas outside, so they would hang out the door even if the wheel were retracted.

When we were finished with that we stood for a moment in the darkness discussing things. The fort was over a mile away and I prayed the generator was still running, making fine background music. Julie crawled under the first plane and looked it over. First she fired shots into the nose tires, which began hissing. Then she fired a bullet into the bottom of each wing tank. Fuel ran out and soaked into the dirt.

There was little danger in this, as Julie well knew. The tanks would not explode unless something very hot went into a mixture of fuel vapor and oxygen: She was putting a bullet into liquid. The biggest danger was that the low-powered pistol bullets would fail to penetrate the metal skin of the wing and the fuel tank. In fact, she fired six shots into the tanks of the second plane before she was satisfied with the amount of fuel running out on the ground.

When she had flattened the nose tires of all of the unbooby-trapped planes and punched bullet holes in the tanks, she walked over to the Humvee, reeking of jet fuel.

"Let's go," she said grimly.

As we drove away I glanced at her. She was smiling.

For the first time, I began to seriously worry that she would intentionally leave me in the desert.

I comforted myself with the fact that she didn't really care about the money she was going to owe me. She could justify the deaths of these men, but if she killed me, she was no better than they.

I hoped she saw it that way too.

*   *   *

She let me out of the Humvee on the road about a quarter of a mile below the fort. From where I stood the road rose steadily and curved through three switchbacks until it reached the main gate.

With my Model 70 in hand, I left the road and began climbing the hill straight toward the main gate. The night was about over. Even as I climbed I thought I could see the sky beginning to lighten up in the east.

The generator was off. No light or sound came from the massive old fort, which was now a dark presence that blotted out the stars above me.

Were they in bed?

The gate was still open, with no one in sight on top of the wall or in the courtyard. That was a minor miracle or an invitation to a fool—me. If they had discovered King Kong's body they were going to be waiting.

I stood there in the darkness listening to the silence, trying to convince myself these guys were all in their beds sound asleep, that the miracle was real.

No guts, no glory, I told myself, sucked it up, and slipped through the gate. I sifted my way past the Land Rover and began climbing the stairs.

I didn't go up those stairs slow as sap in a maple tree this time. I zipped up the steps, knife in one hand and pistol in the other. Maybe I just didn't care. If they killed me, maybe that would be a blessing.

The corridor on top was empty, and the door to the radio shack was still closed. I eased it open and peeked in. King Kong was still lying in a pool of his own blood on the floor, just the way I had left him.

I pulled the door shut, then tiptoed along the corridor toward an alcove overlooking the courtyard.

I heard a noise and crouched in the darkness.

Someone snoring.

The sound was coming from an open door on my left. At least two men.

I eased past the door, moving as quietly as I could, until I reached the alcove.

Nothing stirred in the quiet moment before dawn.

From the rucksack hanging from my shoulder I removed three hand grenades, placed them on the floor near my feet.

And I waited.

Eight

Dawn took its own sweet time arriving. I was sore, stiff, hungry, and I loathed myself. I was also so exhausted that I was having trouble thinking clearly. What was there about Julie that scared me?

It wasn't that she might kill me or leave me stranded in the desert surrounded by corpses. She didn't strike me as the kind to double-cross anyone: If I was wrong about that I was dead and that was that. There was something else, something that didn't fit, but tired as I was, I couldn't put my finger on it.

She stole the V-22, hired me to help her . . .

Well, we would make it or we wouldn't.

I sat with my rifle on my lap, finger on the trigger, leaned back against the wall, closed my eyes just for a moment. I was so tired . . .

I awakened with a jerk. Somewhere in the fort a door closed with a minor bang.

The day was here, the sun was shining straight in through the openings in the wall.

Someone was moving around. Another door slammed.

I looked at my watch. The bombs should have gone off twenty minutes ago. I had been asleep over an hour.

I slowly rose from the floor on which I had been sitting, so stiff and sore I could hardly move. I picked up the grenades and pocketed them. Moving as carefully and quietly as I could, I got up on the railing, put my leg up to climb onto the roof.

The rifle slipped off my shoulder. I grabbed for the strap and was so sore I damn near dropped it.

The courtyard was thirty feet below. I teetered on the railing, the rifle hanging by a strap from my right forearm, the rucksack dangling, every muscle I owned screaming in protest.

Then I was safely up, pulling all that damn gear along with me.

Taking my time, I spread out the gear, got out the grenades, and placed them where I could easily reach them.

I took a long drink from my canteen, then screwed the lid back on and put it away.

The radio that controlled the bombs was not large. I set the frequency very carefully, turned the thing on, and let the capacitor charge. When the green light came on, I gingerly set the radio aside.

Three minutes later, a muffled bang from the bomb behind the shortwave radio slapped the air.

I lay down on the roof and gripped the rifle.

Running feet.

Shouts. Shouts in Arabic.

It didn't take them long to zero in on the radio

room. I heard running feet, several men, pounding along the corridor.

They didn't spend much time in there looking at the remains of King Kong or the shortwave. More shouts rang through the building.

Julie Giraud and I had argued about what would happen next. I predicted that these guys would panic, would soon decide that the logical, best course of action was a fast plane ride back to civilization. I suspected they were bureaucrats at heart, string-pullers. Julie thought they might be warriors, that their first instinct would be to fight. We would soon see who was right.

I could hear the voices bubbling out of the courtyard, then what sounded like orders given in a clean, calm voice. That would never do. I pulled the pin from a grenade, then threw it at the wall on the other side of the courtyard.

The grenade struck the wall, made a noise that attracted the attention of the people below, then exploded just before it hit the ground.

A scream. Moans.

I tossed a second grenade, enjoyed the explosion, then hustled along the rooftop. I lay down beside a chimney in a place that allowed me to watch the rest of the roof and the area just beyond the main gate.

From here I could also see the planes parked on the airfield, gleaming brightly in the morning sun.

Someone stuck his head over the edge of the roof. He was gone too quick for me to get around, but I figured he would pop up again with a weapon of some kind, so I got the Model 70 pointed and flicked off the safety. Sure enough, fifteen seconds later the head popped back up and I squeezed off a shot. His body hit the pavement thirty feet below with a heavy plop.

The Land Rover could not carry them all, of

course. Still, I thought this crowd would go for it as
if it were a lifeboat on the *Titanic*. I was not surprised to hear the engine start even though I had
tossed two grenades into the courtyard where the
vehicle was parked: The Rover was essentially im-
pervious to shrapnel damage, and should run for a
bit, at least, as long as the radiator remained intact.

Angry shouts reached me. Apparently the Rover
driver refused to wait for a full load.

I kept my head down, waited until I heard the
Rover clear the gate and start down the road. Then
I pushed the button on the radio control.

The explosion was quite satisfying. In about half
a minute a column of smoke from the wreckage
could be seen from where I lay.

I stayed put. I was in a good defensive position,
what happened next was up to the crowd below.

The sun climbed higher in the sky and on the
roof of that old fort, the temperature soared. I was
sweating pretty good by then, was exhausted and
hungry . . . Finally I had had enough. I crawled over
to one of the cooking chimneys and stood up.

They were going down the road in knots of threes
and fours. With the binoculars I counted them.
Twenty-eight.

There was no way to know if that was all of them.

Crouching, I made my way to the courtyard side,
where I could look down in, and listen.

No sound but the wind, which was out of the west
at about fifteen knots, a typical desert day this time
of year.

After a couple minutes of this, I inched my head
over the edge for a look. Three bodies lay sprawled
in the courtyard.

I had a fifty-foot rope in the rucksack. I tied one
end around a chimney and tossed it over the wall
on the side away from the main gate. Then I clam-
bered over.

Safely on the ground, I kept close to the wall, out of sight of the openings above me. On the north side the edge of the ridge was close, about forty yards. I got opposite that point, gripped my rifle with both hands, and ran for it.

No shots.

Safely under the ledge, I sat down, caught my breath, and had a drink of water.

If there was anyone still in the fort waiting to ambush me, he could wait until doomsday for all I cared.

I moved downslope and around the ridge about a hundred yards to a place where I could see the runway and the airplanes and the road.

The figures were still distinct in my binoculars, walking briskly.

What would they do when they got to the airplanes? They would find the bodies of three men who died violently and three sabotaged airplanes. Three of the airplanes would appear to be intact.

The possibility that the intact airplanes were sabotaged would of course occur to them. I argued that they would not get in those planes, but would hunker down and wait until some of their friends came looking for them. Of course, the only food and water they had would be in the planes or what they had carried from the fort, but they could comfortably sit tight for a couple of days.

We couldn't. If the Libyan military found us, the Osprey would be MiG-meat and we would be doomed.

A thorough, careful preflight of the bizjets would turn up the bombs, of course. We needed to panic these people, not give them the time to search the jets or find holes to crawl into.

Panic was Julie's job.

She had grinned when I told her how she would have to do it.

I used the binoculars to check the progress of the walking men. They were about a mile away now, approaching the mat where the airplanes were parked. The laggards were hurrying to catch up with the leaders. Apparently no one wanted to take the chance that he might be left behind.

Great outfit, that.

The head of the column had just reached the jets when I heard the Osprey. It was behind me, coming down the ridge.

In seconds it shot over the fort, which was to my left, and dived toward the runway.

Julie was a fine pilot, and the Osprey was an extraordinary machine. She kept the engines horizontal and made a high-speed pass over the bizjets, clearing the tail of the middle one by about fifty feet. I watched the whole show through my binoculars.

She gave the terrorists a good look at the U.S. Marine Corps markings on the plane.

The Osprey went out about a mile and began the transition to rotor-borne flight. I watched it slow, watched the engines tilt up, then watched it drop to just a few feet above the desert.

Julie kept the plane moving forward just fast enough to stay out of the tremendous dust cloud that the rotors kicked up, a speed of about twenty knots, I estimated.

She came slowly down the runway. Through the binoculars I saw the muzzle flashes as she squeezed off a burst from the flex Fifty. I knew she planned to shoot at one of the disabled jets, see if she could set it afire. The fuel tanks would still contain fuel vapor and oxygen, so a high-powered bullet in the right place should find something to ignite.

Swinging the binoculars to the planes, I was pleasantly surprised to see one erupt in flame.

Yep.

The Osprey accelerated. Julie rotated the engines down and climbed away.

The terrorists didn't know how many enemies they faced. Nor how many Ospreys were about. They were lightly armed and not equipped for a desert firefight, so they had limited options. Apparently that was the way they figured it too, because in less than a minute the first jet taxied out. Another came right behind it. The third was a few seconds late, but it taxied onto the runway before the first reached the end and turned around.

The first plane had to wait for the other two. There was just room on the narrow strip for each of them to turn, but there was no pullout, no way for one plane to get out of the way of the other two. The first two had to wait until the last plane to leave the mat turned around in front of them.

Finally, all three had turned and were sitting one behind the other, pointing west into the wind. The first plane rolled. Ten seconds later the second followed. The third waited maybe fifteen seconds, then it began rolling.

The first plane broke ground as Julie Giraud came screaming in from the east at a hundred feet above the ground. The Osprey looked to be flying almost flat out, which Julie said was about 270 knots.

She overtook the jets just as the third one broke ground.

She had moved a bit in front of it, still ripping along, when the second and third plane exploded. Looking through the binoculars, it looked as if the nose came off each plane. The damaged fuselages tilted down and smashed into the ground, making surprisingly little dust when they hit.

The first plane, a Lear I think, seemed undamaged.

The bomb must have failed to explode.

The pilot of the bizjet had his wheels retracted

now, was accelerating with the nose down. But not fast enough. Julie Giraud was overtaking nicely.

Through the binoculars I saw the telltale wisp of smoke from the nose of the Osprey. She was using the gun.

The Lear continued to accelerate, now began to widen the distance between it and the trailing Osprey.

"It's going to get away," I whispered. The words were just out of my mouth when the thing caught fire.

Trailing black smoke, the Lear did a slow roll over onto its back. The nose came down. The roll continued, but before the pilot could level the wings the plane smeared itself across the earth in a gout of fire and smoke.

Nine

Julie Giraud landed the Osprey on the runway near the sabotaged planes. When I walked up she was sitting in the shade under the left wing with an M-16 across her lap.

She had undoubtedly searched the area before I arrived, made sure no one had missed the plane rides to hell. Fire had spread to the other sabotaged airplanes, and now all three were burning. Black smoke tailed away on the desert wind.

"So how does it feel?" I asked as I settled onto the ground beside her.

"Damn good, thank you very much."

The heat was building, a fierce dry heat that sucked the moisture right out of you. I got out my canteen and drained the thing.

"How do you feel?" she asked after a bit, just to be polite.

"Exhausted and dirty."

"I could use a bath too."

"The dirty I feel ain't gonna wash off."

"That's too bad."

"I'm breaking your heart." I got to my feet. "Let's get this thing back to the cliff and covered with camouflage netting. Then we can sleep."

She nodded, got up, led the way into the machine.

We were spreading the net over the top of the plane when we heard a jet.

"Getting company," I said.

Julie was standing on top of the Osprey. Now she shaded her eyes, looked north, tried to spot the plane that we heard.

She saw it first, another bizjet. That was a relief to me—a fighter might have spotted the Osprey and strafed it.

"Help me get the net off it," she demanded, and began tossing armloads of net onto the ground.

"Are you tired of living?"

"Anyone coming to visit that crowd of baby-killers is a terrorist himself."

"So you're going to kill them?"

"If I can. Now drag that net out of my way!"

I gathered a double armful and picked it up. Julie climbed down, almost dived through the door into the machine. It took me a couple minutes to drag the net clear, and took Julie about that long to get the engines started and the plane ready to fly.

The instant I gave a thumb-up, she applied power and lifted off.

I hid my face so I wouldn't get dirt in my eyes.

Away she went in a cloud of dirt.

She shot the plane down. The pilot landed, then tried to take off when he saw the Osprey and the burned-out jets. Julie Giraud used the flex Fifty on him and turned the jet into a fireball a hundred yards off the end of the runway.

When she landed I got busy with the net, spreading it out.

"You are the craziest goddamn broad I ever met," I told her. "You are no better than these terrorists. You're just like them."

"Bullshit," she said contemptuously.

"You don't know who the hell you just killed. For all you know you may have killed a planeload of oil-company geologists."

"Whoever it was was in the wrong place at the wrong time."

"Just like your parents."

"Somebody has to take on the predators," she shouted at me. "They feed on us. If we don't fight back, they'll eat us all."

I let her have the last word. I was sick of her and sick of me and wished to Christ I had never left Van Nuys.

I got a little sleep that afternoon in the shade under a wing, but I had too much on my mind to do more than doze. Darkness finally came and we took the net off the plane for the last time. We left the net, the Humvee, the trailer, everything. I put all the stuff we didn't need over and around the trailer as tightly as I could, then put a chemical fuse in the last of the C-4 in the trailer and set it to blow in six hours.

When we lifted off, I didn't even bother to look at the Camel, the old fortress. I never wanted to see any of this again.

She flew west on autopilot, a few hundred feet above the desert floor. There were mountain ranges ahead of us. She used the night-vision goggles to spot them and climbed when the terrain forced her to. I dozed beside her in the copilot's seat.

Hours later she shook me awake. Out the window ahead I could see the lights of Tangier.

She had the plane on autopilot, flying toward the city. We went aft, put on coveralls, helped each other don backpacks and parachutes, then she waddled forward to check how the plane was flying.

The idea was to fly over the city from east to west, jump over the western edge of the city and let the plane fly on, out to sea. When the fuel in the plane was exhausted it would go into the ocean, probably break up and sink.

Meanwhile we would be on our way via commercial airliner. I had my American passports in my backpack—my real one and Robert Arnold's—and a plane ticket to South Africa. I hadn't asked Julie where she was going when we hit the ground because I didn't want to know. By that point I hoped to God I never set eyes on her again.

She lowered the tailgate, and I walked out on it. She was looking out one of the windows. She held up a hand, signaling me to get ready. I could just glimpse lights.

Now she came over to stand beside me. "Fifteen seconds," she shouted and looked at her watch. I looked at mine too.

I must have relaxed for just a second, because the next thing I knew she pushed me and I was going out, reaching for her. She was inches beyond my grasp.

Then I was out of the plane and falling through the darkness.

Needless to say, I never saw Julie Giraud again. I landed on a rocky slope, a sheep pasture I think, on the edge of town and gathered up the parachute. She was nowhere in sight.

I took off my helmet, listened for airplane noise . . . nothing.

Just a distant jet, maybe an airliner leaving the commercial airport.

I buried the chute and helmet and coveralls in a hole I dug with a folding shovel. I tossed the shovel into the hole and filled it with my hands, tromped it down with my new civilian shoes, then set off downhill with a flashlight. Didn't see a soul.

The next morning I walked into town and got a room at a decent hotel. I had a hot bath and went to bed and slept the clock around, almost twenty-four hours. When I awoke I went to the airport and caught a flight to Capetown.

Capetown is a pretty city in a spectacular setting, on the ocean with Table Mountain behind it. I had plenty of cash and I established an account with a local bank, then had money wired in from Switzerland. There was three million in the Swiss account before my first transfer, so Julie Giraud made good on her promise. As I instinctively knew she would.

I lived in a hotel the first week, then found a little place that a widow rented to me.

I watched the paper pretty close, expecting to see a story about the massacre in the Libyan desert. The Libyans were bound to find the wreckage of those jets sooner or later, and the bodies, and the news would leak out.

But it didn't.

The newspapers never mentioned it.

Finally I got to walking down to the city library and reading the papers from Europe and the United States.

Nothing. *Nada.*

Like it never happened.

A month went by, a peaceful, quiet month. No one paid any attention to me, I had a mountain of money in the local bank and in Switzerland, and neither radio, television, nor newspapers ever mentioned all those dead people in the desert.

Finally I called my retired Marine pal Bill Wiley in Van Nuys, the police dispatcher. "Hey, Bill, this is Charlie Dean."

"Hey Charlie. When you coming home, guy?"

"I don't know. How's Candy doing with the stations?"

"They're making more money than they ever did with you running them. He's got rid of the facial iron and works twelve hours a day."

"No shit!"

"So where are you?"

"Let's skip that for a bit. I want you to do me a favor. Tomorrow at work how about running me on the crime computer, see if I'm wanted for anything."

He whistled. "What the hell you been up to, Charlie?"

"Will you do that? I'll call you tomorrow night."

"Give me your birth date and social security number."

I gave it to him, then said good-bye.

I was on pins and needles for the next twenty-four hours. When I called again, Bill said, "You ain't in the big computer, Charlie. What the hell you been up to?"

"I'll tell you all about it sometime."

"So when you coming home?"

"One of these days. I'm still vacationing as hard as I can."

"Kiss her once for me," Bill Wiley said.

At the Capetown library I got into old copies of the *International Herald Tribune*, published in Paris. I finally found what I was looking for on microfiche: a complete list of the passengers who died twelve years ago on the Air France flight that blew up over

Niger. Colonel Giraud and his wife were not on the list.

Well, the light finally began to dawn.

I got one of the librarians to help me get on the Internet. What I was interested in were lists of U.S. Air Force Academy graduates, say from five to ten years ago.

I read the names until I thought my eyeballs were going to fall out. No Julie Giraud.

I'd been had. Julie was either a CIA or French agent. French, I suspected, and the Americans agreed to let her steal a plane.

As I sat and thought about it, I realized that I didn't ever meet old Colonel Giraud's kids. Not to the best of my recollection. Maybe he had a couple of daughters, maybe he didn't, but damned if I could remember.

What had she said? That the colonel said I was the best Marine in the corps?

Stupid ol' Charlie Dean. I ate that shit with a spoon. The best Marine in the corps! So I helped her "steal" a plane and kill a bunch of convicted terrorists that Libya would never extradite.

If we were caught I would have sworn under torture, until my very last breath, that no government was involved, that the people planning this escapade were a U.S. Air Force deserter and an ex-Marine she hired.

I loafed around Capetown for a few more days, paid my bills, thanked the widow lady, gave her a cock-and-bull story about my sick kids in America, and took a plane to New York. At JFK I got on another plane to Los Angeles.

When the taxi dropped me at my apartment, I stopped by the super's office and paid the rent. The battery in my car had enough juice to start the motor on the very first crank.

I almost didn't recognize Candy. He had even gotten a haircut and wore clean jeans. "Hey, Mr. Dean," Candy said after we had been chatting a while. "Thanks for giving me another chance. You've taught me a lot."

"We all make mistakes," I told him. If only he knew how true that was.

STEPHEN COONTS is the author of eight *New York Times* best-selling novels, the first of which was the classic flying tale *Flight of the Intruder*, which spent over six months on the *New York Times* best-seller list. He graduated from West Virginia University with a degree in political science, and immediately was commissioned as an ensign in the Navy, where he began flight training in Pensacola, Florida, training on the A-6 Intruder aircraft. After two combat cruises in Vietnam aboard the aircraft carrier USS *Enterprise* and one tour as assistant catapult and arresting gear officer aboard USS *Nimitz*, he left active duty in 1977 to pursue a law degree, which he received from the University of Colorado. His novels have been published around the world and have been translated into more than a dozen different languages. He was honored by the U.S. Navy Institute with its Author of the Year award in 1986. His latest novel is *Hong Kong*. He and his wife, Deborah, reside in Clarksville, Maryland.

INSIDE JOB

BY DEAN ING

One

"The longer I live, the more I realize the less I know for sure." That's what my friend Quentin Kim used to mutter to me and curvy little Dana Martin in our Public Safety classes at San Jose State. Dana would frown because she revered conventional wisdom. I'd always chuckle, because I thought Quent was kidding. But that was years ago, and I was older then.

I mean, I thought I knew it all. "Public Safety" is genteel academic code for cop coursework, and while Quent had already built himself an enviable rep as a licensed P.I. in the Bay Area, he hadn't been a big-city cop. I went on to become one, until I got fed up with the cold war between guys on the take and guys in Internal Affairs, both sides angling for recruits. I tried hard to avoid getting their crap on my size thirteen brogans while I lost track of Dana, saw Quent infrequently, and served the City of Oakland's plainclothes detail in the name of public safety.

So much for stepping carefully in such a barnyard. At least I got out with honor after a few years, and I still had contacts around Oakland on both sides of the law. Make that several sides; and to an investigator that's worth more than diamonds. It would've taken a better man than Harve Rackham to let those contacts go to waste, which is why I became the private kind of investigator, aka gumshoe, peeper, or just plain Rackham, P.I.

Early success can destroy you faster than a palmed ice pick, especially if it comes through luck you thought was skill. A year into my new career, I talked my way into a seam job—a kidnapping within a disintegrating family. The kidnapped boy's father, a Sunnyvale software genius, wanted the kid back badly enough to throw serious money at his problem. After a few days of frustration, I shot my big mouth off about it to my sister's husband, Ernie.

It was a lucky shot, though. Ernie was with NASA at Moffett Field and by sheer coincidence he knew a certain Canadian physicist. I'd picked up a rumor that the physicist had been playing footsie with the boy's vanished mother.

The physicist had a Quebecois accent, Ernie recalled, and had spoken longingly about a teaching career. The man had already given notice at NASA without a forwarding address. He was Catholic. A little digging told me that might place him at the University of Montreal, a Catholic school which gives instruction in French. I caught a Boeing 787 and got there before he did, and guess who was waiting with her five-year-old boy in the Montreal apartment the physicist had leased.

I knew better than to dig very far into the reasons why Mama took Kiddie and left Papa. It was enough that she'd fled the country illegally. The check I cashed was so much more than enough that I bought a decaying farmhouse twenty miles and a hundred years from Oakland.

Spending so much time away, I figured I'd need to fence the five acres of peaches and grapes, but the smithy was what sold me. "The smith, a mighty man was he, with large and sinewy," et cetera. Romantic bullshit, sure, but as I said, I knew it all then. And I wanted to build an off-road racer, one of the diesel-electric hybrids that were just becoming popular. I couldn't imagine a better life than peeping around the Port of Oakland for money, and hiding out on my acreage whenever I had some time off, building my big lightning-on-wheels toy.

And God knows, I had plenty of time off after that! Didn't the word get out that I was hot stuff? Weren't more rich guys clamoring for my expensive services? Wasn't I slated for greatness?

In three words: no, no, and no. I didn't even invest in a slick Web site while I still had the money, with only a line in the yellow pages, so I didn't get many calls. I was grunting beneath my old gasoline-fueled Toyota pickup one April afternoon, chasing an oil leak because I couldn't afford to have someone else do it, when my cell phone warbled.

Quentin Kim; I was grinning in an instant. "I thought I was good, but it's humbling when I can't find something as big as you," he bitched.

I squoze my hundred kilos from under the Toyota. "You mean you're looking for me now? Today?"

"I have driven that country road three times, Harvey. My GP mapper's no help. Where the devil are you?"

Even his cussing was conservative. When Quent used my full given name, he was a quart low on patience. I told him to try the road again and I'd flag him down, and he did, and twenty minutes later

I guided his Volvo Electrabout up the lane to my place.

He emerged looking fit, a few grey hairs but the almond eyes still raven-bright, the smile mellow, unchanged. I ignored the limp; maybe his shoes pinched. From force of habit and ethnic Korean good manners, Quent avoided staring around him, but I knew he would miss very little as I invited him through the squinchy old screen door into my authentic 1910 kitchen with its woodstove. He didn't relax until we continued to the basement, the fluorescents obediently flickering on along the stairs.

"You had me worried for a minute," he said, now with a frankly approving glance at my office. As fin de siècle as the house was from the foundation up, I'd fixed it all Frank Gehry and Starship *Enterprise* below. He perched his butt carefully on the stool at my drafting carrel; ran his hand along the flat catatonic stare of my Magnascreen. "But you must be doing all right for yourself. Some of this has got to be expensive stuff, Harve."

"Pure sweat equity, most of it." I shrugged. "I do adhesive bonding, some welding, cabinetry,—oh, I was a whiz in shop, back in high school."

"Don't try to imply that you missed your real calling. I notice you're working under your own license since a year ago. Can people with budgets still afford you?"

"I won't shit you, Quent, but don't spread this around. Way things are right now, anybody can afford me."

It had been over a year since we'd watched World Cup soccer matches together, and while we caught each other up on recent events, I brewed tea for him in my six-cup glass rig with its flash boiler.

He didn't make me ask about the limp. "You know how those old alleyway fire-escape ladders get rickety after sixty years or so," he told me, shifting his leg. "A few months ago I was closing on a bail-jumper who'd been living on a roof in Alameda, and the ladder came loose on us." Shy smile, to forestall sympathy. "He hit the bricks. I bounced off a Dumpster." Shrug.

"Bring him in?"

"The paramedics brought us both in, but I got my fee," he said. "I don't have to tell you how an HMO views our work, and I'm not indigent. Fixing this hip cost me a lot more than I made, and legwork will never be my forte again, I'm afraid."

I folded my arms and attended to the beep of my tea rig. "You're telling me you were bounty hunting," I said. It wasn't exactly an accusation, but most P.I.s won't work for bail bondsmen. It's pretty demanding work, though the money can be good when you negotiate a fifteen percent fee and then bring in some scuffler who's worth fifty large.

While we sipped tea, we swapped sob stories, maintaining a light touch because nobody had forced either of us into the peeper business. You hear a lot about P.I.s being churlish to each other. Mostly a myth, beyond some healthy competition. "I suppose I couldn't resist the challenge," said Quent. "You know me, always trying to expand my education. As a bounty hunter you learn a lot, pretty quickly."

"Like, don't trust old fire escapes," I said.

"Like that," he agreed. "But it also brings you to the attention of a different class of client. It might surprise even you that some Fed agencies will subcontract an investigation, given special circumstances."

It surprised me less when he said that the present circumstances required someone who spoke Hangul, the Korean language, and knew the dockside world around Oakland. Someone the Federal Bureau of Investigation could trust.

"Those guys," I said, "frost my *cojones*. It's been my experience that they'll let metro cops take most of the chances and zero percent of the credit."

"Credit is what you buy groceries with, Harve," he said. "What do we care, so long as the Feds will hire us again?"

"Whoa. What's that word again? *Us*, as in you and me?"

"If you'll take it. I need an extra set of feet—hips, if you insist—and it doesn't hurt that you carry the air of plainclothes cop with you. And with your size, you can handle yourself, which is something I might need."

He mentioned a fee, including a daily rate, and I managed not to whistle. "I need to know more. This gonna be something like a bodyguard detail, Quent? I don't speak Hangul, beyond a few phrases you taught me."

"That's only part of it. Most people we'll interview speak plain American; record checks, for example. The case involves a marine engineer missing from the tramp motorship *Ras Ormara*, which is tied up for round-the-clock refitting at a Richmond wharf. He's Korean. Coast Guard and FBI would both like to find him, without their being identified."

There's an old cop saying about Richmond, California: it's vampire turf. Safe enough in daylight, but watch your neck at night. "I suppose you've already tried Missing Persons."

Quent served me a "give me a break" look. "I don't have to tell you the metro force budget is petty cash, Harve. They're overloaded with domestic cases. The Feds know it, which is where we come in—if you want in."

"Got me over a barrel. You want the truth, I'm practically wearing the goddamn barrel. Any idea how long the case will last?"

Quent knew I was really asking how many days'

pay it might involve. "It evaporates the day the *Ras Ormara* leaves port; perhaps a week. That doesn't give us as much time as I'd like, but every case sets its own pace."

That was another old Quentism, and I'd come to learn it was true. This would be a hot pace, so no wonder gimpy Quentin Kim was offering to share the workload. Instead of doping out his selfish motives, I should be thanking him, so I did. I added, "You don't know it, but you're offering me a bundle of chrome-moly racer frame tubing and a few rolls of cyclone fence. An offer I can't refuse, but I'd like to get a dossier on this Korean engineer right away."

"I can do better than that," said Quent, "and it'll come with a free supper tonight, courtesy of the Feds."

"They're buying? Now, *that* is impressive as hell."

"I have not begun to impress," Quent said, again with the shy smile. "Coast Guard Lieutenant Reuben Medler is fairly impressive, but the FBI liaison will strain your belief system."

"Never happen," I said. "They still look like IBM salesmen."

"Not this one. Trust me." Now Quent was grinning.

"You're wrong," I insisted.

"What do you think happened to the third of our classroom musketeers, Harve, and why do you think this case was dropped in my lap? The Feebie is Dana Martin," he said.

I kept my jaw from sagging with some effort. "You were right," I said.

Until the fight started, I assumed Quent had chosen Original Joe's in San Jose because we—Dana included—had downed many an abalone supreme there in earlier times. If some of the clientele were reputedly Connected with a capital *C*, that only kept folks polite. Quent and I met there and copped a booth, though our old habit had been to take seats at the counter where we could watch chefs with wrists of steel handle forty-centimeter skillets over three-alarm gas burners. I was halfway through a bottle of Anchor Steam when a well-built specimen in a crew-neck sweater, trim Dockers, and tasseled loafers ushered his date in. He carried himself as if hiding a small flagpole in the back of his sweater. I looked away, denying my envy. How is it some guys never put on an ounce while guys like me outgrow our belts?

Then I did a double take. The guy had to be Lieutenant Medler because the small, tanned, sharp-eyed confection in mid-heels and severely tailored suit was Dana Martin, no longer an overconfident kid. I think I said "wow" silently as we stood up.

After the introductions Medler let us babble about how long it had been. For me, the measure of elapsed time was that little Miz Martin had developed a sense of reserve. Then while we decided what we wanted to eat, Medler explained why shoreline poachers had taken abalone off the Original Joe menu. Mindful of who was picking up the tab, I ordered the latest fad entrée: Nebraska longhorn T-bone, lean as ostrich and just as spendy. Dana's lip pursed but she kept it buttoned, cordial, impersonal. I decided she'd bought into her career and its image. Damn, but I hated that . . .

Over the salads, Medler gave his story without editorializing, deferential to us, more so to Dana, in a soft baritone all the more masculine for discarding machismo. "The *Ras Ormara* is a C-1 motorship under Liberian registry," he said, "chartered by the Sonmiani Tramp Service of Karachi, Pakistan." He recited carefully, as if speaking for a recorder. Which he was, though I didn't say so. What the hell, people forget things.

"Some of these multinational vessels just beg for close inspection, the current foreign political situation being what it is," Medler went on. He didn't need to mention the nuke found by a French airport security team the previous month, on an Arab prince's Learjet at Charles De Gaulle terminal. "We did a walk-through. The vessel was out of Lima with a cargo of balsa logs and nontoxic plant extract slurry, bound for Richmond. Crew was the usual polyglot bunch, in this case chiefly Pakis and Koreans. They stay aboard in port unless they have the right papers."

At this point Medler abruptly began talking about how abalone poachers work, a second before the waitress arrived to serve our entrées. Quent nodded appreciatively and I toasted Medler's coolth with my beer.

Once we'd attacked our meals he resumed. Maybe the editorial came with the main course. "You know about Asian working-class people and eye contact—with apologies, Mr. Kim. But one young Korean in the crew was boring holes in my corneas. I decided to interview three men, one at a time, on the fo'c'sle deck. At random, naturally."

"Random as loaded dice." I winked.

"With their skipper right there? Affirmative, and I started with the ship's medic. When I escorted this young third engineer, Park Soon, on deck the poor guy was shaking. His English wasn't that fluent, and he didn't say much, even to direct questions, but he did say we had to talk ashore. 'Must talk,' was the phrase. He had his papers to go ashore.

"I gave him a time and place later that day, a coffeehouse in Berkeley every taxi driver knows. I thought he was going to cry with relief, but he went back to the *Ras Ormara*'s bridge with his jaw set like he was marching toward a firing squad. I went belowdecks.

"A lot of tramps look pretty trampy, but it actually just means it's not a regularly scheduled vessel. This one was spitshine spotless, and I found no reason to doubt the manifest or squawk about conditions in the holds.

"Fast forward to roughly sixteen hundred hours. Park shows at the coffeehouse, jumpy as Kermit, but now he's full of dire warnings. He doesn't know exactly what's wrong about the *Ras Ormara*, but he knows he's aboard only for window dressing. The reason he shipped on at Lima was, Park had met the previous third engineer in Lima at a dockside bar, some Chinese who spoke enough English to say he was afraid to go back aboard. Park was on the beach, as they say, and he wangled the job for himself."

Quent stopped shoveling spicy sausage in, and asked, "The Chinese was afraid? Of what?"

"According to Park, the man's exact English words were 'Death ship.' Park thought he had misunderstood at first and put the Chinese engineer's fear down to superstition. But a day or so en route here, he began to get spooked."

"Every culture has its superstitions," Quent said. "And crew members must pass them on. I'm told an old ship can carry enough leg-ends to sink it." When Medler frowned, Quent said, "Remember Joseph Conrad's story, 'The Brute'? The *Apse Family* was a death ship. Well, it was just a story," he said, seeing Dana's look of abused patience.

Medler again: "A classic. Who hasn't read it?" Dana gave a knowing nod. Pissed me off; I hadn't read it. "But I doubt anyone aboard told sea stories to Park. He implied they all seemed to be appreciating some vast, unspoken serious joke. No one would talk to him at all except for his duties. And he didn't have a lot to do because the ship was a dream, he said. She had been converted somewhere to cargo from a small fast transport, so the crew accommodations were nifty. She displaces maybe two thousand tons, twenty-four knots. Fast," he said again. "Originally she must've been someone's decommissioned D.E.—destroyer escort. Not at all like a lot of those rustbuckets in tramp service."

Quent toyed with his food. "It's fairly common, isn't it, for several conversions to be made over the life of a ship?"

"Exigencies of trade." Medler nodded. "Hard to say where it was done, but Pakistan has a shipbreaking industry and rerolling mills in Karachi." He shook his head and grinned. "I think they could cobble you up a new ship from the stuff they salvage. We've refused to allow some old buckets into the bay; they're rusted out so far, you step in the wrong place on deck and your foot will go right through. But not the *Ras Ormara*; I'd serve on her myself, if her bottom's anything like her topside."

"I thought you did an, uh, inspection," said Dana.

"Walk-through. We didn't do it as thoroughly as we might if we'd found anything abovedecks. She's so clean I understand why Park became nervous. Barring the military—one of our cutters, for instance—you just don't find that kind of sterile environment in maritime service. Not even a converted D.E."

"No," Dana insisted, and made a delicate twirl with her fork. "I meant afterward."

Medler blinked. "If you want to talk about it, go ahead. I can't. You know that."

Dana, whom I'd once thought of as a teen mascot, patted his forearm like a den mother. I didn't know which of them I wanted more to kick under the table. "I go way back with these two, Reuben, and they're under contract with confidentiality. But this may not be the place."

I was already under contract? Well, only if I were

working un-der Quent's license, and if he'd told her so. Still, I was getting fed up with how little I knew. "For God's sake," I said, "just the short form, okay?"

"For twenty years we've had ways to search sea floors for aircraft flight recorders," Dana told me. "Don't you think the Coast Guard might have similar gadgets to look at a hull?"

"For what?"

"Whatever," Medler replied, uneasy about it. "I ordered it after the Park interview. When you know how Hughes built the CIA's *Glomar Explorer*, you know a ship can have a lot of purposes that aren't obvious at the waterline. Figure it out for yourself," he urged.

That spook ship Hughes's people built had been designed to be flooded and to float vertically, sticking up from the water like a fisherman's bobbin. Even the tabloids had exploited it. I thought about secret hatches for underwater demolition teams, torpedo tubes—"Got it," I said. "Any and every unfriendly use I can dream up. Can I ask what they found?"

"Not a blessed thing," said Reuben Medler. "If it weren't for D—Agent Martin here, I'd be writing reports on why I insisted."

"He insisted because the Bureau did," Dana put in. "We've had some vague tips about a major event, planned by nice folks with the same traditions as those who, uh, bugged Tel Aviv."

The Tel Aviv Bug had been anthrax. If the woman who'd smuggled it into Israel hadn't somehow flunked basic hygiene and collapsed with a skinful of the damned bacilli, it would've caused more deaths than it did. "So you found nothing, but you want a follow-up with this Park guy. He's probably catting around and will show up with a hangover when the ship's ready to sail," I said. "I thought crew members had to keep in touch with the charter service."

"They do," said Dana. "And with a full complement of two dozen, only a few of the crew went ashore. But Park has vanished. Sonmiani claims they'll have still another third engineer when the slurry tanks are cleaned and the new cargo's pumped aboard."

"And we'd prefer they didn't sail before we have another long talk with Park," Medler said. "I'm told the FBI has equipment like an unobtrusive lie detector."

"Voice-stress analyzer," Dana corrected. "Old hardware, new twists. But chiefly, we're on edge because Park has dropped out of sight."

Quent: "But I thought he told you why."

"He told me why he was worried," Medler agreed. "But he also said the *Ras Ormara* will be bound for Pusan with California-manufactured industrial chemicals, a nice tractable cargo, to his own homeport. He was determined to stay with it, worried or not. Of course it's possible he simply changed his mind."

"But we'd like to know," Dana said. "We want to know sufficiently that—well." She looked past us toward the ceiling as if an idea had just occurred to her. Suuure. "Sometimes things happen. Longshoremen's strike,—" She saw my sudden glance, and she'd always been alert to nuance. "No, we haven't, but little unforeseen problems arise. Sonmiani is already dealing with a couple of them. Assuming they don't have the clout to build a fire under someone at the ambassador level, there could be one or two more if we find a solid reason. Or if you do."

"I take it Harve and I can move overtly on this," Quent said, "so long as we're not connected to government."

Medler looked at Dana, who said, "Exactly. Low-profile, showing your private investigator's I.D. if necessary. You're known well enough that anyone checking on you would be satisfied you're not us. Of course you've got to have a client of record, so we're furnishing one."

I noticed that Quent seemed interested in something across the room, but he refocused on Dana Martin. "As licensed privateers, we aren't required to name a client or divulge any other details of the case. Normally it would be shaving an ethical guideline."

"But you wouldn't be," Dana said. "You'd be giving up a few details of a cover story. Nothing very dramatic, just imply that our missing man is a prodigal son. Park Soon's father in Pusan would be unlikely to know he's put you on retainer."

Quent: "Because he can't afford us?"

Dana, with the shadow of a smile: "Because he's been deceased for years. I'll give you the details on that tomorrow, Quent. Uhm, Quent?"

But my pal, whose attention had been wandering again, was now leaning toward me with an un-Quentish grin. "Harve," he said softly, "third counter stool from the front, late twenties, blond curls, Yamaha cycle jacket. Could be packing."

"Several guys in here probably are," I said.

"But I'm not carrying certified copies of their bail bonds, and I do have one for Robert Rooney, bail jumper. That's Bobby."

Dana and Medler both looked toward the counter, at me, and at Quent, but let their expressions complain.

"You wouldn't," I said.

"It's my bleeding job," said Quent. "Wait outside. I'll flush him out gently, and if gentle doesn't work, don't let him reach into that jacket."

I was already standing up. "Back shortly, folks. Don't forget my pie à la mode."

"I don't believe this," I heard Medler say as I moved toward the old-fashioned revolving door.

"Santa Clara County Jail is on Hedding, less than a mile from here. We'll be back before you know it," Quent soothed, still seated, giving me time to evaporate.

I saw the bail-jumper watching me in a window reflection, but I gave him no reason to jump. I would soon learn he was just naturally jumpy, pun intended. Can't say it was really that long a fight, though. I pushed through the door and into the San Jose night, realizing we could jam Rooney in it if he tried to run out. And have him start shooting through heavy glass partitions, maybe; sometimes my first impulses are subject to modest criticism.

Outside near the entrance, melding with evening shadow, I listened to the buzz and snap of Joe's old neon sign. I could still see our quarry, and now Quent was strolling behind diners at the counter, apparently intent on watching the chef toss a blazing skilletful of mushrooms. Quent reached inside his coat; brought out a folded paper, his face innocent of stress. Then he said something to the seated Rooney.

Rooney turned only his head, very slowly, nodded, shrugged, and let his stool swivel to face Quent. He grinned.

It's not easy to get leverage with only your buns against a low seat back, but Rooney managed it, lashing both feet out to Quent's legs, his arms windmilling as he bulled past my pal. I heard a shout, then a clamor of voices as Quent staggered against a woman seated at the nearest table. I stepped farther out of sight as Bobby Rooney hurled himself against the inertia of that big revolving door.

He used both hands, and he was sturdier than he

had looked, bursting outside an arm's length from me. Exactly an arm's length, because without moving my feet, just as one Irishman to another I clotheslined him under the chin. He went down absolutely horizontal, his head making a nice bonk on the sidewalk, and if he'd had any brains they would've rattled like castanets. He didn't even pause, bringing up both legs, then doing a gymnast's kick so that he was suddenly on his feet in a squat, one arm flailing at me. The other hand snaked into his jacket pocket before I could close on him.

What came out of his right-hand pocket was very small, but it had twin barrels on one end and as he leaped up, Rooney's arm swung toward me. Meanwhile I'd taken two steps forward, and I snatched at his wrist. I caught only his sleeve, but when I heaved upward on it, his hand and the little derringer pocketgun disappeared into the sleeve. A derringer is double-barreled, the barrel's so short its muzzle blast is considerable, and confined in that sleeve it flash-burnt his hand while muffling the sound. The slug headed skyward. Bobby Rooney headed down San Carlos Avenue, hopping along crabwise because I had held on to that sleeve long enough that when he jerked away, his elbow was caught halfway out.

I'm not much of a distance runner, but for fifty meters I can move out at what I imagined was a brisk pace. Why Bobby didn't just stop and fire point-blank through that sleeve I don't know; I kept waiting for it, and one thing I never learned to do was make myself a small target. Half a block later he was still flailing his arm to dislodge the sleeve, and I was still three long steps behind, and that's when a conservative dress suit passed me. Quentin Kim was wearing it at the time, outpacing me despite that limp. He simply spun Bobby Rooney down, standing on his jacket which pinned him down on his back at the mouth of an alley.

I grabbed a handful of blond curls, knelt on Bobby's right sleeve because his gun hand was still in it, and made the back of his head tap the sidewalk. "Harder every time," I said, blowing like a whale. "How many times—before you relax?" Another tap. "Take your time. I can do this—for hours."

As quickly as Bobby Rooney had decided to fight, he reconsidered, his whole body going limp, eyes closed.

"Get that little shooter—out of his sleeve," I said to Quent, who wasn't even winded but rubbed his upper thigh, muttering to himself.

Quent took the derringer, flicked his key-ring Maglite, then brought that wrinkled paper out of his inside coat pocket and shook it open. "Robert Rooney," he intoned.

Still holding on to Rooney's hair, I gazed up. "What the hell? Is this some kind of new Miranda bullshit, Quent?"

"No, it's not required. It's just something I do that clarifies a relationship."

"Relationship? This isn't a relationship, this is a war."

"Not mutually exclusive. You've never been married, have you," Quent said. He began again: "Robert Rooney, acting as agent for the hereafter-named person putting up bail . . ."

I squatted there until Quent had finished explaining that Rooney was, by God, the property of the bondsman named and could be pur-sued even into his own toilet without a warrant, and that his physical condition upon delivery to the appropriate county jail depended entirely on his temperament. When Quent was done I said, "He may not even hear you."

"He probably does, but it doesn't matter. I hear me," Quent said mildly. A bounty hunter with liberal scruples was one for the books, but I guess Quent wrote his own book.

"How far is your car?"

"Two blocks. Here," Quent said, and handed me the derringer with one unfired chamber. I knew what he said next was for Rooney's ears more than mine. "You can shoot him, just try not to kill him right away. That's only if he tries to run again."

"If he does," I said, "I'll still have his scalp for an elephant's merkin."

Quent laughed as he hurried away, not even limping. "Now there's an image I won't visit twice," he said.

Twenty minutes later we returned from the county lockup with a receipt, and to this day I don't know what Bobby Rooney's voice sounds like. The reason why those kicks hadn't ruined Quent's legs were that, under his suit pants, my pal wore soccer pro FlexArmor over his knees and shins for bounty hunting. He'd suggested Original Joe's to Dana because, among other good reasons, Rooney's ex-girlfriend claimed he hung out there a lot. Since Rooney was dumb as an ax handle, Quent figured the chances of a connection were good. He could combine business with pleasure, and show a pair of Feds how efficient we were. Matter of fact, I was so efficient I wound up with a derringer in my pocket. Fortunes of war, not that I was going to brag about it to the Feds.

Dana and Reuben Medler were still holding down the booth when we returned, Medler half-resigned, half-amused. Dana was neither. "I hope your victim got away," she said. If she'd been a cat, her fur would've been standing on end.

Quent flashed our receipt for Rooney's delivery

and eased into the booth. "A simple commercial transaction, Agent Martin," he said, ignoring her hostility. "My apologies."

She wasn't quite satisfied. "Can I expect this to happen again?"

"Not tonight," Quent said equably.

It must've been that smile of his that disarmed her because Dana subsided over coffee and dessert. When it became clear that Quent would take the San Francisco side—it has a sizable Korean population—while I worked the Oakland side of the bay, Reuben Medler told me where I'd find the *Ras Ormara*, moored on the edge of Richmond near a gaggle of chemical production facilities.

Eventually Dana handed Quent a list of the crew with temporary addresses for the few who went ashore. "Sonmiani's California rep keeps tabs on their crews," she explained. "I got this from Customs."

Medler put in, "Customs has a standard excuse for wanting the documentation; cargo manifest, tonnage certificate, stowage plan, and other records."

"But not you," I said to Dana.

She shook her head. "Even if we did, the Bureau wouldn't step forward to Sonmiani. We leave that to you, although Sonmiani's man in Oakland, ah, Norman Goldman by name, has a clean sheet and appears to be clean. We feel direct contacts of that sort should be made as—what did you call it, Quentin? A simple commercial transaction. Civilians like to talk. If Goldman happened to mention us to the wrong person, the ship's captain for example, someone might abort whatever they're up to. If they see you rooting around, they'll assume it's just part of a routine private investigation."

Maybe I was still pissed that our teen mascot had become our boss. "Implying sloth and incompetence," I murmured.

"You said it, not I," she replied sweetly. "At least Mr. Goldman seems well enough educated that he would never mistake you for an agent."

"You've run a check on him, then," said Quent.

"Of course. Majored in business at Michigan, early promotion, young man on the way up. And I suspect Sonmiani's Islamic crew members will watch their steps around a bright Jewish guy," she added, looking over the check.

Quent drained his teacup. "We'll try to keep it simple; Park Soon could show up tomorrow. Then we'll see whether we need to talk with this Goldman. Is that suitable?"

Quent asked with genuine deference, and Dana paused before she nodded. It struck me then that Quent was making a point of showing obedience to his boss. And his quick glance at me suggested that I might try it sometime.

I knew he was right, but it would have to be some other time. I shook hands again with Reuben Medler, exchanged cards with him, and turned to Dana. "Thanks for the feed. Maybe next time we can avoid a floor show."

She looked at Medler and shook her head, and I left without remarking that she had a lot of seasoning ahead of her.

Two

It was Quent's suggestion that I case the location of the *Ras Ormara* itself, herself, whatever. Meanwhile he made initial inquiries across the bay alone in his natural camouflage, in the area everyone calls Chinatown though it was home to several Asiatic colonies. It was my idea to bring my StudyGirl to record a look at this shipshape ship we'd heard so much about, and Quent suggested I do it without making any personal contacts that required I.D.

StudyGirls were new then, cleverly named so that kids who wanted the spendy toys—meaning all kids—would have leverage with Dad and Mom. Even the early versions were pocket-sized and would take a two-inch *Britannica* floppy, but they would also put TV broadcasts on the rollout screen or play mini-CDs and action games, and make video recordings as well. It was already common practice to paint over the indicator lights so nobody knew when you were videorecording. I'll bet a few kids actually used them for schoolwork, too.

I took the freeway as far as Richmond, got off at Carlson Boulevard, and puzzled my way through the waterfront's industrial montage. Blank-fronted metal buildings with ramped loading docks meant warehousing of imports and exports, and somewhere in there were a few boxcarloads of Peruvian balsa logs. Composite panels of carbon fiber and balsa sandwich were much in demand at that time among builders of off-road racers for their light weight and stiffness. I enjoyed a moment of déjà future vu at the thought that I might be using some of the *Ras Ormara*'s balsa for my project in a few months.

Unless my woolgathering got me squashed like a bug underfoot. I had to dodge thrumming diesel-electric rigs that outclamored the cries of gulls and ignored my pickup as unworthy of notice. Hey, they were making a buck, and this was their turf.

In a few blocks-long stretches, the warehouses gave way to fencing topped with razor wire, enforced isolation for the kind of small-time chemical processing plants that looked like brightly painted guts of the biggest dinosaurs ever. Now and then I could spot the distant San Rafael Bridge through the tanks, reactor vessels, piping, and catwalks that loomed like little skeletal skyscrapers, throwing early shadows across the street. You knew without a glance when you were passing warehouses because of the echoes and the sour, last-week's-fast-food odor that drew those scavenging gulls. The chemical production plants no longer stank so much since the City of Richmond got serious about its air. And beyond all this at an isolated wharf, berthed next to a container ship like a racehorse beside a Clydesdale, the *Ras Ormara* gleamed in morning light. I

wondered why a ship like that was called a "she"
when it had such racy muscular lines, overlaid by
spidery cargo cranes and punctuated by the gleam
of glass. I pointedly focused on the nearby container
vessel, walking past an untended gate onto the dock,
avoiding flatbed trucks that galumphed in and out.
I had my StudyGirl in hand for videotaping, neither
flourishing nor hiding it. In semishorts, argyle socks,
and short sleeves, I hoped I looked like a typical
Midwestern tourist agog over, golly gee, these great
big boats. If challenged I could always choose
whether to brazen it out with my I.D.

I strolled back, paying casual attention to the *Ras
Ormara*, listening to the sounds of engine-driven
pressure washers and recording the logos on two
trucks with hoses that snaked up and back to big
tanks mounted behind the truck cabs. I could see
men operating the chassis-mounted truck consoles,
wearing headsets. Somehow I'd expected more
noise and melodrama in cleaning the ship's big
cargo tanks.

Words like "big" and "little" are inadequate where
a cargo vessel, even one considered small, is concerned. I guess that's what numbers are for. The *Ras
Ormara* was almost three hundred feet stem to stern,
the length of a football field, and where bare metal
showed it appeared to be stainless steel. All that
cleaning was concentrated ahead of the ship's
glassed bridge, where a half dozen metal domes,
each five yards across, stood in ranks well above the
deck level. Two rows of three each; and the truck
hoses entered the domes through open access ports
big enough to drop a truck tire through. Or a man.
Welded ladders implied that men might do just that.

I suppose I could have climbed one of the gang-
ways up to the ship's deck. It was tempting, but
Quent had told me—couched as a suggestion—not
to. It is simply amazing how obedient I can be to a

boss who is not overbearing. I moseyed along, hoping I stayed mostly out of sight behind those servicing trucks without seeming to try. From an open window behind the *Ras Ormara's* bridge came faint strains of someone's music, probably from a CD. It sounded like hootchie-kootchie scored for three tambourines and a parrot, and I thought it might be Egyptian or some such.

Meanwhile, a bulky yellow extraterrestrial climbed from one of those domes trailing smaller hoses, and made his way carefully down the service ladder. When he levered back his helmet and left it with its hoses on deck, I could see it was just a guy with hair sweat-plastered to his forehead, wearing a protective suit you couldn't miss on a moonless midnight. My luck was holding; he continued down the gangway to the nearest truck. Meanwhile I ambled back in his direction, stowing away my StudyGirl.

The space-suited guy, his suit smeared with fluid, was talking with the truck's console operator, both standing next to the chassis as they shared a cigarette. Even then smoking was illegal in public, but give a guy a break. . . .

They broke off their conversation as I drew near, and the console man nodded. "Help you?"

I shrugged pleasantly and remembered to talk high in my throat because guys my size are evidently less threatening as tenors. "Just sight-seeing. Never see anything like this in Omaha." I grinned.

"Don't see much of this anywhere, thank God," said the sweaty one, and they laughed together. "Thirsty work. Not for the claustrophobe, either."

"Is this how you fill 'er up?" I hoped this was naive enough without being idiotic. I think I flunked because they laughed again. The sweaty one said, "Would I be smoking?" When I looked abashed, he relented. "We're scouring those stainless tanks. Got

to be pharmaceutically free of a vegetable slurry before they pump in the next cargo."

"Those domes sitting on deck," I guessed.

"Hell, that's just the hemispherical closures," said
the console man.

"The tanks go clear down into the hold," said his
sweaty friend.

I blinked. "Twenty feet down?"

"More like forty," he said.

The console man glanced at his wristwatch, gave
a meaningful look to his friend; took the cigarette
back. "And we got a special eco-directive on flushing
these after this phase. We have to double soak and
agitate with filterable solvent, right to the brim, fifty-
two thousand gallons apiece. Pain in the ass."

"Must take a lot of time," I said, thinking about
Dana Martin's ability to make people jump through
additional hoops on short notice, without showing
her hand.

"Twice what we'd figured," said Consoleman. "I
thought the charter-service rep would scream
bloody murder, but he didn't even haggle. Offered
a bonus for early completion, in fact. Speaking of
which," he said, and fixed Sweatman with a wry
smile.

"Yeah, yeah," said his colleague, and turned toward the *Ras Ormara*. "For us, time really is money.
But that ten-minute break is in the standard contract. Anyhow, without my support hoses it's getting
hot as hell in this outfit."

"Hold still, it's gonna dribble," I said. I found an
old Kleenex in my pocket, and used it to wipe
around the chin plate of Sweatman's suit, then put
it back in my pocket.

"Guess I'm lucky to be in the wrought-iron biz," I
said. With a smithy for a hobby, I could fake my way
through that if necessary.

"My regards to Omaha," said Consoleman. "And

by the way, you really shouldn't be here without authorization. Those guys are an antsy lot," he said,
jerking his head toward the bridge. It was as nice a
"buzz off, pal" request as I'd ever had.

I didn't look up. I'd seen faces staring down in
our direction, some with their heads swathed in
white. "Okay, thanks. Just seeing this has been an
education," I said.

"If the skipper unlimbers his tongue on you, I
hope your education isn't in languages," Consoleman joked.

I laughed, waved, and took my time walking back
to the gate, stopping on the way to gaze at the much
larger container ship as if my attention span played
no favorites.

When I got back to my Toyota I rummaged in the
glove box and found my stash of quart-sized evidence baggies. Then I carefully sealed that soggy old
Kleenex inside one and scribbled the date and the
specimen's provenance. I'd seen Sweatman climb
out of a cargo tank of the *Ras Ormara* and that fluid
had come out with him. Quent might not do hand-
springs, but the Feebs got off on stuff like that.

I took a brief cell call from Quent shortly before
noon, while I was stoking up at one of the better
restaurants off Jack London Square. The maître d'
had sighed when he saw my tourist getup. Quent
sighed, too, when I told him where I was. "Look, the
Feds are paying, and I keep receipts," I reminded
him.

He said he was striking out in Chinatown, just as
he had in hospitals and clinics, but the Oakland side
had its own ethnic neighborhoods. "I thought you
might want to ride with me this afternoon," he said.

"Where do we meet? I have something off the
ship you might want Dana to have analyzed," I said.

"You went aboard? Harve,—oh well. Just eat

slowly. It's not that far across the Bay Bridge," he replied.

"Gotcha. And I didn't go aboard, bossman, but I think I have a sample of what was actually in the *Ras Ormara*'s tanks, whatever the records might say. You'll be proud of your humble apprentice, but right now my rack of lamb calls. Don't hurry," I said, and put away my phone.

Quent arrived in time for my coffee and ordered tea. I let him play back my StudyGirl video recording as far as it went, and took the evidence baggie from my shirt pocket as I reported the rest. "We have the name of the pressure-washing firm. No doubt they can tell some curious Fed what cleaning chemicals they use. What's left should be traces of what those tanks really carried," I said.

Quent said Dana's people had already analyzed samples of the stuff provided by Customs. "But they'll be glad to have it confirmed this way. Nice going." He pocketed the baggie and pretended not to notice that I made a proper notation on my lunch receipt. We walked out into what was rapidly becoming a furry overcast, and I took the passenger's seat in his Volvo.

Quent said we'd try an Oakland rooming house run by a Korean family. From the list we had, he knew a pair of the *Ras Ormara*'s crew were staying there. "You, uh, might want to draft your report while I go in," he said as he turned off the Embarcadero. "Shouldn't be long."

"I thought you wanted me with you."

"I did. Then I saw how you're dressed."

"I'm a tourist!"

"You're a joke with pale shins. I can't do a serious interview with a foreign national if you're visible; how can I have his full attention when he's wondering whether Bluto is going to start juggling plates behind me?"

I saw his point and promised to bring a change of clothes next time. Quent found the place, in a row of transient quarters an Oakland beat cop would call flophouses. Without a place to park, he turned the Volvo over to me. "I'll call when I'm done," he said, and disappeared into the three-story stucco place.

I did find a parking spot eventually. My printer was at home, but I stored my morning's case report on StudyBint. Quent called not long afterward and, because he wore a frown only when puzzling things out, I hardly gave him time to take the wheel. "Something already?"

He thought about it a moment before replying. "Not on Park. Not directly, at any rate. But I'm starting to understand why our missing engineer was uneasy." When giving Park's name he had mentioned the ship to the rooming-house proprietor, who said she hadn't heard of Park but named the two crew members who were there. The Korean, Hong Chee, she described as taller than average, late thirties. The second man, one Ali Ghaffar, was older; perhaps Indian. Pretending surprise at this lucky accident, Quent asked to speak with them.

Hong Chee was out, but Quent found his roommate Ghaffar in the room, preternaturally quiet and alert. Ghaffar, a middle-aged Paki, was a studious-looking sort wearing one of those white cloth doo-dads wound around his head, who had evidently been reading one of two well-thumbed leather-bound books. Quent couldn't read even the titles though he got the impression they might be religious tomes.

Ghaffar spoke fair English. He showed some interest in the fact that an Asian speaking perfect American English was hoping to trace the movements of an engineer off the *Ras Ormara*. Quent explained that Park's family was concerned enough to

hire private investigators, blah-blah, merely wanted
assurance that Park hadn't met with foul play, et
cetera.

Ghaffar said he had only a nodding acquaintance
with Park. He couldn't, or more likely wouldn't, say
whether Park had made any friends aboard ship,
and had no idea whether Park had friends in the
Bay Area. Ghaffar and Hong Chee had seen the engineer, he thought, the day before in some Richmond bar, and Park was looking fit, but they hadn't
talked. That's when Quent noticed the wastebasket's
contents. He began pacing around, stroking his
chin, trying to scan everything in the room without
being obvious while doing it.

Personal articles were aligned on lamp tables as if
neatness counted, beds made, nothing out of place.
Quent took his nail clippers out and began idly tossing them in one hand as he dreamed up more questions, and he just happened to drop his clippers into
the wastebasket, apologizing as he fished them out
with slow gropes of bogus clumsiness.

Quent realized that Ghaffar was waiting with endless calm for this ten-thumbed gumshoe to go away,
volunteering little, responding carefully. Quent said
he'd like to talk with Hong Chee sometime if possible and passed his cell-phone card to Ghaffar, who
accepted it solemnly, and then Quent left and called
me to be picked up.

"So I ask you," Quent said rhetorically: "What
would a devout Moslem, who adheres to correct
practices alone in his room, have been doing in a
gin mill, with or without his buddy? Not likely. I
don't think he saw Park, I think he wanted me to
think Park was healthy. And you haven't asked me
about the trash basket."

"Didn't want to interrupt. What'd you see?"

"Candy wrappers and an empty plastic pop bottle.
Oh, yes," he added with studied neglect, "and an

airline ticket. I didn't have time to read it closely, but I caught an Asian name—not Hong Chee's—Oakland International, and a departure date." He paused before he specified it.

"Christ, that's tomorrow," I said.

"I'm not through. Ghaffar is on the crew list as the ship's machinist. You ever see a machinist's hands?"

"Sure, like a blacksmith's. Like he force-feeds cactus to Rottweilers for kicks."

"Well, at the least they're callused and scarred. Not Ali Ghaffar. He may know how to use a lathe, but I'd bet against it."

"Then who's the real machinist? Ships have to have one."

"Do they? From what Medler and you tell me, and from what I saw on your video, the *Ras Ormara* might go a year without needing that kind of attention."

He checked some notes and drove silently across town like he knew where he was going. Presently he said, as if to himself: "So Hong Chee has dumped what looks like a perfectly good airline ticket for somebody out of Oakland. Wish I'd seen where to. More particularly, I wish I knew how he could afford to junk it. And why he knows to junk it the day before the flight."

"Me, teacher," I said, putting up a hand and waving it. "Call on me."

"Tell the class, Master Rackham," he said, going along with it.

"Somebody else is funding him better than most, and he's changed his departure plans because La Martin and company have put the brakes on whatever he had in mind."

"Take your seat, you've left the heart of my question untouched. Is he worried for the same reasons as Park?"

"Suppose we give him a chance to tell us," I said.

"Maybe we'll do that. But I'm not sure he's making plans for his own departure. Another Asian?"

"At a guess, I'd say the name is unimportant. How many sets of I.D. might he have, Quent?"

After a long pause, he exhaled for what seemed like forever. "Harve, you are definitely paranoid—I'm happy to say. Now you've torn the lid off this little box with a missing engineer in it, and I find a much bigger box inside, so to speak. And there wasn't a second ticket there—so Ghaffar may still intend to go back aboard. Or not. But I'll tell you this: Our machinist is no machinist, and he certainly isn't spending his time ashore as if he had the usual things in mind."

I couldn't fault his reasoning. "So where are we headed?"

"Korean social club. Maybe we'll find Hong Chee there."

"And not Park Soon?" All I got was a shrug and a glance, and I didn't like the glance. Quent found a slot for the Volvo in a neighborhood of shops with signs in English and the odd squiggles that weren't quite Chinese characters; Hangul has a script all its own. "You might try calling Dana while I'm inside," Quent said. "Let her know we've got a gooey Kleenex for her."

So I did, and was told she was in the field, and I tried her cell phone. She sounded like she was in a salt mine and none too pleased about it. She perked up slightly at my offer of the evidence. "I'll pick it up when we're through here," she said, and sneezed. "I thought the incoming cargo might be dirty, but the spectral analyzer says no. A few pallets are too heavy, though. My God, but wood dust is pervasive!"

"You're in a warehouse," I said, glad that she couldn't see me grinning. Climbing around on pallets of logs probably hadn't been high on her list of adventures when she joined up. "I haven't seen the stuff, but if it's that dusty maybe it's not plain logs. Probably rough-sawn, right?"

She said it was. "What would you know about it?"

"I've seen how balsa is used in high-tech panels. The stuff is graded by weight per cubic meter and it varies from featherweight, which is highly prized, to the density of pine. In other words, pallets could vary by a factor of three or so."

"Well, damn it to hell," she said. "Excuse me. Scratch one criterion. What's the significance of its being sawn?"

"Just that it may make it easier for you to see whether some of it's been cut lengthwise with a very fine kerf and glued back."

"What's a kerf?"

"The slot made by a saw. Balsa can be slitted with a very thin sawblade. It occurs to me that it might be the lighter timbers you should be checking for hollowed interiors. Bags of white powder aren't that heavy, Dana."

I think she cussed again before she sneezed. She said, "Thanks," as if it were squeezed out of her.

"But I don't think you'll find anything," I said.

She demanded, "Why not?" the way a kid says it when told she can't ride behind the nice stranger on his Superninja bike.

"I just feel like whatever's being delivered, if anything, hasn't been. The monkey wrench your people threw into their schedule didn't delay those pallets— gesundheit—but they're behaving as if you did delay something. They're waiting, apparently with patience."

She said she'd get back to me and snapped off. To kill time, I played back our conversation on StudyBabe. Dana had a spectral analyzer with her? I had thought they were big lab gadgets. Right, and computers were room-sized—once upon a time.

While I was still muttering "Duhh" and thinking about possible uses of Dana's gadgetry, Quent came down out of a stairwell in a hurry. He motioned for me to drive, pocketing his phone. "You love to drive like there's no tomorrow, and I don't. Please don't bend the Volvo," he begged. "Just get us across the bridge to Jackson and Taylor."

While I drove, he filled me in on his fresh lead. He'd struck out again upstairs, but had just taken a call on his cell phone from Ali Ghaffar. His buddy Hong, said the Paki, had returned. Ghaffar had asked about Park. Oh, said Hong, that was easy; back at the gin mill, Park Soon had said he was considering a move to a nice room in San Francisco for the rest of his time ashore. Corner of Jackson and Taylor.

"Smack-dab middle of Chinatown. Didn't say which corner, I suppose," I said, overtaking a taxi on the right.

"No such luck. But there can't be more than a half dozen places with upscale rooms on or near that corner. We can canvass them all in twenty minutes."

I tossed a look at Quent. "You speak directly to Hong?"

"Watch the road, for Christ's sweet sake," he gritted. "I asked, but Ali said he was gone again. Very handy."

"That's what I was thinking," I said, swerving to miss a pothole on the way to the Bay Bridge on-ramp.

Quent closed his eyes. "Just tell me when we get there."

To calm him down I played my conversation with Dana. It pacified him somewhat, and I turned down the Volvo's wick nearing Chinatown, which was a traffic nightmare long before the twenty-first century.

I chose a pricey parking lot near Broadway, and we jostled our way through the sidewalk chaos together. By agreement, Quent peeled off to take the two west corners of the intersection. Because some of the nicer little Chinatown hotels aren't obvious, I had to ask a restaurant cashier. When she hesitated, I said I had a job offer for an Asian gent and knew only that he'd taken a nice room thereabouts. I said I hadn't understood him very well.

Evidently, Asiatics have their own privately printed local phone books, but she didn't hand it over and I couldn't have read what I saw anyhow. She gave me five addresses, and three of them were on Quent's side. I tipped her, hoping I'd remember to jot it down, and found the first address almost next door.

If there's a small Chinatown hotel on a street floor, it's one I never saw. I climbed three narrow flights before I saw what proved to be a tiny lobby through a bead curtain. A young Asiatic greeted me, very courteously, his speech and dress yuppily American. He heard my brief tale sympathetically. Sorry, he said, but no young person of either gender had registered in several days. Would I mind describing the employment I had to offer?

I said it was a marine engineer's job, and I swear he said, "Aw shit, and me a journalism major," before he wished me good day, no longer interested in my problems.

I crossed the street and began to search for the second address when my phone clucked. "Bingo," Quent said with no preliminaries. "But no joy. Meet me at the car in ten. Until then you don't know me." No way I could mistake the implication.

He didn't sound happy, and when I saw him on the street he had turned away, heading down Jackson. It's a one-way street, and he walked counter to the traffic flow, something you do when you suspect someone may be trying to tail you in a car.

So I did the same on Taylor, which is also one-way, doubling back after a long block to approach Quent's car on Jones—again counter to one-way traffic. If anyone followed me on foot, he was too good for me to make him.

I had paid the lot's fee and was waiting in the Volvo when Quent appeared. "Oakland it is," he said, racking his seat back to disappear below the windowsill. As I sought an on-ramp he said, "A man calling himself Park Soon rented a room for a week, not two hours ago; one flight up, quiet, expensive. Told the concierge he might be staying with a friend for a night or so but please to hold his messages and take names."

"He's not hard up for cash," I said.

"He's also about my height and age," said Quent, who was five-eight, pushing forty.

I'd had Park's description. "The hell he is," I said.

"The man who rented that room with a cash advance is," Quent said. "Unless the lady was pulling my leg. And why would she if she wanted me to think it was Park? Park Soon is five-three. What's wrong with this picture, Harve?"

"I might know if I got a look inside that room."

"That was my thought, but it's a risky tactic in a subculture that's understandably wary, so I didn't even try. The Feds can do it if they want to. They know how to lean on people to, ah, I think the phrase is, 'compel acquiescence.' "

"Our own little Ministry of Fear," I observed.

"Everybody's got 'em, Harve. I even have one," he said with a half smile, and pointed a finger at my breast. "And if I had to choose between Uncle's and the ones run by people who call him the Great Satan, I choose Uncle.

"Meanwhile, we don't know who's pushing our buttons, waiting for us to show up, and watching us flail around all over hell. But I'd bet someone is, and I'd just as soon they didn't pin a tail on us."

I nodded, pointing the Volvo onto the Bay Bridge. "You don't think Park could somehow be in on this," I suggested.

"Not in any way he'd like. I don't think Park is where anyone will find him anytime soon," Quent replied grimly. "Whoever tried to create a fresh trail for him would probably be pretty confident he's not leaving his own trail of crumbs. I really don't like that idea, Harve. Well, maybe I'm wrong. I hope so."

"When are we gonna drop that one on Dana?"

He levered himself and his seat erect; opened his phone. "Right away. She's probably still in the field. I will bet you a day's expenses Mr. Ghaffar knows who took that room for Park; the description fits Hong, of course."

I nodded. "Should we go back and have a talk with him now?"

"Not yet, I want to be very calm for that, and at the moment I am peeved. I am provoked."

"You are royally pissed," I supplied. He nodded. "Me too," I added, as he punched Dana's number.

It was nearing rush hour by that time, but with a few extra twists and turns, I managed to satisfy myself that we weren't tailed while Quent spoke with our pet Feeb. She said she'd meet us in twenty at the boathouse on Lake Merritt, in residential Oakland.

She was as good as her word, looking as frazzled as she'd sounded earlier but even more interesting, which irked me. No Feeb had the right to look that good. She took the perimeter footpath and we caught up to her, two visitors hitting on a cutie. When we found a park bench, she plopped her shoulder bag next to me. "If that specimen's bagged, stuff it in here," she said.

"And if not, where do I stuff it?"

She simply looked toward my partner. "While he figures out the answer to his own question, Quent: We've still drawn blanks at every bus terminal, airport and rail connection between Vallejo and Santa Clara. What's your best guess on Park?"

Quent told her while I put my evidence in her bag. At his bidding I let her review the video I'd made. He described the timing of the connections we'd made and blunted the conclusions he and I had reached together. "Wherever Park is, and for whatever reason, I just have a suspicion he won't surface again in the Bay Area," he said. Then he described the Chinatown lead and told her flatly why he believed it was fugazi, a false trail.

She turned to me. "You're uncharacteristically silent. What do you think?"

"Much the same. And I think Quent ought to borrow your spectral analyzer, if it's small enough to put in a Bianchi rig."

"Mine won't fit in any shoulder holster I've seen," she said, "but some will. The covert units are slower, though. Encryption-linked to a lab in Sunnyvale, which is why they can be so small. I've seen one implanted in a LOC-8. And they are very, very expensive," she added. A LOC-8 was one of the second-generation GPS units with two-way comm and a memory just in case you wondered where you'd been. Combined with a linked-up analyzer it would be worth a new Volvo.

"You want me to ship out on the *Ras Ormara* or something," Quent said to me, amused.

Dana turned to him again. "Better you than King Kong here. You look the part, and you could talk with the crew more easily."

Quent: "You're not serious."

Dana: "Not actually shipping out, but you might try getting aboard while the new cargo is being loaded. A spectral analyzer needs no more than a whiff to do its job, and I'd hate to try to guess all the ways a cargo can be falsified."

Quent was silent for a time. Then, "I'd never get aboard without the rep's authorization, or the captain's. There goes one layer of our deniability but yes, I could try it. Or Harve could, in a pinch."

We kicked the idea around a bit, and then she excused herself and walked off a ways to use her phone while Quent and I watched boats slice the lake's surface under psychedelic bubbles of sail. When she turned back, she was nodding. "You'll need to learn how to use it," she said.

Quent said if it was anything like the one she carried, she could show us using the specimen I'd collected. She simpered for him and said she should've thought of that herself. We found a picnic table and, sandwiched between me and Quent, Dana pulled a grey, keyboard-faced polymer brick from her bag and opened my evidence baggie next to it.

She stuck her forefinger into a depression labeled CRUCIBLE in the brick and pressed the CRU key. When she withdrew her finger its tip was covered by a filmy shroud, which she quickly stuck into my soggy tissue. Then she pushed the fingertip into another depression and pressed SAMPLE, and the brick whirred very faintly for an instant. Dana withdrew her finger, stripped the film off, and let it drop to the tabletop, an insubstantial wisp. Then after a silence, the brick's little screen began to print gibberish at a rate too fast to follow.

"Essentially, a carbon ribbon wipes a bit of the specimen off the film—don't ask me why it's called a crucible—and analyzes it," Dana murmured.

"What if you're testing the air," Quent asked.

"Wave your finger around for a moment. They say

the crucible has microscopic pores on its surface," she explained.

"And how many of those little mouse condoms are inside," I asked, unrolling the discarded wisp for a better look.

"Rackham, you are a piece of work," she said under her breath. Then more loudly, "A hundred or so. By that time the battery needs replacing." When the little screen quit printing Martian, it showed a line with several numbered pips of varied height. She showed us how to query each number, which could be shown as chemical symbols or in words.

The biggest pip was for water, the next was for a ketone solvent, then cellulose, then something called Biopol.

I put my finger out and touched the screen. "Bad actor?"

"No. A polymer from genetically altered canola," she said.

"How in the hell would you knew that," I demanded.

She let me stew for a moment. Then, "Customs. Biopol was the plant extract on the manifest. Quent would've figured that out and told you anyway," she added grudgingly.

The trace of $C_{10}H_{18}O$, according to the screen, was eucalyptol. Dana pointed out that the heavily aromatic tree hanging over us was a eucalyptus. "So you see it's pretty accurate."

I said no it wasn't, or it would've told us what the little condom was made of. She said yes it was and positively beamed, explaining that the analyzer knew to ignore the crucible's signature. I gave up. The damned thing was pretty smart at that.

"At least we know the cargo was as advertised," Quent said.

Dana nodded. "Including those pallets of wood. We 'scoped enough of it. So now we focus on the

next cargo because no one has come ashore with
sizable contraband, and the incoming cargo was
clean."

"Unless they'd already pumped it out into those
trucks I saw," I said.

"They didn't," said Dana. "One of the cleanout
crew is one of ours. You don't need to know which
one. The *Ras Ormara* crew are watching him carefully enough to make us even more suspicious."

"I wasted my time then," I said.

"You proved the wharf isn't all that secure,"
Quent mused, and checked his wrist. "If you're going to spring for a couple of those analyzers, ma'am,
we should get to it."

She reminded him that it was a loan, and there'd
be only one. Thinking ahead as usual, he said as
long as we were going to show our hand overtly as
a P.I. team, he'd feel better going aboard if I went
along. That meant I could contact the Sonmiani rep
myself for the authorization and save some time.

"If you drop me off at my Toyota right away," I
said, "I might catch this Goldman guy before he
leaves his office."

We quick-marched back to the Volvo and Dana
agreed to meet Quent back at the Sunnyvale lab in
the South Bay.

I knew I was cutting it close for normal working
hours but StudyBimbo found the Sonmiani number
while Quent drove me to my pickup. I was in luck;
better luck than Quent would find. One Mike Kaplan answered for Sonmiani Shipping, and put me
through without rigamarole. That's how my brief
platonic fling began with my friend, Norman Goldman.

Three

When you first meet someone of your own sex that you like right away, no matter how hetero you are, you tend to go through something resembling courtship. When the other guy is equally outgoing, ordinary things sink into a temporary limbo: time, previous appointments, even mealtimes.

That's how it had been with me and Quent, and it happened again with Norm. The reason he and his staff assistant had still been at the office was that the Goldman suite and Sonmiani's office were over-and-under, in one of the smaller of those old Alameda buildings respiffed in the style they call Elerath Post-Industrial. I guessed that Sonmiani did a healthy business because the whole two-story structure was theirs.

It was a few minutes after five, but Goldman had said he'd leave the front door unlocked. Following

the signs, I moved down a hallway formed by parti-
tioning off a strip from the offices, which I could
see through the glassed partition. One man was still
in there, wearing a headset and facing a big flat
screen. He looked up and waved, and I waved back,
and he motioned for me to continue.

The place must have once doubled as a warehouse to judge from the vintage—now trendy again
and clean as a cat's fang—freight elevator. I obeyed
its sign, tugging up on a barrier which met its descending twin at breastbone height. It whirred to life
on its own, a bit shaky after all those years of service,
and a moment later I saw a pair of soft Bally sandals
come into view under nicely creased allosuede
slacks. A pale yellow dress shirt with open collar followed, and finally I saw a tanned, well-chiseled face
looking at mine. Hands on hips, he grinned. I
couldn't blame him; I'd forgotten how I was
dressed.

We introduced ourselves before he jerked a
thumb toward the glass door of what might have
been an office, but turned out to be his digs. "Sorry
about the time," I said, as he ushered me into a big
airy room with an eclectic furniture mix: futon,
modern couch, inflatable chairs, and a wet bar. And
some guy-type pictures, one of which had nothing
to do with ships. I thought it would stand a closer
look if I got the time. "I tend to forget other people
keep regular hours," I added.

"Couldn't resist your opening," he said, with a
wave of his hand that suggested I could sit anyplace,
and I chose the couch. "Anyone looking for the
same crew member I'm looking for, is someone I
want to meet. Besides, I've never met a real live—
ah, is 'pee-eye' an acceptable buzz phrase?" He had
heavy expressive brows that showed honest concern
at the question, and big dark eyes that danced with
lively interest. "And if it's not, would some sour

mash repair the damage?" His accent was Northeast, I guessed New York, and in Big Apple tempo.

"Maybe later," I said. "But P.I. is a term always in vogue."

"As long as I'm on Goldman time, I'll have a beer," he said, and bounced up like a man who played a lot of tennis. He uncapped a Pilsener Urquell from a cooler behind the bar, dipped its neck toward me, then took a swig of the brew before sitting down again. "We've about given up on Park, by the way. Do you suppose the dumb slope has gotten himself in some kind of trouble?"

I admitted I didn't know. "That's what the client wants us to find out. At this point, we're hoping his personal effects aboard ship might point us in some direction. With your authorization, of course, Mr. Goldman. That's what we had in mind."

He nodded abstractedly. "Don't know why not. And hey, my father is Mr. Goldman, God forbid you should mix us up." His grin was quick and infectious. "It's Norm; okay?"

I'd intended to keep this on a semiformal level but with Norm it was simply not possible. I insisted on "Harve," and asked him if he ever felt ill at ease dealing with Moslem skippers. He got a kick from that; a ship's captain might be Allah on the high seas, said Norm, but they knew who signed their checks. "No, it's the poor ragheads who aren't all that easy about me." He laughed. "But Sonmiani's directors include some pretty canny guys. As long as I keep cargoes coming and going better than the last rep, what's to kvetch about?

"Actually the skipper probably will anyway. Gent with a beard, named something-Nadwi. A surly lot, Harve, especially when they're behind schedule." He stopped himself suddenly, shot a quick glance at me. "I don't suppose it's my bosses who put you onto our man's trail. Nobody's told me, but they don't always tell the left hand what its thumb is doing. In a way I hope it is them."

"Against my charter to identify a client, but let's just say it's someone worried about a young guy who's a long way from home," I said. A hint that broad was, as Quent had said, bending the rules a bit but that wasn't why I felt a wisp of guilt. I felt it because I knew our real client wasn't a deceased Korean.

Norm was understanding. He said he'd seen Park Soon exactly once, and that, while he was making his own inquiries, a couple of the crew who had their papers had claimed they saw the engineer in a bar. "They may have been mistaken. Or—hell, I don't know. You couldn't pick a more suspicious mix than we have on the *Ras Ormara.* Schmucks will lie just for practice. You can't entirely blame them, you know. Some skippers skim company food allowances intended for the crews, though I don't believe Nadwi does. I won't have it, by God, and our skippers know it. There's a backhander or two that I can't avoid in half the foreign ports. A lot of their manning agencies are corrupt—"

"Backhander?"

"Kickback, bribe. It's just part of doing business in some ports, and the poor ragheads know it, but they never get a dime of the action. Same-old, same-old," he chanted, shook his head, and took another slug of Urquell.

His shirt pocket warbled, and he tapped it without looking. "Goldman," he said, not bothering to keep the conversation private from me. I was struck by the openness of everything, the offices, Norm's apartment, his dealings with people.

"I'm about squared away here, guv," said a voice with a faint Brit flavor. "Thought I'd nip out for a bite."

"Why not? You've been on Kaplan time for,"

Norm consulted a very nice Omega on his wrist, "a half hour. Oh! Mike, would you mind running up here a minute first? Gentleman in an unusual business here I want you to meet."

The voice agreed, sounding slightly put-upon, and after he rang off I realized it must be the man I'd seen in the office. It was obvious that Norm Goldman had the same view of formalities that I did, but something about his decisive manner said he might crack a whip if need be. I decided he was older than I'd first thought; maybe forty, but a very hip forty.

Then I took a closer look at that framed picture on his wall, a colorful numbered print showing one formula car overtaking another as a third slid helplessly toward a tire barrier. It was the Grand Prix of Israel, Norm said, adding that he was a hopeless fan. I said I shared his failing; worse, that I had half the bits and pieces of an off-road single-seater in my workshop awaiting the chassis I'd build. He crossed his arms and sighed and, beaming at me, said he might have known.

A quick two-beat knock, and Mike Kaplan entered without waiting. He was swarthy and slim, with very close-cropped dark hair and a nose old-time cartoonists used to draw as a sort of Jewish I.D. His forearms said he'd done a lot of hard work in his time. I got up. Norm didn't, waving a hand from one of us to the other as we shook hands. "Mike Kaplan, Harve Rackham. Mike's my second, and when we're both out of the office, our young tomcat Ira Meltzer holds down the fort. Ira's not in his rooms—where the hell is Ira—as if it were any of my effing business," Norm added with a smile.

Mike said how would he know, and Norm shrugged it off. "Let me guess," Mike said to me. "Wrestler on the telly?"

"That's me," I said, and pulled up my pants. "Harve, the Terrible Tourist."

"Come on," Mike said, because Norm was chuckling.

"I didn't know they existed anymore, Mike, but you are looking at a private eye. In disguise, I hope," said his boss, enjoying the moment. When Mike didn't react, he said, "As in, private investigator. You know: Sam Spade."

Mike Kaplan's face lit up then, and his second glance at me was more appraising and held a lot more friendly interest. "Personally, I'd be inclined to tell him whatever he wants to know," he said to Norm. I must have outweighed him by fifty kilos.

"If you knew, you might. But that would more likely be the job of the *Ras Ormara*'s skipper," Norm replied. "You're better at those names than I am."

Mike shook his head in mock censure. "If you worked at it as I do, you'd get along better with them," he said. "Captain Hassan al-Nadwi, you mean." As Norm nodded, Mike Kaplan went on, "And what do we need from that worthy?"

I told him, and admitted we needed to look at the engineer's effects as soon as possible—meaning the next day.

Mike allowed as how al-Nadwi would put up a pro forma bitch, but it shouldn't really be a problem if I didn't mind a lot of silent stares, and people on board who suddenly seemed to know no English at all. He said he'd call the skipper, stroke him a little, lean on him a little. Al-Nadwi knew who held the face cards. Piece of cake, he said.

Norm said he gathered I wasn't working alone, and I told him about Quentin Kim, apologizing for the oversight. "If Park Soon left any notes in Hangul," I said, "it'd be Quent who could read them. He speaks Korean, of course; that's probably why he got the case. I'd be just as useful chasing down other leads."

Norm donated a quizzical look. "I didn't realize there were other leads."

New friend or not, there are times when you see you're about to step over the line. That can reach around and bite you or your friend sometimes in ways you can't predict. I said, "There may not be. If there were, I couldn't discuss them. 'Course, if Quent stumbled on one, it wouldn't surprise me if you got wind of it later." I let my expression say, *the game's a bastard but rules are rules.*

"I respect that. Can't say I understand it, but I respect it," said Norm.

"Good," I said. "So for all I know, Quent may come alone to the ship and send me off in another direction."

Norm's reaction warmed my heart. "But—I was going to go along because you were," he said. "Spring for lunch, pick your brains about racing,— uh-unh; you've got to go along, Harve."

"I'll try, but it's Quent's call. He's my boss," I said.

A sly half smile, and one lifted brow, from Norm. "Well," he said softly, reasonably, "just tell him the real call is Norm Goldman's. And Goldman is an unreasonable asshole."

Mike Kaplan laughed out loud and jerked his head toward Norm while looking at me. "I've been saying that for ages," he said.

After Kaplan promised to set up a visit to the ship for me and Quent, he left us. I told Norm that just about cleared my decks for the day, and said I'd take one of those Czech beers if the offer was still open. We jawed about our tastes in racing—I couldn't see his fascination with dragsters; he thought karts were kid stuff. He showed me around his place while we discussed Norm's good luck in falling heir to a floor of rooms that split so nicely into three apartments. Whatever Sonmiani paid their seamen, Norm and his staff obviously were in no fiscal pain. Finally, we bonded a little closer over the fact that both of us placed high value in working with people we liked.

I promised Norm he'd like Quent because they shared a subdued sense of humor, though he might find my old pal oddly conservative considering the career he chose. That was the chief way, I said, that Quent's ethnicity showed.

Norm said believe it or not, I'd find Kaplan had a touch of the prude. He added that it couldn't be the man's Liverpool upbringing, so maybe it was the Sephardic Jew surfacing in him. It was a comfort, he said, to know he could be gone a week and feel confident that the office was secure in the hands of Mike Kaplan. I'd find Ira Meltzer a frank Manhattan skirt-chaser, he said, which could get a bit wearing but Ira was a real *mensch* for hard work.

I tried to call Quent about the good news, but got his tape. I didn't call Dana Martin because I didn't want to seem secretive, and I sure wasn't going to talk with a Fed in front of Norm.

And when he suggested we go looking for dinner—on him, or rather on Sonmiani, he reminded me—I said it might be better if we called a pizza in because I was tired of people looking at me funny. I was catching on to his dry humor by then, and laughed when he said with a straight face that he couldn't imagine why they might.

"Pizza's a good idea," he said, "but we could order it from anywhere. How about from your workshop?"

He was as serious about it as most race-car freaks, and the idea of a forty-minute drive didn't dismay him. It was long odds against a deliveryman finding my place, I said, but we could pick that pizza up on the way. He'd be driving back alone for the first few miles on dark country roads, I cautioned. He said he had a decent Sony mapper, so he was up for it if I was, but if I had any objection we could do it another time.

Objection? Hell, this would be the first time I could recall that I'd had two guests in one week, and I said as much while we rode the rocking old elevator down.

Eventually, using our phones while he followed me out of town in his enviable, cherried-out classic black Porsche Turbo, I suggested we save time by my cobbling up a couple of reubens on my woodstove. He agreed, and when we hit the country roads I tried Quent again without success.

Now I could call our pet Feeb, who sounded slightly impressed that I was still at work. She liked it even better that Sonmiani's people were receptive to our private search and would help us snoop aboard ship, the next day.

Quent, she said, had taken the Loc-8 with its hidden spectral analyzer after playing with it under lab tutelage. She thought he might be cruising around Richmond trying to find crewman Hong Chee. Reception, especially in some of the popular basement dives, wasn't all that reliable. I told myself Quent could cruise the ethnic bars better as a singleton and besides, I was working in a way, schmoozing with a guy who could hinder or help us. No doubt Quent would call me when he was ready.

Dana wasn't so happy with my suggestion that the Feds canvass airline reservation lists scheduled for the next few days, just to see if they got any hits on the *Ras Ormara*'s crewlist. Did she think it was pointless? Maybe not entirely, she admitted, before she hung up. I still think Dana was simply pissed because she hadn't already gotten around to it.

No need to worry about Norm Goldman's ability to keep my pickup in sight. He stayed glued to my back bumper, perhaps to prove that he had a racer's soul. But Jesus! A Pooch Turbo tailing an old Toyota trash hauler? My sister Shar could've done it. Even so, he must've bottomed his pan following me up the lane to my place. A moment later my phone chirped.

I hoped it was Quent, but, "Harve? Is this a gag? How much farther is it," asked a slightly subdued Norm.

I asked if he could spot the old white clapboard farmhouse past the orchard ahead, and he said yes. "That's it. We're on my acreage now," I said. With hindsight, I think he had started to wonder whether his new friend had something unfriendly in mind for him.

My workshop was still more than half smithy then, a short walk from the house, and we parked beside it. I toggled a key-ring button that unlocked the side door, and its sensor lit the shop up for us as I approached.

Norm stepped inside with the diffidence of an acolyte in a cathedral, ready to be awed by a genuine racing-car shop. It may have been a disappointment. The most significant stuff I had on hand was the specialized running gear, protectively bagged in inert argon gas, but he spent more time studying my half-sized chassis drawings and the swoopy lines I had lofted to show the body shells I hadn't molded yet. When I saw him rubbing his upper arms I realized it was chilly for him. "You might enjoy looking at some recent off-road race videos," I said, "while I get the kitchen stove warmed. Or you could sit on top of the stove," I cracked. "Takes about ten minutes to get that cast-iron woodhog of mine up to correct temperature."

So we closed up the shop and I used my century-old key to get us past the kitchen door. I explained my conceit, keeping the upstairs part of the house turn-of-another-century except for a few sensible improvements: media center, smoke and particulate detectors, a deionizer built into a squat wooden 1920s icebox. I couldn't recall whether I'd left any notes on my desk or screen downstairs, so I didn't mention my setup there.

I showed Norm to the media center in my parlor, swore to him that the couch wouldn't collapse, and left him with a holocube of the recent Sears Point Grand Prix. I'd be lying if I said I was worried about Quent, but while rustling up the corned beef, cheese, and other munchables necessary to a reuben I kept expecting him to call. I thought he might wind up his day by driving out, and we could all schmooze together. I thought wrong.

Just for the hell of it, I opened a bottle of Oregon early muscat for our sandwiches. A bit on the sweet side, but, to make a point, I reminded Norm that Catalonians serve it to special guests and I admired their style.

After supper we skimmed more holocubes and played some old CDs, and I was yarning about the time I had to evade a biker bunch when I heard my phone. It had to be Quent, I thought; and in a way it was. I said, "Sorry, you never know," to Norm, went into the back bedroom, and answered.

It was Dana, terse and angry. "You won't like this any better than I do," she warned me, and asked where I was.

I told her, and added, "I sure don't like it when I don't know what's up, boss lady. Tell me."

She did, and a flush of prickly heat spread from the back of my neck down my arms. I only half heard the essentials, but every word would replay itself in my mind during my drive back to Richmond.

"Give me a half hour," I said. "The Sonmiani rep is here with me. He might be some help tracing some of the crew's movements if there's a connection."

"Say nothing tonight; Sonmiani might be one of those firms that demand advocacy no matter what."

"Firms like yours," I said grimly, and regretted it in the same moment. "Forgive me, I'm—I need to go out and slug a tree. See you in thirty."

Norm must have been sensitive to body language because he stood up as I stumped through the parlor door. I told him I had to drive back into town as soon as I changed clothes. To his question I said it wasn't anything he could help with; just a case that had taken a new turn. He asked whether my Korean boss let me go along on the *Ras Ormara* thing. I replied that there wasn't much doubt I'd make it, and promised to give him an early-morning call. Then I hurried into my bedroom for a quick change, my hands shaking.

As I slapped the closures on my sneakers I heard the Porsche start up, and Norm was long gone when my tires hit country-road macadam. Not so long gone that I didn't almost catch him nearing Concord. I hung back enough to let him find the freeway before me. After all, there wasn't any need for breaking records now; hard driving was simply the only way I could use up all that adrenaline before I met the Feds off the freeway in East Richmond, near the foothills. I kept thinking that from downtown Richmond to some very steep ravines was only five minutes or so. And wondering whether my buddy Quent had still been alive during the trip.

Linked to Dana by phone, I found the location a block off the main drag, a long neon strip of used-car lots and commercial garages. Evidently Dana's people had shooed the locals away, though a pair of uniformed cops still hung around waiting to control the nonexistent crowd, and I seemed to be it.

The guys doing the real work wore identical, reversible dark jackets. I knew that "F B I" would be printed on the inner surfaces of those jacket backs and, when Dana waved me forward, a strobe flash made me blink.

I saw the chalk outline before I spotted the partially blanketed figure on a foldable gurney in the extrawide unmarked van. The chalk lines revealed that Quent had been found with his legs in the street, torso in the gutter, head and one arm up on the curb. The stain at the head oval looked black, but it wouldn't in daylight.

We said nothing until I followed Dana into the van, sitting on jump seats barely out of the way of a forensics woman who was monitoring instruments while she murmured into her headset. The gadget she occasionally used looked like my StudyFrail but probably cost ten times as much. I leaned forward, saw the misshapen contours of a face I had known well. I knew better than to touch him. I think I moaned, "Awww, Quent."

"He was deceased before he struck the curb, if it's any consolation," said Dana. "Long enough before, that he lost very little blood on impact. Presumption is that someone dropped him from a moving vehicle."

I couldn't help wondering what I'd been doing at the time. Nodding toward the forensics tech, I managed to mutter, "Got a time of death?"

Dana said, "Ninety minutes, give or take." I would've been licking my fingers right about then. "We thought it might have been accidental at first."

"For about ten seconds," said the tech dryly. She wasn't missing anything. Her gloved hand lifted Quentin Kim's lifeless wrist. It was abraded and bruised. She pointed delicately with her pinkie at the bluish fingertips. The nails of the smallest two fingers were missing. The cuticles around the other nails were swollen and rimmed with faint blood-stains, and the ends of the nails had been rough-ened as if chewed by some tiny animal. "He still had a heartbeat when this was done," she added.

"Pliers," I said, and she grunted assent. "Some-body wanted something out of him. But how could pulling out fingernails be lethal," I asked, shudder-ing by reflex as I tried to imagine the agony of my close friend, a friend who had originally hired me for physical backup. Fat lot of good I had done him. . . .

The tech didn't answer until she glanced at Dana, who nodded without a word. "Barring a coronary, it couldn't. But repeated zaps of a hundred thousand volts will give you that coronary. Zappers that pow-erful are illegal, but I believe Indonesian riot con-trol used them for a while. The fingernails told me to look for something else. Nipples, privates, lips, other sites densely packed with nerve endings."

"I'll take your word for it," I said. She was imply-ing torture by people who were good at it, and I lacked the objectivity to view the evidence.

"But that's not where I found the trauma," said the tech. "It showed up as electrical burn marks in a half dozen places where a pair of contact points had been pressed at the base of the skull, under the hair. Not too hard to locate if you know what you're looking for. The brain stem handles your most basic life support; breathing, that sort of thing. Electro-cute it hard, several times, and it's all over."

"It's not over," I growled.

"It is for him," the woman said, then looked into my eyes and blinked at whatever she saw. "Got it," she mumbled, going back to her work.

"Under the circumstances," Dana said, not un-kindly, "you may want to break this one off without prejudice. Even though there may be no connection between this and the particular case you're working.

Quentin had other active cases, and we know he's not above working two at once, don't we?"

"I resent that word 'above.' We also know how we'd bet, if we were betting," I said.

"You *are* betting, Rackham. And stakes don't go much higher than this."

Neither of us could have dreamed how wrong she was, but I could dream about avenging my pal. I said, "I'm feeling lucky. Where's that Loc-8 with the analyzer? I'll learn to use it by tomorrow. Maybe Norm Goldman can divert some people's attention. He'll be with me."

She said she'd be glad to, if she knew where it was. "It might be in Quentin's Volvo; the Richmond force is on it, too. It could turn up at any time," she said.

She led me out of the van again and into its night-shadow. "There's not much point in going aboard that ship until we find you an analyzer. Preferably the one Quent had. Don't contact Goldman's people again until we do."

"He might call me. We hit it off pretty well, and he could be an asset," I said.

"He may be, at that," she said as if to herself, then sighed and shifted her mental gears with an almost audible clash. "You may as well go home, there's nothing you can do here. I called you in only because I knew you two were close." A pause. "You'd have told me if Quentin had called you tonight. Wouldn't you?"

"About what?"

"About anything. Answer my question," she demanded.

Before that tart riposte was fully out of her mouth I said, "Of course I'd tell you! What is this, anyway?" When she only shook her head, I went on, "I kept my phone on me at all times because I kept hoping he'd call. I was getting uncomfortable because, normally, he'd have called just for routine's sake. I called *him* a couple of times, that's easy enough for you to check. I'd like to know where you're going with this."

"So you don't feel just a touch of, well, like you'd let him down, left him waiting? A little guilty?"

Her tone was gentle. In another woman I might've called it wheedling. And that told me a lot. "Goddamned right I feel guilty! I did let him down, but not because I put him off when he called. He never called, Martin. Why don't you just say 'dereliction of duty' and be done with it? And be glad you're half my size when you say it."

I turned and stalked off before she could make me any madder, wondering how I was going to get any sleep, wishing Quent had called in so I'd know where he'd gone. Wishing I had that Loc-8 so I'd have a reason to go aboard the *Ras Ormara*. And suddenly I realized how important it was that I find the gadget for its everyday use. Hadn't Dana said she'd be glad to lend me the damn thing if she knew where it was?

I was pretty sure where it would be: in the breakaway panel of the driver's side door in the Volvo. Quent had padded the pocket so he could keep a sidearm or special evidence of a case literally at hand.

But the Volvo was missing. If it were downtown, it should already have been spotted. If it was a Fed priority, the Highway Patrol would have picked it up five minutes after it hit a freeway. Very likely someone had hidden it, maybe after using it to dump poor Quent along Used Car Row. Maybe it was in the bay. Maybe parked in a quiet neighborhood, where it might not be noticed for a day or so. Maybe in a chop shop someplace, already being dismantled for parts for other used cars. . . .

Used Car Row! What better place to dump an upscale used car? I fired up my Toyota and drove slowly past the nearest lot, noting that a steel cable stretched at thigh height from light pole to light pole, with cars parked so that no one could cruise through the lot or hot-wire a heap and cruise out with it. Or dump a stolen car there.

Several long blocks later I lucked out, not in a car lot but at the end of a row of cars outside a body-and-fender shop. I hadn't remembered the license; it was that inside rearview of Quent's that stretched halfway across the windshield just like mine did, one of those aftermarket gimmicks every P.I. needs during a stakeout or traffic surveillance.

Pulling on gloves, I parked the pickup out of sight and flicked my pocket flash against the Volvo's steering column. The keys were in the ignition. Knowing Quent as I did, I avoided touching the door plate. In fact, though the racket should have brought every cop in town, I didn't touch the car until, on my fourth try, the old bent wheel rim I'd scrounged managed to cave in the driver's side window, scattering little cubes of glass everywhere.

By that time the alarm's *threep, threep, whooeeeet, wheeeoot* parodied a mockingbird from hell and for about thirty seconds I expected to see gentlemen of the public safety persuasion descending on the scene. Only after I got the keys out and unlocked the driver's side door did the alarm run out of bird-seed and blessed silence overtook the place once more.

Fed forensics are better than most folks think, so while I intended to tell Dana what I'd done, I wanted it to be at a time of my choosing. That's why I didn't climb inside the car. I just opened the driver's door and checked the spring-loaded door panel.

And good old Quent, following his procedures as always, had squirreled away the Feds' tricky little

Loc-8 right where it would be handy, and whoever had left the Volvo there hadn't suspected the break-away panel. I pocketed the gadget, left the keys in the ignition again, and drove like a sober citizen back to the freeway and home. I could hardly wait to check out the Loc-8's memory. Every centimeter of its movements through the whole evening would have been recorded—unless Quent or someone else had erased it.

The normal functions of the Loc-8's little screen hadn't been compromised, so I was able to scroll through its travels beginning with Quent's depar-ture from the Sunnyvale lab early in the evening. I brewed strong java and sipped as I made longhand notes with pen on paper at my kitchen table. Say what you will about old-fashioned methods, nothing helps me assemble thoughts like notes on paper.

Quent had driven back via the Bay Bridge to Rich-mond at his ordinary sedate pace, and the Volvo had stopped for two minutes or so halfway down a block in the neighborhood where he had spoken earlier in the day with the so-called machinist. If he hadn't found a parking slot, I guessed he had double-parked.

Next he had driven half a mile, and here the Loc-8 had stayed for over an hour. At max magni-fication it showed he must have used a parking lot because the Volvo had been well off the street. I noted the location so I could interview the parking attendant, if any. From the locale, I figured Quent had been cruising the ethnic bars and game palaces, maybe looking for our missing engineer or, still more likely, the machinist's roomie. Then the car had left its spot, found the freeway, and headed south through Oakland to the Alameda, not in any special hurry.

But when the Volvo's trail traversed a long block

for the second time, I checked the intersections. There was no mistake: Quent had circled the Sonmiani offices a couple of times, then parked in an adjacent alleyway, the same one Norm used for his Porsche as access to the garage entrance of the first-floor offices. As well as I could recall, I hadn't been gone from there long when Quent arrived to do his usual careful survey of the whole layout before committing himself. That would fit if he'd intended to meet someone like Mike Kaplan or the other guy I hadn't met—Meltzer. Someone whose phone number he didn't have. Maybe he had been confident I was still there.

But if he had been trying to contact me, why hadn't he just grabbed his phone? Obviously he hadn't thought it was necessary. That meant he wasn't worried about his safety, because Quent had told me up front that he'd rented me, as it were, by the pound of gristle. And, like most P.I.s, Quent worked on the premise that discretion was the better part, et cetera. The P.I. species is often bred from insurance investigators, a few lawyers, ex-military types, and ex-cops. Guess which ones are most willing to throw discretion in the dumper. . . .

Despite the lateness of the hour, my first impulse was to call Norm and ask him a few questions about what, or whom, Quent might have met there. But what would he know? He'd been tailgating me out past Mt. Diablo at that time. Another thing: Nearing my place I had called Quent to no avail. Had he gone inside by then? Or he could have met someone in another car. Illegal entry wasn't Quent's style. I decided that if he had been looking for me, he'd have called before parking there. The car had stayed there for about five minutes and then its location cursor virtually disappeared, but not quite. With its signal greatly diminished, it said the Volvo had been driven into Norm's garage. There it had stayed for about an hour.

Then when the cursor suddenly appeared with a strong satellite signal, the Volvo went squirting through the Alameda as if someone were chasing it. It would've been dark by then as the cursor traced its way up the Nimitz Freeway to the Eastshore route, taking a turnoff near Richmond. I was feeling prickly heat as I keyed the screen back and forth between real time and fast-forward, because in real time Quent never drove with that kind of vigor.

I concluded he hadn't been driving by then. The Volvo had gone some distance up Wildcat Canyon near Richmond's outskirts, now driving more slowly, at times too slowly, then picking up the pace as it turned back toward the commercial district. There was no doubt in my mind where this jaunt would end, and for once I nailed it. The Volvo sizzled past the spot where a chalk outline now climbed a boulevard curb, turned off the main drag, and doubled back and forth on a service road before it stopped. The site was approximately where I had found the Volvo.

The screen said more than two hours passed before the cursor headed toward my place, duly recording the moment when I stole the gadget— recovered it, I mean; Dana had clearly said she wished she could lend it to me. Had she been lying? Probably, but it didn't matter. I had the gimmicked Loc-8 and I had time to fiddle with its hidden functions, having watched while Dana showed another one off while sitting on a park bench between me and Quent.

And I had something else: a cold hard knot of certainty that someone working for my new friend Norm Goldman was no friend of Quent's. Or of mine.

Four

I did sleep, after all. Worry keeps me awake but firm resolve has a way of grinding worry underfoot. I woke up mad as hell before I even remembered why, and then I sat on the edge of my bed and shed the tears I never let anyone see.

Then I dressed for a tour of the *Ras Ormara*. I'm told that the Cheyennes used to gather before a war party and ritually purge their bellies. They believed it sharpened their hunting instincts, and I know for a fact that if you expect a reasonable likelihood of serious injury, your chances of surviving surgery are better on an empty stomach. For breakfast I brewed tea, and nothing else, in memory of my friend.

Around nine, I called Norm Goldman and asked if my visit was on. He said yes, and asked if my Korean boss would be coming, too. I told him I hadn't been able to raise Quent, before I realized the grisly double entendre of my reply. We agreed to meet at the slip at ten-thirty. I went downstairs and made a weapons check. Assuming the guys who took Quent down were connected with the ship—and I did assume it—somehow it just seemed a natural progression for them to make a run on me on what was their turf. Especially if Quent, in his agony, had admitted who was running the two of us.

I ignored my phone's bleat because its readout didn't identify the caller and there was no message, and I figured it might be my Feebie boss with new orders I didn't want to follow.

With my StudyChick in one jacket pocket, the Loc-8 in the other, my Glock auto in its breakaway Bianchi against my left armpit and the ex-Bobby Rooney derringer taped into the hollow of my right armpit, I felt like the six-million-gadget man. My phone chortled at me as I drove into town. Still no ident for the caller, and I didn't reply, but this time there was a message and it was clearly Dana's voice on the messager.

She was careful with her phrasing. "The car's been found, but not our property. Whoever has it is asking for a grand theft indictment. But the real news is, someone with political pull back East has complained at ministerial level about the, and I quote, unconscionable interference with Pacific Rim commerce. We're now obeying a new directive. Absent some solid evidence of illegal activity by the maritime entity—and nothing ironclad is present—we're terminating the operation. Of course last night's felony will be pursued by the metro force.

"I want you to report to me immediately. After what's happened, it makes me nervous not to know whether you're still pursuing the operation. If I knew, it would probably make me even more nervous. Just ask yourself how much your license is worth." No cheery good-byes, no nothing else.

I wanted to answer that last one, though not
enough to call her back. While my license was worth
a lot to me, it wasn't worth Quentin Kim's life. She
might not know it, but I could make a decent living
as a temp working under someone else's license. If
Dana Martin's people dropped out, whatever the
Richmond homicide detail found they'd almost certainly discover that their suspects had sailed on the
Ras Ormara. Good luck, Sergeant, here's a ticket to
Pusan and the damnedest bilingual dictionary you
ever saw . . .

I played the recording back again, trying to listen
between the lines. If Dana had been thinking how
her message would sound when replayed for her local SAC, she'd have said just about what she did say.
Did she suspect the Volvo's window had been busted
by clumsy ol' Harve, who had the Loc-8 and was now
en route to the docks? If so, she evidently wasn't
going to share that suspicion with her office.

She had also made it plain that I'd have bupkis
for backup, leaving an implication that until I got
her message, I was still on the case. Or I could just
be reading into it what I wanted to read.

What I wanted to read at the moment were my
notes, not an easy task in what had now become city
traffic.

With twenty minutes to burn, I pulled over beside
a warehouse near the wharf and scrolled over my
notes hoping to identify the next cargo. The stuff
Sonmiani wanted to load was something called par-
aglycidyl ether, a resin thinner. Quent had checked
a hazmat book on the off chance that it might be
really hazardous material.

The classic historic screwup along that line had
been the burning shipload of ammonium nitrate in
1947 that was identified only by its actual intended
use as fertilizer. However, Quent had found that this
cargo wasn't a very mean puppy though it was flam-

mable; certainly not like the old ethyl ether that puts your lights out after a few sniffs.

When I checked the manufacturing location I found that the liquid was synthesized right there, not merely there in Richmond but in one of the fenced-off chemical plants with an address off the boulevard facing me. I drove on and found a maze of chemical processing towers, reactor tanks, pipes, and catwalks a half mile past the *Ras Ormara*. A gate was open to accept a whopping big diesel Freightliner rig that was backing in among the storage tanks, carrying smaller tanks of its own like grain hoppers. For a moment I thought the driver would bend a yellow guide barrier of welded pipe and wipe out the prefab plastic shed that stood within inches of the pipe. Near the shed stood a vertically aligned bank of bright red tanks the size of torpedoes. I recognized the color coding, and I didn't want to be anywhere near if that shed got graunched.

The driver stopped in time, though. He was no expert, concentrating on operating his rearview video instead of using a stooge to damned well direct him, and I thought he looked straight at me when he was only concentrating on an external mirror directly in front of him. He didn't see me any more than he would've seen a gull in the far background.

It was Mike Kaplan.

I couldn't be wrong about that. Same caricature of a beak, same severe brush cut and intense features. And why shouldn't it be him? Okay, using a desk jockey to drive a rig might be unusual, and I had thought Kaplan was slated to take the ship tour with me. But if the Fed-erected barriers to Pacific Rim commerce had come tumbling down during the morning as Dana claimed, an aggressive bunch of local reps might be pitching in to make up for lost time.

I wondered what, if anything, Kaplan might be able to tell me about what had happened in that office building early on the previous night. He had left before Norm and I did, but how did I know when he had come back? The third guy—Seltzer? Meltzer!—was one I hadn't met, but without any positive evidence I had already made a tentative reservation for him on my shit list.

It was only a short drive back to the gate that served the *Ras Ormara*. This time the gate was manned, but Norm Goldman, in a ritzy black-leather jacket, leaned with a skinny frizzle-haired guy against the fender of his Turbo Porsche, just outside the fencing. Norm recognized me with a wave and called something to the two guys at the gate as I parked beside the swoopy coupe.

The skinny guy with Norm turned out to be Ira Meltzer, who spoke very softly and had a handshake that was too passive for his work-hardened hands, and wore a denim jacket that exaggerated his shoulders. When Meltzer asked where my partner was, I said he hadn't answered my calls, so I figured he wasn't coming.

Neither of them seemed to find anything odd about that. If Meltzer knew *why* Quent wasn't coming, it was possible that Norm might know. I didn't like that train of thought; if true, it made me the prize patsy of all time. And if they had learned from Quent who it was that had been giving him orders, they would assume I already knew what had happened to him. While I thought about these things, the three of us stood there and smiled at one another.

Then Meltzer said, "By the way, aboard ship it's the captain's little kingdom—except for government agencies. And you're private, am I right?"

I agreed.

"Then if I were you, I wouldn't try to go aboard

with a concealed weapon." His smile broadened. "Or any other kind."

He didn't actually say I was carrying, and it took a practiced eye to spot the slight bulge of my Glock, but I didn't need an argument with the honcho on board. "Glad you told me," I said, and popped the little black convincer from its holster. I unlocked the Toyota and shut my main weapon in the glove box. "I carry my GPS mapper; it's a Loc-8. And I've got a StudyGirl for notes. That a problem?"

Meltzer looked at Norm, who made a wry grimace. "Shit, Ira, why would it be? In fact, you might carry one of 'em openly in your hand, Harve. I'll do the same with the other, and I'll give it back once we're aboard. I don't think al-Nadwi will get his shorts in a wad. I'm supposed to carry a little weight around here, even with these ragheads."

Meltzer said he supposed so, and I handed over StudySkirt, carrying the Loc-8 in one hand. We left our vehicles near the gate and walked in side by side toward the *Ras Ormara*.

The commercial cleanup outfit I had previously seen on the wharf was finally leaving, a bright yellow hazmat suit visibly untenanted in a niche near the truck's external console. I recognized two of the three guys in the truck's cab, and Consoleman, now the driver, waved. When Sweatman, the guy who had worn the suit, pretended he didn't notice us I knew which of them the Feds had co-opted on the job. I would've given a lot to talk with him alone right then.

Norm waved back, his good spirits irksome to me though I couldn't very well bitch about it. He kept looking around at the skyline and the wheeling gulls, taking big breaths of mud-flavored waterfront air that I didn't find all that enticing. Wonderful day, he said, and I nodded.

As we walked up the broad metal-surfaced ramp

leading to the ship, Norm made a casual half salute toward the men who stood high above on deck to meet us. Other men in work clothes were shouting words I couldn't understand as they routed flexible metal-clad hoses around forward of the bridge. A couple of them wore white head wraps.

The skipper took Norm's hand in his in a handshake that seemed clumsily forced, but he shook mine readily enough, unsmiling, as Norm made formal introductions.

Captain Hassan al-Nadwi had a full beard and an old sailor's rawhide skin, bald forward of his ears, but with chest hairs curling up from the throat of his work shirt. He wore no socks, and the soles of his sandals must have been an inch thick.

He spoke fair English. "You want see engineer quarters? Go. Much much work now," he said, friendly enough though shooing me with gestures. He gave an order to one of the two men, evidently officers, who stood behind him, then turned away to watch his work crew.

"You come, okay. I show where Park, eh, sleep," said the Asian, a hard-looking sort whose age I couldn't guess. He led us quickly through a portal, Norm giving me an "after you" wave, and down a passageway sunlit by sealed portholes. Another doorway took us through a room dominated by a long table surrounded by swiveling chairs that seemed bolted in place. Finally, we negotiated another passage with several closed doors, and as the crewman opened the last door I had a view of the skyline through the room's portholes.

The Asian stood back to let us in, pointing to one of three bunks in the room. "Park, okay," he said, and paused, with a sideways tilt of his head. Somewhere in the ship a low thrumm had started, and I could feel a hum through the soles of my shoes. He seemed to talk a bit faster now as he stepped quickly to a bunk with a half-filled sea bag on it. "Park, okay," he said, then moved to a table secured to the metal. Wall? Bulkhead? Whatever. "Park, okay," he said again. I recalled Quent saying once that all Korean kids took English courses. I figured maybe this guy had cheated on his exams.

I pulled out the table's single drawer, which was so completely empty in a room shared by three guys that it fairly screamed "total cleanout job." "Okay," I said. At my reply the crewman turned on his heel, obviously in a hurry to be off. "Wait," I said. The crewman kept going.

Ira Meltzer said something singsong. The crewman stopped in the doorway, not pleased about it. Meltzer looked at me.

"Ask him if there was any other place Park kept any of his personal effects," I suggested.

"I'll try," he said, and then said something longer. The crewman said something else. Meltzer said, "*Nae*," which was damn near all the Korean I knew, meaning "yes."

The man said something else; glanced at Norm as if fearing eye contact; then, when Meltzer nodded, left hurriedly. "He doesn't know of any. I guess this is all," he said, and nodded at the bunk.

As I unlatched the hasp that closed the sea bag, I could hear quick footfalls of a running man in the corridor. Norm laughed. "Skipper keeps the crew on a tight leash," he commented.

"I don't doubt it," I said. I knew he was explaining the Korean crewman's hellacious hurry to me. And I wasn't sure if that was the best explanation. In fact, I sat down on the bunk so that I wouldn't have my back to my trusty guides while I carefully pulled out the contents of the bag to inspect them, one by one.

A small cheap zippered bag held toilet articles, soap, and a prescription bottle of pills with instructions in Spanish. After that, a pair of worn Avia cross-trainers; socks; a set of tan work clothes, and a stained nylon windbreaker. A heavy hooded rainproof coat; a couple of girlie mags; two pairs of work gloves, one pair well worn. A small, pre-palmtop book full of engineering tables, which I flipped through without finding any handwritten notes.

I saw Meltzer take a peek at his watch, so I decided to use up some more time. "Norm, you have that StudyGirl of mine?"

He handed it over. "You find something?" In answer I shook my head. He squatted for a closer look and, I figured, to see what notes I might make.

I used the audio function, first citing the date and location. As I placed each item back in the big bag I described it, and asked if Norm could translate the label on the pill bottle.

He couldn't, but Meltzer could. While I spelled out "methacarbamol," he said, "Muscle relaxant," practically running his words together.

I announced for the audio that this was my complete audit of Park Soon's effects left aboard ship. I added, in traditional P.I. third-person reportage, "The investigator found nothing more to suggest the subject's itinerary ashore, or whether he intended to return. In the investigator's opinion, the value of the bag's contents would not exceed a hundred dollars." By the time I'd latched the bag and placed it back on the bunk, the combined silences of Norm and Meltzer hung like smoke in the little room. They were being nice, but clearly they wanted me the hell out of there.

And just as badly, I wanted to stick around. I hadn't found anything suspicious to use the analyzer on, and in any case these guys were right at my elbow. Norm stepped into the corridor and waited expectantly.

"Just one more thing," I said, following him into

the corridor. "I wonder if the captain would let me see Park's workstation. You never know what he might've left lying around."

Meltzer exhaled heavily as we retraced our steps. Norm shot me a pained smile. "I'll ask. In case you're wondering, they just got their clearance this morning, so they're hoping to get under way today. I'd like to see them do it, Harve."

"Message received," I said. "I guess that's why Mike Kaplan isn't with us."

"He's doing three men's work in the office this morning," said Norm.

And as I tried to read Norm's expression, Meltzer saw my glance and chimed in, "It's always like this at the last minute. He isn't even taking calls."

So he lies and you swear to it, I thought. Aloud I said, "I promise to keep out of the way. I just need to cover all the bases." *And one base is the discovery that my new friend may not be that good a friend.*

We found our way back on deck. A faint, musky odor lay on the breeze, reminding me of rancid soy protein. The rushing thrum in the ship's innards was more pronounced as we neared the bridge. It seemed to be coming from those big cargo tank domes that protruded from the forward deck plates. "Wait here," said Norm.

Meltzer stopped when I did. He pulled out a cigarette and, as he lit it, I could see that his hands trembled. It wasn't fear, I decided; not a chill, either, because of the way he was smiling to himself.

It was suppressed excitement.

And when the phone in my pocket gave a blurt, Ira Meltzer jumped as if I'd goosed him. "It's probably Quent," I said. "Let me take it over here." By now I was virtually certain he knew Quentin Kim would not be making any more phone calls. But maybe he didn't know that I knew.

I walked back far enough for privacy, unfolding

my phone, casually holding my StudyWench at my side so that its video recorded Meltzer. "Rackham," I said. I didn't want to pull the Loc-8 out until I could make it look like a response to this call. I'd lugged the damn thing aboard to no purpose.

"Your location is known," said Dana Martin. Sweatman had evidently done me a favor. "Are we clean?" Meaning, 'is our conversation secure?'

Meltzer was watching my face. "More or less. Our Mr. Park didn't leave anything aboard that might tell us—" I said.

Until her interruption I had never heard her speak with a note of controlled panic. "Get out of there aysap. A.T.F. liaison tells us that ether compound can be converted in the tank to a component of a ternary agent. Do you understand?"

I smiled for Meltzer. "Not exactly. Where are you?"

"Sunnyvale. We have to arrive in force, and that could take an hour. *Listen to me!* Binary nerve gas isn't deadly 'til two components are mixed. A ternary agent takes three. A relatively small proportion of an ether derivative is one. Our other asset just confirmed that the second component is already aboard. No telling how much is there, but to be effective, it's needed in far greater amounts than the ether derivative."

The rushing noise aboard the *Ras Ormara* and the deep vibrations abruptly resolved themselves in my mind into a humongous pump, dumping something into those newly cleaned cargo tanks. A hell of a lot of something. "Does it stink like bad tofu?"

"Wait one."

"Make it quick," I muttered with a smile for Meltzer, seeing Norm as he walked back toward me, a sad little smile on his face.

I was still waiting when Norm showed me a big shrug and headshake. "I'm sorry. Park didn't even have a particular workstation anyway," he said.

On the heels of this came Dana's breathless, "That's what you're smelling, Rackham. Judging from the order form for ether, and assuming they intend to convert it to another compound, we predict an amount of ternary agent that is—my God, it staggers the imagination. Component three is a tiny amount of catalyst, easy to hide. If they have it, you're on a floating doomsday machine."

Norm Goldman now stood beside me. "Copy that," I said, with a comradely pat on Norm's shoulder to show him there were no hard feelings. "Hell of a secretary you are if you don't even know where Quent is. Look, I expect I'll be having lunch with a friend. I'll call in later." With that, I folded my phone away.

Norm took my arm, but very gently. "Part of my job is knowing when not to bug the troops, Harve. Sorry." We moved toward the gangway ramp.

Somewhere in the distance, the double-tone beeps of police vehicles dopplered off to inaudibility. I hoped the audio track of my StudyBroad was picking up the sound of whatever it was that surged into those huge tanks, and then I released the button and pocketed my gadget. If the ether component was still being loaded for transfer, or if its conversion was complicated, there might be some way to slow them down. "About lunch," I began, as Meltzer followed us down to the wharf.

"Hey, listen, I'll have to take a rain check on that," said Norm, as if answering my prayer. "Mike will need help in the office. Before the clearance came through I even had a lunch reservation for a nice place where I run a tab, up in San Rafael. Promise me you'll do lunch there today anyway. My treat. Just give 'em this," he said, fishing a business card from his wallet, scribbling a Mission Avenue address in San Rafael on the back of the card. "Have a few drinks on me. Promise me you'll do that."

"It's a promise," I said, as we walked toward our vehicles. Hey, if he had lied to me I could lie to him. . . .

Because San Rafael lay to the northwest, I gave a cheery wave and drove off as if keeping my promise, tugging on my driving gloves. Then I reached over and retrieved my Glock as I doubled back toward the place where I'd seen Mike Kaplan loading up. Minutes later, while I redlined the Toyota along the boulevard, I managed to call Dana. "I'm circling around to where they're loading ether into a big rig," I said over the caterwaul of my pickup. "Why not call the Richmond force and get them to meet me there until you show up? Someone should've already thought of that."

"They have casualty situations in both high schools at the other end of town, called in almost simultaneously ten minutes ago. Perps are adults with automatic weapons. It's already on the news and traffic is wall-to-wall there. And we're having trouble getting compliance with metro liaison staff."

That was weasel-talk for getting stonewalled by city cops who have had their noses rubbed in their inferiority by Fed elitists too many times and who might not believe how serious the Mayday was. I didn't take time to say, "what goes around comes around." Of course that sort of rivalry was stupid. It was also predictable.

I growled, "I'll give odds those perps are decoys to draw SWAT teams away from here. Bring somebody fast. Strafe the goddamn ship if you have to; I'll try to delay the load of ether. Am I sanctioned to fire first?"

A two-beat pause. "You know I can't authorize that. Let me check with our SAC," she said.

I made a one-word comment, dropped the phone

in my pocket, and swung wide to make it through the open gate.

Fifty feet inside was the nose of the Freightliner, and behind it two guys in coveralls and respirator masks stood on its trailer fooling with transfer hoses. A guy in street clothes stood near the gate, jacket over his arm, and it barely registered in my mind that the guy was Ira Meltzer. The yellow-pipe barrier, protection for that long utility shed, ran from beside the rig almost to the gate. I made a decision that I might not have made if I'd had time to think.

My Toyota weighed something over a ton, and was still doing maybe thirty miles an hour. The Freightliner with its load might've weighed over twenty tons, but it wasn't in motion. I figured on moving it a little, probably starting a fire. I popped the lever into neutral as my pickup blew past the open-mouthed gate guard, then tried to hit the pavement running. Meanwhile my Toyota screeched headlong down the guide barrier, which kept nudging my vehicle straight ahead. Straight toward the nose of the towering Freightliner.

The scrape of my pickup's steel fender mixed with shouts from the gate man, and I lost my balance and went over in a shoulder roll. Inertia brought me back to my feet and nearly over again, and I heard a series of reports behind me just before my poor old pickup slammed into the left fender of the Freightliner with an earsplitting *wham* that was almost an animal scream.

Guttural little whines told me someone's ricochets were hitting distant metal, and I somehow managed to clear that knee-high barrier of four-inch pipe without slowing. I ducked—actually I tripped and fell—behind the utility shed, and saw the common old lock on its door. I was in full view of the diesel rig and turned toward it, drawing my Glock.

I had expected an instant fireball, but I was

wrong. Big rigs have flame-resistant fiberglass fenders these days, and only one fat tire on each side up front. The Toyota's entire front end was crammed up into the splintered shreds of truck fender, and the cab leaned in the direction of my four-wheeled sacrifice. With a deflated front wheel, that Freightliner wasn't going anywhere very fast.

And the reason why nobody was shooting at me from the truck was that the Toyota's impact had shoved the entire rig back, not by much, but enough to crimp the already tight fit of transfer hoses. The guys in respirators were wrestling with a hose and shouting, though I couldn't understand a word. As I stood unprotected in the shadow of the shed Meltzer pounded up, an Ingram burp gun in hand. I guess he didn't expect me to be standing so close in plain sight as he rounded the shed.

Because Meltzer was six feet away when he pivoted toward me, it was an execution of sorts. The truth is, we both hesitated; but my earlier suspicions about his dealings with Quent must have given me an edge. Meltzer took my first round in the chest with a jolt that made dust leap from his shirt, and went down backward after my second round into his throat, and I risked darting farther into the open because I needed his weapon.

A burst of three or four rounds grooved the pavement as I leaped back. I saw a familiar face above a black-leather jacket, almost hidden behind the remains of the Freightliner's fender, holding another of those murderous little Ingrams one-handed. I fired once, but only sent particles of fiberglass flying, and Norm Goldman's face disappeared.

He called, "Majub!"

I heard running footsteps, and whirled to the shed's metal-faced door before they could flank me. With those big red tanks standing nearby I had a good idea what was in the shed, so I put the muzzle of my Glock near the hasp and angled it so it *might* not send a round flying around inside. The footsteps halted with my first round, maybe because the guy thought I could see him. I had to fire twice more before the hasp's loop failed, and took some scratches through my glove from shrapnel, but by the time I knew that, I was inside the shed fumbling with two weapons. A drumming rattle on the shed didn't sound promising.

From behind the Freightliner's bulk, Norm's voice: "You couldn't leave it alone, could you?"

I didn't answer. I was scanning the shed's interior, which was lit by a skylight bubble. About half of the machinery there was familiar stuff to me: big battery-powered industrial grinders and drills, a hefty Airco gas-welding outfit, a long worktable with insulated top, a resistance-welding transformer, and tubes with various kinds of wire protruding, welding and brazing rod. Above the table were ranks of wrenches, fittings, bolts, a paint sprayer—the hardware needed to repair or revise an industrial facility.

And I could hear Norm shouting, and voices answering. Simultaneous with gunshots from outside, several sets of holes appeared in both sides of the shed at roughly waist height.

Norm yelled again, this time in English. "Goddammit, Majub, don't waste it!"

And the response in another slightly familiar voice and genuinely English English: "Sorry, guv. We do have the long magazines." So Mike Kaplan's name was also Majub. *What's in a name? Protective coloration*, I thought. Noises like the tearing of old canvas came from somewhere near. I squatted and lined up one eye with a bullet hole, but not too near the hole. By moving around, I caught sight of my wrecked Toyota. Norm and a guy in coveralls were ripping the fiberglass away as best they could. It might take them ten minutes to change that tire if I let them.

I darted to the end of the shed nearest the action and put a blind short burst from the Ingram through the wall, with only a fair guess at my targets. Because I stood three feet from the plastic wall, I didn't get perforated when an answering burst tore a hole the size of my fist in the wall.

I had taken out one man and there were several more. They seemed partial to Ingrams, about thirty rounds apiece, meaning I was in deep shit. And when I heard the hiss of gas under pressure, the hair stood up on my nape. Those big red torpedoes just outside were painted to indicate acetylene. I hadn't noticed where the oxygen tanks were, but they had to be near because of the long twinned red and black hoses screwed into the welding torch.

And acetylene, escaping inside that shed from a bullet-nicked hose, could blow that entire structure halfway to Sunnyvale the next time I fired, or when an incoming round struck a spark. I darted toward the hiss, wondering if I could repair the damage with tape, and saw that it was the black oxygen hose, not the red one, which had been cut. A slightly oxy-rich atmosphere wasn't a problem, but if I'd had any idea of using a torch somehow, it was no longer an option.

Outside, angry jabbers and furious pounding suggested that Goldman's crew was jacking up the Freightliner's left front for a tire change. It would be only a matter of minutes before they managed it, and another round through the shed reminded me that Kaplan was deployed to keep me busy. From the shafts of sunlight that suddenly appeared inside when he fired, I could tell he was slowly circling the shed, clockwise.

That long workbench with its insulated top must have weighed five hundred pounds, but only its

weight anchored it down. If I could tip it over, it
should stop anything short of a rifle bullet if and
when Kaplan tried to rush the door, and I could fire
back from cover. Maybe.

I took off my jacket to free my shoulders and tried
to tip the table quietly, but when I had the damn
thing halfway over, another round from Kaplan
whapped the tabletop a foot from me and I flinched
like a weenie. The muted slam of the tabletop's
edge was like a wrecking ball against the concrete
floor. My shirt tore away under the arms so badly
that only the leather straps of my Bianchi holster
kept it from hanging off like a cape.

Then I scurried behind the table and tried to vi-
sualize where Kaplan might be. Ten seconds later
another round ricocheted off a vise bolted to the
tabletop. But I saw the hole where the slug had entered, made a rough judgment of its path, and recalled that Kaplan was still moving clockwise. He
had fired from about my seven o'clock position, so
I used Meltzer's Ingram and squeezed off three
rounds toward seven-thirty. The astonished thun-
derstorm of his curses that followed was Wagnerian
opera to me, but his real reply was a hysterical burst
of almost a dozen rounds. A whole shelf of hardware
cascaded to the floor behind me, and I crouched
on the concrete.

Maybe I hadn't hurt Kaplan badly, but he didn't
fire again for a full minute. A handful of taps, dies,
and brass fittings rolled underfoot, the kind of fittings that were used for flammable gases because
brass won't spark. I stood up and found that I could
see through the nearest bullet hole toward the
Freightliner. My good buddy Norm was barely visible, wrestling a new tire into position. I thought I
could puncture it, too, then recalled that late-model
tires would reseal themselves after anything less
than an outright collision. Then I noticed that the

end of that four-inch railing of brightly painted yellow pipe was within a foot of the truck. The pipe was capped; one of those extra precautions metalworkers take to prevent interior corrosion in a salt-air environment.

And that made me rush to another hole at the end of the shed to see if the other end was capped.

It was.

Which meant, if there weren't any holes in the rail of pipe, I just—might—be able to use it as a very long pressure tank.

I duck-walked back behind the overturned table and routed the hoses with the welding torch along the floor, where they couldn't be struck again. Among all the stuff underfoot were fittings sized to match those that screwed the hoses into the torch, and taps intended to create threads in drilled holes of a dozen sizes. Five minutes before, they'd all been neatly arranged, but now I had to scavenge among the scattered hardware. Not a lot different, I admitted to myself, from the chaos I sometimes faced in my own workshop. My best guess was that I'd never face it again.

Another round from Kaplan struck within inches of the big battery-powered drill I was about to grab, and the new shaft of sunlight sparkled off a set of long drill bits, and I gave unspoken thanks to Mike-Majub while promising myself I would kill him.

I knelt and used a half dozen rounds from the Ingram to blow a ragged hole in the wall at shin height, hearing a couple of ricochets. My Glock wasn't all that big, but its grip gouged me as I wallowed around on my right side, so I laid the weapon on the floor where it would still be handy.

Lying on my side, I could see the near face of the pipe rail in sunlight six inches away, with bright new bullet scars in its yellow paint. Like the big acetylene tanks outside, its steel was too thick to be penetrated by anything less than armor-piercing rounds. That's what carbide-tipped drill bits are for.

One of the scars was deep enough to let me start the drill bit I eyeballed as a match for the correct brass fitting, and while I was chucking the long bit that was the thickness of my pinkie, I heard Mike-Majub yelling about the "bloody helo." A moment later I understood, and for a few seconds I allowed myself to hope I wouldn't have to continue what seemed likely to become my own personal mass murder-and-suicide project. The yelling was all about the rapid *thwock-thwock-thwock-thwock-thwock* of an approaching helicopter.

It quickly became so loud the shed reverberated with the racket from overhead, so loud that dust sifted from the ceiling, so loud I couldn't even hear the song of the drill as it chewed, too slowly, through the side of the pipe rail just inches outside the shed wall. Someone was shouting again, in English I thought, though I couldn't make out more than a few words. A few single rounds were fired from different directions and then the catastrophic whack of rotor blades faded a bit and I could understand, and my heart sank.

". . . Telling you news crews don't carry fucking weapons, look at the fucking logo! Don't waste any more ammunition on it," Norm yelled angrily.

So it was only some TV station's eye in the sky; lots of cameras, but no arms. As a cop I used to wish those guys were forbidden to listen to police frequencies. This time, as the noise of the circling newsgeek continued in the distance, I gave thanks for the diversion and hoped they'd at least get a close-up of me as I rose past them.

The bit suddenly cut through and I hauled it back, burning my wrist with the hot drill bit in my haste to fumble the hardened steel tap into place. Of course I couldn't twist the tap in with my fingers, but in my near panic, that's what I tried.

Another round hit the shed, and this time the steel-faced door opened a few inches. Bad news, because now the shooter could see inside a little. I wriggled to my knees and looked around for the special holder that grips a tap for leverage. No such luck. But another round spanged off the door, and in the increased daylight I spotted that bad seed among good tools, a pair of common pliers. They would have to do.

Because I was on my knees at the end of the overturned table and reaching for the pliers when Mike-Majub rushed the door, I only had time to grovel as he kicked the door open and raked the place with fire. I don't think he even saw me, and he didn't seem to care, emptying his magazine and then, grinning like a madman, grabbing a handgun from his belt as he dropped the useless Ingram.

Meanwhile, I had fumbled at my Bianchi and then realized the Glock lay on the floor, fifteen feet behind me. But I was sweating like a horse, and the irritant in my right armpit was now hanging loose, and the tatters of my shirt didn't impede my grasp of Bobby Rooney's tiny palmful of bad news. Tape and all, it came away in my hand as I rolled onto my back, and the grinning wide-eyed maniac in the doorway spied my movement. We fired together.

Though chips of concrete spattered my face, he missed. I didn't. He folded from the waist and went forward onto his knees, then his face. The top of his head was an arm's length from me and I had made a silent promise to him ten minutes previous and now, with the other barrel, I honored it.

Blinking specks of concrete from my vision, eyes streaming, I grabbed the pliers, stood up, vaulted over the tabletop, and kicked the door shut before scrambling back to the mess I had made. Pliers are an awful tool for inserting a steel tap, but they'll do the job. Chasing a thread—cutting it into the material—requires care and, usually, backing the tap out every turn or so. I wondered who was moaning softly until I realized it was me, and I quit the backing-out routine when I heard the Freightliner's starter growl.

Then Norm Goldman called out: "Let him go, Majub, it won't matter."

The tap rotated freely now. I backed it out quickly. "If he answers, I'll blow his head off," I shouted, and managed to start the little brass fitting by feel, into the threaded hole I had made. When it was fingertight I forced it another turn with the pliers. Then I pulled the torch to me with its twinned slender snakes of hose, one of them still hissing. To keep Norm talking so I'd know where he was: "Some Jews you turned out to be," I complained. "Who am I really talking to?"

The Freightliner snicked into gear, revved up, and an almighty screech of rending metal followed. The engine idled again while Norm shouted some kind of gabble. Then, while someone strained at the wreckage and I adjusted the pliers at the butt of the torch: "I am called Daud al-Sadiq, my friend, but my true name is revenge."

"Love your camouflage," I called back. Now a louder hiss as the acetylene fitting loosened at the torch while I continued to untwist it. With the sudden unmistakable perfume of acetone came a rush of acetylene, which has no true odor of its own. The fitting came loose in my hands and I shoved the hose through the hole, to fumble blindly for the fitting. "I especially like that 'my friend' bullshit," I called.

"In my twenty years of life in the bowels of Satan I have been a true friend to many," Norm-Daud called back in a tone of reproach, everything in his voice more formal, more rhetorical than usual. Now it became faintly whimsical. "Including Jews. You'd be surprised."

"No I wouldn't," I called, knowing that if a hot round came through now it would turn me into a Roman candle. My own voice boomed and bellowed in the shed. "How else could you learn to pass yourself off as your own enemy?" I tried to mate the fittings without being able to see them. Cross-threaded them; felt sweat running into my eyes; realized some of it was blood; got the damned fittings apart and began anew.

The Freightliner's engine revved again. Norm-Daud called, "Not the real enemy. Western ways are the enemy, but I could be your friend. Heaven awaits those of us who die in the struggle; do you hear me, Majub? What can this man do but send you to your glory an hour sooner?"

I knew he was goading his buddy into trying to jump me or to run. "He's just sitting here with the whites of his eyes showing," I lied, to piss my friend-enemy off. The sigh of escaping acetylene became a thin hiss, then went silent. In its place, a hollow whoosh of gas rushing unimpeded into an empty pipe fifty feet long, starting slowly but inevitably—if the bank of supply tanks was full enough, and if there weren't any serious leaks—to fill that four-inch-diameter pipe that was now a pressure tank.

"We will all find judgment when I reach the *Ras Ormara*," Norm-Daud called happily.

"The Feds know about your ternary agent, pal, and they're on the way. That tub isn't going anyplace," I called.

That set his laughter off. "So you've worked that out? Fine. I agree. And no one else will be going anyplace, downwind, from the Golden Gate to San Jose. What, two million dead? Three? It's a start," he said, trying to sound modest.

Then the Freightliner's engine roared, and the

rending of metal intensified. The big rig was shoving debris that had been my Toyota backward. I didn't know how fast my jury-rigged tank was filling, and if I misjudged, it wouldn't matter. I grabbed up my Glock and the burp gun and darted to the door I had kicked shut.

I had jammed it hopelessly.

I began to put rounds through the wall, emptying my Glock in a pattern that covered a fourth of an oval the size of a manhole cover. When I'd used that up I continued with the Ingram until it was empty. The oval wasn't complete. That's when I went slightly berserk.

I kicked, screamed, cursed and pounded, and the oval of insulated wall panel began to disintegrate along the dotted line. With insulation flying around me, the Freightliner grinding its way toward the boulevard in a paroxysm of screaming metal, I saw the oval begin to fail. I could claim it wasn't hysteria that made me intensify my assault, but my very existence had focused down to shredding that panel. When it bent outward, still connected at the bottom like the lid of a huge tin can, I hurled myself into the hole.

For an endless moment I was caught halfway through, my head and shoulders in bright sunlight, an immovable target for anyone within sight. But I was on the opposite side of the shed from the big rig, and when the wall panel failed I found myself on hands and knees, free but without a weapon.

Twenty feet away stood a huge inverted cone on steel supports, and beyond that a forest of braces and piping. As I staggered away behind the pipes one of Norm-Daud's helpers saw me and cut loose in my direction, ricochets flying like hornets. Meanwhile the Freightliner moved inexorably toward the open gate, the Toyota's wreckage shoved aside, the massive trailer trundling its cargo of megadeath along with less than a half mile to go. I hadn't so much as a stone left to hurl at it.

But I didn't need one. Funny thing about a concussion wave: when that fifty-foot pipe detonated alongside the trailer, I didn't actually hear it. Protected by all that thicket of metal, I felt a numbing sensation of pressure, seemingly from all directions. My next sensation was of lying on my side in a fetal curl, a thin whistling in my head. Beyond that I couldn't hear a thing.

I must have been unconscious for less than half a minute because unidentifiable bits of stuff lay here and there around me, some of it smoking. The trailer leaned drunkenly toward the side where my bomb had exploded, every tire on that side shredded, and gouts of liquid poured out of its cargo tanks from half a hundred punctures. Still addled by concussion, I steadied my progress out of the metal forest by leaning on pipes and supports. I figured that if anyone on the truck had survived, I'd hear him. It hadn't yet occurred to me that I was virtually stone deaf for the moment.

Not until I saw the blood-smeared figure shambling like a wino around to my side of the trailer, wearing the remnant of an expensive black-leather jacket. He was weaponless. One shoe was missing. He threw his head back, arms spread, and I saw his throat work as he opened his mouth wide. Then he fell on his knees in a runnel of liquid chemical beside the trailer, and on his face was an unspeakable agony.

A better man than I might have felt a shred of pity. What I felt was elation. As I stalked nearer I could see a headless body slumped at the window of the shrapnel-peppered Freightliner cab. Now, too, I could hear, though faintly as from a great distance, a man screaming. It was the man on his knees before me.

Standing three feet behind him, I shouted, "Hey!" I heard that, but apparently he didn't. I put my foot on his back and he fell forward, then rolled to his knees again. I would have hung one on him just for good measure then, but one look at his face told me that nothing I could do would increase his suffering. Even though his bloody hair and wide-open eyes made him look like a lunatic, a kind of sanity returned in his gaze as he recognized me.

Still on his knees, he started to say something, then tried again, shouting. "What did this?"

I pointed a thumb at my breast. "Gas in a pipe. Boom," I shouted. He looked around and saw the long shallow trench that now ran along the pavement. The entire length of the shed wall nearest the pipe rail had been cut as if by some enormous jagged saw, and of course the pipe itself was nowhere. Or rather, it was everywhere, in little chunks, evidence of a fragmentation grenade fifty feet long.

He looked up at me with the beginnings of understanding. "How?"

I could hear him a little better now. "Acetylene is an explosive all by itself," I shouted. "Can you hear me?" He nodded. "You store it under pressure by dissolving it in acetone. Pump it into a dry tank and it doesn't need any prompting. As soon as it gets up to fifteen or twenty pounds pressure—like I said: boom," I finished, with gestures.

He showed his teeth and closed his eyes; tears began to flow afresh. "Primitive stuff, but you would know that," he accused in a voice hoarse with exhaustion.

I nodded. "The new model of Islamic warrior," I accused back, "so all you know is plastique. Ternary agent. The murder of a million innocents."

"There are no innocents," said the man who had been, however briefly, my friend. Why argue with a man who says such things? I just looked at him.

"There are many more like me, more than there are of men like you," he said, the words rekindling something fervid in his eyes. "The new model, you said. Wait for us. We are coming."

My eyes stung from the tons of flammable liquid around us. When I reached out to help him up, he shook his torso, fumbling in his pockets. "Get away," he said. "Run."

Only when I saw that he had pulled a lighter from his pocket did I realize what he meant. I scrambled away. An instant later, the whole area was ablaze, and for all I knew the tanks on the trailer might explode. Daud-al-Sadiq, alias Norm Goldman, knelt deeply and prostrated himself in the inferno as though facing east in prayer as the flames climbed toward his warrior's heaven.

The metro cops got to the scene before anyone else, and after that came the paramedic van. Aside from cuts on my face and arms and the fact that the whistle would remain in my head for hours, I had lucked out. I could even hear ordinary speech, though it sounded thin and lacked resonance.

Captain Hassan al-Nadwi and several of his crew weren't so lucky in my view but, in their own view, I suppose they found the ultimate good luck. Using automatic weapons, they had tried to prevent a boarding party. One competence the Feds do have is marksmanship. No wonder the remaining crew were so hyperactive that morning; they were going to heaven, and they were going *now*.

Dana Martin pointed out to me after I handed over her cracked, useless Loc-8 gadget an hour later, that there had probably never been any intention on the part of the holy warriors to sail beyond the Golden Gate again. Their intent was evidently to start up their enormous doomsday machine and, if possible, set it in motion toward San Francisco's

crowded Fisherman's Wharf. The crew would all be
dead by the time the *Ras Ormara* grounded; dead,
and attended by compliant lovelies in Islamic
heaven while men, women, kids, pets, and birds in
flight died by the millions around San Francisco
Bay.

Dana said, "We came to that conclusion after we
found that all the Korean crew members but one
had reservations of one kind or another to clear out
of the area," she told me. "They knew what was coming. Once we realized how much of the major component they must have to react with all that stuff on
the trailer, we knew they were using the ship itself
as a tank. An external hull inspection wouldn't pick
that up."

"You lost me," I said.

"You know that most ships are double-hulled?
Well, the *Ras Ormara* is triple-hulled, thanks to a re-
build by the Pakistanis. The main component of the
ternary agent was brought in using the volume between the hulls as a huge cargo tank. I think Park
Soon must have found the transfer pipes, and they
couldn't take a chance on him."

"Three hulls," I muttered. "Talk about your basic
inside job. You think the entire crew knew?"

"Hard to say, but they wouldn't have to. It doesn't
take but a few crewman to pull away from the slip.
The North Koreans helped set the stage, but most
of them don't believe Allah is going to snatch them
up to the highest heaven," she said wryly.

"I don't get it. Which one of them did," I
prompted.

"The one who was an Indonesian Moslem," she
said. "He was on the truck crew with the perp who
passed himself off as Norman Goldman."

"Then he's a clinker over there." I nodded across
the boulevard toward the still smoking ruin. "Really
keen of you people, assuring me what a great guy

Norm Goldman was. Who did your background checks: Frank and Ernest?"

She didn't want to talk about that. Journalists had a field day later, second-guessing the Feds who failed to penetrate the "legends," the false bona fides, of men who had inserted themselves into mythical backgrounds twenty years before. And in twenty years a smart terrorist can make his legend damned near perfect.

Dana Martin preferred to concentrate on what I had done. I had already set her straight on the carnage at the chemical plant. She had it in her noggin that I had started the fire. The truth was, that's exactly what I would have done first thing off, if I'd had the chance. I didn't say that.

"I still don't see exactly how you detonated your bomb," she said. I responded, a bit tersely, by telling her I didn't have to detonate the damned thing. Acetylene doesn't like to be crowded in a dry tank, and when you try, a little bit of pressure makes it disassociate like TNT.

"I'm no chemist," she said, "but that sounds like you're, ah, prevaricating."

"Ask a welder, if the FBI has any. If he doesn't know, don't let him do any gas welding. End of discussion."

Her big beautiful eyes widened, not even remotely friendly. I knew she thought I'd been carrying some kind of incendiary device, which has been a sore point with Feds for many years, ever since the Waco screwup. She kept looking hard at me. Well, the hell with her—and that's what I said next.

"You're under contract to us," she reminded me.

"You offered to cut me loose early today," replied. "I accepted, whether you heard me or not. Keep your effing money if you don't believe me. Oh, don't worry about sweeping up," I said into her astonished frown. "I'll testify in all this; I've got nothing to hide."

And while she was still talking, I walked away from there with as much dignity as a man can muster when his clothes are in tatters and his only vehicle lies in smoking shreds.

Actually I did have something to hide: gratitude. I didn't want to try explaining to Dana Martin how I felt about the brilliant, savage, personable, murderous Daud. I wasn't sure I could if I tried.

There was only one reason why he would've made me promise to drive the miles to San Rafael for lunch: to make certain I wouldn't be a victim of that enormous, lethal cloud of nerve gas that would be boiling up from the *Ras Ormara*. And while he could have grabbed my ankles when he set himself alight, he didn't. He told me to run for it.

He would kill millions of people he had never seen, yet he felt something special for a guy who had befriended him for only a few hours. I didn't understand that kind of thinking then, and I still don't.

I do understand this: A man must never trust his buns to anyone, however intelligent and friendly, who believes there's a bright future in suicide. And as long as I live, I will be haunted by what Daud said, moments before he died. There are more of us, he said. Wait for us. We are coming.

Well, I believe they'll come, so I'm waiting. But I'm not waiting in a population center with folded hands. I'm recounting the last words of Daud al-Sadiq to everyone who'll listen. I'm also erecting a cyclone fence around my acreage, and I'm in the process of obtaining a captive breeding permit. That's the prerequisite for a guard animal no dog can ever match.

DEAN ING has been an interceptor crew chief, construction worker on high Sierra dams, solid-rocket designer, builder-driver of sports racers—his prototype Magnum was a *Road & Track* feature—and after a doctorate from the University of Oregon, a professor. For years, as one of the cadre of survival writers, he built and tested backpack hardware on Sierra solos. His technothriller, *The Ransom of Black Stealth One*, was a *New York Times* best-seller, and he has been finalist for both the Nebula and Hugo awards. His more humorous works have been characterized as "fast, furious, and funny." Slower and heavier now with two hip replacements and titanium abutments in his jaw, he pursues his hobbies, which include testing models of his fictional vehicles, fly fishing, ergonomic design, and container gardening. His daughters comprise a minister, a longhorn rancher, an Alaskan tour guide, and an architect. He and his wife, Gina, a fund-raiser for the Eugene Symphony, live in Oregon, where he is currently building a mountainside library/shop.

Harve Rackham and Dana Martin have appeared in two previous novellas, "Pulling Through" from the collection of the same name, and "Vital Signs" which appeared in the science fiction series *Destinies*.

SKYHAWKS
FOREVER

BY BARRETT TILLMAN

ACKNOWLEDGMENTS

Wynn Foster, Rick Morgan, George Olmsted, Larry and Janet Pearson, Robert Powell, Dwight Van Horn, Phil Wood, Jack Woodul, Lucy Young, the Skyhawk Association, and Training Squadron Seven.

One

The Boat

"Well, now I almost believe it," exclaimed Michael Ostrewski to his fellow flight instructor from Advanced Training Associates.

"Believe what?" Eric "Psycho" Thaler stood beside him on the flight deck of the former USS *Santa Cruz.*

Ostrewski pointed about him. "That we're really going to carqual on this boat. I mean, as long as she was mothballed in Bremerton, she was just an old Forrestal-class carrier. But now that she's an active ship, here in Long Beach, it looks like we're in business."

Thaler, who with "Ozzie" Ostrewski had gone to war aboard one of *Santa Cruz*'s sisters, envisioned this flight deck in its glory years: when aircraft carriers were named for battles or historic ships rather than mere politicians. He visualized thirty knots of wind over the deck, steam roiling from the catapults, and dozens of sailors milling in organized chaos as twenty-ton aircraft slammed onto the deck at 130 knots. He asked his colleague, "Did you talk to the navy yard guys yet? I mean, about the old girl's condition?"

Ostrewski nodded. "Yeah, just a little. One of the engineers was still aboard after the cruise from Bremerton. He says they worked up to twenty-four knots, but they expect to make thirty by the time we start trapping."

"What about the jobs that weren't finished there?"

"Well, they concentrated on what we'd need to operate six jets. Besides main plant and electrical, we have two good catapults, the arresting gear, and fuel systems. The condensers aren't up to speed, so there'll be limited water, and some of the radars aren't operational. But the mirror system checks out so the LSOs will be happy." He flashed two thumbs up.

Thaler looked around the 328-foot-wide deck where American and Chinese military personnel and civilians were busily engaged. "I guess the chinks will have a smaller crew and air wing, huh?"

Ostrewski nodded. "Smaller air wing fershure, dude. They plan on two Flanker squadrons plus a couple of helo outfits for starters. I don't know how many bodies that means, but a lot less than one of our wings. Probably about two thousand for ship's company, to start."

"Oz, I don't really understand something. This isn't a commissioned naval vessel yet, and far as I know the Chinese haven't paid for it in full. Who's actually responsible for this bird farm? I mean, do they have two captains or what?"

"Yeah, they do. Admiral Rhode at NavAir says the official skipper is Captain Albright, who's about to retire. He has a Chinese opposite number with an exec and department heads on down the line, and most of them have American supervisors. But a lot of the crew is civilian contract labor because there aren't enough white hats available after all that 'right sizing.' "

"They still going to send some talent out from Pensacola?"

Ostrewski nodded. "Yeah, I guess Rocky Rhode and others are nervous about of a bunch of civilians driving a carrier up and down the California coast, and retired guys like us landing on her. We're getting an instructor from the LSO school and a couple of TraCom instructors to monitor our procedures."

"Well, I'm glad to see the Chinese are running their part of it." Thaler waved a hand toward the carrier's island, where a gutted Flanker airframe was secured to the deck by tie-down chains. Even with its outer-wing panels folded, the sixty-eight-foot-long fighter, with its twin tails reaching eighteen feet high, took up a lot of space. The ATA instructors watched "Flight Deck 101" in progress as Chinese sailors rehearsed aircraft handling and servicing in the unaccustomed carrier environment.

"Think they'll get the hang of it?" Thaler asked.

"Yeah. This first class is a mix of navy and air force. The sailors handle the basic chores and the blue-suiters do the aircraft maintenance. They already knew the Flanker systems."

Psycho Thaler was skeptical. "Man, they're sure jumping in with both feet. I'd hate to have to learn everything they need to in a few weeks."

Ostrewski pointed to the sailor doing most of the talking. "See the petty officer who's lecturing? Mr. Wei, our Chinese liaison, told Terry Peters that this bunch started training ashore back in China. They knew all the moves before they got here: the yellow gear, the deck cycle, all that stuff. They even had full-size flight deck and hangar deck mock-ups to practice moving airplanes." He shook his head in appreciation. "Makes sense when you think about it."

Deep in thought, Ostrewski toed a tie-down on the nonskid deck surface. "What is it?" Thaler asked.

"Oh, I don't know." Ozzie looked up again at the bustle around him. "I can't quite get used to the idea of us selling the Commies an operational carrier, then teaching them how to use it." He grinned self-consciously. "Even if our company has the contract."

Thaler nudged his colleague. "Careful—if Terry Peters hears you, it's bad enough. If Jane hears you . . ." He allowed himself a grin. "Besides, like we always said in the navy—it's way above our pay grade. Congress and the administration signed off on it three years ago, so just be thankful that we got the job." Psycho grinned at his former *Langley* shipmate. "Besides, how'd you like to watch some other civilian contractor get a sweetheart deal like this?"

Thaler noticed a stocky Caucasian detach himself from the Chinese. "Hey, there's Igor Gnido. He's the lead pilot with the Sukhoi transition team."

The Russian waved at the Americans, and Thaler greeted him. "Hey, Igor." Ozzie was less effusive; he merely nodded. The Only Polish-American Tomcat Ace respected Gnido's reputation as an aviator but could not bring himself to like the former Soviet combat pilot.

"Good morning to you," Gnido ventured with a smile that Thaler took as genuine. The Flanker pilot waved a hand toward the Chinese sailors. "They getting good start on flight deck pro-cee-dures."

"We were just discussing that," Thaler replied. He watched as a group of "grapes"—sailors in purple jerseys—moved a fuel hose toward the Sukhoi's port wing. "Did the factory specially build this airplane to accept American hose fittings? I mean, like they built the nose gear to fit the catapult shuttle?"

Gnido leaned close, trying to ensure that he understood the question. Thaler made a circle with his left thumb and forefinger and a probe of his first two right fingers. The Russian nodded. "Ah, *da, da.*" He nodded decisively. "Nose gear yes. Fuel fittings, not exactly." He shook his head. "All Soviet aircraft were being designed to take your hoses, you know?" He hid any edginess in mentioning a NATO–Warsaw Pact conflict. "Plan was, take European airfields and use equipment already there, you know?"

Ostrewski, whose Polish roots ran deep, absorbed that knowledge and worked his professionalism around the ethical thorns. "Well, I guess that makes sense, if you're going to invade the next country."

Thaler felt moved to intervene. "Does that cause any problems with maintenance, Igor? I mean, having both English and metric systems in the same airplane."

Gnido shrugged eloquently. "Is not being much problem. Just way it is, you know? Like cockpit instruments. In air force Flankers, all is metric. In this airplane for navy, airspeed is knots, altitude meters. Besides, pretty soon America is being all metric, like rest of world. Best for everybody, yes?"

Thaler demurred. "Igor, you'll get an argument about that, I guarandamntee you."

Two

Scooter

Half a dozen staffers of Advanced Training Associates lazed away the shank of the afternoon, sipping slowly and speaking rapidly. The animated atmosphere in ATA's office spaces probably had not been seen since Williams Air Force Base became Williams Gateway Airport south of Mesa, Arizona.

Despite the beer-call military ambience, the atmosphere was post–Cold War business; a corporate foundation overlaid with a lather of friendly rivalry.

One of the partners, Zack Delight, had told an active-duty friend, "Here there be morale." A former Marine aviator, he had retired as a reserve lieutenant colonel, flew for Delta, and now was on his second or third career, depending on how they were reckoned. Pushing sixty, he was stocky, well built, and studiously irreverent. He sat on a barstool, scratching the Vandyke beard he had cultivated to cover a scar obtained in a motorcycle "incident." Now, with the unaccustomed beard, "Pure" Delight said he was still getting accustomed to "that mean-looking bastard glaring at me in the mirror every morning."

Next to Delight was Robert "Robo" Robbins, a retired navy commander and former landing signal officer. Slightly younger, he wore a perpetual smile as if savoring a private joke at the expense of the world around him. Aside from their previous part-time work for ATA, both staffers shared a passion for World War I aviation. They haunted The Aerodrome web site, exchanged arcane information and esoterica, and constantly critiqued each other's alternating chapters in an epic titled *Duel over Douai.*

Delight and Robbins were joined by Ozzie Ostrewski, just back from Long Beach. New to ATA, he was known as an exceptionally fine fighter pilot. Rumor and gossip swirled around Ozzie. Reportedly he had scored multiple kills as a USS *Langley* F-14 pilot during a classified dustup in the Indian Ocean a few years before. He steadfastly declined all efforts to elicit details, both overt and otherwise. Not even his shipmate Psycho Thaler would discuss it; he had been there as well.

"Hey, Oz," said Delight. "Lemme buy you a drink, god damn it." Pure and Robo traded sideways smiles. They knew Ostrewski as a nonimbiber, non-blasphemer, and devout Catholic—a rara avis in military aviation.

"And the horse you rode in on," Ostrewski replied evenly. He was getting good at bowdlerizing. He reached over the bar and pulled a root beer from the ice chest. "Any word yet?"

"Naw," said Robbins. He knew what Ostrewski meant. "The boss is still in the office with the new kid. But I think he's gonna hire her."

"Damn!" Ostrewski slammed his bottle down on

the bar harder than intended. It was the direst expletive the normally composed aviator allowed himself. "That's one reason I got out of the navy—the damn double standards and all that bu . . . siness." Delight suddenly realized how upset the instructor really was.

Robbins nudged him. "C'mon, Oz, how bad can it be?"

Ozzie inhaled, held his breath, and exhaled. "Look, it's the accumulation of all this stuff. I don't know about you guys, but I really don't like the idea of teaching Chinese Communists how to land on carriers, let alone go bombing and strafing with them. Add in the trouble we're bound to have with girl aviators, and what was a dream job is going to get screwed up."

"The world's changing, my boy," Robo said solicitously.

"Yeah, I know, I know . . . it's just not *my* world anymore. Not even my same country."

Michael Ostrewski wore his heart on his flight jacket. His friends knew he was intensely proud of his Polish heritage and its Old World values.

"Attention on deck!"

Delight, Robbins, and the others turned in their seats. Striding through the door was Terry "Hook" Peters, six-foot-three-inches of enthusiasm and what the navy called command presence. Peters saw his wife in the room and winked. Jane Peters, five-foot-five-inches of feistiness, blew a kiss at the once-gangly kid who earned an ironic call sign when he forgot to lower his tailhook for his first night carrier landing. A former Blue Angels commander, he and Jane had invested most of their savings in ATA, and now it had paid off with the Chinese training contract.

With him was a brown-eyed brunette, about five-foot-nine and 135 pounds. She glanced around, noticed Jane Peters, and gave her a shy smile. Jane had liked her immediately and told Terry Peters that Elizabeth Vespa got Jane's vote among the four applicants for the new slot. The fact that Liz and that nice Ozzie Ostrewski were single had not escaped her attention.

"Gang," Terry explained, "I'd like to introduce our new instructor—Liz Vespa, call sign Scooter."

Cheers, applause, and laughter greeted Elizabeth Vespa. A few ATA staffers chuckled at the nickname. Ostrewski muttered to Robbins, "Cute."

"Yeah, she is, kind of," Robbins replied.

"I meant the call sign," Ozzie said in a monotone.

Peters continued the introduction. "Liz comes to us from TraCom. She left active duty as a lieutenant commander, and the navy's loss is our gain. She was an A-4 CarQual instructor before going to T-45s, and that's part of the reason I selected her now that we're progressing with the Chinese students. She's more current on carrier qualifications than any of us, and now, having flown with her, I can say that she's a good stick." He turned to Vespa and grinned. "Liz, welcome aboard!"

Vespa blushed slightly at the attention. Standing with her hands behind her back, she said, "Thanks, Captain Peters." She scanned the room, taking in the faces. "There's no place else I'd rather be than here, flying with you guys." More applause and laughter skittered through the room—except from the crew cut, gray-eyed instructor at the bar who met her gaze without blinking. Even from that distance, Liz Vespa could read the flight jacket patch that said OZZIE.

Three

As Good As It Gets

Peters and Delight watched the two Skyhawks accelerate as Ostrewski led Vespa in a section takeoff. Zack turned toward his partner. "You sure this is a good idea, Terry?"

Peters's gaze never left the TA-4s. "It's Jane's idea. She said that when any of her third-graders didn't get along, she put 'em at the same desk." He shrugged. "Eventually they made up and became friends."

Delight shook his head. "Child psychology applied to fighter pilots." He unzipped a wry grin. "Works for me."

Three miles over Gila Bend, Ozzie keyed his mike. "Ah, Wizard Two, let's go in trail. Over."

Liz smiled in anticipation. That was the agreed-upon signal. "Let's go in trail" actually meant, "The

chase is on; see if you can stay with me, cowgirl."
But privately she rankled at Ozzie's self-confident
call sign: "The Wizard of Oz."

She double-clicked her mike button in acknowledgment.

Two seconds later Ozzie half snapped to inverted
and sucked the stick into his stomach. From sixteen
thousand feet, Wizard One responded in a mind-
numbing split-ess, the Gs building quickly to the
grayout stage. His vision grew fuzzy around the
edges, narrowing to a thirty-degree cone. In several
seconds he would regain full vision and swivel his
head to see if he had made any money on Scooter
Vespa.

Liz had expected an abrupt move, but the sud-
denness caught her off guard. She lost a hundred
fifty yards before she rolled over and followed Ozzie
downward. It was much as she expected: On the
ground, Michael Ostrewski was a complete gentleman. Up here, man to man, he was a mongoose. No
quarter asked or given.

And damn sure no preferential treatment for
girls.

Wizard One pulled through the bottom of the
split-ess, and as the nose reached the horizon Ozzie
rolled into a ninety-degree bank, still pulling hard.
He sensed the Skyhawk approaching the onset of
buffet, but a minute adjustment sustained his rate
of turn. He felt he was getting maximum performance out of the bird.

From experience and conditioning, Ostrewski was
comfortable at four Gs. He looked back over his
right shoulder, in the direction of his turn. Vespa's
Wizard Two had lost some of its original dead-six
aspect, but the contest was far from over.

Ostrewski's testosterone-rich brain was convinced
that no woman could stay with him in a sustained
high-G contest. He determined to make Sir Isaac

Newton his chief ally, wearing down Vespa by the unrelenting pressure of gravity. Besides, it was an accepted fact in squadron ready rooms: Girls can fly, but they can't hack the G.

With her throttle two-blocked, Liz focused her powerful concentration not only on Wizard One, but on its projected path. She knew that Ozzie was unlikely to telegraph his punches, and he could be trusted to do the unexpected, but the laws of physics permitted no amendments; they were enforced equally upon all contenders.

As both jets came around the circle, completing their first 360, Liz perceived that the relative separation had stabilized. Ozzie's initial move had netted him perhaps fifteen degrees. By common consent, the fight would end one of two ways: reaching the artificial "hard deck" of ten thousand feet, or when one of them could track the other in the gunsight for at least three seconds.

Passing through magnetic north, Ostrewski nudged bottom rudder, sliding the TA-4 downward to the right. Liz saw the motion and, momentarily perplexed, jockeyed stick and rudder to follow. She was suspicious; Delight had confided that Ozzie seldom made an error of technique.

As Liz slid down toward Ozzie's six o'clock, he abruptly half rolled to the left, pausing almost inverted. Liz could either try to match the move or risk closing to dangerous range. She followed, smoothly coordinating her controls. The G had abated a little, but the oppressive load still pressed on her body.

Ostrewski smiled to himself as he completed an elegant slow roll, stopped the motion, then stomped left rudder and continued around the circle, sliding outside Vespa's field of view in a lopsided barrel roll. When he rolled wings level he looked up to his left—about 9:30—and was gratified with a view of

Two's belly. He retarded the throttle and hit the button. His speed brakes extended into the slipstream, incurring welcome drag that slowed him further.

With airspeed and G relatively undiminished, Wizard Two edged ahead of One. Liz sensed more than knew what had happened—there was only one way to explain Ozzie's disappearance—and she knew it was seconds before his triumphant "Guns" call ruined her day.

Her mind raced. *He's behind my trailing edge, slowing and expecting me to overshoot. But I've got more energy.*

Liz began a hard left turn, realizing that Ozzie would be cleaning up his speed brakes and adding power before putting his gunsight pipper on her tailpipe. But instead of continuing the turn, she forced the Skyhawk three-quarters of the way around, completing 270 degrees of roll. She stopped the wings nearly vertical to the horizon, then pulled right. She surprised herself with her calmness. *Gosh, I hope we don't collide.*

Ostrewski gaped at the plain view of Wizard Two crossing his nose two hundred feet ahead. With Liz's superior momentum at that point, he realized she would continue the turn into his rear hemisphere before he could regain comparable energy. *Smooth move, Scooter!* He had no chance to make a "Guns" call.

"Hard deck. Knock it off!" Liz Vespa knew the contest was a draw, but her voice carried the ring of triumph.

Ninety minutes later, following the debrief, Ozzie Ostrewski and Scooter Vespa regarded one another across the bar in the Skyhawk Lounge. He clinked his root beer against her Coors Light. "Here's to good times." Clearly the frost had melted.

"Long may they wave." She clinked back.

Ozzie looked at her. "You seem pretty darn pleased with yourself, Miss Vespa."

Feeling flirtatious, she cocked her head. "Why not, Mr. O? I just outflew The Only Polish-American Tomcat Ace."

"Did not."

"Did too."

"Did not!"

"Did too!"

He grinned back at her. "Okay, you made a righteous move after I was kicking your butt. Where'd it come from?"

She set down her beer. "Well, because I made a human being of you, I'll tell you." She pretended to ignore his feigned indignation. "Daddy's best friend flew F-86s in Korea. When I got my wings, he told me about his fights in MiG Alley."

Ozzie nodded vacantly, staring at the mural above the bar. "You know, it's odd. I've seen that move before, too."

"Really? Where?"

His eyes returned to her face. He shrugged.

"Oh." She thought. *They still won't talk about the Langley cruise.*

"Well," he said, "it was a great hop, Scooter. You can be my wingman anytime—in Wizard Flight."

She giggled more than she intended. "And like Maverick said to Iceman: 'Bullshit. You can be *my* wingman—in Scooter Flight.'"

Ostrewski gave a noncommittal grunt as he finished his root beer. Two minutes passed before he worked up enough nerve to ask Liz to go dancing.

Four

Gonna Wash
That Man . . .

Orbiting at sixteen thousand feet, Liz Vespa relished being alone in a jet. Hawk Twelve was one of four A-4Fs owned or leased by ATA, and the powerful little single-seater was a joy to fly—as Zack said, "Pure delight." Lighter than the two-seat trainers with almost thirty percent more thrust, it was the sports car of Skyhawks.

Nearing the end of the two-week air-to-ground phase, the instructors anticipated live ordnance for qualification. Vespa smiled beneath her molded gray oxygen mask—the feds had gone spastic at the mere suggestion of five-hundred-pound bombs being loaded on civilian aircraft. But ATA's certification with State and DOD, plus some high-level arm twisting on behalf of the Chinese, had resulted in issuance of approval for "owning" and proper storage of destructive devices. Vespa marveled at Terry

Peters's patience with fearful, overbearing federal inspectors.

Vespa switched channels on her VHF radio and checked in with the Gila Bend controller. She was advised to watch for two F-16s outbound—Fighting Falcons of the Fifty-sixth Tactical Fighter Wing based at nearby Luke Air Force Base. Moments later she caught them, swift darts rocketing above her to the southwest. For a moment Liz envied the Falcon pilots their high-performance fighters, then mentally berated herself. *I've already got one of the best flying jobs on earth.* She keyed the mike. "Gila, this is Hawk Twelve. I see them. Are we clear?"

"Roger, Hawk. Your range time begins in three minutes."

She acknowledged and switched to ATA's common frequency. "Hawk Lead from Hawk Twelve. Zack, do you read?"

The carrier wave crackled in her earphones as Delight's New Mexico drawl came to her from twenty miles astern. "Twelve from Lead. I gotcha, Scooter. I'm inbound with four good birds. Will proceed as briefed. Out."

Vespa now knew that Pure Delight had launched with three other TA-4Js, all with four Mark 82s beneath the wings. Acting as range safety officer, she would clear the flight into the operating area and coordinate with the ground controller in keeping other aircraft away from the impact zone. She was authorized to cancel operations at any time with a knock-it-off call.

In her fifteen years in the navy, Liz Vespa had seldom seen live ordnance expended. Most of her flying had been in C-9 transports and TraCom T-34s or TA-4s. The closest she had got to tactical operations had been qualification as an A-4 adversary pilot, but even that coveted slot ended when all but two of the squadrons were disestablished.

Quitcherbitchin' she told herself. She leveled the Foxtrot, nosed down slightly, and executed a precise four-point roll. Then for no reason at all she wondered what it would be like to kiss Michael Ostrewski. *Do you, Scooter, take Ozzie . . .*

Liz made a clearing turn to port, expecting to see Hawk Flight inbound. She forced herself to focus on the job at hand, upset that she had allowed her mind to wander in the air. That had seldom happened. It was one of the factors that separated her from so many other aviators, male or female. Her flight evaluations had repeated entries: "excellent situational awareness, full concentration, highly professional." Now she found herself humming the refrain from *South Pacific,* her favorite musical. *Gonna wash that man right out of my hair, and send him on his way . . .*

She told herself she was not in love with Ozzie Ostrewski or anyone else, which was true. She knew that Ozzie had recently met "a nice Catholic girl" at a midnight Mass and presumably he was dating her. Once or twice Liz had thought of asking offhandedly, "Hey, Oz, how's your love life?" She had demurred because she knew that The Only Polish-American Tomcat Ace would certainly interpret it as jealousy. *Men are such swine. Well, at least some men. If only he weren't such a good dancer . . .*

"Hawk Twelve from Hawk Lead. I gotcha, Scooter. I'm about three miles back at your eight. Over."

Damn it! Liz, get your shit together. She was angry at being "caught" by Zack Delight, flying in the backseat of one of the trainers. Vespa felt she should have made the first tally-ho on a four-plane flight instead of being tagged as a single. She knew that, despite his red-meat exterior, Delight was too polite to mention it again, but she also knew she had just dropped a point in the unrelenting tacit competition among aviators.

"Lead from Twelve. Roger, Zack. I'm clearing you onto the range. Check in with Gila Control before your first run."

"Right-o, Scooter."

Resuming her orbit, Liz awaited Delight's initial bombing pass. Each Skyhawk would make four runs: one each from five thousand feet at sixty degrees; seven-thousand at thirty degrees; and two from the low-level pop-up pattern at forty-five degrees. She and Delight would mark the hits on their knee-boards for comparison with the data received from the range personnel before debrief.

Moments later Delight was on the air again. "Gila Control, this is Hawk Lead. Rolling in hot."

Glancing down, Liz saw the jet roll over and slant into its sixty-degree dive toward the northerly target, an ancient truck. She knew that Wang was flying, with Zack observing in the rear seat. The other three Chinese—Deng, Yao, and Hua—were solo.

The lead Skyhawk tracked straight down its cho-sen path. Liz judged it a decent run, maybe a bit shallow, but the little delta-winged jet smoothly pulled up after making its drop. Wang's lilting ac-cent came to her ears, "Lead is pulling off." Below and behind the TA-4 an orange-white light erupted near the truck, spewing smoke and dust into the air.

Deng was next down the chute with a "Two is in" call. Liz watched with pride as her pupil put his first bomb near the target at five o'clock. If anything, he had released a little high. She imagined him flip-ping the master arm switch to safe as he recovered and called, "Two off."

"Three going in," came from Yao. Liz rolled port wing low to follow his run. She knew that Ozzie had literally taken the taciturn Chinese under his wing, and evidently the instructor's extra attention had borne fruit. Mr. Yao would never be the best bomber in the class, but he showed steady improvement. For a moment Liz wondered if Ostrewski had invested the effort for Yao, or for himself. She literally shook the thought from her mind, snapping her head left and right. *I've got to get him out of my mind for a while.*

Yao was pressing, no doubt about it. Delight had just called "Three, you're . . ." when Yao dropped. The hit was about thirty feet out at one o'clock. Zack came back on the air. "Too low, Yao. You were probably below twenty-five hundred." There was no reply, so Delight added, "Acknowledge." The hick on the turnip truck was gone from his voice, replaced by the Leader of Men.

"Acknowledge." Liz could tell that Yao resented the rebuke.

As Four rolled in, Delight was climbing back to the perch, leading an aerial daisy chain of pirouetting Skyhawks. Vespa tracked each through the seven-thousand-foot pattern and the first pop-up, observing one hit for each pilot. On his fourth run, however, Hawk Lead pulled out without releasing; Delight had a hung bomb. Clearing the immediate area, he called Vespa. "Liz, I can't get shed of this thing. We're gonna have to divert to Luke. Over."

Vespa realized that Zack Delight had no choice. The FAA had balked at permitting ATA jets to take off with live ordnance; there was no question of allowing anyone to return to a civilian field with a potentially armed bomb aboard, whatever the master switch position. "Roger, Zack. I'll finish the cycle here."

Deng's fourth bomb was the best yet—it obscured the deformed old vehicle. As he called off and clear, Liz directed him to dog in the holding pattern until the others were finished. She wanted to lead a four-ship flight back into the break, "lookin' good for the troops."

Yao called "Three in" and made an aggressive

move in his second pop-up. It was immediately apparent at the apex that he was too steep. Liz realized that Mr. Yao was determined to get a center hit, and the onerous Mr. Delight's departure only encouraged the student. She thumbed the mike button. "Three, you're too steep! Pull out!"

The TA-4J continued its plunge toward the chalky circle on the desert floor. Liz felt her cheeks flush. "Hawk Three, this is Hawk Lead. You are ordered to pull out. Now, mister!"

Yao's Skyhawk never wavered in its dive. With her thumb still on the transmit button, Liz watched aghast. *My god, he's going right in . . .*

She was already forming the thought "target fixation" for the postmortem when Yao released. Liz estimated he dropped at less than two thousand feet above the ground, and the lethal blast pattern extended to twenty-two hundred. His nose had barely come level when the Mark 82 detonated.

Five

Thumbs-Down

Hawk Three was obscured in the mushrooming smoke and dust of the explosion. Vespa gave a sigh of relief, surprised to see the Skyhawk recover. She realized he had been caught in the frag pattern. *He must have damage.* She ordered priorities in her mind.

"Knock it off, knock it off. This is Hawk Twelve to all Hawks. Safe all your master arm switches. Acknowledge."

Wang in Hawk Four, the only one still with ordnance, chirped a response at least two octaves high. Liz had Yao's jet padlocked in her vision as she pushed over to join him. Briefly she switched frequencies. "Gila Control from Hawk Twelve. We may have a damaged aircraft. I'm stopping operations."

"Ah, roger, Hawk. We read you. Standing by."

She was back to the common freq. "Hawk Three from Twelve. Yao, do you read me?"

Something rapid and garbled came from the two-seater now less than two thousand yards ahead of Twelve. Liz waited clarification, got none, and called again. "Yao, this is Vespa. I am a mile in trail, overtaking you to port." She could see the stricken jet was streaming something, fuel or hydraulic fluid. Or both. The plane was in level flight, slowly turning northerly, toward Williams.

Yao's gentle turn allowed Vespa to close more easily. She slid up on his left wing and surveyed the damage. Small holes were hemorrhaging vital fluids from the wings and empennage. The Skyhawk's "wet wing" held three thousand pounds of fuel, and most of it was venting through holes in the bottom. It occurred to Liz that this sight had been familiar to aviators of Hook Peters's generation: a battle-damaged A-4 trying to reach home before it bled to death.

She remembered to speak slowly, modulating her voice. "Yao, this is Vespa. Can you transmit? Over."

She saw the student's head turn toward her briefly, a faceless entity beneath the oxygen mask and sun visor. He tapped the side of his helmet, then he nodded vigorously. Placing his left hand on his mask, he shook his head left and right. *He can receive but not transmit.* She rocked her wings. "All right, Yao. Keep this heading." She paused. "Break-break. Four, do you copy?"

"Yes, Miss Vespa. Copy."

"Wang, I want you to safe your bomb and drop it on the nearest bull's-eye. Then join Deng and return to base. Clear each other for hung ordnance before landing. Acknowledge."

Wang replied, then Liz was back to Yao. "Three, this is Vespa again. Let's do a systems check. Show me a thumb's-up, thumb's-down, or thumb's-level for a declining state." She allowed him to absorb the procedure, then began.

"Hydraulics." Thumb down.

"Utility." Thumb level. *Damn, he's losing his controls.*

"Fuel." Thumb level. *He's bleeding fuel and hydraulics.* Vespa was frustrated, uncertain how long Yao could stay in the air.

"Electric." Thumb up.

"Yao, I can clear you for a straight-in approach or you can eject in a safe area." Yao motioned toward the north, nodding for emphasis. "You can maintain control long enough for a landing?"

Yao nodded again, less vigorously.

"All right. I'm calling the tower to declare an emergency."

Assured that the fire trucks were rolling, Liz took stock. Fifteen miles out, it was still possible for Yao to eject into the row crops south of Williams, or she could talk him down.

The steps came to her like multiplication tables. "Yao, get ready. To compensate for hydraulic loss, you'll have to pull the T-handle. First, be sure you're below two hundred knots." Liz glanced at her own airspeed indicator: 210.

She saw him lean down in the cockpit, then straighten. He nodded. "All right, Yao. You're flying by cable now. The stick forces will be very high—especially the ailerons—but you can compensate somewhat with electric trim."

The abused J52 began spitting intermittent smoke. Liz noted that the white mist in the slipstream was nearly gone. *He's about to run out of fuel.* "Yao, listen. You need to switch to the fuselage fuel tank. Do it now."

Yao nodded, then flashed a thumbs-up. Vespa asked, "Fuel flow steady?" Another nod, followed by a thumb level. Liz assumed problems with the fuel pump, but at fifty pounds per minute the fifteen hundred pounds in the fuselage tank would get the wounded Skyhawk home.

Vespa's mind raced, trying to stay ahead of the airborne crisis proceeding at three and a half miles per minute.

He's getting pretty low; he's going to drag it in. "Yao, you're losing altitude. Can you add power and hold what you got?"

Hawk Three seemed to respond, then visibly decelerated. Liz glanced at her altimeter: barely two thousand feet above the ground. *It's gonna be awful close.*

"Yao, listen. I think you're having fuel feed problems. Switch to manual fuel control." A brisk nod acknowledged the order. "Okay, good. Now slowly advance your throttle to eighty-eight percent. Let me know how that works."

Long moments dragged by before Yao gave a thumb's-up.

"All right, Mr. Yao. You're doing fine. Listen, we're going to make a low cautionary approach. I want you to maintain 160 knots indicated, okay?" The two jets jockeyed in relation to one another, speed stabilizing at 165 by Vespa's airspeed indicator.

"Now, one more thing, Yao. I need you to put 110 mils on your gunsight. Understand? At the end of the runway, you will aim for the thousand-foot marker and fly onto the runway. Okay?"

Yao reached up and put the setting on his sight. He looked at Vespa and displayed his left thumb again.

Liz waited a few more moments, trying to gauge Yao's rate of descent against the remaining distance. *Damn it! I need to talk to him.* She waited several seconds more, then regretted the time she spent pondering. "Yao, this is Hawk Lead." She sought to reassert her authority. "You need to decide right away if you can land or if you should eject." She emphasized each syllable for clarity. Yao squirmed on his seat as if trying to make a decision. Following several rapid pulses, he pointed straight ahead.

There's the runway! Vespa could see the perimeter fence and the two-mile-long concrete strip running into the midday mirage. She knew that Yao could stand some good news. "Three, this is Vespa. I have the runway in sight. Come left about fifteen degrees." Slowly, the TA-4 complied, steadying up on the runway heading. Barely two miles now.

Then Yao depressed the landing-gear knob and pulled the emergency gear extension handle. The nosewheel and both mains fell forward, locking under their own weight, incurring horrible drag. Liz Vespa's heart sank. There was no retracting them. "Yao! You're settling too fast! Power, power, power!"

The abused J52-P8 had no more power to give. As the last of the engine oil siphoned overboard, bearings and blades exceeded design limits and the jet began shaking itself apart in its mounts. At best, Liz saw that Hawk Three would impact between the fence and the gravel overrun at the threshold. The extra drag coupled with the straining engine and ponderous controls conspired with gravity to defeat lift. The "zero-zero" specifications of the IG-3 ejection seat flashed on her mental screen: wings level with no rate of descent. *But there's no time!* "Yao, eject, eject, eject!"

The TA-4 shuddered, wavered for a long ephemeral moment, and the airspeed dropped through 110 knots. The canopy shot upward and away from the airframe as Yao began the ejection sequence—two seconds too late. Hawk Three fell to earth and exploded with a low, rolling *carrumph.*

Scooter Vespa landed through the smoke of Yao's pyre.

Six

Post Mortem

Terry Peters was first up the boarding ladder of Hawk Twelve. He ensured the seat was safe, then waved the line crew away.

Liz pulled off her helmet and fumbled for the bag. Peters took the blue-and-white hardhat with the ATA logo and *Scooter* in gold script across the back. "Oh, Terry," she croaked. "It was awful . . ." She choked down a sob and rubbed her watery eyes with a gloved hand. He stretched his right arm between her neck and the headrest and awkwardly hugged her, allowing his forehead to touch hers. "I know, babe. I know."

Slowly she unstrapped and followed him down the yellow ladder. They stood by the nose gear, smelling the smoke and hearing the mindless wailing of the sirens. Peters decided against any preliminary questions. There would be plenty of those, but he felt that Mr. Wei, the program manager, undoubtedly would declare a regrettable loss wholly to pilot error. In this case, the PRC officer would be right.

Liz ran a hand through her raven hair. In that motion she seemed transformed from a shaken young woman into a professional aviator who had just sustained a loss. She looked at her employer with eyes still misted but calm. "We didn't have full comm," she said in an even voice. "He could receive but not transmit, so I gave him the lead. He signaled that he was losing utility and fuel, but he still thought he could make the field. About two miles out I saw he might not make it and I asked if he . . ." She ran out of breath. Inhaling, she continued. "I asked if he didn't want to eject while he had time. But he continued the approach, and . . ." She cleared her throat. ". . . and he dropped the gear too soon. He started a high sink rate, and then he lost power and the bird went in." She dropped her right hand, palm down. "Just like that. He pulled the handle just as he hit."

Peters nodded. "I know, Liz. We heard most of it on squadron common. I don't know what else you could have done . . ." His voice trailed off.

He won't say that I should have ordered Yao to eject sooner. She realized that eventually some of the others might be less reluctant to voice that opinion. With a start, she thought of Delight and Wang, who probably now were landing at Luke. "Does Zack know?"

Peters shook his head. "Negats, unless he monitored our freq, which I doubt. Anyway, I don't want to distract him when he has to land with hung ordnance."

Liz realized that ATA still had a lesser emergency

to sweat out before the day could be put behind them. She looked at Peters again. "Ozzie?"

Peters's blue eyes went to the pavement before meeting hers again. "He knows."

Seven

Slaying Dragons

"Ozzie?"

"Yes."

"This is Liz."

Ostrewski's pulse briefly spiked, then returned to his normal fifty-five. But his grip tightened on the phone while he thought of something to say.

"Hi, Liz." He never asked "How are you?" unless he meant it. Whatever his faults, insincerity was not among them.

Her breath was measured, controlled. "Listen, Michael. I really think we should talk. Could I come over?"

"Well, yeah. I mean . . . tonight?"

"Yes, if that's all right."

No point putting it off. "Okay. Ah, sure." He paused, collecting his thoughts. "You're still shook about Yao?"

"He's dead, Ozzie. But you and I haven't said ten words since yesterday morning. The investigation and everything . . ." She swallowed. "I just felt you didn't want to talk to me, you know."

He swallowed hard. "Why, of course I'll talk to you."

"Thanks. I'll be there in twenty minutes."

" 'Bye, Scooter." He hung up. "Damn!"

Fourteen minutes later the doorbell rang at Ostrewski's condo. Before he opened the door, he inhaled, closed his eyes, and did a five count. He did not want to do this—he would rather tangle with two of Colonel Li's MiG-29s again—but he recognized the only way out was straight ahead.

"Hi, Liz. C'mon in." He managed a smile.

"Thanks." She stepped inside and looked around. "Gosh, this is nice. I've never been here before." *Oh, that's original, Liz. Talk about stating the obvious!*

Ozzie showed her to the living room, where he had some ice and soft drinks. "Well, I haven't done much entertaining, you know. At least not before I met Maria."

Liz sat on the sofa, trying to appear nonchalant. "Oh, when do we get to meet her?"

Ostrewski sat in the chair at right angles to the sofa. He poured a Coke for himself and a Tab for Liz. "Oh, I'll prob'ly bring her around one day. We're just now going steady." *Got that out of the way.*

She sipped her drink, trying to decide how she felt about that information. "Mmmm . . . what's she do?"

"She's an MBA; manages the family business—construction. It's a large family, sort of like mine." He waved to a series of color photos on the wall behind the sofa.

Liz turned to study the Ostrewski family portraits surrounding a simple crucifix. A big, happy Polish clan with lots of aunts, uncles, and cousins. The only other photo was a large framed shot of an F-14 squadron. It was labeled "VF-181 Fightin' Felines, USS *Langley*," and the date. Suddenly Liz felt on safer ground. "Was that your combat cruise?"

"Yeah. The CO was Buzzard McBride. That's me and Fido Colley behind the skipper."

She leaned forward, hands in her lap. "I'd really like to hear about it sometime, Ozzie. As much as you can tell."

He leaned back, a defensive gesture. "I can't say much, Liz. There's a twelve-year hold. I don't even know why. Something to do with intel sources and diplomacy."

"But that's crazy. A lot of people know what happened."

He smiled. "Like the GS-20 said, 'There's no reason for it—it's just our policy.' "

Vespa recognized a no-win setup and changed the subject. She looked him full in the face. "I need to know what you think about Yao."

Well, there it is. "Liz, I think he screwed up—twice. He pressed too low and he stayed with a dying jet too long."

"Some of the Chinese think I'm partly to blame. Damn it, Ozzie, I have to know what *you* think. What you *really* think. He was your student and I lost him . . ." She had sworn she would not cry; she held back the tears. For ten seconds. Then the dam broke.

Michael Ostrewski, who had dueled with the Tiger of the North, shot eight Front-Line aircraft out of the sky, and held the Navy Cross, felt helpless with a weeping female. It was one more Guy Thing.

"Ah, Liz . . ." He moved beside her on the sofa, awkwardly patted her shoulder, then wrapped both arms around her. She leaned into him and let the sobs out.

Nearly three and a half minutes trickled by, two

hundred seconds, each with a beginning, middle, and an end. Abruptly she sat up, wiped her eyes with the back of one hand and sniffed a few times. He handed her a Kleenex.

"Thank you. I'm all right now." She blew her nose and Ostrewski had no idea what to say. Instead, he picked up her glass and passed it to her.

She drained the soda, set it down, and looked at him through misted eyes. "I really do need to know, Ozzie. Do you think I could have saved Yao?"

He took her hand. He realized that she needed to know another professional's opinion of her judgment. "Liz, I think if I'd been there I'd probably have told him to pull the handle. But I wasn't there. I didn't know what you knew, and you didn't know what I knew about him."

"What do you mean?"

"Well, I brought him along, that's all. I think I got inside his head. He was insecure about his bombing, and my guess is that he thought by saving the jet he could sort of make up for, you know, screwing up."

Liz dabbed at one eye with the hankie. "Did you like him?"

"What?"

"I mean it. Did you like Yao as a person?"

"Well . . . gee, I don't know. I didn't think of him as an individual human with friends and maybe a family. He was a student who was my responsibility." He shrugged. "It was a professional relationship, that's all." Ozzie looked at her again. "Do you like Deng?"

She smiled. "Yeah, I do. The way he wears his Stetson everywhere. And he has that shy quality about him, you know?" Ozzie nodded. He didn't know.

"But he's a good student, Liz. He follows orders."

"You know they were friends? They'd been squadronmates for about four years."

"He seems to be taking it okay."

She gulped an ice cube. "Better than me, evidently."

"Liz, didn't you ever lose anybody in TraCom?"

"No, not like this. A classmate of mine was killed instructing in T-34s at Whiting, but this was different." Ostrewski shrugged again. "Ozzie, why didn't you talk to me when Yao was killed?"

He exhaled, slowly letting the air out of his lungs. "I didn't know what I felt, Liz. I guess . . . I guess I didn't trust myself to say anything to you before I learned the details because I wondered if you *had* screwed up, and I was even more afraid that *I* had screwed up. Maybe I missed something with Yao. I just don't know." He rubbed her arm. "I'm sorry that I caused you any extra pain. I should have been thinking beyond myself."

"You had your own dragons to slay."

"How's that?"

She smiled. "It's a Chinese saying or something. We all have our emotional dragons to slay." She laughed. "You were one of mine."

Ozzie's eyes widened in apprehension at the implication. *High buffet, airspeed bleeding off. Unload, bury the nose and go to zone five 'burner.* He recovered nicely. "Consider that dragon slain, Scooter."

Ozzie walked Liz to her car and made a point of hugging her again. They kissed good night the way friends do.

Eight

Dead Eyes

There was a little delay in the pace of training after Yao's death. As Peters predicted, Mr. Wei had declared the incident closed long before the FAA, the Air Force, or anyone else had reached the obvious conclusions: Mr. Yao had ignored the minimum recoverable altitude when using live ordnance and had tried to land the aircraft instead of ejecting while he still had control. "Consider it another lesson learned," Wei had said. His next words bespoke his mission-oriented mind-set: "I expect you will proceed with strafing next week."

Sitting with the other IPs in the Skyhawk Room, Robo Robbins absorbed the implication. "Did you ever notice Wei's eyes?" he asked. "He's got dead eyes, like a shark."

"Be that as it may," Peters said, "we're now going to be dead eyes with our guns." There were exaggerated groans at the pun. "To tell you the truth," Peters added, "I'd just as soon wrap up the air-to-ground phase and get on to the tactics syllabus."

Delight rubbed his beard, and asked, "Terry, are we condensing the gunnery syllabus to make up time?"

"Affirm. I talked to Rocky Rhode and held his hand long-distance. He's concerned that the loss would delay carquals and upset Lieu and some others back in D.C. so we're throwing in an extra simulator session with two live-fire hops instead of three."

Peters searched the audience. "Gunner, where are you?"

Warrant Officer Jim Keizer raised a laconic hand at the back of the room. He was a tall, well-built career sailor in his late thirties. Peters continued, "Now that we're done with bombing, your ordies can concentrate on the twenty millimeters. Then you can all go back to Kingsville and rejoin the Navy."

"What? And lose all this per diem? Not likely, sir!" Keizer's retort drew appreciative laughter. Ordnancemen qualified to arm and load bombs and maintain the A-4s' cannon were a premium commodity. Like all seadogs, they knew how to turn their per diem expenses into a profit by careful shopping and gratuitous mooching.

"All right," Peters continued. "We have three days before the first gunnery flights. Jim's crew has done the boresighting, but we need to test the guns on the jets we'll be using in this phase. That's eight launches a day. We have range time tomorrow and the next day to confirm that both guns work in each bird. Everybody gets one hop to fire fifty rounds per gun. Any malfunctions, and I may exert my authority and take the extra flights myself."

Catcalls and two paper cups pelted Hook Peters. Fending off the assault with crossed arms, he intoned, "Hey, it's not my fault. Jane said either she gets a gunnery hop or I sleep on the couch."

Nine

Manly Man Night

"*El Cid*," began Delight, standing at the Skyhawk Bar. "Greatest six-minute sword fight ever filmed—duel to the death for possession of the whole danged city of Calajora. Single-combat warriors like Tom Wolfe wrote about in *The Right Stuff*." He wiggled his eyebrows suggestively. "And Sophia Loren . . ."

"*Fighting Seabees*," countered Robbins. "Burly construction guys who drive bulldozers and earthmovers. They level mountains for airfields while killing Japs and hardly break a sweat."

"Okay, *The Vikings*. You can't get no more manly than they were. Sail the Atlantic in an open longship, then go raping and pillaging—real Manly Man stuff. And remember Ernest Borgnine? Ragnar's feasting hall where they swill mead from horns and throw battle-axes at each other and ravish the serving wenches . . ." Delight grinned hugely. "Come to think of it, kinda reminds me of Animal Night at Miramar . . ."

Robbins nearly choked on his drink, rerunning the long-gone Friday frivolity at Fighter Town USA. He thought fast. "*Taras Bulba*. Those cossacks were really Manly Men—jumped their horses over a huge ravine to prove who was right or wrong." He struck an heroic pose and emulated Yul Brynner. " 'I am Taras Bulba, colonel of the Don Cossacks. Put your faith in your sword, and your sword in the Pole!' " He glanced across the room at Ostrewski. "Oops, sorry, Oz. No offense."

Ozzie, conversing with Vespa and Thaler, flipped him off without looking back.

"*Conan the Barbarian*." Delight flashed a gotcha smile, confident he could not be topped.

"Beeeeep," went Robbins. "You lose. Conan doesn't count 'cause he isn't real."

Terry Peters entered the lounge with Jane on his arm. He turned to his wife. "Oh, no," he groaned. "They're at it again."

She looked around. "At what again?"

"Richthofen and Brown over there. They play a game called Manly Man Night. One starts by naming a movie and the other has to respond with an equally macho flick until one of them runs out of titles. I think Zack just lost."

Delight saw the Peterses enter the lounge and joined them at a table. "Hi, guys. You're just in time—the party's rolling."

Jane regarded the former Marine, a suspicious pout on her face. "Things never change around here. The monthly Friday night gathering and poor Carol's over there with the rest of the aviation widows." She glanced at the far corner where Carol Delight sat in animated conversation with Kiersten Thaler, Marie Robbins, and some other ATA wives.

Delight waved a placating hand. "Hey, it's an old-married-person trick. You spend the whole evening talking to everybody else so you have something to say to your spouse during the drive home." He looked back and forth between Terry and Jane Peters. Keeping a straight face, he added, "Didn't you know that?"

Jane patted his cheek. "That's all right, dear. I'm sure you have a comfortable couch somewhere." She joined the other ladies, knowing that her husband wanted to speak to their partner.

Peters motioned Delight into a corner. "Zack, I got a call from Congressman Ottmann this afternoon. He wants to meet me for a face-to-face with one of his people day after tomorrow. I should be back Monday night."

Delight nodded. "Sure. You taking the red-eye to Dulles?"

"No, I'm hopping Southwest to Wichita." He looked around to ensure no one overheard. "Look, if anybody asks—and don't volunteer it—I'm looking at a twin Cessna at the factory. Ottmann stressed that we keep this as low-key as possible. I don't know exactly why, but that's how he wants it."

"Okay." Delight thought for a moment. "You figure it has something to do with the Chinese?"

"I don't know what else. Anyway, I'll get back ASAP."

Delight punched Peters's arm. "Okay, pard. You got it." He returned to the bar, where Robbins was still holding forth.

Liz Vespa, intrigued by the arcane male ritual under way, edged closer to Delight and Robbins. Zack offered her the ice bucket. "Hey, Scooter. You need a refill?"

"No, I just wonder how you tell which movie is most manly."

Delight's warning receiver began twitching. He

knew that Liz Vespa could kid a kidder. "Well . . . it's, like, a Guy Thing."

"Sort of common consent," added Robbins. His perennial grin seemed to indicate that girls would not understand.

"You want to know what Manly is?" Vespa did not await an answer. "I'll give you Manly. It's PMS . . . actually, it's *flying* with PMS."

Robbins braced himself. *Here it comes. The Girl Speech.*

"Imagine feeling bloated from all the water you're retaining. Then add a migraine headache, plus nausea. Then throw in stomach cramps—the kind that make you just want to curl up and go to sleep." She leveled her gaze at both men. "Now, with all that, imagine making an instrument approach in rough air, at night." Privately, Delight recalled when he *had* felt that way.

Vespa was warming up. "Now, after you've fought off vertigo in an instrument descent, aggravated by your headache and nausea, consider this. You feel that same way during an air-combat hop, pulling four or five Gs and doing that twice a day for a week."

Liz drained the last of her vodka tonic and set the glass on the bar with a decisive clunk. "Gentlemen, I'm here to tell you: only Manly Men can fly with PMS."

The men watched her walk away, too astonished for a reply.

Robbins found his voice first. "Wow! What got into her?"

Delight turned to Thaler, who joined his friends at the bar. "Hey, Psycho. What were you guys talking about with Liz?"

"Well, Ozzie said that he and Maria are getting engaged." Thaler cocked his head in curiosity. "Why do you ask?"

Ten

Almost Human

Mr. Wei Chinglao sat across the desk from Terry Peters and played the game. Producing a pack of cigarettes, he politely asked, "Do you mind if I smoke?" In the months he had been working with ATA, he hardly could have missed the "No smoking" signs, let alone Robbins's hand-lettered "Oxygen in use" beside the WW II LSO paddles on his wall.

Hook Peters had quit smoking three decades before, between Vietnam deployments. He had told his wingman, "If I'm ever about to get captured, you'll have to shoot me. I'd tell the gooks *anything* after two days without a smoke."

Now, Peters regarded Wei's request. *He knows I don't smoke; he knows there's no smoking in the building. If I turn him down, he probably thinks I'll feel I owe him something.* "If you don't mind, Mr. Wei, I'm allergic to tobacco smoke. That's one of the reasons we post the signs in our spaces here."

Wei nodded. "Ah, yes. Please excuse me." He put the Camels back in his shirt pocket. Americans: such a peculiar race. Well, not even a race, he told himself, as mongrelized as they had become. Asia's homogeneous populations had blessedly escaped most of those problems. And such concerns over trivia! The cartoon animal used to advertise Wei's favorite cigarettes had been virtually banned by the U.S. government. All things considered, America was a mishmash of contradictions: constant meddling in the affairs of other nations but unwilling to control its own borders; puritan ethics constantly exposed to public hypocrisy; a vicious civil war fought to free the slaves, the descendants of whom still suffer in economic servitude; a constitution proclaiming supremacy of the individual but steadily eroded by the power of the state. If not for its technological genius, Wei was convinced that America never could have come to world prominence.

"I am preparing a report for Mr. Lieu at the embassy," the program manager explained. "Now that our pilots are nearing the end of their carrier-landing training, I am required to provide a preliminary assessment of their progress."

Peters turned in his chair toward the "howgozit" chart on the wall. Each PRC flier's name and grades were neatly inked in for each phase of the program. Where a pilot had failed the course was an abrupt, final red X indicating that he had departed. Two, Peters thought ruefully, had departed this life.

"Well, sir, the figures are right there for you. Overall, I think your pilots have done pretty well." He turned back to Wei. "Actually, I was surprised that we didn't lose more pilots or planes before now. The weapons and especially the aerial-tactics refresher programs had the greatest potential for losses, but Yao's incident was the only one directly involved in our training program." He did not need to add that the first loss had involved wake turbulence from a Boeing 757 landing at Williams.

Wei's dark eyes scanned the chart, evidently reading the small, neat letters from fifteen feet. "Mr. Yao brought disaster upon himself, Mr. Peters. My report made that clear." The normal brisk tone of his voice softened perceptibly. "I trust that you know we hold your firm completely innocent in that event."

"Thank you."

"Now, I have been following the field-landing practice as much as possible, and I believe most of our pilots are doing reasonably well. But how many might not achieve your own standards before going to the ship?"

"I was discussing that with Mr. Robbins. We noted four pilots who were inconsistent in the simulated carrier-landing pattern. Two of them have improved this week; the others remain erratic."

"And they are?"

"Mr. Zhang and Mr. Hu."

"I mean, Mr. Peters, who are the four?"

"Oh." Peters was taken aback; he knew that Robbins was inclined to give the first pair "a look at the boat." He referred back to the list. "Mr. Chao and Mr. Wong. But I should note that Mr. Robbins believes they are making satisfactory progress."

Wei scribbled a note, then looked up. "Even if Chao and Wong do not complete the course, we regard this as an acceptable completion rate." He almost smiled. "You have done well."

Peters was surprised; outright praise from Wei Chinglao was unprecedented. "Well, thank you, sir. Of course, we won't know the actual results until after the qualification period aboard the *Santa Cruz*." He opened his mouth, then thought better of it.

"Yes?" Wei prompted.

No point kidding this guy. "To tell you the truth, sir, I'm surprised and impressed with how well your group has done here. They've done quite a lot better than most of us expected."

Wei leaned back—an unaccustomed, almost relaxed, posture. "Mr. Peters, now I will tell you the absolute truth. These pilots are the product of a screening process completely unprecedented in our military history. Not only did we require exceptional pilots by our standards, but exceptional individuals. The language study alone eliminated several of our most experienced aviators."

"Well, yes, sir. We knew that this group . . ."

"Excuse me, Mr. Peters. In all candor, your Navy was told as little as possible about these men. It was considered necessary as a security measure at the time." He looked down, as if composing his thoughts. "When my government accepted your government's ah, *suggestions* as to our internal affairs, there was much resentment. But it was judged worthwhile because of the greater access to American trade and programs such as this."

Peters sat silently, astonished at Wei's candor.

"Now, there is a reason for our pilots' success here," Wei continued. "You know that most of our aviators only fly about one hundred hours a year—roughly half of what most Americans do. But once we selected our people for this program, they were given that extra hundred hours, much of it under Russian instruction. Therefore, some of our people flew far less than one hundred hours. Additionally, the prospective carrier fliers were exempted from most political requirements. Each year the army is mobilized to help bring in the crops when necessary, but none of these men did so." He paused, looking directly into Peters's eyes. "You realize what that meant?"

Peters waved a hand. "Certainly, sir. It meant they were expected to succeed here."

"Precisely. And thanks to your staff, the large majority have done so." Wei stood up, preparing to leave. Peters leapt to his feet as well, ruefully thinking that he had mistaken the man's intentions with the cigarette gambit.

"One final thing, Mr. Peters. You must suspect that I have some aviation background. Therefore, I wish to ask one thing."

"Yes, sir?"

"At a convenient time, may I ask the favor of making a carrier landing in the backseat of your Skyhawk?"

Peters did not even try to conceal his pleasure. He extended a hand, which Wei solemnly grasped. "It's a deal, sir."

Wei bowed slightly and walked out the door as Delight looked in. "Any problems, Hook?"

Peters shook his head. "Just that I'm afraid Wei is starting to act human." He looked at his friend. "And that scares me."

Eleven

Things Unsaid

From seven thousand five hundred feet on a crystalline night, the Phoenix Valley was a splash of multihued color from millions of lights strewn across the black carpet of the Sonoran Desert.

Returning to Williams Gateway after a series of instrument approaches to Sky Harbor, Hawk Six descended through the night sky, running lights strobing from wingtips and fuselage. In the front seat, Liz Vespa concentrated on her approach plate. She knew that she had done well on the instrument-check ride, though not quite as well as she would have liked for this particular check airman. Ozzie Ostrewski rode in the back, keeping notes for the debriefing.

Northwest of the field, Ozzie unexpectedly waggled the stick. "I got it, Liz."

Vespa raised her hands, speaking into the hot

mike. "You have it." She wondered if she had missed something, committed a mental error.

"Let's take a look out desert way," Ozzie offered. "I always like to see the desert at night, away from the lights."

"Okay," she replied. *Something's on his mind,* she told herself as the TA-4J banked more to the east. *Ozzie's usually all business once he's strapped into the jet.*

The Skyhawk settled on course 090, south of the Superstition Freeway. Apache Junction and then Gold Canyon slid past the port wingtip before her scan returned to the cockpit, where her practiced gaze registered normal indications in the red night lighting.

Minutes passed without further conversation. Vespa was becoming slightly concerned when Ostrewski was back in her ears. "Maria and I have set a date: two months from now."

Though it was physically impossible, Liz tried to turn her head to look at Ozzie. The fittings on her torso harness prevented her from shifting her shoulders more than a few inches. "Wow. That's great, Ozzie." *He's really going to do it.* "Congratulations." Her voice was flat.

"Thanks. We want to have a church wedding, you know? It'll take a while for my family to make travel arrangements out from Chicago."

Liz's pulse was back under seventy. As seconds passed, she reminded herself to scan the instruments again: fuel flow, engine RPM, tailpipe temperature, the TA-4's own vital signs.

"Michael."

"Yeah?"

"Why did you wait until now to tell me? I mean, why not before we launched? Or after the debrief?"

"Hell, Liz . . . I guess I don't really know. Maybe it just seemed important that we have a little time . . . you know, without anybody else around."

She almost laughed. "Well, this is as private as it gets."

"Ah, I just thought that maybe you'd sort of like some time to, you know, maybe, talk."

She forced her feminine fangs back; she would not coyly ask, *Gosh, Ozzie, talk about what?* "That's sweet of you, Michael."

Liz mentally cataloged everything she did and did not want to say—and everything that she could never again discuss with her friend and rival. In two months there would be no going back.

"I'm going to miss you, Michael."

He knew exactly what she meant. "Thank you, Liz. But Ozzie will still be here. And you'll still be Wizard Two."

"Does Maria understand that?"

He thought for several seconds. "Maybe not quite. But she will. It's part of my job as her husband."

"Roger. Break-break."

Again, Michael Ostrewski perfectly read the intent of Elizabeth Vespa. Ozzie waggled the stick and said to Scooter, "You have it. Come right to two four zero. Descend and maintain four thousand five hundred feet."

Hawk Six banked into a thirty-degree turn in the night sky, leaving something more than jet exhaust in its wake.

Twelve

Who Needs Oxygen?

Four Skyhawks were announced by the Pratt and Whitney whine that once was an ordinary sound at Marine Corps Air Station El Toro, south of Los Angeles. Peters looked up from the flight line, where ATA and the Sukhoi delegations were quartered. "Well, that's the last of them."

The TA-4Js broke up for landing interval, gear and flaps coming visible during the 360-degree overhead break. In a descending spiral, line astern, each pilot allowed sufficient distance behind the plane ahead.

"Lookin' good," Peters commented.

"Damn straight," added Robbins.

Peters shielded his eyes with one hand. "I guess Zack had his division up for practice before they left Williams." He looked back toward the parking lot adjacent to the flight line.

"Expecting somebody, boss?"

"Yeah, Rob. I told Jane about Zack's ETA. She and Carol were going to be here for for his arrival."

Robbins worked his eyebrows. "I thought there was some doubt if Carol would even come."

"There was, up until a couple days ago. I guess it took some begging on a pretty thick rug, but Zack convinced her she'd be better off here with us than waiting back home."

"Roger that." Robbins did not need to elaborate. He had persuaded his own wife to accompany him rather than stay alone in their condo—too many people did not want the program to proceed.

As Hawk Ten taxied into the chocks, Delight waved from the cockpit, his rear seat occupied by one of Chief Dan Wilger's maintenance men. The other three A-4s parked beside Delight's, their noses gently bobbing on the long nose-gear oleos.

The boarding ladder was barely in place before a car horn sounded behind Peters and his entourage. Jane Peters and Carol Delight alit from the rented Ford, waving to the crowd as two security men emerged from the front seat. Delight scrambled down the yellow ladder, tugging off his helmet. He met his wife halfway across the ramp, scooped her up in both arms, and carried her back to their friends. "You fool, put me down!" Carol's demand lacked conviction.

"Hi, sweetheart," Zack cooed. He kissed her warmly, then turned to face Jane Peters. "You too, honey." He leaned forward to touch lips with her.

"Pure, what the hell are you doing?" Hook Peters knew perfectly well what his partner was up to.

"I'm ravishing two gorgeous women at the same time," he declared. "It's a Manly Man kind of thing."

Carol Delight settled more comfortably in her husband's arms, both hands around his neck. "I'm glad you're in a manly mood, dear," she said sweetly.

"Jane took me shopping on the way back from John Wayne Airport."

Delight shifted her weight in his arms. "That's as manly an airport as there is. I hope you spent a lot of money."

Carol cocked her head, as if studying him. "Did you get enough oxygen on the way over here?"

"Darlin', I don't need oxygen as long as I've got you."

That saccharine statement prompted a chorus of "Yuuuk" sentiments when Chief Wilger appeared. "Excuse me, folks," he intoned. "You might want to come listen to the portable radio."

"What is it?" Peters asked.

"Well, apparently the Chinese and the Vietnamese are shooting at each other."

At eight that night most of the instructors and their wives gathered in the Peters's suite at the old visiting officers' quarters. Two security guards from the firm contracted by Wei stood outside, guarding the door.

"I want you all to know what's going on in Vietnam and how it affects us," Peters began. He stood by the television set that was turned on but muted. The news graphic headlined, "War in the Tonkin Gulf."

"First, apparently it isn't really a war. It seems to be a limited naval action involving the same area that was disputed several months ago. China and Vietnam both claim the area where petroleum was found, and Vietnam has been drilling there for a few years. You've heard the same news reports I have, but a couple of my D.C. contacts have more detail."

Peters paced a few steps, staring at the carpet. "Congressman Ottmann is coming out here tomorrow or the next day at the latest. So are a couple of Navy representatives involved with the PRC carrier program. From them, I've learned that Chinese marines occupied two of the three drilling platforms."

Robbins interrupted. "Terry, what's Washington say about the Chinese carrier program? If the chinks are the aggressors, won't that result in some kind of sanctions?"

"I'm just coming to that, Rob. Washington has chosen to treat this as a local feud. Even though Beijing is technically the aggressor, the State Department waffles it enough to say that both sides should stand down." He raised his hands. "That's just diplomatic BS. The president and Congress are in bed with the Chinese too far to back out. The bottom line is markets and money, and in that contest, Hanoi loses every time."

"So you're saying we'll continue with the CarQual schedule?" Ostrewski sat on the floor between Vespa and Thaler.

"Well, as of now I haven't heard anything different. Rob, you were out to the boat yesterday. How'd it look?"

"Fine. Captain Albright was happy with things, and he said he can give us twenty-eight knots. Oh, we heard from Pensacola. Two landing signal officers are inbound tomorrow. They're supposed to clear us instructors for preliminary CarQuals before the Chinese begin trapping."

Peters scanned the crowded room. "Any other questions?"

Liz Vespa voiced the thought in a dozen minds. "Only about a hundred, skipper."

Thirteen

The Truest Test

Peters convened the briefing in Ottmann's suite. Zack Delight, Rob Robbins, Ozzie Ostrewski, Psycho Thaler, Liz Vespa, and Chief Wilger were seated around the dining-room table.

"First," Peters began, "for those who haven't met Congressman Tim Ottmann, I'll introduce him by saying he's on the House Military Affairs Committee. He chairs the Tactical Airpower Subcommittee, which has oversight of the Chinese carrier program. Before that, Skip made a poor but honest living as an Eagle driver." Ottmann shared the group's laughter.

"Before Skip explains the reason for this meeting, one thing has to be clear." As usual when he wanted to make a point, Peters paused. "Everything that's said here stays here. What we're planning is potentially dangerous, and the legal implications are not clear-cut. Zack and I are in, but you have to make your own decisions. So, before we continue, anybody who wants to withdraw, do so now." Peters waited but nobody stirred. Peters then turned to Ottmann, standing at the head of the table.

"Thanks, Terry." Ottmann cleared his throat. "Folks, in no more than seven days Mainland China will invade Taiwan."

Vespa's hand instinctively sought Ostrewski's. Chief Wilger voiced the unspoken sentiment of everyone else. "Holy shit."

"I know your first concern," Ottmann said. "You wonder why the Chinese would pick fights with Vietnam and Taiwan at the same time. Well, the Vietnam feud is strategic deception—a manufactured crisis to draw our attention away from Taiwan.

"The real reason behind the upcoming invasion is, well, time. The old guard in Beijing—the hardline Maoists—are dying off. They want China 'reunited' before they go to Marxist valhalla. The new generation is more pragmatic." Ottmann gave an ironic smile. "By 'new generation,' I mean those who don't remember the Long March in 1936.

"Now, they've been very patient. They went along with the so-called internal reforms we wanted because they needed American technology. But there is nothing to prevent the Communist Party from reverting to its old ways once it has what it wants—control of Taiwan. It's a purely cynical view, but remember, these folks insist that Mao Zedung was 'too great a man to be bound by his word.'" Ottmann shrugged. "It's a cultural attitude that we can't change."

Ostrewski leaned forward. "Mr. Ottmann, I don't know much, but I know if China invades Taiwan, there'll be war with the U.S."

"Previously, I'd agree with you, but things have changed." Ottmann stopped to organize his thoughts, then continued. "The reason the PRC has initiated its so-called reforms is to increase its influence here. You all know about the scandals that never went anywhere. Well, by making themselves financially necessary to three administrations, the Chinese bought themselves more than political influence. They bought political souls."

Robbins was tempted to mutter, "No such thing" when Liz Vespa spoke up. "My God, how did it ever go this far?"

"Well," Ottmann said, "the Bush administration continued normal relations after Tiananmen Square. Clinton, who hammered Bush for his China policy in the campaign, not only continued that policy, but expanded it." He grinned sardonically. "Hey, Washington runs on hypocrisy like jets run on JP-4.

"Anyway, besides the millions of dollars in campaign money, you had major corporations clamoring to do business with one-third of the human race. After all, most other Western nations already were in bed with Beijing, and our CEOs didn't want to be left out. So they leaned on their politicians, and things just snowballed."

Robbins raised his voice. "Sir, how do we fit into this?"

"Okay. Beijing knows that America can't just lean back while PRC troops walk over Taiwan. There has to be a publicly acceptable reason for us to sit it out and pass some window-dressing sanctions. We'll probably impose embargos again.

"However, the Chinese are hedging their bet. They have a new long-range missile, the DF-41, with technology we either sold them or they stole from us. France and Israel also contributed, by the way. So, in the next few days we expect China to launch a 'test' that'll hit about two hundred miles off the Washington coast. That'll be a warning shot that says, 'America, you don't have any better missile defense than we do.' So ICBMs are a standoff.

"Now, that's where you folks come in. A Malaysian-registered freighter is headed this way with a Chinese crew. Its manifest lists petroleum products. It does not list five backpack nukes."

Ostrewski merely emitted a low whistle.

"No kidding holy shit," Wilger said in a hushed voice.

"We're tracking this ship, the *Penang Princess*, and we expect it to arrive off Long Beach day after tomorrow. The plan calls for her to transfer the nukes to several smaller vessels that will bring them ashore in different places. But one of them will be delivered, minus detonator, to the Chinese consulate in San Francisco. There, the president and secretary of state will be invited to see it, with a promise that four more have been distributed around the country. At that point, China wins. No American politician is going to defend an Asian island at the expense of thousands of American lives—maybe tens of thousands. It's in his interest, and Congress's, to keep the lid on. No overt acts, no hysterical commentary, and damn sure no scandal about giving in to blackmail." Ottmann shook his head admiringly. "You got to admire the plan—it's a beaut. Right out of Sun-Tzu."

"Sun who?" asked Wilger.

"Sun-Tzu, an ancient Chinese military philosopher. He said the truest test of a general is to win without fighting."

"Okay," Robbins interjected. "So what do we do?"

Ottmann looked directly at the LSO. "You sink that ship."

Fourteen

Questions

The responses came with machine-gun rapidity.

"We don't have ordnance!"

"How do we *know* the nukes are aboard?"

"What about the Navy or Coast Guard?"

And, on everyone's mind, "How do we stay out of prison?"

Ottmann raised his hands, asking for silence. "I'll answer as many of your questions as possible, folks. First, we know the backpacks are aboard because one of our sources helped load them. Most of our intel has been back-channel between unofficial contacts on both sides. I can't tell you more for obvious reasons—you were all military professionals. But I'm convinced the intel is real.

"Second, we're not involving the Navy because the people in DC who know about this plan need 'plausible deniability.' That's a buzzword that means you're lying and everybody knows you're lying but nobody will prove it because everybody else lies, too. The *Santa Cruz* is perfect: officially it's not a U.S. or a Chinese ship. It's not yet commissioned in either navy, it has a mixed crew, including civilians, and there's been no transfer ceremony."

Zack Delight spoke up. "Tim knows I'm an all-up round for this plan. But how about explaining the legality?"

"Right. The plan is to launch you during your first qualification period with thousand-pounders that'll be loaded aboard right before the ship leaves the dock. You'll have the location of the *Penang Princess* inside our twelve-mile limit, and a full briefing on her. You'll land back aboard before the *Santa Cruz* returns to U.S. waters, which is a legal technicality, but it preserves the appearance of American neutrality."

"But, Congressman," Vespa interjected, "we'll still have sunk a neutral ship. People will probably be killed. Aren't we—pirates or something?"

Ottmann smiled as he reached inside his sport coat. From the pocket he produced several folded sheets. "These are full pardons, exonerating you for everything since Adam. They're signed by the president but undated. You'll have your copies, notarized by the attorney general, before you take off from here to land aboard the ship. If everything goes well, you won't need them. If things go wrong, you're covered."

Vespa locked eyes with the New Yorker. "So the president . . ."

". . . still denies involvement." Ottmann smiled again.

"Excuse me, sir," Robbins said, "but how do we know these papers are valid? We might be set up, and you wouldn't know it."

"Well, Rob, I could just say, 'Trust me.' But if one

of you goes to prison, I'll be there waving bye-bye when you finally walk out the front gate. As deep as I am in this, I'd never see daylight again."

Robbins's blue eyes had a little-boy gleam. "You just told me that you've got the president by the . . ."

"By the plausible deniability." Ottmann grinned.

"A couple of other things," Robbins continued. "If I was smuggling nukes into this country, I wouldn't put 'em all in one basket, and I wouldn't wait until a few days before I might need 'em. Doesn't that seem kind of suspicious?"

"Geez, Robo. You ever consider a career in politics?" Ottmann chuckled at the sentiment. "Your instincts are good, but we know that the Chinese decided not to risk discovery of the backpacks until almost the last minute. And actually they're not putting them all in one basket. As I said, some or all of them will be put in other boats before unloading. That's why we need to sink the ship at a specific time and place."

"We're going to recover them?"

"We're sure not going to leave them on the bottom of the ocean. Tactically, it'd make more sense to sink the ship in deep water beyond our limits. But this way, the U.S. government has full authority over recovery and salvage operations. I believe that a Coast Guard cutter will accidentally be nearby to pick up all survivors—and whatever they get off the ship."

Ozzie gave an appreciative whistle. "Sounds like you have it all doped out, sir."

"Well, it's been a long time planning. But in any operation like this, there's always the Oscar Sierra factor. Just remember that if things do turn to shit, you're covered legally.

"Anything else?" Ottmann asked. Liz Vespa's frown caught Ottmann's attention. "Miss Vespa?"

"Liz," Scooter corrected. "You know, all this seems

really well planned, but I don't understand something. Why are the Chinese blackmailing us with ICBMs or backpacks? They must know we can't stop them from taking Taiwan—we don't have the people, the airlift, or the sealift anymore. So if they're willing to accept the political fallout, why not just go?"

"Good strategic question. I wish I could tell you what I know, but I can't right now." He looked around. "Yes, Ozzie."

"With everything involved in a big operation like occupying Taiwan, the folks on that island must know what's coming. I mean, PRC bases for shipping, airfields, and several infantry and armored divisions—all of that's got to draw attention. Why haven't we heard anything from them or the UN?"

"Hell, the UN doesn't matter since China has a veto. As for Taiwan, they've lived in the shadow of the PRC for about fifty years—their military is on constant alert. Also, the Chinese have American politicians in their hip pocket. There hasn't even been any contingency planning for operations involving the PRC for several years now." He snorted his contempt. "Hell, dozens of White House staffers don't even submit to presumably mandatory security checks, so don't expect the military to buck policy. Maybe it would help if some senior uniformed people would stand up and risk their careers, but there aren't any left." He looked around the room full of former military professionals. "There just aren't any left."

Fifteen

Answers

Hijacking a moored aircraft carrier is no small task. It requires planning, cunning, and most of all, nerve.

It also helps to have well-placed contacts.

Representative Tim Ottmann announced a later meeting after the first one broke up. He impressed upon Terry Peters the importance of having everyone involved in the program present to take a tour of the Chinese and Russian facilities at El Toro.

"Have you talked to Captain Albright?" Ottmann asked Peters.

"Yes, he'll be here with his exec. I also told our active-duty instructors to attend. That's Lieutenants Arliss and Horn plus Lieutenant Commander Cartier from the LSO school." Peters inclined his head slightly, regarding the New Yorker with amused suspicion. "You're up to something."

Ottmann made a small come-hither gesture with two fingers. Though they were alone in the room, Peters stepped closer. "I want the Chinese and everyone else to think that we're having a last conference here before qualifications begin day after tomorrow. As far as you and anyone else knows, there'll be a reception until late tonight in my suite. Wei and his students will attend, and I've even invited some of the Russians."

"Okay."

"While the *Santa Cruz*'s captain and exec and the active-duty guys are here, including your LSO, there's not much chance of anyone thinking the ship's going to sail, is there?"

Peters's eyes gleamed in admiration. "You're a sneaky bas . . ."

"Thanks. A helo will pick you up here at 2230. Would it be suspicious if you and Robbins both disappeared at that time?"

"Hell, I don't know, Skip. Are you going to serve booze?"

"All the adult beverages anybody wants to consume. Except your guys, of course. As soon as I get word from you that the ship's under way, I'll tell Zack your overhead time. His flight will land aboard, load ordnance, and get the final brief."

Peters nodded. "Sounds like your plan hasn't changed much."

"Now, there's one more factor in our favor. The harbor pilot is one of our guys, Ben Tolleson. He's a master mariner and probably could run the ship without much help. Except for flight operations, of course. But you'll be in full command once you exit the harbor." Ottmann searched his fellow conspirator's face. "Are you really sure you can drive that boat?"

"Well, it's been quite a few years, Tim. I conned

Independence before she entered the yard. But yes, I'm sure."

"Okay. Now, while we still have time, I need to let you know about our inside source."

"Why tell me? Do I really need to know?"

Ottmann smiled. "Oh yeah, you really need to know. He's flying in one of the two-seaters tomorrow morning." Ottmann rapped on the wall of the adjoining bedroom. After a few seconds the door opened and Terry Peters gaped at Mr. Wei Ching-lao.

Sixteen

Half-Truths and White Lies

Tim Ottmann invited Wei to take the most comfortable chair while the Americans sat on the couch. Wei produced a cigarette holder and inserted a Camel before lighting up. He blew two near-perfect smoke rings before he began to speak.

"Mr. Peters, I have not been completely truthful with you. However, you will understand the need for security."

"Certainly, sir."

The old MiG pilot put down his cigarette. "Mr. Peters, the primary Chinese trait is patience. We take the long view of history, but now, in the twenty-first century by your reckoning, some of us realize that events have accelerated far beyond our accustomed pace. The world economy and global communications have forced a radical change upon us. Unfortunately, most of the venerable leaders in

Beijing are unable to grasp that fact. Tiananmen Square was just one example.

"Frankly, various American administrations have made the task of reform-minded Chinese more difficult. Your politicians tried to have things both ways: supposedly opposing the successors of Mao while trying to exploit China's emerging economy. The hypocrisy of Republican and Democrat administrations has left China convinced that America stands only for profit and expediency. That attitude has, ironically, reinforced the old men's determination to seize Taiwan. They believe that after an initial flurry of protests, Sino-American relations will return to the status quo ante."

"Will they, sir?"

Wei looked at Ottmann, who nodded. "Most assuredly. As far as America is concerned, I shall explain the consequences for China. But first, I concede that China has too much influence in your internal affairs to prevent, as you say, business as usual. Too many public figures have accepted illegal contributions; too many are compromised in other fashions." Wei shook his head. "You would not believe how many people or how many ways."

Peters felt a small shiver between his shoulder blades.

"Now," Wei continued, "you ask why my colleagues and I are working with men like Mr. Ottmann. The reason is that we are Chinese patriots. Oh, some of us still believe in Marxism, but that is almost irrelevant. Instead, we look at this Taiwan folly and see unnecessary risks. Therefore, we decided to upset the nuclear blackmail part of the plan. Without the assurance of American capitulation, the operation is too dangerous to proceed. Even if it succeeds, the rest of Asia would unite against us, economically and militarily. We would be forced into the type of military spending that ruined the Soviet Union."

Peters ingested the revelation, emotionally breathless at the implications. "Mr. Wei, why don't the Politburo and the Chairman understand these things?"

Wei dismissed the concept with the wave of a hand. "You know of America's so-called Beltway mentality, Mr. Peters? We have the same thing in Beijing. From there, the world appears logical and orderly, bound to fit the outmoded perceptions of the office holders. Our 'wise old men' still view the world through Marxist prisms, even though many of them are political pragmatists. They know their time is running out, and they are determined to cling to their attitudes until the last moment."

Peters leaned back, rubbing his eyes as if in disbelief of what he had heard. He rolled his shoulders and faced Wei once more. "All right, sir. You convinced me. How do we proceed?"

"Our intention is to have the *Santa Cruz* at sea without anyone knowing of it here until the last possible moment. Surprise will be important in sinking the *Penang Princess*, and we must assume that her captain will have some form of communication with agents here at El Toro or in Long Beach."

"That's right," Ottmann added. "Remember the original plan, Terry? We were going to have your instructors qualify in one day and stay aboard that night. Then the Chinese pilots supposedly would fly out the next day with some of the other instructors to begin the main qualification period."

Peters snapped his fingers. "And we're going to launch the strike the same day as the instructors' CarQuals."

"Exactly, Mr. Peters. However, in our long-range planning we only had a time frame. We knew the best time of year for an invasion of Taiwan, and we knew the decision had been made to insert the nuclear weapons a few days before that date." He raised his hands in a semihelpless gesture. "Therefore, our planning could not be as precise as we hoped."

"All right," Peters replied. "But Mr. Wei, I don't understand something. You got a promise from me to get you a carrier landing. How does that fit into the plan?"

Wei almost smiled. "I made it known to my pilots that I wanted to share their experience. Now, if they see me in one of your aircraft, they are unlikely to be suspicious. But it also suits our larger purpose. First, your government and my faction wish to emphasize the Chinese participation in this operation while minimizing American involvement. My authority is accepted among the Chinese aboard the ship, and will not be questioned.

"Therefore, in keeping with the Chinese emphasis, we will need PRC pilots. I am one; Mr. Hu will be the other."

Peters glanced at Ottmann, then back to Wei. "Why Hu? He's one of those who was almost cut from the program."

"Mr. Peters, Hu is my sister's son. I trust him."

Ottmann could almost hear the wheels clicking in Peters's skull. "Terry, when Mr. Wei says we need Chinese on the mission, it's part of the plausible deniability. No active-duty Americans are involved, and we emphasize that PRC pilots flew the mission."

"I see. We ATA folks are retired while the flight-deck troops are Chinese or inactive American reservists." Peters winked at the congressman. "A half-truth isn't quite the same as a white lie."

Ottmann made a point of shaking hands. "Terry, welcome to the wonderful world of politics."

Seventeen

One of Our Carriers Is Missing

It was just past midnight, but the floodlights on the flight deck, and those along the pier on F Avenue, provided ample illumination for the Jet Ranger that Wei had leased. The pilot, who had flown SH-60s, was more than willing to set down directly on *Santa Cruz*, saving Peters and Robbins a long walk from Navy Landing a mile and a half away. They waved good-bye, then turned and entered the island en route to the bridge.

"Think they'll miss us at Wei's reception?" Robbins asked.

"Not likely, with all the free booze and fresh crab. Did you see how our boy Igor was sucking it up?"

On the O–9 level Peters entered the red-lit bridge. He saw an older man, graying with a two-day crop of stubble, talking to the watch officer. "Mr. Tolleson? I'm Terry Peters."

"That's me," the harbor pilot replied. He regarded Peters openly, assessing the aviator who would take this ship to sea. They shook hands. "Our friend told me to expect you."

"Well, it's early for the usual watch change, but I think we'll do all right."

"I hope so, skipper. I've never hijacked a carrier before!" Tolleson smiled. "By the way, do you know your officers of the deck? Mr. Odegaard and Mr. Mei. Gentlemen, this is Captain Peters. He'll be relieving Captain Albright today."

Peters greeted the American and his Chinese counterpart. "Yes, I've met both these gentlemen." He knew that Odegaard was a retired reserve commander; Mei had been aboard destroyers and frigates; reputedly he was an above-average ship handler.

"All right, gentlemen, let's get started. Captain Albright said to expect four boilers on line and four standing by, provisions for two days, and a full complement sufficient for carrier qualifications tomorrow. We're running under our own power without connections to shore. Also, I'm told we have tugs standing by. Is that correct?"

"All correct, Captain." Odegaard nodded toward Mei. "We've checked with the department heads and we're ready to go."

"Very well." Peters inhaled, held the breath, then let it out. "On the bridge, this is Captain Peters, I have the conn." He turned to Robbins. "Robo, check with the weapons officer—Medesha? I want you to eyeball the Mark 83s before we push off."

"You got it, boss." He disappeared down the ladder.

Peters turned back to his bridge watch. "We'll light off the other boilers as we clear the channel, but right now it's important to get under way without drawing too much attention."

"Aye, aye, sir," Odegaard replied. "The plant is lined up in parallel. We'll use those four boilers to provide steam for the main engines."

"Good. Ah, let's see . . . I know the elevators are raised. Are they locked?"

"Yes, Captain. We can confirm that with the deck division if you prefer."

"Not necessary." Peters strode to the starboard side of the bridge, assessing the topography of his new domain. He turned to the watch standers. "Let's test the rudders. And I'd like to confirm that we have up radar plus navigation and comm."

The helmsman was a retired merchant marine and active yachtsman who relished steering eighty thousand tons of steel. He tested the tiller and reported that he had full control of the two rudders.

Mei came to attention. "Captain, I have personally inspected the navigation equipment. I also consulted the communications watch officer. We are ready."

"Very well, gentlemen." He looked to Tolleson. "Captain, request you make up the tugs, sir."

"Right, Cap'n." While Tolleson communicated with the tugs that would pull the carrier's deadweight outboard against the onshore breeze, Peters saw to the pierside procedure. He waited for word from Robbins before the remaining brow was wheeled back from the starboard quarterdeck. The call quickly came from the weapons division.

"Weps to bridge."

Odegaard responded, leaning into the speaker. "Bridge aye."

"This is Robbins. Tell the captain we're cocked and locked."

Peters grinned beneath the brim of his "A-4s Forever" ballcap. "Cocked and locked" was verbal shorthand for the occasion: Robbins had seen the thousand-pound bombs and confirmed that there were suitable fuzes on hand.

At a nod from Peters, Odegaard broadcast over the 1-MC general-announcing system. "Set the special sea and anchor detail. Single up all lines and make all preparations for getting under way."

Peters waved to his de facto executive officer and the harbor pilot. "Mr. Odegaard, Mr. Tolleson. We'll move to Aux Conn." While they stepped eight feet aft to the auxiliary conning station, sailors on the pier removed the first of two heavy lines securing the carrier to each of eight stanchions along the ship's 1,046-foot length. Meanwhile, Tolleson directed both "made-up" tugs into position at the bow and stern.

Taking nothing for granted, Peters leaned out of Aux Conn, looking fore and aft to confirm that all was ready. He called behind him, "Let go all lines." The order was repeated, echoing metallically through the moist maritime darkness as pierside personnel released the final eight hawsers linking *Santa Cruz* to shore.

Peters turned back inboard to face his bridge crew. "Gentlemen, I see no reason to stand on ceremony. Captain Tolleson, you'll give your orders directly to the helmsman, if you please." He chuckled slightly. "We do things differently in the Skyhawk Navy."

Tolleson scratched his beard, beaming his approval of the nonregulation procedure. "Right you are, Cap'n." He waited until he judged the ship forty to fifty feet from the pier, then said, "Son, give me left standard rudder." As the helm swung through fifteen degrees of arc, Tolleson announced, "Back one-third on number one and two; ahead two-thirds on three and four."

Peters watched the "spinning" maneuver move the bow away from the pier, ponderously swinging to port. The watch officer, peering through the window, called to Tolleson. "We're fair, Pilot."

Tolleson spoke into his walkie-talkie, clearing the tugs of their chore.

As the big ship maneuvered in the turning basin, Tolleson called, "All ahead one-third." *Santa Cruz* grudgingly edged up to five knots as Tolleson smoothly coordinated rudder commands and orders to the tugs. With the bow properly positioned, he turned back to Peters. "She's all yours, skipper."

Peters warmly shook hands with the friend of Wei Chinglao. "Nicely done, sir. You'd better catch your taxi if you don't want to make this cruise."

Tolleson laughed. "I might enjoy it at that." He slapped Peters's arm and disappeared through the hatch, en route to the stern, where he would take a jacob's ladder down to the tug.

Captain Terence Peters, USN (Retired), felt the faint throbbing of the engines through the soles of his brown aviator shoes. Peering ahead into the Pacific darkness, he modulated his voice in what he intended to resemble confident authority. "All ahead two-thirds."

Eighteen

Ready Deck

The A-4s dropped their tailhooks and entered the Delta pattern two thousand feet overhead the ship in a descending left-hand carousel. Thaler, Delight's wingman, crossed his leader's tail from the left to establish right echelon beside Ostrewski with Vespa outboard.

Delight reached the initial point three miles astern of the carrier, approaching parallel to her starboard side. He looked down from eight hundred feet and felt a rumble of excited satisfaction in his belly. After months of planning and training, there was the former USS *Santa Cruz* with a ready deck, steaming upwind and eager to receive him. Zack led his little formation ahead of the ship's white-foamed bow. He checked his airspeed—steady on three hundred knots—and prepared for his break turn.

Ahead of the ship, Delight laid the stick over to

port, brought the throttle back to 80 percent, hit the speed brakes, and pulled. His vision went gray at the periphery, but he rolled wings level about a mile and a quarter off the port side, descending through six hundred feet while headed aft.

Delight's left hand automatically found the gear and flap handles, and he felt his A-4F decelerate through 220 under the additional drag. He shot a glance at the angle-of-attack indicator, cross-checking with airspeed.

As the LSO platform seemed to slide past him, Delight turned left, adding power to maintain 130 knots. Turning his head, he saw the mirror's meatball halfway up the deck. He crossed the wide white wake, sucked off a bit of throttle, and stabilized his angle of attack with minute adjustments of the stick.

Meatball, angle of attack, lineup, Delight chanted to himself. He knew that a good start and small corrections were the keys to success. He felt as if the A-4 were balanced on a pencil tip, and forced himself to fly smoothly—too much muscle meant over-controlling that did bad things to landing grades.

"Pure, this is Rob. Come back." Robbins was avoiding standard LSO phraseology in case somebody was listening.

"Read you, Robo."

"Lookin' good, keep it coming."

Delight liked to fly his approach half a ball high. If he began to settle in close, he could catch it without a fistful of power, and it worked. He added a little power and the meatball stabilized nicely in the center. As his wheels impacted the deck he crammed on full throttle in case of a bolter—and was thrown against his straps as the hook snagged the four wire.

Did it! he exulted. He retarded throttle, tapped his brakes, and raised the hook. Up ahead a yellow-shirted crewman was into his manic arm-waving routine, gesturing Hawk One to the elevator.

Behind Delight, Psycho boltered, shoved up the throttle, and went around. Ozzie snagged the two wire; Liz flew a near-perfect OK-3. Thaler trapped the three wire on his next pass.

The ordies began loading weapons on the hangar deck.

Nineteen

Face of a Stranger

Zack Delight stood at the head of the ready room with the doors closed and guards posted outside. The passageways on either side were blocked with plastic tape, forcing anyone transiting the area to detour around the area.

Delight looked over his bobtailed "squadron" seated in the first row: Ostrewski, Thaler, and Vespa, plus Robbins the LSO. Wei and Hu sat in the second row. On the board behind him was an overhead view of *Penang Princess*, carefully drawn to scale.

Delight mussed his graying hair and grinned to himself. "Never thought I'd be in a ready room again, wearing Nomex and briefing a strike with live ordnance against a real target."

"Neither did we," exclaimed Ozzie. He winked at Liz, who smiled back.

"I never thought I'd brief a strike against a real target at all," she added.

"Okay, folks. Here we go." Delight's face seemingly morphed before his tiny audience, passing in one heartbeat from peace to war. Liz felt a tiny thrill somewhere deep inside her. She realized she was seeing a man she had never met before.

Delight quickly passed through the basics: launch, rendezvous, and the route outbound. Then he addressed communications.

"You have your UHF and VHF frequencies, but we need to run this thing under total EmCom if at all possible. If you do have to transmit, no names or call signs on the radio—no Zack or Pure or Ozzie. We are Papa Flight, for 'Pure.' I'm Dash One, Ozzie's Dash Three and so on. The backseaters are Two Bravo and Four Bravo. The helos are Hotel One and Two.

"If anybody has to abort, keep off the radio. That's only for no-shit emergencies. Just rock your wings and break off. We'd rather not bring live ordnance back aboard, but if you can't find a safe place to jettison your bombs, just be damn sure they're safed. If possible, dog overhead the ship until everybody else is back aboard." He paused. "Any questions?"

Robbins waved a hand. "Zack, let's play Oh shit, like we talked before."

"Right." Peters looked from Robbins back to the front-row aviators. "Over the past couple of days, Terry and Rob and I discussed some of the things that might go wrong. For instance, suppose the guys on that ship know we're coming. Maybe they'll have SAMs or even Triple A. Well, two A-4s will have flare pods and chaff dispensers, and there's no need to conserve them."

Ostrewski piped up. "What if the *Penang* doesn't

show up on time? Or we can't find her?"

"Well, in that case our part is over. We return to the boat or land at El Toro. You'll have to recover ashore if you get a hung bomb."

Robbins spoke again. "You want to discuss SAR at this point?"

"Coming to that, Robo." Delight leaned on the rostrum, checking his notes. He picked up the paper and extended it to arm's length, ignoring chuckles from the other pilots. "If anybody has to make a controlled ejection, try to get as close to the carrier as possible. We have two helos aboard, but only one is fully equipped for rescues, so be aware that we need to keep that one nearby as plane guard."

Thaler waved a pen. "Since the *Boorda*'s in the area, what about diverting to land on her?"

Scooter shot a glance at Psycho. "That's right, I forgot. I have a Pensacola classmate aboard, flying Hornets." Vespa's tone told the males that there was probably little love lost between the two women. Ostrewski, who had met slender, blond Lieutenant Commander Jennifer Jensen—"Jen-Jen" the ice princess and admiral's daughter—knew that Vespa resented her rival's influence in getting a coveted fleet assignment.

Delight shook his head at Thaler. "Nope, not unless there's something entirely unexpected. We'd rather you eject and write off a jet rather than show the U.S. Navy what we're doing."

With no further questions, Delight turned back to the board. "Now, here's the crunch. When we positively ID the target, we'll conduct a dual-axis attack with roll in from about twelve thousand feet. Put 112 mils on your sight, and include that in your precombat check. I recommend that you pickle no lower than forty-five hundred feet. Like we practiced at Gila Bend: a five-G pull gets you level by three thousand feet.

"I'll take Psycho in from the bow. That's the best way to attack a ship because it forces you to get steep, and we'll be making sixty-degree dives. By attacking along the fore and aft axis of the target, we have a better chance of getting hits with shorts and overs." He jotted pinpoints along the deck of the *Princess* with his Magic Marker, indicating random hits.

"Ozzie, you and Liz will pull around to the stern. If there's no opposition, wait until you've seen the result of our attack. The fuzes are one-tenth of a second delay, but there'll still be smoke and probably flames. Otherwise, time your roll-in so you're down the chute as we're pulling off." He scrawled two arrows breaking to port from their attack.

"Now, if there's opposition—either SAMs or Triple A—Psycho and I will try to strafe, time permitting. I'll tell you what I'm doing. If we do this right, it'll be the only radio call of the whole mission, because we want to stay zip-lip from startup to attack." He scanned the audience, emphasizing his words with his tone.

"When I roll in, I'll start popping flares whether there's any shooting or not. Ozzie and I in the A-4Fs both have enough flares in our pods to cover this short an attack.

"Mr. Wei, Mr. Hu." The two Chinese sat attentively upright in their seats. "You can help your front-seaters by keeping your heads moving the whole time. Let them know if you see anything unusual. When the attack starts, your video cameras need to stay on the target as long as possible. It may be the best damage assessment we get for a while."

"Except for Eyewitness News," Ozzie ventured.

Wei raised his hand from the second row. "Yes, sir," Zack responded.

"Mr. Delight, perhaps you should describe the return to port."

"I was just coming to that. As soon as we're back aboard, all ATA personnel will jump in both helos and we'll be flown to a vacant lot near Tustin. Two or three cars will be waiting there, and we'll return to El Toro. From that point on, we don't know nothin'." He looked around the room again, noting each flier's face. The Chinese were impassive, whether from temperament or familial trait he could not guess. Robbins was completely relaxed, a professional "waver" waiting to do his job. Ozzie fidgeted slightly; Delight attributed it to excess energy. As for Liz Vespa—well, she was smiling.

Twenty

Been There, Done That

Terry Peters stepped into the ready room, unexpected and unannounced. Liz Vespa saw him first. Partly from impulse, partly from abiding respect, she reverted to naval custom. "Captain on deck! Atten-hut!"

Almost in unison the green-clad aviators shot to their feet. Wei and Hu, untutored in such things, followed the example.

Peters felt a warm rush inside him—something close to love. "Thank you, gent . . . ah, *lady* and gentlemen. Please be seated."

Striding to the front of the room, he collected his thoughts. *A short speech is a good speech,* he told himself. He exhaled, wet his lips, and began speaking. "I just wanted to say how proud I am of you guys—all of you. When we started this project, I had no more of an idea how it would turn out than anyone else. Now that it's about to end, and considering what's at stake, well . . ." He blinked away something and shook his head. ". . . I wouldn't be anywhere else on earth today, or with any other people."

"Neither would we, pard." Delight's eyes were beginning to mist over, too.

"Damn straight," added Robbins.

"Well," Peters concluded, "I'd better get back to the bridge. But first I want to wish good hunting to everyone here." He trooped the line, warmly shaking the hands of his friends and colleagues, squeezing Liz in a bear hug, and solemnly greeting Wei and Hu. Then he stepped back three paces, standing erect. "This isn't regulation the way we were brought up, but this ship is in *our* navy, isn't it?" Peters brought his heels together and whipped his right hand to the brim of his ball cap in a slicing arc that might have left a vacuum in its wake. His aviators returned the gesture for the first time in their lives, as it was contrary to U.S. Navy practice when uncovered. Then he was gone.

Eric Thaler began zipping his torso harness and survival vest while Robbins and Hu helped Wei with the unfamiliar garments. Ostrewski caught Vespa's attention and motioned to the far corner in the back of the compartment.

"How do you feel, Liz?"

She arched her eyebrows. *Now he thinks I'm going to wimp out!* "I'm fine, Ozzie. Just fine. Why?"

He glanced away from her and saw Delight's head turned toward them. Equally quickly, Delight averted his gaze. *Like Ward Bond in* The Searchers *watching John Wayne and his sister-in-law,* Ostrewski thought.

"Well, it's just that this is the only combat mission we'll ever fly together . . ." His reticence finally melted in a rush as he heard himself say, "Ah, hell, Liz." He wrapped his arms around her, awkwardly

pulling their bodies together despite the bulky flight
gear. Her arms encircled his neck, compressing the
collar of his flotation device.

"Michael . . ."

They kissed one another with a tender aggressive-
ness that trod the neutral zone between the foundation of friendship and the dawning of desire. It
lasted an eternal four seconds.

"Now hear this! Pilots, man your planes."

The squawk box on the bulkhead repeated the
ritual command, focusing aviators' attention and
shattering peaceful thoughts.

Ostrewski pulled back, locking eyes with Vespa. "I
love Maria, Liz. I'm going to spend my life with her.
But I needed to do that, especially today."

She patted the front of his vest. "So did I, Michael."

He managed a laugh. "Okay—been there, done
that."

"Good," she added. "Now, let's sink us a ship."

The pilots emerged from the base of the island and
strode onto the flight deck. Wearing helmets with
visors lowered, they were unidentifiable to anyone
who did not know them well.

As the aircrew approached the yellow boarding
ladders on four Skyhawks, each of the fliers paused
to look at the thousand-pound bombs beneath each
wing. Delight touched a kiss to one of his; Vespa ran
a loving hand along the ablative surface of hers.
Plane captains and ordnancemen scrambled with
last-minute checks as catapult crews stood by.

Lowering himself into the blue-and-white A-4F
now called Papa One, Delight glanced up at the
bridge. He saw Terry Peters's face in one of the windows and perceived a smart wave. Delight tossed a
nonregulation salute to the former deep-draft skipper who had missed his chance to drive a flat-roofed

bird farm. Twisting slightly to his right, Zack saw the diamond-design Foxtrot flag snapping from its halyard, indicating flight operations under way. Higher up the mast, appearing in stark contrast to the striped banner he was accustomed to seeing, flew the jolly roger. The leering white skull with crossed leg bones on the black field sent an electric thrill through his body. Below it, expressing no less heartfelt a sentiment, was the light blue ensign of the Tailhook Association.

Zack Delight clasped his hands over his head in a gesture of undiluted rapture. At fifty-nine years of age, he knew that he would never again feel as good as this day and this hour. He felt gleefully giddy as his mind defaulted to the frontier tales of his Southwest youth. *Ya-ta hay!* he exulted. *It is a good day to die!*

Twenty-one

The Oscar Sierra Factor

The beeper sounded on Peters's cell phone, pulling him back from the disappearing A-4s that had been the focus of his existence. He pulled the handset from the Velcro pouch on his belt, hit the button, and said, "Peters."

"Terry, thank God!" Jane was almost breathless.

"Honey, what is it?"

"Terry, I don't know how, but the Chinese here know what you're doing! They've roped off their hangar and they're rounding up people and holding them inside." She paused to inhale. "There's been some shooting, and I saw two bodies on the ground. I think they were security guards."

Peters slid off the captain's chair. "Are you all right?"

"Yes, I'm okay. So's Carol and everyone else I've seen."

"Jane, where are you?" He waited three seconds. "Jane!"

"I'm, ah, I don't think I should say over the phone, darling. We're safe for now, and we're keeping out of sight. But they're guarding the parking lot."

"Have you called the police?"

"No, I called you first."

"Jane, honey, there's nothing I can . . ."

"God damn it, Terry! Listen to me!" The venom in her voice silenced him like a piano smashing a Walkman. "Are you listening?"

"Yes." His voice was muted.

"One of the ordnancemen is with us, Ron. He saw the Chinese loading ammunition in two A-4s, and we heard them taxi out."

"Oh, no . . ."

"There's more."

"They're arming more A-4s?"

"No, honey." She inhaled. "The Russians kept the Flankers fueled, and Ron said they were hanging missiles on the rails."

Peters's eyes widened, saucerlike. "Call me again in ten minutes." He broke the connection, belatedly regretting not asking about Skip Ottmann, about the security men who might be dead—and not telling her that he loved her. But now, sorting priorities, he flipped the switch to the communications division.

"Radio, this is the captain."

"Yes, sir."

"Call Papa Flight and tell them at least two A-4s are launching from El Toro with live ammo. Our people are to assume they're hostile. Get an acknowledgment—to hell with EmCon."

"Yes, sir."

"Wait, there's more. Tell them . . . tell them the

Flankers are spooling up, too. And they're armed with missiles."

"Yes, *sir*!"

Peters sat back in his chair, sorting through the phone numbers stored in his Powerbook. He scrolled down the listings until he reached NavAirPac, then punched in the number.

It was forty seconds before he got a tone, and the phone rang four times before the watch stander finally answered. "GoodmorningCom-NavAirPacPetty-OfficerStroudspeakingthisisanonsecurelinemayI-helpyou?" Peters barely understood the rapid-fire babble that seemed mandatory in the modern Navy. He wanted to scream, "Shut up, you bitch!" Instead, he did a fast three count.

"This is Captain Peters, commanding the aircraft carrier *Santa Cruz*, steaming off Long Beach. I am declaring an emergency and I need to speak with Admiral Paulson. *Right now*."

Petty Officer Stroud seemed taken aback; she had never heard of USS *Santa Cruz* and had no idea of the protocol involved in a ship declaring an emergency. "Sir, the admiral's at a conference."

"Then I'll speak to the senior watch officer. Immediately."

"Sir, what shall I say is the nature of the emergency?"

"Listen to me, Petty Officer! You have about twenty minutes before a backpack 'nuke' detonates under your rosy red ass. Now, what part of 'nuke' don't you understand?"

"Lieutenant Commander Paglia. What is your emergency, sir?"

"This is Terry Peters. I'm in command of the *Santa Cruz*, conducting CarQuals off Long Beach. Listen carefully, son."

"Yes, sir?"

"I have four A-4s airborne with live ordnance, operating under orders from the national command authority. Their mission is to sink a Malaysian freighter carrying nuclear weapons into this country." He paused for effect. "Do you understand, Commander?"

Peters could almost hear Anthony Paglia swallow hard. "Yes, sir. Ah, may I request verification . . ."

"Commander, I have no verification. And there's no time for you to call the White House and get it. Is there?"

"Well, I suppose . . ."

"Fine. Here's the situation. My flight is about to be intercepted by two Chinese-flown A-4s trying to prevent us from sinking the *Penang*. Okay? That's not the problem—my guys can take care of themselves. But the Russians who're here to CarQual their Flankers are loading missiles at El Toro this minute."

"Ho-ly . . ."

"Right. So here's what I need you to do, Commander. I assume there's an alert flight on the pad at Miramar." *Please tell me there is!* "I need you to scramble them, get 'em up here at the speed of heat, and contact my mission commander on Baker Channel. He answers to Papa One. Your flight can talk to me on 308.2. Tell your people that under *no* circumstance are they to shoot a Skyhawk. Any Flanker—I repeat, *any* Flanker in the air or on the ground at El Toro is a legitimate target. The ROE is: shoot on sight."

"Sir, are you authorized to establish rules of engagement?"

Peters did not even blink. "Absolutely. Definitely. You can check with CNO. But for now, you have your orders, Commander Paglia. Acknowledge."

"Uh, yessir."

"Fine. Call me back as soon as you know about the Hornets."

"Aye, aye, sir."

Robbins appeared at Peters's side. "How bad, Terry?"

"The Oscar Sierra Factor just kicked into afterburner."

A low whistle escaped the LSO's lips. "What else can we do?"

Peters slumped into his swivel chair. "Wait."

"What do you think about Miramar? Will they scramble or will that O–4 go through channels?"

Peters tipped back his cap, biting his lip. "I don't know, Rob. He seemed like a good kid, but . . ."

"But his career's on the line in a situation that's not covered in the *Watch Officer's Guide*." Robbins folded his arms, leaning against the thick glass overlooking the flight deck. "And initiative's been bred out of the system. The 'zero defect' mentality just stifles risk taking, doesn't it?"

Peters closed his eyes. "It doesn't get this way under good leadership."

"Yeah," Robbins replied, "and look who's been 'leading' us recently." He etched quote marks in the air with both hands.

"Bridge, Radio."

Peters leapt to the console. "Captain speaking."

"Captain, we just heard from Papa One."

"Yes?"

"Sir, they can't find the target."

Twenty-two

An All-Up Round

In Papa One, Zack Delight ran his precombat checklist, still savoring the memory of the kick in the small of the back as the catapult threw him off the deck, accelerating the A-4 from zero to 120 knots in three seconds. He confirmed the mil setting on his sight, ensured that his master arm switch was off, and scanned his gauges in one practiced sweep of his eyes. He was, as he liked to say, an all-up round.

Delight raised his right leg and withdrew the chart. After nearly a century of powered flight, the human thigh remained the best map holder yet invented.

The Los Angeles area navigation chart was folded to show *Penang Princess*'s most likely location, given her expected arrival time. Delight had bounded the search sector in red crayon—a twenty-mile-by-ten-mile rectangle beginning five miles offshore. At two thousand feet altitude, he could see fifty-five miles in any direction, haze and smog permitting.

Delight glanced down again, taking in the multitude of ships and vessels approaching or departing the Middle Breakwater. Even allowing for the possibility that her company's green hull and beige deck had been repainted, none of the aged thirty-thousand-ton freighters matched his target's configuration.

With a rising flush of ambivalence, Zachary Delight felt frustrated and proud. *I'm like Wade McClusky at Midway,* he thought. *I've got Heinemann-designed airplanes at my back, looking for a target that's not at the briefed intercept point.* The kinship he felt with the *Enterprise* air group commander nearly sixty years before was diluted by the growing doubt that the mission could be accomplished—and bandits were inbound.

He made a decision and keyed his mike. "Papa Three, look north and west of the track. I'll swing south and west."

"Roger." Ozzie's voice was crisp, professional. He eased into a right bank, leading Liz Vespa parallel to the coast.

The cell phone buzzed and Peters whipped it out of the pouch. "Talk to me!" *Whoever you are!*

"Terry, it's Jane."

"You okay?"

His wife's response was delayed a fraction longer than he had grown to expect in twenty-nine years. He had time to wonder if he had hurt her feelings with his abrupt tone.

"We're still all right. I wanted to tell you that Skip's been on the phone to Washington. He called the Pentagon—he has a cell phone—and now he's talking to somebody at NavAir."

"Rocky Rhode?"

"I don't know, honey. It's ... awful ... confusing ..."

"What about the Flankers?"

"What?"

Peters closed his eyes, forcing composure upon his growing anger and frustration. "Jane ... honey ... I asked, what about the Flankers?"

There was no reply. Peters lowered the handset from his ear to look at it, willing the inanimate thing to explain itself. He raised it again and spoke slowly, clearly. "Jane, this is Terry. Do you hear me?"

The line clicked twice and went dead.

Delight and Thaler completed their sweep down the east side of the search area, again coming up empty. Zack's cockpit scan took in his fuel state: twenty-four hundred pounds. *Enough for a little while*, he thought. *Then we'll have to abort.* At his altitude, necessary to ID the target, fuel was going fast.

Decision time, Delight realized. *Either we continue trolling this area or we look elsewhere.* He waggled his wings, signaling Eric Thaler that they were heading east to hunt along the coast. He motioned for Psycho to spread out, expanding the visual limits of their horizon.

"Do you know any satisfying profanity?"

Robbins wondered if Terry Peters would recognize Walter Brennan's line from *Task Force*. The LSO sought any method of easing his friend's gnawing concern about his wife, if only for a few seconds.

"Lots of profanity, Rob. None satisfying." Peters bit his thumbnail and stared northward, as if trying to see inland thirty miles to El Toro from fifteen miles at sea. The uncertainty, the concern, the growing fear all eroded his cultivated composure. Aviator cool was one thing—the modulated voice during an in-flight fire or engine failure. Standing here, feeling 280,000 horsepower throbbing impotently beneath his feet, was an appallingly new experience. He paced a few steps back and forth, hardly noticing that he forced Odegaard and Mei out of the way.

"Why the hell haven't we heard from AirPac or Miramar?"

"I don't know, Terry. Shall I give 'em a call?"

Peters spun on one heel, his face eerily alight. "I should've thought of it before, Rob! The Chinese A-4s!"

Robbins shook his head. "What about 'em?"

"They probably know where the *Penang* is! So would the Flankers. If ATC . . ."

"I'm gone!" Robbins seemed to vaporize as he exited the bridge.

"Captain?" Odegaard stood near the helmsman, wearing a querulous expression.

"I should've thought of it before!" Peters smiled for the first time in an ephemeral eternity. "If air traffic control can break out those A-4s and track them, it'll tell us where the target is!"

The watch officer nodded. "Mr. Robbins is talking to ATC?"

"No, Mr. Odegaard. I suspect he's screaming at them."

Twenty-three

Whiskey Tango Foxtrot

"Peters, what the hell is going on out there?"

Nice to hear from you, too, Rocky. "I don't have much time, Admiral. Tell me what you know and what you can do to help."

A continent away, Rear Admiral Allen Rhode nearly sputtered at the flippancy from a retired captain. Instead, the Vice Chief of Naval Operations gripped the phone harder and fought to control his anger. "Mr. Lieu just called to tell me that *Santa Cruz* has been taken over by a bunch of Chinese dissidents, that they're going to bomb merchant vessels, and you're helping them!"

Peters almost gasped. *So Lieu's behind it! Why didn't Wei tell us?*

Rhode was back inside Peters's ear. "Then Skip Ottmann called. He says you and Wei are going to sink a Malaysian ship with nukes, that he's trapped with your wife at El Toro, that A-4s are taking off, and the goddam Russians are loading goddamn AA-11s on their goddamn Flankers!"

"Okay, Admiral. You got the picture, right? Lieu's the fly in the ointment, and Wei's with us. Now, what're you doing to keep those Flankers off my guys? Hell, they're probably gear up by now."

Rhode's voice came back more modulated. "Yeah. I heard from AirPac that you need a scramble from Miramar."

"Well?" *So Rob called it. Paglia's a wimp.*

"Terry, the Marines don't maintain an alert. At best it'd take them a half hour to upload ordnance. I've given the order, but this'll be over by then."

Peters's heart sank. *Maybe Paglia's not such a wimp.* "What help *can* you get us, then?"

Rhode paused, and Peters uncharitably imagined N-88 calculating the odds of how best to play the hand. "Listen: the *Boorda's* headed for the SoCal Operating Area. Most of the air wing just flew aboard from Lemoore; they deploy in two days."

Peters's mind raced. The new Nimitz-class CVN with Air Wing 18 would be even closer than MCAS Miramar. "A really tactical guy like Baccardi Riccardi might have a couple of Toms or Hornets on Alert Five."

"Hook, I already made the call. I don't know their deck status, but they'll be talking to you directly. It's best if I stay out of the loop, you know . . ."

Yeah, I know, Rocky. If anything goes wrong . . . "Thanks. I'll try to keep you informed." Peters hung up, then turned to the speaker. "Radio, this is Peters."

"Aye, Captain."

"Rob, tell me something."

Robbins's voice shot back. "Terry, I'm talking to ATC at LAX. They're working the problem, but I think they're more concerned with diverting commercial traffic than finding our bogeys."

"Any joy at all?"

"They had a couple low-level skin paints out around Tustin but nothing definite. The A-4s aren't squawking, of course."

Peters bit his lip. The Chinese interceptors naturally would stay low to evade radar while avoiding transponder identification. "Rob, we need a Hawk-eye or another AWACS—something that can break a bogey out of the ground clutter. I need to talk to *Boorda*."

"Rog, boss. I'll keep after the feds."

Peters straightened up, and Odegaard approached him. "Excuse me, Captain. I was just wondering—couldn't our own radar pick up the Chinese?"

"Not over land—too much background clutter. Over water, maybe, depending on their altitude and distance. Otherwise . . ."

"*Santa Cruz, Santa Cruz.* This is USS *Boorda*." The power of the transmission was such that Mei turned down the volume on the bridge console.

Peters answered in person, speaking bridge to bridge. "Lima Delta, this is *Santa Cruz*, Captain Peters speaking." He used the CVN's generic call sign to demonstrate his knowledge and authority. "Good thing we worked with these guys at Fallon," he explained to Odegaard and Mei.

"Ah, yeah, Terry. This is Ben Spurlock. Listen, I'm putting you through to CAG Riccardi in strike ops. Call sign Chainsaw. You copy?"

Peters grinned. Captain Spurlock had been Lieutenant Commander "Spurs" Spurlock in Peters's air wing. "Hey, Ben. Sure thing, put Baccardi through."

". . . ardi here, Terry. You read me?"

"Affirmative, Chainsaw. I guess you know our situation?"

"I understand you have four A-4s on a SinkEx for

a Malaysian freighter hauling nukes, that a couple of Chinese A-4s are looking for them, and one or two Flankers are involved. Right?"

"That's right. As yet we haven't found the target, Tony. Now, I'm not worried about the Chinese A-4s 'cause that'll be a straight-out gunfight that my guys will win. But the Flankers . . ."

"Concur. They're the threat. Terry, I'm launching two Hornets right now with a couple Toms several minutes behind them. I'm also trying to get an E-2 up, but that'll take longer. Probably too long."

"That's okay, CAG. Just be sure they know that they shouldn't shoot any A-4s. The odds are seventy-five percent that they're friendly."

"Consider it done. Chainsaw, out."

Peters turned to Odegaard and Mei. "At least there's something going right. Now if . . ."

"Bridge, Radio." It was Robbins's voice.

"Rob, what've you got?"

"LA Center has been in touch with Dougherty Field at Long Beach. Between them they've got a plot on two low-level fast movers headed offshore."

Peters's eyes widened. "Send it!"

Twenty-four

Bogies

"Papa One, this is *Santa Cruz*. Over."

Delight's pulse spiked. *God, I hope they have something for us.* "Papa One here. Go."

"Pure, this is Rob. Listen, *amigo*, LAX and Long Beach both got fixes on two low-level fast movers. They're feet wet at Anaheim Bay."

Delight did the geometry in his head. From El Toro, the Chinese Skyhawks had to overfly the Seal Beach naval weapons station and the wildlife refuge. *They'll get FAA violations fershure*, Delight mused. He pressed the mike button. "Roger, Robo. I'm northbound." He paused for two seconds. "Break-break. Papa Three from Lead. Over."

"I heard it, Lead." Ostrewski's voice came through crisp and clear. "We're inbound."

"Papa Lead, Robo here again. The bogies are

climbing, orbiting the area around Island Chaffee. Your signal is Gate."

"Roger." Delight glanced over at Thaler, nodded briskly, and shoved the throttle almost to the stop—"through the gate" as it was known in the propeller era. Almost immediately Thaler called, "Lead, gimme a percent." Delight nudged off a skosh of throttle to allow his wingman to keep up.

In a fast climb, Delight led his section toward one of the four small islands in San Pedro Bay. He marveled that *Penang Princess* could have come so far so soon, apparently to drop anchor virtually within sight of the pier from which *Santa Cruz* had sailed the night before. Subconsciously checking his A-4's vital signs, he began thinking ahead in time and space.

Let's see . . . if they're climbing, it's because they want to intercept us before we roll in. They'll be waiting at twelve thousand feet or higher, probably a little south of the ship. He punched the button again. "Papa Three, Lead."

"Three here."

"I'm going in high, Oz. If you see we're engaged, ingress below the fight. We'll buy you some time."

"Three copies. Out."

On the bridge of his hijacked aircraft carrier, Captain Terry Peters rubbed his chin, staring north into the Los Angeles Basin's perennial smog and haze. Emotionally he was split between his friends, airborne and about to engage in an old-fashioned gunfight and dive-bombing attack, and his wife, who was—what? He began allowing himself to consider the possibility that he might no longer have a wife.

"Captain?" Odegaard was at his side.

Peters was startled by the intrusion. He visibly flinched. "Yes?"

"Well, sir, Mr. Mei and I were looking at the chart.

The only way the *Princess* could have got this far north was if she'd been running about three or four hours ahead of schedule. I mean, there wasn't a specific arrival time, but it was a pretty narrow window if they were going to off-load as planned."

Peters felt himself growing short-tempered. "Yeah. So what's your point?"

"Well, sir, presumably the Chinese didn't have time to divert the freighter because they only learned about us this morning. And they couldn't follow their original plan because they know that their leased facility at Long Beach is compromised. But here they are, still one step ahead of us. That means, either they intentionally built this fudge factor into the equation, or . . ."

"Or what?"

"Or they planned to transfer the nukes to other boats all along."

Peters shook his head as if avoiding a nettlesome insect. "What are you saying?"

Mei stepped forward. "Captain, we don't know how long the *Princess* has been offshore. It is possible the backpacks are not aboard her anymore."

Peters slumped in his chair, chewing on his thumbnail, pondering the prospects of his watch officers' assessment. He felt that he should have considered the likelihood himself, and he knew why he had not. *Jane, where are you?*

Finally, he shook his head. "Negative, I don't think so. Otherwise, there'd be no reason to scramble the A-4s and cap the freighter. We'll know more once Zack gets a visual."

Odegaard was dubious enough to press his point. "Skipper, I think we're obliged to notify the Coast Guard or the harbor patrol. At least they could board the *Princess* and . . ."

Peters shot a laser glance at Odegaard. "No, absolutely not! If the nukes are still aboard, the crew is bound to resist, and there'll be casualties. And if there's a patrol craft alongside, more innocent people will get killed. No, Mr. Odegaard. We have to play it out."

Odegaard's eyes widened. "You mean, you'd order the attack even with a Coast Guard vessel right there?"

"I mean that Zack Delight and Ozzie Ostrewski will hit their target unless I call them off. And I won't do that."

"Captain Peters, I wish to object. I still think we have options to . . ."

"Noted. Log it, and I'll sign it. You too, Mr. Mei."

The Chinese officer exchanged glances with his American counterpart. "You mean, Captain, you are accepting full responsibility?"

"It goes with the territory, son."

Peters swung his chair outboard, slightly surprised to find that he cared very little about what happened to *Penang Princess.* Jane's face came to him at the same time as Robbins's voice.

"Terry, I'm still in Radio. I'm hitting Baker Channel."

Psycho Thaler's voice was high-pitched in alarm: "Bogies, one o'clock high!"

Twenty-five

Bandits

Zack Delight had seconds to decide his tactics. Psycho's call told him all he needed to know—the Chinese had altitude on him. He could split the section, relying on his A-4F's superior performance to hold off the hostile Juliets while Thaler bombed, but Delight was the one with flares to deceive heat-seeking SAMs. Or he and Thaler could jettison the two tons of weight penalty they each carried, shoot it out with the bandits, and buy time for Ostrewski and Vespa. Four Mark 83s could sink the ship, but six or eight offered far better prospects. Then there were the Flankers to consider . . .

I'll never get this chance again, he realized. *A pure guts and gunfight; no radar or missiles.* "Two, I'm engaging. ID the target and attack." Delight quickly unlocked the drum on his gunsight, dialed in thirty mils, and locked the lever. At one thousand feet range his sight reticle now subtended thirty feet, slightly more than the wingspan of an A-4. He double-checked his armament switches even as Thaler acknowledged, "Dash Two is in."

Two and a half miles below, riding at anchor off Island Chaffee, was a dark-hulled freighter with light-colored deck and upper surfaces. But Delight's attention was focused on the two Skyhawks slanting toward him from his right front. He resolved to keep his bombs as long as possible, hoping that Psycho could drop, rejoin, and even the odds.

The lead bandit tripped off a short burst of 20mm rounds, accurate in elevation but wide to the right. Delight two-blocked the throttle, resisting the temptation to squeeze off a burst in reply, and wrapped the little Douglas into a shuddering, high-G turn as the aggressor pulled off high and left.

Delight felt an emotional shiver when his opponent zoom-climbed for the perch. It was an unwelcome message: *This guy wants an energy fight; I can't match him with my current airspeed.* He glimpsed the Chinese wingman rolling over and diving after Papa Two. *Well, I can't go vertical with my guy; I'll go down.*

Delight retarded the throttle and rolled over. Through the top of his canopy he caught a view of Thaler's TA-4J diving toward the ship. As Delight pulled his nose through, aligning his illuminated sight with the target, he saw one, then two lights streak upward, corkscrewing awkwardly. "Yeah!" he exulted. *It's gotta be the* Princess *all right!*

The SA-7s shot almost vertically from the stern. One wobbled, perhaps uncertain which heat source to home on, and belatedly tried to correct back toward Papa Two. By then, Thaler was down the chute, tracking for the five seconds he needed. Both bombs came off the hardpoints, stabilized, and accelerated toward the ship.

The second man-portable SAM passed twenty feet

beneath Psycho Thaler's aircraft before detonating.

Delight saw the white smoke of detonation, noted Papa Two wobble in its dive and begin a shallow pullout. A human noise chirped in Delight's earphones—something unintelligible. The Chinese A-4—"Gomer Two"—had veered away from the two SAMs, giving Thaler some maneuvering room. However, Gomer One—the intelligent bastard somewhere above and behind Delight—was positioned to kill one or both Americans.

Delight knew he was poorly placed to get hits. His roll-in after avoiding the Chinese leader was too far astern for a high-angle attack, and his sight was calibrated for air-to-air. He quickly reset 112 mils with Stations Two and Four selected. Recognizing he was shallow in his dive, he held half a diameter high, hit the red "pickle," felt the Mark 83s leave the racks, then punched the flare button four times. Beneath Station Five, outboard on his starboard wing, four magnesium flares arced downward, silent sirens competing for the attention of the next SA-7s.

Two blows rocked the A-4, then another. Without needing to look, Delight knew that Gomer One was in range and gunning. The Marine kicked right rudder, slewed to starboard, and pulled the stick into his lap. His left hand shoved up the power and began accelerating through 430 knots.

Now long-forgotten, Thaler's two half-ton bombs smashed into *Penang Princess* just aft of amidships. One punched through the deck, exploding two compartments down. The other hit slightly to port, dishing in three-eighths-inch steel plates and destroying a speedboat lashed alongside. The splintered Chris Craft, minus four feet of its bow, flooded and sank as far as its lines permitted.

Delight's bombs struck thirty feet aft of the stern. One was a dud, victim of fuze failure. The other strewed water and steel splinters in a wide radius, adding to the confusion aboard the Malaysian vessel.

Zack pulled off target, coming nose level at three thousand feet, and looked left. Gomer Two was turning in behind Thaler, whose TA-4J was streaming something white—smoke or fuel. Briefly Delight wondered what Mr. Wei must be thinking in the rear cockpit. Then the former Marine was coordinating his controls, feeling some slack in the rudder, cutting the corner on Gomer Two and rotating his sight drum back to thirty. He knew that Gomer One was still back there, but Papa Two needed help.

"Papa One, this is Three. We're rolling in hot."

Thank you, God! Delight forced himself to keep the hostile TA-4 padlocked as Island Freeman careened into view. With Ozzie and Liz now attacking, Gomer One probably would let Delight go, trying to disrupt the greatest threat to the *Princess*.

Probably.

Delight keyed his mike. "Psycho, come right and drag 'im for me."

There was no reply, but Papa Two reversed from left to right, turning northerly toward Island White and the Belmont Pier. Gomer Two fired and missed astern, big 20mm slugs churning the water into tall geysers as the fight descended through one thousand feet. *He underdeflected!* Delight exulted.

The Chinese pilot, either unaware of his peril or boldly ignoring it, followed the turn. Delight, twelve hundred feet back and three hundred feet higher, knew the Gomer would pull deflection on Thaler and Wei after another thirty degrees of turn. But as the hostile Skyhawk crossed his nose and the deflection angle narrowed to nearly zero, Delight nudged back his stick, set the pipper one mil over the canopy, and pressed the trigger.

Beneath his feet, Delight felt the twin Colts pounding out three-quarter-inch-diameter shells at a combined rate of thirty-two per second. He kept the trigger depressed for two seconds, expending one-third of his ammunition.

Gomer Two absorbed fifteen rounds across the top of the fuselage and wings. Delight saw shattered canopy glass glinting briefly in the sun, followed by gouges of aluminum, streams of fuel, and just plain junk whipping in the slipstream. The little jet rolled right, dropped its nose, and went straight in.

Zachary Delight pulled up, savoring the dirty brown-white geyser marking his kill, and screamed an atavistic shout of warrior joy that pealed off Valhalla's golden dome.

At least that was how he felt at that exact moment.

A microsecond later he was back in control of himself. He rolled hard right, turning into Gomer One, who had vanished. Leaving the throttle against the stop, he began climbing back toward the likely roll-in point. Delight could do nothing more for Thaler, but still felt an obligation. "Eric, Zack. You better plant that thing."

"Roger, Zack. Ah . . . I'm losin' fuel, but I think I can make the boat."

"Good luck, pard."

Climbing back to the east, Delight rolled his port wingtip down for a better view. He was just in time to see two more bombs explode amidships of *Penang Princess.*

Three seconds later, missile tracks arced out of the haze, passing well above him on a reciprocal course. Then his friend and coauthor was back on the radio. "Papa Flight, be advised. We have Flankers inbound from the east and Hornets from the west."

Twenty-six

Gomer One

"Four, you bomb the ship. I'll block for you."

With that, Ozzie Ostrewski rolled over and slanted down from thirteen thousand feet. He already had spotted the hostile TA-4 trying to cut off the bomber's roll-in point. Confident that Vespa would hit the target, he intended to tie up the Chinese long enough to afford her a clear shot.

Scooter Vespa flipped MASTER ARM, confirmed her sight setting, and nosed over. She forced herself to concentrate on the fundamentals rather than all that had gone wrong. *We were going to make a coordinated attack on a moving target miles from here, without enemy interceptors.* She came back on the throttle, recalling Zack Delight's combat motto: *No plan survives contact.*

The ship was listing slightly to port, with smoke partly obscuring the stern. From a twelve-thousand foot roll-in, Vespa stabilized her TA-4 at 450 knots. She remembered to tell Hu in the rear seat, "Keep the camera going." She received a grunt of acknowledgment.

Elizabeth Vespa had all the time in the world— ten seconds of time in which to trim out her dive, align the sight with the aim point, and track smoothly to the release point. *This is good,* she told herself. *This is very . . . very . . . good.* She marveled at how . . . ordinary . . . it seemed.

At forty-five hundred feet she thumbed the button.

Ostrewski met Gomer One head on—Ozzie going downhill, Gomer headed up. At six thousand feet they passed, slightly offset, and Ozzie pressed the bomb release. With the fuzing switch on SAFE, both Mark 83s slanted toward the water, ridding Papa Three of unwanted weight and drag.

Ozzie honked back on the stick, using his greater momentum to zoom-climb for the perch. He knew that he had the fight in the bag. His opponent, nose-high with energy bled off from the climb, had nowhere to go. The Chinese pilot's only move was to bury the nose, accelerate away, and try to evade.

That was exactly what Deng Yaobang decided to do.

Gomer One rolled into a diving port reversal, looking for the best cover available. He saw it less than three miles ahead.

Barely a mile away, Zack Delight saw the developing fight. He keyed his mike. "Papa Three or Four, this is Zack. I'll take the Gomer. You guys finish the ship."

Without his bombs, Ostrewski could do no more than shoot holes in *Penang Princess*'s hull. Frustrated at giving up a gun kill—the universal fighter pilot's wet dream—he recognized the wisdom of Delight's call. *At least I might split the defenses for Liz's attack.* He reversed course, expending some of his excess energy in a high-speed descent back toward the target.

Delight came hard aport, cutting the corner on Gomer One, who was leaving a 350-knot wake on the water. The hostile Skyhawk flashed across the bow of the Catalina Island cruise ship, drawing appreciative responses and Kodak Moments from the passengers. Delight was six seconds back.

Deng banked fifteen degrees left to thread his way through the channel between the Downtown Marina to starboard and *Queen Mary* to port. Leaving a rooster tail behind him, he flew under Queensway Bridge, popped up long enough to clear the 710 exit, Anaheim Street and Pacific Coast Highway bridges, then bunted his nose down toward the Los Angeles River.

Delight, with his teeth into his former tormenter, followed Deng beneath the Queensway Bridge without thinking about it. Only when the hostile Skyhawk popped up to clear the next three spans did it really occur to him what he had done. Willow Street, Wardlow, and the 405 all disappeared below their white bellies at six and a half miles per minute.

Delight tried to put the TA-4's tailpipe in his reticle. Down low, with the river channel providing a natural barrier, he thought it might be safe to shoot, but Gomer One's jet wash made steady aiming almost impossible. Even within the confines of the flood-control channel, Delight knew there would be misses and ricochets. *Besides,* he told himself, *if I do hose the sumbitch, he's likely to crash on the Long Beach Freeway.* Route 710 North lay an eighth of a mile off their port wingtips.

As if reading Delight's mind, Deng abruptly laid a hard right at the 710/91 interchange. Scooting along the Artesia Freeway, he quickly departed North Long Beach, entered Bellflower at fifty feet

altitude, and felt safer in a residential area. Delight
followed.

Liz Vespa felt the thousand-pounders fall away,
counted *One potato*, then began a steady, hard pull.
She tensed her abdominal and thigh muscles, straining as six times the force of gravity forced her deep
onto the unyielding ejection seat. While her vision
narrowed, somehow her hearing improved; she
heard Hu's grunts over the hot mike.

With the horizon seemingly descending to meet
her jet's nose, Vespa extended her left arm, locking
the elbow. The J52 spooled up from 80 to 100 percent. She regained full vision and scanned the
panel. *All in the green. Now, where's the ship?*

Vespa kept three G on the aircraft, turning back
toward the target so Hu could resume videotaping.
Coming parallel to the burning, smoking vessel, the
TA-4J was rocked as a white shock wave radiated outward from the hull. One second later the aft sixty
feet jackknifed, paused an ephemeral moment, then
dropped back in a cascading eruption of smoke,
flames, and spray.

Scooter Vespa's eyes widened behind her visor.
"Secondary explosions, Hu! Are you getting this?"

"Yes, miss! Hold this angle." She thought she
heard him laugh. "This is wonderful!" He depressed
the zoom button to get a closer view of the confla-
gration.

Liz shared the laugh. She felt almost giddy. "We
have a saying in this country, Mr. Hu."

"Yes, miss?"

"Film at eleven."

Delight scanned his instruments. RPM, fuel flow,
and tailpipe temperature were in the green, but he
felt himself losing ground on Gomer One. He rea-
soned that the battle damage had torn gouges in his

jet's aluminum skin, imposing a drag penalty. He was down to nine hundred pounds of fuel, and Gomer seemed headed back to El Toro. *Nothing I can do there*, he thought. Reluctantly, Delight pulled up, briefly wagging his wings in tacit tribute to a bravura low-level performance. As he climbed to a more fuel-efficient altitude, the last he saw of the Juliet was a fast white dart making 400 mph in a 65 zone.

Ozzie called for a joinup; he wanted mutual support in case more bandits arrived. "Papa Four, this is Three. I'll meet you over Freeman. Angels eight."

Liz hedged for a moment. "Ah, Four, we're getting BDA. Please wait one."

Ostrewski fidgeted on his seat. He understood Vespa's wish for bomb damage assessment, but the *Princess* was beyond help. For a moment he wondered about the heat-resistant qualities of bootleg backpack nukes.

From long habit, he turned his head through almost two hundred degrees. Looking upward to his left, he froze for two heartbeats. Coming from seaward was the track of an air-to-air missile streaking inland.

Twenty-seven

Light to Moderate

"Missile inbound! Left eleven o'clock!"

"My God! It's . . ."

"Tommy, break! Break left!"

The voices on the VHF circuit overlapped in rising octaves and decibels as twelve miles from the burning, sinking *Penang Princess*, a female section leader screamed at her male wingman. Liz Vespa, hearing the garbled transmissions, fought to make sense of it amid her elation at putting both bombs square amidships.

"Tommy, eject!" The female voice was nearly hysterical now. "My God, oh my God . . ." The hoarse contralto descended into an audible sob before the thumb slid off the mike button.

Five heartbeats later, the voice was back. "This is Bronco Three-Zero-Four broadcasting on guard.

Three Oh Six . . . exploded. I'm off Palos Verdes. Send a helo!"

Elizabeth Vespa felt a shiver between her shoulder blades. *My God . . . Jen-Jen!*

Flying alone in Flanker One at sixteen thousand feet, Igor Gnido had an idea that he was too late. That black smoke roiling off Long Beach looked ominous for the prospects of *Penang Princess,* and he could only hope that her cargo had been off-loaded. In truth, there had been little chance of making a timely interception.

Furthermore, the R-73M2s and R-77s had necessarily been in deep storage, and it took time to upload the missiles, especially with the Sukhoi factory crew unaccustomed to handling ordnance. Furthermore, Deng and Li obviously had failed to prevent the carrier-based A-4s from attacking.

Gnido glanced again to the south, where the freighter seemed to be burning itself out. He sucked in more oxygen, mentally tipping his hardhat to Miss Scooter. Not long ago he had plans of bedding her; now he might have to kill her. *Or maybe it will not be necessary, and I will kill her anyway.*

Igor Gnido literally possessed a license to kill. He chuckled at the thought of his diplomatic passport from the Russian government, plus his credentials as a trade representative of the People's Republic of China. The mirth he felt at his present situation—controlling the airspace over Los Angeles, California—was mixed with contempt for politicians and diplomats who made such a condition possible.

The first American fighter had been ridiculously easy to destroy. The R-77—what NATO called the AAM-AE "Amraamski"—had been fired well within range and performed as advertised. The haze made it difficult to discern the fireball fifteen nautical miles away, but the big Sukhoi's sophisticated radar clearly showed the southerly target destroyed. Gnido knew that it had to be a Tomcat or Hornet, and from the its unvarying course he wondered if the pilot had been using his radar-warning receiver. Not that it would have mattered very much; R-77 was a fire-and-forget weapon like the U.S. AMRAAM.

Gnido banked into a tight orbit above Terminal Island, awaiting events. He felt confident that the Americans would not return fire as long as he was over land, where aircraft wreckage or missiles would cause casualties and damage on the ground. However, with his look-down, shoot-down radar, he could easily track anything over water.

To the northwest the radar picture was a cluttered mess. Gnido laughed again at the thought of the panic he must have caused at LAX, where a flock of jetliners was scrambling like a covey of quail. *Ladies and gentlemen, we regret to announce the cancellation of Flight 123 owing to occasional Flankers and light-to-moderate missiles in the area.* It occurred to him that he could hide in the LAX traffic pattern, essentially holding hostage any commercial traffic still there.

A pity I only have three missiles left, he gloomed. There had been no time to load more.

"Papa Three or Four, this is Lead."

Ozzie heard the call and replied first. "Zack, this is Oz. Where are you?"

"Ah, I'm halfway to home plate on the zero three five radial. Getting skosh on fuel. How 'bout you?"

"Dash Four and I have seen missile plumes, Zack, and there's a splash on guard channel. You hear it?"

"Negative. I been kinda busy." There was a pause while Delight sorted priorities. "Four, you copy?"

"Four here. Go!" Vespa sounded calm, even eager.

"You have a visual on Three?"

"Yes, I'm closing on his four o'clock."

Delight mentally computed the relative positions of the three Skyhawks. Ostrewski and Vespa would be below and behind him, still offshore. "Okay. Break-break. *Santa Cruz*, this is Papa One. What dope on Dash Two? Over."

Moments passed before the watch officer replied. "Ah, Papa One, be advised. Papa Two is aboard with a bent bird. Pilot and backseater are both okay. Your signal is Charlie on arrival."

"Roger. See you on deck."

Lieutenant Commander Jennifer Jensen fought to control the palsied trembling of her hands and forearms. For the first time in her naval career she was forced to confront the fact that she was out of her depth, facing a situation that neither seniority nor contacts would alleviate.

That knowledge, combined with the fiery death of her wingman, meant that she was deep-down, bone-chilling *scared*. Just how scared she might have to admit eventually—how else to explain the switchology error in firing a Sidewinder after designating the suspected Flanker for an AMRAAM shot?

Now, with the range closing at six miles per minute, she was barely one minute from the merge with that supremely arrogant Russian. Belatedly, Jensen realized she had not made the obligatory "Fox Two" call, indicating an AIM-9 shot. She knew that she had been too rattled to follow procedure, but with a little luck she might still retrieve the situation. Which would be fortunate indeed, considering that she had not yet received the "Weapons free" call from *Boorda*'s strike operations center.

She inhaled deeply, sucking oxygen into her lungs with the faint molded rubber scent of her mask. She willed herself to project the ice princess tone in her voice as she called Strike Ops. "Chainsaw

Strike from Bronco Three-Zero-Four. Request weapons free. Repeat, weapons free."

"Three-Zero-Four, stand by."

God damn it, I can't afford to stand by! "Strike, Bronco. I'm looking at multiple bogies on my nose. My wingman is down, and I'm outnumbered!" Immediately, Jen-Jen Jensen regretted the tremor in her voice—the guys would say she choked—but she realized it could work to her advantage. *Admiral, I was in reasonable fear of my life. My God, they had just killed Tommy Blyden!*

Interminable seconds crawled past. During that infinity of time, Jensen fought a cosmic battle of Ambition against Fear. Ambition whispered in her ear, hinting at glorious rewards that might yet be hers if she succeeded. Fear screamed the banshee wail, the dirge that the only reason that Flanker pilot had not yet destroyed her was his willingness to toy with her until he tired of the game.

"Bronco, Strike. Two Tomcats are launching at this time. You are cleared to fire only in defense of yourself or other aircraft. VID is required. Acknowledge."

Jensen was appalled. *Visual identification? He'll kill me before I ever see him!* Then, like a gambling addict laying her last dollar on the table in hope of beating the house odds, she heard herself say, "Three Zero Four. Acknowledge."

Gnido sought to sort out the confusing radar picture. Amid the multitude of blips on his screen, one American fighter had gone down, another continued toward him, briefly painting him with fire-control radar. At least three more aircraft were below him to the south. He assumed the latter were A-4s but had no way of knowing which were friendly or hostile. One was climbing out to sea, probably returning to the carrier, and that one likely was an

American. Gnido placed his cursor on the blip and toyed with the idea of locking it up. *If I had a full loadout . . .*

But he needed to keep his remaining R-73 for the main threat—the fighter pressing inland over the Palos Verdes peninsula. He remained confident that no American officer would allow a BVR engagement over a densely populated area. Therefore, he retained control of the situation, willing and even eager to test his aircraft and close-range weapons against a competent opponent. Whatever the political fallout from the *Penang Princess* debacle, Igor Gnido felt that he stood to gain exceptional benefits both from his Russian employers and his Chinese patrons. "Yes, it was terrible what happened at Long Beach," arms merchants would say, "but did you notice what one Su-30 did to three or four U.S. Navy fighters?"

American businessmen talked of "cutthroat competition." *The comfortable, dilettante bastards.* How could they compare to Igor Gnido, who was turning into a world-class salesman?

Jennifer Jensen was thinking better now. She had broken lock on the presumed Flanker, lest the pilot get nervous and spear her with another long-range Archer. She was willing to go to visual range, which would probably be under three miles in this murk, and if the bogey—no, make that bandit—made a threatening move, she would would use her remaining AIM-9M.

Following the "bandit box" in her heads-up display, Jensen turned slightly to port, keeping the threat on her nose. It was an eerie feeling, knowing that somewhere within the HUD square superimposed on infinity lay the source of the death of Lieutenant Thomas Blyden.

*   *   *

Elizabeth Vespa craned her neck, trying to glimpse
the high-performance jets jousting inland. She ap-
proved of Ostrewski's decision to remain low on the
water, relatively safe from radar detection, but it was
about time to head for the boat. The temptation to
ask Papa Three his intention was powerful, considering that their survival might be at stake, but
Scooter Vespa knew that Ozzie Ostrewski would
think less of her for it.

And Scooter was like every other tactical aviator.
She would much rather die than look bad.

Gnido had had enough of groping through the
murk. Since the carrier aircraft approaching him apparently had not fired, nor even continued target-
ing him, he realized that his premise was correct.
The Americans will not engage beyond visual range! But
he was under no such stricture. He thumbed his
weapon selector to the helmet sight detent, confirmed the symbology, and prepared to fire. As soon
as the target emerged from the smog and haze, he
would shoot, then decide whether to deal with one
of the low-flying targets. A BVR kill, a short-range
kill, and then perhaps a low-level over-water kill
would look very convincing in the sales brochures.

The Hornet appeared slightly offset to starboard
as Gnido's blue eyes focused on the dark shape.
Range four point five kilometers, good enough. He
pressed the trigger.

In Bronco 304, Jensen felt her blood surge as she
saw the big Sukhoi. She already had her starboard
Sidewinder selected, finger on the trigger, ready to
fire. There was the tracking tone chirping in her
earphones . . .

And the smoke trail of an AA-11 igniting beneath
the Flanker. One four-letter word strobed in her

brain as she reacted. Stick hard over, throttles against the stops, and pull.

The Hornet pirouetted about its axis and the nose arced abruptly downward.

Twenty-eight

Two V One V One

Ozzie's experienced eyes picked the Archer out of the sky. He would not have seen it had it performed normally—that is, if it had killed Jennifer Jensen—but its rocket motor described a swirling, corkscrewing path below the haze.

"Papa Four, heads up. Missile shot five o'clock, way high." He thought to add, "No threat. Yet."

Vespa looked over her left shoulder and scanned the upper air. She saw the errant missile a few seconds later. "It's gone ballistic?"

"I think so." Ostrewski estimated the geometry of the situation and decided to face the potential threat. He led Vespa into a forty-degree banked turn, climbing back toward the north-northwest.

Jennifer Jensen rolled wings level at four thousand feet and began her pull. She remembered to call the ship. "Chainsaw! Heshotatmeheshotatme! Iwill-returnfire!"

"Bronco, Chainsaw. Say again? Repeat, say again."

Jensen barely heard the response to her panicked transmission. She fought the oppressive G that she loaded on herself as the Hornet's nose rose through the horizon, her vision tunneling through a gray mist.

As her vision returned to normal, her adrenaline-drenched brain perceived a dark spot almost straight ahead. Her richly oxygenated blood put her in a survival mind-set—eyes dilated, blood pressure, pulse, and respiration elevated. Psych 101, fight or flight. It did not occur to Jensen that the aerodynamic shape approaching her through the HUD symbology was far lower than the threat aircraft that had just launched against her.

She heard the AIM-9 Mike's seeker head tracking the friction heat generated by the 320-knot airspeed of the target airframe. *They said there might be two Flankers!* With the range down to two and a half miles she pressed the trigger, remembering to call "Fox two!"

From his perch above and behind the plummeting Hornet, Igor Gnido watched in fascination. The sight presented to him was almost enough to erase the anger he felt at the malfunctioning R-73 that had narrowly missed the F/A-18. *The pilot is mad,* Gnido told himself. For the life of him, the Russian could not conceive what the Hornet was shoot-ing at. He eased off some power, brought his nose up, and bided his time.

Ostrewski's combat-experienced mind screamed at him even as his rational side denied what was happening. He heard something garbled on the radio, vaguely imagined it was Vespa, then began dealing with the lethal reality accelerating toward him.

Ozzie shoved up the power and abruptly rolled into a right turn, better to gauge the Sidewinder's aspect and closure rate. Head-on it was nearly impossible to determine the range until too late.

As the smoky trail corrected slightly to rendezvous on him, he told himself to wait. He punched off four or five flares, none of which seemed to deceive the Mike's improved logic board. *Not yet . . . not yet . . . Now!*

It is not enough to change vectors in one dimension to defeat a missile. The trick is to alter both heading and altitude simultaneously, forcing more G onto the mindless killer than its small wings can accept.

Ozzie's stomach was bilious in his mouth, constricting his throat. He did not realize that he stopped breathing.

He snapped the stick back, pitching up abruptly while coordinating aileron and rudder. His high-G barrel roll, executed with less than two seconds leeway, forced the winder to cut the corner at too acute an angle to continue tracking. As its seeker detected that the range was opening, the warhead detonated.

"Knock it off, knock it off! Hornet, knock it off! You just shot at a friendly!" Vespa's voice was a high-pitched mixture of astonishment and outrage. She had no idea who was listening to her frequency, and at that moment she was not inclined to be charitable. She saw Papa Three reappear beyond the smoke of the Sidewinder's explosion, apparently unharmed, but Michael Ostrewski had been forced on the defensive. If the Hornet pressed its advantage . . .

She turned in, savoring the Skyhawk's superb roll rate. *If he turns into Ozzie, I'll shoot.* She remembered

Hu in the backseat. "Hu, watch for other planes. We
don't know who these people are."

In a Topgun "murder board," the debriefer would
have faulted Jensen for turning back to engage. The
school solution was to blow through, extend away
from the immediate threat, reassess the situation,
and set up for another missile shot.

Jennifer Jensen pulled her nose above the horizon, anxious to observe the result of her shot. She
needed to know that her opponent had either been
destroyed or driven into a vulnerable position for a
reattack. As she neared the peak of a chandelle,
seeking the target through the top of her canopy,
she allowed her airspeed to bleed off more than she
intended. By the time she caught sight of the target,
which she recognized as an A-4, she was down to
285 knots. She tapped the afterburners, pulling
through into a 135-degree slicing turn, ruefully recalling that she had no more Sidewinders. Too close
for an AMRAAM, she flicked the selector and her
HUD indicator changed from HEAT to GUN.

Something's wrong, she realized. *That's not a Flanker.*
She eased off some of the G, retarding throttles
slightly to gain more time to evaluate the potential
threat.

"Liz, cut him off!" Ostrewski's evasive roll had depleted much of his energy. He stuffed his nose
down, pulling back into the threat, but knew he
lacked the "smash" to go vertical.

With 375 knots on the dial, Vespa committed to
an all-or-nothing gamble. She gauged the distance
by the Hornet's size in her thirty-mil reticle, waited
three vital seconds, then pulled up. Vespa felt oddly
calm, almost as she had during adversary training
missions with VC-1 in Hawaii. Tracking the F/A-18
from eight o'clock low, she remembered to fly the

pipper through the target, allowing a full ring of
deflection.

At nine hundred feet range, she pressed the trigger and held it down.

Gnido shook his head in bemused contempt for the
American's folly. How could he allow himself to be
sandwiched between two potentially hostile aircraft?
And then to compound it by turning back again to
repeat the error! The Sukhoi pilot decided to watch
the outcome of the Hornet's clumsy attack. Depending on what happened, he would kill the win-
ner, return to El Toro, and try not to smile too
broadly when waving his diplomatic passport on his
way out of this amazing country.

Jen-Jen Jensen had no idea what was happening.
Something like hailstones on a tin roof hammered
the airframe behind her. The canopy shattered two
feet aft of her headrest. Her initial emotion was con-
fused disbelief; only after the Hornet lurched
abruptly and began an uncommanded roll did she
realize she had been hit by an unseen assailant. *The
other Flanker!* she raged.

Jensen shot a wide-eyed glance at her instrument
panel. Master caution, fire warning, and system-
failure lights strobed at her in red-and-yellow
hues. Wind-fed flames waved angrily orange in her
rearview mirrors. For an indecisive moment she
wondered whether she should risk taking time to
point the nose out to sea, away from the Alamitos
Bay Yacht Club. Her father's voice came to her.
*Honey, don't ever hesitate in an emergency. The Navy can
always buy another airplane.*

The crippled strike fighter dropped into a mind-
numbing spiral barely a mile over San Pedro Bay.

"Bronco Three Zero-Four! Mayday, mayday!"

Lieutenant Commander Jennifer Jensen pulled the black-and-yellow-striped handle.

As Vespa passed below and behind the doomed Hornet, Ostrewski had an unforgettable view. In a nose-down spiral the canopy separated, the seat fired with its rocket motor glaring white-hot, and the parachute deployed, pulling the pilot violently erect.

"*Santa Cruz*, this is Papa Three. Be advised, we have an F/A-18 down about one mile off Long Beach Marina. The pilot has a good chute. He'll splash about two miles south of Pier J."

"Roger, Three. We're alerting the . . ."

Vespa's voice chopped off the rest of the message. "Ozzie! Above you! Flanker at six o'clock!"

Taking the warning on faith, Ostrewski responded the only way he could. He turned into the threat.

Igor Gnido saw the nearer Skyhawk reverse its turn, hauling around the corner in a ninety-degree bank. The Russian had not intended to shoot yet, but he relished sparring with what was certainly a more competent opponent than that idiot in the Hornet. He added power, pulled up and executed a high yo-yo, keeping the A-4F on the defensive. The TA-4J was still too far off to pose any danger.

Topping out of his four-thousand-foot pitch-up, Gnido half rolled and brought his nose over the top, toward the southern horizon. He looked rearward between his twin tails, found the Skyhawk where he expected, and retarded his throttles.

Ostrewski had padlocked the big Sukhoi, conserving his available energy for the right moment. *Like a Topgun free-for-all*, he thought: *two versus one versus one*. When he saw Gnido's nose pull through, he pitched up, momentarily spoiling the Flanker's tracking. Both pilots had a chance for a gun snap shot; neither took it.

As they passed one another, offset two hundred yards at twenty-five hundred feet, Ostrewski stomped right rudder, shoved the stick over, and buried his nose. He gained fifteen degrees angle on the Flanker before it rocketed upward again in that awesome climb, this time pulling its vector toward Papa Four. His rapid turn caught Ostrewski by surprise—Papa Three could practically join on his wing, almost too close to shoot.

"All stations, all aircraft over Long Beach Harbor. This is USS *Boorda* on guard. Be advised, two F-14s are inbound. They are armed and cleared to fire at any threat. All aircraft: You will comply with any directions from the mission commander. Out."

Gnido cursed fervently. With most of his weapons gone, he was in no position to tackle two Tomcats. He decided to kill one Skyhawk, disengage, and streak for El Toro at low level.

He felt he was managing the two Skyhawks nicely. Without missiles, they had to gain a close-range tracking solution on him, and as long as he kept both of them off his nose—or well below him—he could not be hurt.

The A-4s could not say the same thing. Gnido had selected his last R-73M2. With the Archer's seeker slaved to his helmet-mounted sight, he could kill up to sixty degrees off his nose; he put the reticle on the two-seater running in from ten o'clock. A sideways glance to his right showed the single-seater to be no threat. It was going to pass close aboard and slightly high, too near for more than a fleeting snap shot.

Gnido pressed the trigger and felt his last Archer come off the rail. He was tracking the TA-4J smoothly, knowing that as long as he kept the Sky-hawk in his forward hemisphere it was doomed.

Ostrewski saw the smoke plume as the rocket motor ignited, sending the AA-11 toward Papa Four. His heart was raw in his throat; he knew that Liz possessed neither the time nor the countermeasures to defeat the missile. With thrust vectoring, it was perhaps the most agile air-to-air weapon in the world.

Without room for a decent shot, without time to extend away before turning back in—and without conscious thought—Ozzie made his move.

Vespa saw the smoke trail, knew it for what it was, and rolled nearly inverted. She intended to wait until the last possible instant before pulling into her belly and loading maximum positive G on her aircraft. From 135 degrees of bank, her world was a crazy quilt of three-dimensional geometry with the Russian missile eating up the last quarter mile of airspace.

She shut her eyes, saw her mother's face, and pulled.

Gnido saw the evasive maneuver, admiring the pilot's last-ditch effort while knowing it was futile, and awaited the explosion.

Michael Ostrewski's last view was a windscreen full of Flanker. The two-tone gray paint scheme loomed at him, and his final willful effort was to clamp down on the trigger.

His cannon had hardly begun to fire when the little Douglas speared the big Sukhoi squarely behind the cockpit.

Liz fought the G, realizing that she had bottomed out of her desperate split-ess, knowing that the very realization meant life. *I'm alive. How?* She craned her head, seeking the Flanker that had to be above and behind her, positioned to shoot again.

The first thing she noticed was a corkscrewing smoky spiral as the Archer, devoid of guidance, followed its ballistic path to destruction. Vespa reversed into the threat that now was nonexistent. The visual footprint led to a dissipating fireball suspended in space, shedding fuel, flares, and aircraft parts.

Her pulse spiked at the knowledge that Michael Ostrewski somehow—*somehow*—had gained enough room to pull lead on the Flanker. A warm deluge of adrenaline-rich adoration flooded her veins. *Ozzie, you are one* superb *fighter pilot!* She pressed the mike button. "Three, this is Four. Climbing through four thousand."

She waited several seconds for the reply, believing that the Only Polish-American Tomcat Ace must be savoring his triumph. When no response came, she tried again. And again. Finally, she said, "Hu, look around. Do you see Ozzie?"

The Chinese pilot turned in his seat, swiveling his head across the horizon. "No, miss."

Realization descended on Vespa's brain, draining downward in a chilling cascade that coagulated into a hard, insistent lump in her stomach.

She spoke to the windblown smoke and drifting shards. "Oh, Michael. What did you do?"

Twenty-nine

Last One Back

Peters and Delight were on the bridge, digesting three versions of what had happened to the renegade Sukhoi. Delight, still in his flight suit and torso harness, was coming off an adrenaline high following his kill.

"I still think Ozzie gunned the sumbitch and ejected."

"Zack, radar saw the plots merge. And we have a secondhand report from the Coast Guard reporting a midair collision." Peters slumped against the bulkhead, arms folded. Staring at the deck, he intoned, "They're searching, but . . ."

". . . but Ozzie's probably dead."

Peters nodded.

"TA-4 on downwind, Captain!" Odegaard lowered his binoculars and pointed to port.

With gear and flaps down, Scooter Vespa broke

at "the ninety" while Robo Robbins, Psycho Thaler, and Mr. Wei watched from the LSO platform.

Vespa rolled wings level a mile and a quarter from the ramp, making minute adjustments to keep on glide slope. Robbins, with the phone in one hand and the "pickle switch" held aloft in the other, waited for her call.

"Skyhawk ball," she said. "State point six."

Robbins and Thaler silently regarded one another. With six hundred pounds of fuel, she would have only two chances at the deck. "Lookin' good, Liz. Keep it comin'," Robbins called.

Thaler had the binoculars on the TA-4, serving as Robbins's watcher. "Hook!" He turned to look at Robbins. "No hook!"

Robbins made a conscious effort to keep his voice calm. "Liz, drop your hook."

Vespa chided herself for missing the crucial item. *Damn it—I've never done that before!* She reached down for the hook-shaped handle, missed twice, and had to look in the cockpit. When she returned her gaze to the mirror, the ball was a diameter high and she was angry with herself almost to the point of tears.

"Waveoff, Liz. Take it around!"

Vespa knew that she could recover and probably catch a four wire, but obedience to the LSO's command was too deeply ingrained. She shoved up the power and ignored the usual procedure. Instead, she wrapped into a hard left turn, leaving gear and flaps down, rejoining the circuit slightly downwind of the ninety.

Thaler leaned into Robbins's shoulder. "I think she could've made it, Rob."

"I know. But she's gotta be shook about Ozzie,

and this way there's less doubt in her mind."

As a landing signal officer, Robbins also was a working psychologist. He knew how frustrated and anxious the pilot must be, especially with a passenger aboard. He keyed the phone. "Don't worry, Scooter. We'll catch you this time."

Vespa scanned the instruments once more, pointedly ignoring the fuel gauge. Over the hot mike, she said, "Mr. Hu, brace yourself for possible ejection. If I miss this pass I'll climb straight ahead and give you as much notice as I can."

"Yes, miss." His tone sounded neutral.

As Vespa rolled out of her oblong-shaped 360-degree turn, the ball was half a diameter low. She called "Skyhawk ball," omitting her fuel state, and added throttle to intersect the glide slope. She barely heard Robbins's "Power" call.

As the ball rose slightly she led it with pitch and power, stabilizing her airspeed at 122 knots to compensate for the light fuel load. *Santa Cruz*'s 328-foot-wide deck was irrelevant to her now. What mattered was the eighty-foot-wide landing area with the life-saving arresting wires, though Vespa aimed within three feet of centerline.

For the next ten seconds Elizabeth Vespa's attention was riveted on the glowing amber meatball. From the the backseat, Hu appreciated the fact that it remained nailed in the middle of the datum. He heard Robbins's only additional transmission. "Good pass, hold what you got."

Papa Four impacted the deck at eleven feet per second sink rate, the landing gear oleos compressing under pressure as the tailhook snagged the third steel cable. As Vespa added power in event of a bolter, the TA-4J was dragged to a stop.

Mr. Wei Chinglao broke all decorum and hugged Robo Robbins. Psycho Thaler pounded both of them on the back, bouncing on the balls of his feet.

Robbins turned to his writer. "Papa Four, low-state recovery, rails pass. Underfunckinglined OK-3!" As a group, they turned and ran up the the deck to the parking area.

Vespa sat in the front seat, listening to the J52 unspool with its vacuum-cleaner whine. She wanted time to absorb what had happened to Ostrewski, and what she had just done. Hu already had descended the ladder, standing with his camcorder, intending to record his pilot's triumph. He was immediately joined by a crowd of plane handlers, ordies, and the LSO contingent, plus Peters and Delight from the bridge.

Liz dropped her helmet over the side, where the plane captain caught it. She beaned a smile she did not quite feel, blew a kiss at Hu's camera, then pinched her torso harness restraints and eased out of the cockpit. She backed down the ladder but had not reached the bottom before she felt eager hands plucking her up and away. She was afloat on a raucous sea of male faces, borne shoulder high toward the island. For the tiniest instant she thought back to her high-school senior prom and the condescending look of triumph that Christine LaMont had shot her as the tiara was set on the queen's head. *Take that, Christine.*

The men grasping Vespa's legs and thighs allowed her slide off their shoulders. She alit in front of Peters, who grasped her in a crushing hug. When he pulled back he exclaimed, "I am so proud of you."

She blinked back what was rising inside her and managed to keep her voice calm. "Ozzie?"

Peters wanted to avoid her eyes. Instead, he focused on her face and shook his head. "No word, Liz. I think he's gone."

"Scooter."

Liz turned at the sound of her call sign. Delight stood by her left shoulder, and she leaned into him. "Oh, Zack." She wrapped her arms around his neck. He patted her back, exactly the way he had reassured his grandchild after a bicycle spill twenty years ago.

"Did you see it?" He knew what she meant.

"No, hon. I was . . ." He cleared his throat. "I was in the pattern about that time. But . . ."

"But my God, Zack. He died for me!" Her eyes were clear and dry, but she choked on her words. "He died for me . . ."

Delight grasped her by both shoulders. "Listen to me, Liz. Listen to me!" They both were aware of the crowd melting away. The deckhands recognized that this was a moment between friends who had shared something exceptional. "If he was still here, he'd be just as proud of you as . . . we are." Delight allowed her to grasp that sentiment. "Liz, you just sank a ship and got a gun kill on the same mission. Do you realize nobody's done that in about fifty-five years?"

She allowed herself a grim smile. "You got a kill, too."

Delight looked at Peters. "Hook and I both flew a couple hundred missions in Vietnam and never got close to what happened today. But, hell, my mom could have hosed that gomer from six o'clock."

Vespa realized that she had instructed the dead Chinese pilot. "Do we know who was in that airplane?"

"No," Peters replied. "But we'll find out fairly soon."

Delight shook his head, marveling at the pilot he had chased. "I'll bet the ranch that my guy was Deng. I don't think anybody else in the class could've flown that way."

Robbins forced his way through the dispersing

crowd. He leaned around Delight and kissed Liz on both cheeks. "Scooter, that was the best pass I've seen in years. You got an underlined OK-3." He grinned hugely. "And after a hell of a mission."

Some of the giddiness was returning even as she wondered, *Have they forgotten that Michael's dead?* But she heard herself responding to the banter. "Even with the low start, Rob?"

He punched her arm. "Hell yes. That was a great recovery, and since *I'm* the only LSO aboard, it's a perfect OK-3."

"Captain from bridge." Odegaard's voice snapped over the 1-MC speaker. Peters looked up at the 0–9 level where a khaki arm waved at him. "Sir, the phones are working at El Toro and your wife's on the horn. She and Mrs. Delight want to know if you will both be home for dinner."

Thirty

Shakeout

"How many federal agencies can there be, anyway?"

Representative Tim Ottmann grinned ruefully at Delight's plaintive query. "Hell, Zack, don't blame me. I voted against every new bureau and agency that ever came up for funding. Even tried to make a couple of 'em go away, but it did no good."

Peters looked around the hotel suite, assessing the collective mood. Besides himself and Jane, the Delights and Ottmann, were Vespa, Robbins, Thaler, Wei and Hu, plus two Washington attorney friends of Ottmann's. One of them, a former A-7 pilot named Brian Chappel, specialized in transportation law, including maritime and aviation. He was cordially detested by the Navy Department and the Department of Transportation.

"In the two days since the excitement, I've heard from the following," Chappel said. "DOT including

FAA and the Coast Guard, FBI, ATF, and DEQ. That doesn't count state and local agencies."

Robbins raised his head. "DEQ? What's their take on this?"

"Something about protection of coastal waters. They say that bombing is bad for the fish, and the *Penang*'s oil spill caused some concern."

Peters was anxious to wrap up the meeting. "Okay, Brian. Where is all this likely to lead?"

"My guess is that it'll mostly disappear in a couple of weeks."

"Really?" Jane Peters was reluctantly eager to believe it.

"Yes, Mrs. Peters. Really." Chappel gave her a convincing smile. "Look, the bottom line is this: Everybody on both sides wants the same thing. To make this go away. State and DOD are red-faced over the way things turned to . . . hash . . . with their Chinese program. The way that heavy ordnance like bombs and missiles were smuggled into this country, or actually purchased here, could force Congress to ask a bunch of embarrassing questions." He looked at his D.C. colleague. "Right, Skip?"

Ottmann gave two thumb's-up. "Guarantee it."

Thaler picked up his glass and slurped the last of his lemonade through the straw. "Mr. Chappel, I understand the PR angle—the government's got to look like it's investigating all this. But you know that the fix is already in with the president and the administration. Those pardons that Skip got for us, in case we need them."

"Yes, that's right."

"So what'll happen in Taiwan?"

"Oh, that plan is canceled. With the assistance of Mr. Ottmann, Mr. Chappel, and some other well-placed individuals, the names and roles of certain prominent PRC officials are being made known on a confidential basis in Washington."

"Which means"—Ottmann grinned—"that the papers and news networks will have all the details in time for today's five o'clock news. With what we can release about bribes, kickbacks, and influence peddling, neither the U.S. nor Chinese governments will risk losing billions of dollars in trade and revenues."

Vespa spoke for the first time. "Mr. Ottmann, what about the backpacks? Are they being recovered?"

"I shall answer that," Wei interjected. The old MiG pilot regarded the American woman frankly. At length he said, "Under utmost secrecy, I confide to you what few people will ever know. There were no nuclear weapons."

Liz involuntarily shuddered; Jane felt the tremors in Vespa's body and put an arm around her shoulders. Liz leaned toward the Chinese. "Michael died for *nothing*?" Her hands clenched into frustrated, vengeful fists.

"Not at all, my dear. Not at all. He played a vital role in carrying out the most important part of our plan. When I said that we knew the weapons were aboard because one of my people helped load them, that was the same information that went to the Premier and the Politburo. Oh yes, packages were placed in the *Penang Princess's* hold, and they would have showed a reading if exposed to a Geiger counter. But they were, ah, your word is—a placebo."

"A fake pill to make the patient feel better." Peters slowly shook his head, marveling at the subtle complexity of Wei's plan.

"Exactly, Mr. Peters. In this case, the patient was the premier and his Stalinist cabal. Now that their 'plot' has been defeated and exposed, China may move on to more productive endeavors."

Liz grappled with the cooling anger she felt. At

length she asked, "But what about the people on that ship? Eric and I . . ."

"Miss Vespa, Mr. Thaler, please." Wei managed a note of sympathy in his voice that still seemed out of place for the man. "You knew that people would die when you accepted the mission. The rationale was that a far greater number might be saved. Well, nothing has changed. The eleven men who were killed and the twenty or so injured must be balanced against the losses that would occur in an invasion of Taiwan."

While Vespa allowed herself to accept the fact that she had been skillfully used in a geopolitical chess game, Delight intruded on the hushed silence. "One thing I'd like to ask, Mr. Wei. What caused the secondary explosions after Liz's hits?"

"Explosive charges set near the presumed weapons, Mr. Delight. We wanted to ensure that an independent agency confirmed the presence of nuclear materials. Your emergency disaster crews have reported trace elements in the atmosphere and water—far below any hazardous level, but enough to ensure that protests and diplomatic consequences will result in Beijing." He allowed the ghost of a smile. "Your Navy will 'recover' the weapons."

Thaler swirled the ice in his glass, still shaking his head at the revelations. "How were the charges set?"

"Again, Mr. Thaler, I require utmost discretion. But you have treated me and Mr. Hu with uncommon courtesy, and provided me with the most exhilarating day of my life." He almost smiled again. "When the attack began, one of our operatives set off a timer. Then he escaped over the side."

"And the pleasure craft alongside?" Thaler asked.

"You may consider your effort well spent," Wei responded. "That was a Mexican drug smuggler hired by the PRC agents in Long Beach. He was to disperse the backpacks to other agents throughout the area."

Ottmann noticed Chappel closing his briefcase. "Well, I guess that's about it. Brian, you have anything else for these folks?"

"No, just the usual lawyer-client warning." He smiled at the audience. "The spin doctors will take the lead, but people, please remember this. Don't say a damn thing to anybody without consulting me first."

Peters stood up, resting one hand on Jane's shoulder. "Then I guess we can all go home."

Wei and Hu looked at each other in a way that had nothing to do with family ties. "Not all of us, Mr. Peters," Wei intoned. "Not all of us."

Thirty-one

Scooter Flight

The memorial service at St. Francis Catholic Church was smaller than the wedding would have been. The testimonials had been spoken, the elegy delivered by Terry Peters, the rites performed by Ostrewski's priest.

The mourners rose following the benediction and slowly filed out. The ATA contingent stood by while Maria Vasquez accepted greetings and condolences from friends and relatives.

"By the way," Peters said, "Tim Ottmann is recommending Ozzie for a special orders Medal of Honor. With the political horse trading, he figures it's a cinch for a Navy Cross."

"Oz already had a Navy Cross," Delight replied without irony. "Besides, you know how he felt about this country for the past several years."

Peters chose to ignore the sentiment. "Additionally, everybody else on the mission probably will get a Silver Star."

"I've got a Silver Star," Delight replied—with irony.

Carol Delight leaned over the pew. "I don't understand something. Everybody involved was civilian. How can military medals be awarded?"

"Actually there's precedent—industry tech reps, even war correspondents have received combat decorations. Besides, Tim said something about a videotape of a former secretary of the Navy with a sheep." Delight shrugged, then smiled. "Maybe Skip was exaggerating—I couldn't say."

Maria Vasquez turned from the front row, her obsidian eyes searching the pews. "Mrs. Peters," she whispered. "I don't see Elizabeth. I can't believe she would miss this."

Jane patted the young woman's hand. "Don't worry, dear. She'll be here—I promise." She nodded to her husband, who strode up the aisle in that long, ground-eating gait.

"But the service is over."

"Not exactly, Maria." Jane took her arm. "Let's step outside, shall we?" On their way to the exit, Maria glimpsed Terry Peters speaking into a handheld radio.

Thirty seconds later the screech of low-level jets echoed off the surrounding buildings. "There!" somebody shouted, pointing to the south. Other witnesses followed the gesture and clapped or cheered—or merely shielded their eyes against the glare.

With the effortless grace of jet-propelled flight, the finger-four Skyhawk formation glided eight hundred feet overhead. In unison, they dropped their tailhooks in salute.

"It's illegal as hell," exclaimed Carol Delight. "How'd you swing that?"

Zack whispered in her ear. "Don't ask, don't tell!"

Maria leaned against Jane Peters, one hand to her lips and the other dabbing at her eyes. Jane hugged her close. "That's Liz, Maria. With Eric and Rob and Tim."

From eight hundred feet over downtown Mesa, Arizona, Scooter Vespa added power and abruptly pulled up from the number one position while the others continued straight ahead. The vacant space—the missing man—was obvious to everyone on the ground.

As she laid the stick to starboard, inducing a series of vertical aileron rolls into a cloudless blue sky, Liz Vespa made the call to Hook Peters.

"Wizard Flight, off and out." She paused. "Break-break. Scooter Flight, returning to base."

BARRETT TILLMAN is the author of four novels, including *Hellcats*, which was nominated for the Military Novel of the Year in 1996, twenty nonfiction historical and biographical books, and more than four hundred military and aviation articles in American, European, and Pacific Rim publications. He received his bachelor's degree in journalism from the University of Oregon in 1971, and spent the next decade writing freelance articles. He later worked with the Champlin Museum Press and as the managing editor of *The Hook* magazine. In 1989 he returned to freelance writing, and has been at it ever since. His military nonfiction has been critically lauded, and garnered him several awards, including the U.S. Air Force's Historical Foundation Award, the Nautical & Oceanographic Society's Outstanding Biography Award, and the Arthur Radford Award for Naval History and Literature. He is also an honorary member of the Navy fighter squadrons VF-111 and VA-35. He lives and works in Mesa, Arizona.

Look for

COMBAT 3

———

featuring
James Cobb
Harold W. Coyle
Ralph Peters
Rogelio J. Pineiro

at your local bookstore
March 2002

CYBERKNIGHTS

———

BY HAROLD W. COYLE

One

---

combat.com

The secluded community just outside of Valparaiso, Chile, slumbered on behind the high walls and steel-reinforced gates that surrounded it. Other than the lazy swaying of branches stirred by a gentle offshore breeze, the only sound or movement disturbing the early-morning darkness was that created by the rhythmic footfalls on the pavement of a pair of security guards patrolling the empty streets of the well-manicured community. The two armed men did not live in any of the homes they were charged with protecting. Even if either one of them had been fortunate enough to possess the small fortune that ownership of property in the tiny village required, neither had the social credentials that would permit him to purchase even the smallest plot of ground within these walls. If they harbored any resentment over this fact, they dared not show it. The pay was too good and the work too easy to jeopardize. Their parents had taught them well. Only fools take risks when times were good and circumstances didn't require it.

Still, the guards were only human. On occasion a comment that betrayed their true feelings would slip out during the casual conversation that they engaged in during the long night. Upon turning a corner, one of the security guards took note of a flickering of light in a second-story window of one of the oversize homes. Slowing his pace, the hired guardian studied the window in an effort to determine if something was out of kilter. Belatedly, his partner took note of his concern. With a chuckle, the second guard dismissed the concerns of the first. "There is nothing going on up there that we need to bother ourselves with."

"And how would you know that?" the first asked as he kept one eye on the window.

"My sister, the one who is a cleaning woman, chatters incessantly about what she sees in each of these houses. That room, for example, is off-limits to her."

Rather than mollify his suspicions, these comments only piqued the first guard's interest. "And why is that? Is it the personal office of the owner?"

Letting out a loud laugh, the second guard shook his head. "Not hardly. It is the bedroom of a teenage boy."

Seeing the joke, the first guard let out a nervous chuckle. "What," he asked, "makes the bedroom of a teenage boy so important?"

"The boy is a computer rat," came the answer. "My sister says he has just about every sort of computer equipment imaginable cluttering the place."

"What does your sister know about computers?" the first asked incredulously.

Offended, his partner glared. "We are poor, not ignorant."

Realizing that he had unintentionally insulted his comrade, the first guard lowered his head. "I am sorry, I didn't mean to . . ."

"But you did," the offended guard snapped. "What goes on in those rooms is not our concern anyway. We are paid to guard against criminals and terrorists, not speculate about what our employers do within the confines of their own homes." With that, he pivoted about and marched off, followed a few seconds later by his partner.

Neither man, of course, realized that the only terrorist within miles was already inside the walls of the quiet little community. In fact, they had been watching him, or more correctly, his shadow as he went about waging an undeclared war against the United States of America.

Alone in his room, Angelo Castalano sat hunched over the keyboard of his computer, staring at the screen. As he did night after night, young Angelo ignored the pile of schoolbooks that lay strewn across the floor of his small room and turned, instead, his full attention to solving a far more interesting problem. It concerned his latest assignment from the commander of the X Legion.

The "foot soldiers" in the X Legion were, for the most part, the sons of well-to-do South American parents, people who could be correctly referred to as the ruling elite. While Angelo's father oversaw the operation of a major shipping business in Valparaiso owned by a Hong Kong firm, his mother struggled incessantly to keep her place in the polite society of Chile that was, for her husband, just as important as his business savvy. Like their North American counterparts, the information age and modern society left them little time to tend to the children that were as much a symbol of a successful union as was a large house in the proper neighborhood. That Angelo's father had little time to enjoy either his son or house was viewed as a problem, nothing more. So, as he did with so many other problems he faced, the Chilean businessmen threw money and state-of-the-art equipment at it.

A computer, in and of itself, is an inert object. Like a projectile, it needs energy to propel it. Young Angelo and the electricity flowing from the overloaded wall socket provided that energy. But engaging in an activity can quickly becomes boring if there is nothing new or thrilling to capture a young, imaginative mind, especially when that activity involves an ultramodern data-crunching machine. Like the projectile, to have meaning the exercise of power must have a purpose, a target. That is where the X Legion came in.

The X Legion, properly pronounced Tenth as in the roman numeral, was a collection of young South and Central American computer geeks who had found each other as they crawled about the World Wide Web in search of fun, adventure, some sort of achievement. In the beginning they played simple games among themselves, games that involved world conquest, or that required each of the participants to amass great wealth by creating virtual stock portfolios. Slowly, and ever so innocently, the members of the X Legion began to break into the computer systems of international companies, not at all unlike those owned or operated by their own fathers. They did this, they told each other, in order to test their growing computer skills and engage in feats that had real and measurable consequences. "We live in a real world," a legionnaire in Argentina stated one night as they were just beginning to embark upon this new adventure. "So let us see what we can do in that world."

At first, the targets selected for their raids were chosen by the legionnaires themselves, without any controlling or centralized authority. This, quite naturally, led to arguments as fellow members of their group ridiculed the accomplishments of another if they thought the object of a fellow legionnaire's attack had been too easy.

"Manipulating the accounts of a Swiss bank must have more meaning," a Bolivian boy claimed, "than stealing from a local candy store." Though intelligent and articulate, no one had a clear idea of how best to gauge the relative value of their targets.

To resolve this chaotic state of affairs, a new member who used the screen name "longbow" volunteered to take on the task of generating both the targets to be attacked by the members of the legion and the relative value of those targets. Points for the successful completion of the mission would be awarded to the participants by longbow based upon the security measures that had to be overcome, the creativity that the hacker used in rummaging around in the targeted computer, and the overall cost that the company owning the hacked site ultimately had to pay to correct the problem the legionnaire created. How longbow managed to determine all of this was of no concern to the young men like Angelo who belonged to the legion. Longbow offered them real challenges and order in the otherwise chaotic and shapeless world in which they lived, but did not yet understand.

When they were sure he was not listening, which was rare, the rank and file of the legion discussed their self-appointed leader. It didn't matter to Angelo and other members of the X Legion that longbow was not from South or Central America. One of the first clues that brought this issue into question was the English and Spanish longbow used. Like all members of the X Legion, longbow switched between the two languages interchangeably. Since so many of the richest and most advanced businesses using the World Wide Web communicated in English, this was all but a necessity. When it came to his use of those languages, it appeared to the well-educated legionnaires that both Spanish and English were second languages to their task-master. Everything about longbow's verbiage was too exact, too perfect, much like the grammar a student would use.

That longbow might be using them for reasons that the young Latin American hackers could not imagine never concerned Angelo. Like his cyber compatriots, his world was one of words, symbols, data, and not people, nationals, and causes. Everything that they saw on their computer screen was merely images, two-dimensional representations. In addition to this self-serving disassociated rationale, there was the fear that longbow, who was an incredible treasure trove of tricks and tools useful to the legion of novice hackers, might take offense if they became too inquisitive about longbow's origins. The loss of their cyber master would result in anarchy, something these well-off cyber anarchists loathed.

While the security guards went about their rounds, protecting the young Chilean and his family from the outside world, Angelo was reaching out into that world. As he did each time he received a mission from longbow, Angelo did not concern himself with the "why" governing his specific tasking for the evening. Rather, he simply concentrated on the "how."

Upon returning from school that afternoon, Angelo had found explicit instructions from longbow on how to break into the computer system of the United States Army Matériel Command in Alexandria, Virginia. This particular system, Angelo found out quickly, handled requests for repair parts and equipment from American military units deployed throughout the world.

The "mission" Angelo had been assigned was to

generate a false request, or alter an existing one, so that the requesting unit received repair parts or equipment that was of no earthly use to the unit in the field. Knowing full well that the standards used to judge the success of a mission concerned creativity as well as the cost of the damage inflicted, Angelo took his time in selecting both the target of his attack and the nature of the mischief he would inflict upon it. After several hours of scrolling through hundreds of existing requests, he hit upon one that struck his fancy.

It concerned a requisition that had been forwarded from an Army unit stationed in Kosovo to its parent command located in Germany. The requesting unit, an infantry battalion, had suffered a rash of accidents in recent months because of winter weather and lousy driving by Americans born and raised in states where the only snow anyone ever saw was on TV. Though the human toll had been minimal, the extensive damage to the battalion's equipment had depleted both its own reserve of on-hand spare parts as well as the stock carried by the forward-support maintenance unit in-country. While not every item on the extensive list of replacement parts was mission essential, some demanded immediate replacement. This earned those components deemed critical both a high priority and special handling. With the commander's approval, the parts clerk in Kosovo submitted a request, via the Army's own Internet system, to the division's main support battalion back in Germany to obtain these mission-essential items.

As was the habit of this particular parts clerk, he had waited until the end of the normal workday before submitting his required list of repair parts. In this way the clerk avoided having to go through the entire routine of entering the system, pulling up the necessary on-screen documents, and filling out all the unit data more than once a day. Though parts that had been designated mission essential and awarded a high priority were supposed to be acted upon as soon as they landed on the desk of the parts clerk, lax supervision at the forward-support unit where the clerk worked permitted personnel in his section to pretty much do things as they saw fit. So it should not have come as a great surprise that the parts clerk in Kosovo chose to pursue the path of least resistance, executing his assigned duties in a manner that was most expedient, for the clerk.

This little quirk left a window of opportunity for someone like Angelo to spoof the United States Army Matériel Command's computer system. Since the request was initiated in Kosovo and relayed to the forward-support battalion's parent unit after normal working hours in Kosovo, the personnel in Germany charged with reviewing that request were not at their desks. Those personnel had the responsibility of reviewing all requests from subordinate units to ensure that they were both valid and correct. They then had to make the decision as to whether the request from Kosovo would be filled using on-hand stocks in Germany or forwarding back to Army Matériel Command to be acted upon using Army-wide sources.

All of this was important, because it permitted Angelo an opportunity to do several things without anyone within the system knowing that something was amiss. The first thing Angelo did, as soon as he decided to strike here, was to change the letter-numeric part number of one of the items requested to that of another part, an item which Angelo was fairly sure would be of no use to the infantry unit in Kosovo.

The item Angelo hit upon to substitute was the front hand guards for M-16 rifles that had been cracked during one of the vehicular accidents.

Switching over to another screen that had a complete listing of part numbers for other weapons in the Army's inventory, Angelo scrolled through the listings until he found something that struck his fancy. How wickedly wonderful it will be, the young Chilean thought as he copied the part number for the gun tube of a 155mm howitzer, for an infantry unit to receive six large-caliber artillery barrels measuring twenty feet in length instead of the rifle hand guards that it needed. Just the expense of handling the heavy gun tubes would be monumental. Only the embarrassment of the unit commander involved, Angelo imagined, would be greater.

Selecting the item to be substituted, then cutting and pasting the part number of the artillery gun tube in its place, was only the beginning. The next item on Angelo's agenda was to move the request along the chain, electronically approving it and forwarding it at each of the checkpoints along the information superhighway the request had to travel. Otherwise, one of the gate-keeping organizations along the way, such as the parent support battalion in Germany, the theater staff agency responsible for logistical support, or the Army Matériel Command in Virginia, would see that the item Angelo was using as a substitute was not authorized by that unit.

To accomplish this feat Angelo had to travel along the same virtual path that such a request normally traveled. At each point where an organization or staff agency reviewed the request, the young Chilean hacker had to place that agency's electronic stamp of approval upon the request and then whisk it away before anyone at the agency took note of the unauthorized action. This put pressure on Angelo, for he had but an hour or so before the parts clerks in Germany and the logistics staffers elsewhere in Germany switched on their computers to see what new requests had come in during the night. Once he had cleared those gates, he would have plenty of time to make his way through the stateside portion of the system since Chile was an hour ahead of the Eastern time zone.

It was in this endeavor that the tools and techniques that longbow had provided the legionnaires came into play. By using an account name that he had been given by longbow, Angelo was permitted to "go root." In the virtual world, being a "root" on a system is akin to being God. Root was created by network administrators to access every program and every file on a host computer, or any servers connected to it, to update or fix glitches in the system. Having root access also allows anyone possessing this divine power the ability to run any program or manipulate any file on the network. Once he had access as a root user on the Army computer system that handled the requisitioning and allocation of spare parts, Angelo was able to approve and move his request through the network without any of the gates along the way having an opportunity to stop it. In this way the request for the 155mm artillery howitzer gun tubes for the infantry battalion in Kosovo was pulled through the system from the highest level of the United States Army's logistical system rather than being pushed out of it from a unit at the lowest level.

To ensure that there was no possibility that the request would be caught during a routine daily review, the Chilean hacker needed to get the request as far along the chain as he could, preferably out of the Army system itself. To accomplish this little trick, he used his position as a root operator within the Army Matériel Command's computer to access the computers at the Army's arsenal at Watervaliet, in New York State. It was there that all large-caliber gun tubes used by the United States Army were produced.